# FIERCE FORGETTING

Therese felt the heat of Anthony's breath, heard his inchoate murmur. Suddenly she moved closer, and some impulse made her touch the skin of his neck with the tip of her tongue.

He gave a groan and his hold tightened. She melted into his strength, flowing to him and around him.

She could think of nothing now, nothing but the thought: *We cannot let each other go.* Nothing was real to her; she moved with the watery motions of someone in a dream, half-closing her eyes. He unfastened her dress. Rustling, it fell into a fiery pool on the carpet, looking like a huge blown flower. She stepped from the silk like a dancer; his breath caught at the sight of her body in its thin cambric and foaming lace.

It was only later, much later, when Anthony said, "We belong to each other now. For always," that she remembered.

And said, "I am married to another man. . . ."

# Grand Design

## Patricia Strother

A SIGNET BOOK

**NEW AMERICAN LIBRARY**

*For my cousins*
*Frances Porter Seier,*
*Irvine C. and Sarah Lathrop Porter*

## PUBLISHER'S NOTE

This book is a work of fiction. Names, characters, places, and incidents
either are the product of the author's imagination or are used fictitiously,
and any resemblance to actual persons, living or dead, events, or locales
is entirely coincidental.

Copyright © 1988 by Patricia Strother

SIGNET, SIGNET CLASSIC, MENTOR, ONYX, PLUME, MERIDIAN
and NAL BOOKS are published by NAL PENGUIN INC.,
1633 Broadway, New York, New York 10019

First Printing, April, 1988

1  2  3  4  5  6  7  8  9

PRINTED IN THE UNITED STATES OF AMERICA

# Acknowledgments

Many thanks to Mrs. Nancy Broussard and Mrs. Renee Reaux, Lafayette Parish Convention and Visitors Commission, Lafayette, Louisiana

# 1

## 1857

Therese held her breath to listen for Charl'.
Through the cabin window, built narrow and high to check wet bayou wind, she heard nothing but the chuckle of nightbirds, a 'gator croaking like a big bullfrog.

Nothing else outside. Not yet. In the room the sighs of Amelie and Elianne, the little one, came in even rhythm. Therese shifted under the covers; cold excitement scraped inside her stomach. The rest of her was warm in her next-best dress. Even at October's end, the swamp nights kept their Indian-summer haze.

Straining again to listen, Therese heard the sound she was waiting for—the sound of her brother stealing, hardly louder than a rabbit, down the outside stairs from the attic *garçonnière* allotted to the boys.

She turned back the cover and got up warily. On the other side of the bed, her sister Amelie was as still as the leaves before a storm; three-year-old Elianne lay quiet in her bed, small fists curled on either side of her black, mussed hair. Therese's heart misgave her: she might never see either one of them again.

But there was no choice anymore. She had to go with Charl'. And there wasn't an instant to waste.

Therese felt for her shoes, grabbing them by their heels and clamping them together in one hand. Her hand was slick with the moisture of fear. If her father, Michel, should wake up . . . But no. He got up with first light. By now he had to be past hearing.

Therese bent, grabbed the knotted mouth of the croker sack hidden under the bed, and pulled. The harsh burlap wheezed against the bare cypress planks

1

of the floor. Therese's heart bumped. But both her
sisters still slept, Elianne with the catlike concentration of her three short years.

Therese let out her breath. Padding to the door, she
opened it awkwardly with the hand that held her shoes.

The part most *difficile*, most terrifying, lay ahead—
getting past her parents' door and out of the cabin. All
the other doors opened right into the common room
that served the Pavans as kitchen, workroom, and
sitting-place.

"Oh, Lord, I scared, *mois*," she whispered, using an
expression she hadn't used since she was little, since
the nuns had taught her how to talk the Anglo way.

But she went on, stiff with dread, past the closed
door of her mother and father, Berthe and Michel.
Nothing happened. Therese shook all over with relief.

Then at the front door a small noise from the
*garçonnière* above unnerved her; her younger brother,
César, was a light sleeper. Therese stopped in her
tracks.

The sound was not repeated. Gathering all her courage, she unlatched the front door and pulled it slowly,
blessing her father's skill at building things. The door
opened as silently as a moccasin slid from the marsh
into the water, and then she was closing the door,
avoiding the one creaking plank on the porch, scurry-
ing down the front steps to the spongy ground.

It was good that she was so light, because she would
not disturb the nightbirds much, but she prayed she
wouldn't step on the big, wriggly worms that came out
at night when the day birds stopped hunting . . . or on
a snake, in her stocking feet. But she had gotten this
far and must go the rest of the way. Her body would
not keep its secret much longer. If her father found
out her disgrace, he would either kill her or make her
marry Hector Rocaille. Either way Therese Pavan would
be dead.

She started running toward the water.

By the light of the full moon Charl' had awaited for
their journey, she could see his lean torso silhouetted

against the live-oaks' dappled shadows. He was already sitting in the pirogue.

Therese could not make out his face, though, until a waft of air moved the eerie gray mosses on the oaks' big limbs. Then she saw his sweet, nervous smile. "*Vite,*" he called out softly.

He held one wiry hand out for her sack and stowed it in the pirogue beside a smaller bundle. Therese slipped on her shoes and stepped into the narrow boat which Charl' had made from a single cypress log. It was barely wider than Michel's massive body, but Therese and Charl', with their sparse haunches, had more than enough room.

She eased down, trembling in her relief.

Neither of them spoke as Charl' thrust the pole into the murky water, pushing the boat out from among the reeds. It slipped so quietly over the black stream that she could hear the rustle of birds disturbed in the rushes, the timid belching of frogs. All of a moment, her fear was gone, and with it, some of her sadness. In the full moon's golden light, Charl's movements had the rhythm of music, of a song that sang: *We are going, We are getting away*.

In three days they would be in New Orleans; both of them would see and maybe even have things that had always been beyond their reach. Therese yearned to tell her thoughts to her brother, but he was so intent, so grim, that she kept quiet. The effort of poling had already soaked his shirt with sweat; they would not be really safe until they were out of the lagoon and on the narrow river.

Everybody in Côte Blanche Bayou knew the Pavans; almost every Acadien, she thought, was *parenté* to them—*cousin* and *cousine, tant'* or *nonc*.

Therese watched Charl's shoulders rise and fall with each strong thrust of the pole, loving him, loving the way they had always been so like each other. He hated the trapping as much as she did; hated the sight of the small, pathetic carcasses spread over the boats and the piers and the porch of the cabin, hated the always-present metallic smell of the animals' blood. And Charl' understood Therese and the things she wanted, because he wanted too; he read and dreamed, like her.

Looking around at the mossy oaks, the towering cypresses shooting their trunks above the surrounding trees, and the palmettos growing in little clumps from earth that looked firm, but where it was never safe to rest your feet, Therese knew for the first time in her life how much she hated the bayou. She would probably never see it again.

Or Petit Anse. And Nicholas.

With a sense of wonder she realized that she had not thought of Nicholas for days, had not let herself think of him.

Or the baby.

All her thoughts, and Charl's, had gone into planning the journey.

She peered at him again. His whole body strained with the effort of poling faster and faster away from the familiar lagoon. Finally, when it seemed that there were miles behind them, Charl' steered the boat toward the land and fastened it to a sturdy overhanging vine, his shoulders heaving with exhaustion. When he turned, she saw the sweat pouring down his face, over the proud features so like hers.

Her brother was *famille*, more than her mother and father, or any of the others. Certainly more than Nicholas Adair had been or ever could be. An ache caught in her throat. But Charl' was smiling at her and so she managed to smile back. It had been so hard for him, doing the extra work in Jeanerette to get them a little money without letting their father know; finding ways to hide them a store of food and making their own pirogue in secret. Not for anything would she cry now and spoil his night of glory.

Charl' lowered himself into the pirogue and got his breath back. He wiped his face with his hands. "We can rest here awhile, Tez. No one knows about this place but me, not even Michel."

To his face, their father was *père*; but between themselves Therese and Charl' called him Michel. They belonged more to their mother, and looked like her with their smaller, pointed features and deep black eyes. Michel's face was broad, with a big nose and mouth and cold gray eyes. Outwardly their mother, Berthe, minded Michel and spoke softly to him. But on the inside she was strong, she resisted. And in her way she'd let Therese and Charl' go their own paths, as much as they were able. Berthe knew Charl' was a man, even if he hated trapping, and understood when Therese slighted her chores so she could do her drawings.

It would be so strange, Therese thought, to be away from her mother. "She will miss us," she said abruptly. "We were always her favorites."

"Yes." Charl' sounded drowsy and weary and absent. And they still had so far to go. She must not speak any more of sad things. "Did you sleep at all?" she asked softly.

"Not a wink." He broke out laughing. "I was too excited. Did you?"

"No. And I don't care." She was pleased that he looked so happy when she said that. "Oh, Charl', is it really so splendid in New Orleans?"

"Yes. I told you. There are hundreds of ladies that look just like the ladies in the book I brought you back from the last trading trip."

"The *Godey's*. I have it in my sack."

The moonlight caught his eyes; they were shining. "And what else did you bring?"

"My drawings, of course. And the paper and pencil you brought me. My nightgown . . . the red dress and the striped cloak I made for the *fait do-do*."

"Lord, what a night that was," he said, grinning. "When we had to fight the Thibauxes . . . for saying our sister had her mattress on her back. A very suggestive remark."

"Well," she retorted, "mattress ticking was all I had, you know. And you have to admit it looked every bit as good as the cloak in *Godey's*."

"Better," Charl' said in his loyal way. His face was serious when he added, "Maybe that is what you should do in New Orleans, Therese—make dresses and cloaks.

The ladies in New Orleans will pay you a lot of money. It will be just the thing to do when you . . . when the baby is getting . . ." He stopped, chagrined.

"Bigger," she finished matter-of-factly. There was a tight little silence between them as she remembered how angry Charl' was at Nicholas. To get his mind off that, she urged him, "Tell me again about Odalie's house."

Brightening, he detailed the wonders of the house on Rampart Street paid for by Odalie Verrett's rich white protector. "Old Emile says everything there is very bright and pretty. There are pictures, and rugs from Turkey. Not like the little rugs we have at home, the rag rugs and the reed rugs, but big ones, with designs. And there's a tub where she can bathe every day, *twice* a day if she wants to."

"Twice a day," Therese repeated, marveling. In the Pavans' cabin the girls bathed twice a week while the men were outside, with just sponge baths between. In the free settlement of color, Odalie had lived with her family in a mud hut. The house she now had sounded like a mansion. Therese smiled to remember Odalie, the *"griffe"*—the name whites gave to the fairest-skinned black people, lighter by far than *melif*, octoroon and quadroon. Charl' had told Therese the *griffe* women in New Orleans were highly valued for their beauty.

"And that's not all," Charl' went on. "But you'll see it for yourself soon."

"Oh, I wish you could stay there too."

*"Quelle idée,"* he teased her. "I can imagine what her protector would say to *that*. Besides, I am a man. I don't need things like rugs and bathtubs and sewing machines."

"Where will you stay?"

"Anywhere." His reply was easy, confident. "I can do anything, you know—roustabout work on the levee, carpentry. I can go out with the fishermen. Lord, it will be grand to be *paid* for my work!"

"Yes. Oh, yes." All his life, since he was seven, Charl' had worked so hard for Michel. Their father was losing his best workman, she realized darkly. "Will he come after us, Charl'?"

"He might, Tez." She was sorry she'd said that, because all of the light had gone out of his face again and he looked anxious and hunted. "We'd better get going. When daylight comes we'll stop somewhere and sleep. Are you all right?"

"Yes, Charl'. I am fine." She spoke with more confidence than she felt. Much as she wanted to sleep, it was scary to think of sleeping on the ground, with all the snakes and worms and lizards.

She watched Charl' unfasten the boat and push them out again into the current. Therese's eyes felt heavy, and for a minute she was afraid the splashing of the pole and the lullaby of frogs would put her to sleep. A person had to stay wide-awake in a pirogue: you couldn't lie down, and you could easily unbalance the boat or fall over the side.

Therese widened her eyes, fighting drowsiness. A bumpy mound, shinier than a log, cut the surface of the black water. It was a 'gator. Charl', wise in the creatures' ways, steered the boat around the mound, far enough so the 'gator couldn't grab the pole with his teeth. If that happened a man either had to let go of the pole or be jerked into the swamp with it. She shivered.

But it was all right. Charl' had missed the 'gator completely and went plowing on in the moon-dappled dark with Therese sitting stiffly behind him.

When he stopped to rest again, he took some dried fruit and salt pork from his bundle. "It isn't *jambalaya*, or crawfish pie," he said apologetically. "But we had to travel light. I couldn't bring any coffee, even."

She thought of three days without the black, strong coffee. "*N'importe*, Charl'."

Nothing was important anymore besides New Orleans. Maybe their father wouldn't come after them; it was so far away, more than a hundred miles. She would tell people her husband was dead.

Her husband.

Nicholas should be her husband. But he never would be.

And just like that, she could see his face before her eyes—that proud English face, and his yellow hair as bright as the meadow in the mornings; it had smelled like lemons when she had held his head against her breast.

She had tried so hard to put those pictures out of her mind, because they hurt the way a fishhook hurt her once when she had gotten it caught in her finger.

But she would never forget that day last summer when she first crossed the waving meadow to Petit Anse. . . .

That morning her father and Charl' were going to Jeanerette, where they would trade crawfish and muskrat skins for flour, coffee, and rice.

With the porch half-swept, Therese paused and propped the broom against the outside wall of the cabin, calling out, "*Père*! Take me with you!" She asked more out of stubborn habit than in hope.

As usual, Michel didn't even look at her; he kept on loading.

She came down the steps and wandered toward the water.

Her brother Charl' asked gently, "Where would we put you?"

Charl' bent his head toward the slender pirogue; there was barely room now for him and their father.

"I can squeeze in," she persisted. "I'm thin."

Still not looking at her, Michel said gruffly, "A sight too thin for a half-grown woman."

Therese smarted; nothing about her pleased her father. He was always saying she'd be better off with more meat on her bones and fewer silly ideas in her head.

"Please, *père*," she repeated.

"Go back to your work." At last her father looked at her and his pale gray eyes were cold. "You do little enough as it is. And you go to Jeanerette every Sunday to Mass. What are you deviling me for?"

She knew better than to answer, but she blurted out, "It isn't the same!"

"No. All the stores are closed then, and you can't waste my money on gewgaws. Get back to the house; leave me alone." Michel's face was red. Suddenly he drew back his huge hand and slapped Therese across the face.

The blow was so jarring she thought her head would come off her neck; the force of it unbalanced her and she fell to the ground.

Through her tears she saw Charl' stiffen, his hands balling into fists. Oh, my God, she thought, Charl' is going to fight him. And their father was so strong he could kill Charl' with one blow. Her brother was strong too, but slender and wiry; Michel's neck was as wide as a bull's and his fists like small hams.

Her brother's eyes frightened her: they were like black, burning coals, and his face was white.

He leapt out of the pirogue and came to her, helping her up. "Are you all right, *petit*?"

"Yes. Please, Charl' . . . forget it."

"Come here, boy," Michel growled. "Are you going to let me do all the loading by myself?"

Charl' did not answer, but returned to the boat, his posture as stiff as his face as he resumed his task.

I hate him, I hate him, she raged in silence.

She walked slowly back to the cabin and picked up the broom, sweeping the porch savagely. Her face still stung from the slap.

When they were through loading, her father sat down in the pirogue with his broad back to her.

Charl' waved to her, push-poling the boat into the sluggish current.

She watched until the pirogue disappeared around the bend of the stream and there was nothing left except the moss-hung cypresses and the willows leaning in the teeming mud of the bank, no sound except the whooping of the cranes and the *aigrettes'* cry.

The heat-haze covered Therese's skin like flannel. She remembered she'd promised to help her mother and sisters pick moss today. Marie Lavalle, one of

their cousins, was getting married in August, and the
women were busy making mattresses. They needed
more moss to stuff them.

Feeling hot and rebellious, Therese decided she'd
just disappear. Berthe wouldn't scold her; she'd be too
happy, having the cabin to herself and the children
tonight. Michel would get drunk in Jeanerette, the
way he almost always did, so he and Charl' might not
be back before the morning. Until tomorrow they
would all be free.

Therese shaded her eyes and stared at the chimneys
of the big house on the hill beyond, on the "island" of
Petit Anse. It wasn't an island at all, just a hill that
rose out of a waving sea of meadow grass that moved
like water in the wind. The big house belonged to the
Adairs, who owned the whole island.

They were Anglo Yankees, and people in the bayou
said the old man was crazy. He sheltered egrets and
cranes, and even the muskrats and the nutrias. Michel
and the other trappers hated him.

But Therese had always wanted to see a man like
that, a man who hated the trapping too. Therese cried
to see the animals struggle in their mud traps, and she
would run away so she wouldn't have to see the clubbing. Old man Adair, she thought, wouldn't call her a
"fool girl" the way Michel did when she ran away.

And today she was going to sneak onto the island
and see where the birds and animals were.

Therese looked back at the cabin; there was no one
outside yet. César had gone off to fish, and Berthe
and Amelie would be attending to the house.

Therese grinned. Amelie would be grumbling, because it was Therese's turn to wash the dishes and
sweep. Well, this morning she just wouldn't.

She began to run toward the meadow. There was a
little breeze now, and the grasses, yellow-green in the
bright sun, did for a fact look just like water, like the
ocean Therese imagined but knew only as a big piece
of blue in the geography book at the school kept by
the nuns.

Therese crept across the grass-waves and started up

the hill. The sun was hot, and she could feel her old dress sticking to her back; the grasses stung her bare ankles and her cotton drawers felt heavy. Her shoes felt hot and heavy too, and she wished she could run through the grass in her bare feet, even though the grass stung. But nobody went barefoot much around the bayou; you never knew what you'd step on.

When she got her first good sight of the house, she forgot everything else in her wonder: it made her gasp for breath. It was enormous, bigger than any house she could have imagined; three times as big as the church, even, in Cameron, and so white in the sun she had to blink. There were tall white columns all around the structure. Porches encircled the whole house on the first and second floors, and were enclosed by a lacy-looking fence as high as her waist.

And suddenly the meadow had become a soft, smooth, bright green yard, a yard so sweet to step on, it could have been a rich cloth described in *Godey's*, fit for a fancy dress. Therese stopped, dismayed. Maybe the Adairs shot people who trespassed on their property.

But no. Surely a man like old man Adair, who was kind to muskrats and to birds, would not allow them to do that.

And she just had to see the inside of the house.

It was so quiet. There seemed to be no one around the front of the house. As Therese crept nearer, she heard faint laughter from somewhere to the rear. The sound must come from the servants in the kitchen, she supposed. She'd heard that only three people lived there: Mr. and Mrs. Adair and their son.

Therese looked up at the house again. If that was so, it was a marvel. Only three people in this big, big house. Maybe . . . maybe they were away just now. Charl' said the old man spent a lot of time outdoors in his "sanctuary." Well, she would try to see in—she might never have this much courage again.

She stole up the smooth, sloping lawn toward the lower porch at the side of the looming mansion. But the lacy iron fence was too high to climb over. *Mon Dieu*, she would have to go right in the front door.

She took off her shoes and hid them under one of the spicy cedars that grew in thick profusion along the front of the house.

No one in the bayou planted cedar trees except in the cemetery. They said if you planted a cedar tree in your yard, somebody you loved would die as soon as the tree was tall enough to shade a grave. Therese shivered, smelling the cedar. This was a spooky house. She must be *fou* to think of entering. But she just had to.

The worst they could do was to tell her to go away. She skirted the cedars and went up the front steps and onto the long, shaded porch.

Several tall, skinny windows stood open to the warm air. She went to one and peeked in. What she saw made it almost hard to breathe: through white, filmy curtains, as sheer as a bride's nightgown, she saw a glittering room, with flowered carpets and shiny fabrics on curly chairs and couches. And a harp. A golden harp like those played by the angels of heaven. Hypnotized, Therese stepped through the French window.

The carpet felt like clouds beneath her bare feet, and there was a heavenly smell of flowers. On the mantelpiece, over a pale gray, carved fireplace, was a vase full of blood-red roses, and there was a basket of them in the cold hearth too.

Therese looked up again at the roses over the mantel and gasped. A wide-eyed girl with a mass of dark, tangled hair was staring back at her; the girl's small, full lips were parted and her white face was flushed with heat.

The girl was herself. Therese was looking into an enormous mirror, as clear as water, which hung over the mantel. She had never seen so much of herself so plainly before. The little looking-glasses in the cabin were nothing like this. She had never really known what she looked like. The surprise made her forget everything else for a minute, and she stared, fascinated, at her image.

Why, she was *belle*, just as that *cochon* Hector told her, just as her mother said. Therese hadn't believed them—Hector told her that so he could kiss her, or worse; and all mothers said that about their own children. Now Therese saw by the bright, gleaming light that it was true. Her black hair, for all its disorder, shone; her black eyes in their thicket of soft, long lashes were large and luminous. She'd never realized her skin was so clear, or her mouth so red.

Startled, she caught a motion behind her in the glass, heard a boy's deep voice. "Who are you . . . a dryad?"

Transfixed, she observed the tall image beyond hers—a golden-haired boy with fine features and blue-gray eyes. He was smiling and his eyes were warm.

Therese was mortified to be caught out, standing there gaping at herself like an *imbécile*, barefoot, in her sweaty tan dress. She was in for it now. At the same time she felt resentment: no boy could be allowed to call her names, no matter how rich he was.

"Don't call me that. I am Acadien. I am Therese Pavan." She said it as proudly as if her name were Marie Antoinette.

The tall boy grinned at her answer and bowed. "Nicholas Adair, *mademoiselle*. Of Adair's Island."

He came forward until he stood right before her. He was beautiful in his open-necked white shirt with full sleeves. The same kind of shirt she had seen in pictures of the famous pirate Jean Lafitte. But Nicholas Adair was nothing like Lafitte; he was a perfect Anglo, with his princely features and narrow mouth. His fair skin had only been touched by the sun, and his eyes were the color of a stormy sky.

She could smell the delicious odor he gave off, a combination of fine, clean cloth and lemons. Underlying that was another scent, one that she had never noticed in her father or her brothers, or the malodorous Rocailles. It was a scent that made her tremble inside.

But she wished that she had not left off her chemise, for coolness, because he was looking down now at her body. The thin cotton of her shift clung to her small, shapely breasts; she was very developed, Berthe said, for a girl of fifteen.

Suddenly she became fully aware of where she was, and who they were—an intruder and the son of the house. "I have trespassed," she said quietly. "You will excuse me now." She began to sidestep him, moving toward the open window.

"Please," he said urgently. "Don't go." He put out a slender, long-fingered hand and laid it on her moist, bare arm.

His touch had an astonishing effect. She'd never known anything like it—again, the inner trembling, a shivering cold swoop of her insides, then a prickle of heat just below her ears.

When she hesitated, he said once more, "Please. Let me show you the gardens. You will like them. And it is so much cooler there. Come."

He had the ways of a *remède* man, she marveled. The way the *remède* man could see a person's sickness, Nicholas Adair could see into her hesitation, seem almost to read her feelings. There was something magical in his bright, peculiar eyes with their alien Anglo blueness.

This time he didn't touch her, only gestured toward the French window. Unable to help herself, Therese walked ahead of him through the window onto the long porch, intimidated by his courtly manner; then let him show her to the first of the wonderful gardens, fragrant and vivid and cool with blood-red roses.

"Tez."

Her pet name reached Therese from the strangest distance, as if calling her out from a dream. The memory of Nicholas had been so real she felt as if she had left her very body and was walking with him again among the summer roses in the gardens of the Adairs.

"See?" Charl' said. "The night is going."

Therese looked up at the sky in surprise. It was hard to believe that they had traveled so far and so long, even if they had left only a few hours before day.

Grayness washed the sky; then there was the abrupt golden-rose brightness of the swift bayou morning.

Charl's tongue was thick with sleep, but he sounded buoyant. "We can rest now. We will stay here."

He poled them toward a small rush-covered island where a fringe of mangroves grew. *Aigrettes* clamored and an osprey dived over the live-oak trees. The morning painted the wheeling birds a pale, breathtaking pink as the pirogue glided through a wide expanse of water, carpeted by purple-blue water hyacinths for as far as the eye could journey.

Still half inside her waking dream, Therese thought: Someday I will sew dresses the color of the birds, the color of the hyacinths.

With a jolt the pirogue struck mud, and she was fully awake again. This was real. They were fugitives, just like the runaway slaves that the people talked about in the free settlement of color along the Côte Blanche.

Charl' tied the boat to one of the mangrove branches and thrust the pole in the mud to test it. The pole wobbled and sank: the shifting mud was as soft as grits.

Charl' drew the pole out and tossed it onto the shore beyond the rushes. "We'll have to jump it." His bundle followed the pole. He picked up Therese's sack and leapt over the mud into the rushes.

Turning, he held out his hand. "Careful now."

Therese pulled up her skirts and leapt, but her legs were not as long as Charl's, so she landed short, in the black, sucking mud. Her brother lunged forward and caught her by both arms, pulling them so hard they hurt, dragging her to safety.

They both collapsed on the rushes, laughing a little.

*"Bon!"* Charl' gasped. "It's a rough place, but that's why I chose it. We shouldn't have too many visitors."

Therese grinned at him, heartened by the prospect of really stretching out. She ached in every muscle, partly from being so anxious, partly from sitting so long in the narrow boat. She also ached for sleep. When Charl' stood up and retrieved the pole and her sack, she picked up his smaller bundle, following him to a clearing in the rushes.

*"Pas mal,"* Charles said, yawning. He beat against the rushes to scare away snakes. "Better take your cloak out, Tez, and wrap yourself in it. The ground's damp."

She hated to get the cloak dirty: it was her pride and joy. It was inspired by a "Saragossa" cape she had seen in the *Lady's Book*, made out of splendid stuffs she had never even heard of. But the cape was striped, and so was mattress ticking. She had persuaded Berthe to buy some extra ticking when they were buying the fabric for Marie's mattresses, and made her cloak out of that. She had made it by instinct, going just by the *Godey's* drawing, but the cloak, with its stripes of off-white and gray, turned out beautifully.

She had been so proud of it; it looked fine over her cherry-red dress at the *fait do-do*—the party whose name the Anglos made such fun of. *Fait do-do* meant "take a nap." It was the Acadien word for a dance at which the children took a nap in another room while the grown-ups danced the night away.

The cloak was her only connection with *Godey's Lady's Book*, that bible of everything lovely and elegant and refined, the very opposite of the crude, ugly dresses of the bayou and her stingy, needy life on Côte Blanche.

Reluctantly Therese spread the cloak on the ground.

Charl' offered her some more dried fruit and dried beef. She shook her head.

She lay down full-length on the cloak, luxuriating in the extra space. After he had eaten, Charl' made a pillow of his sack and lay down beside her, sighing with gratification.

"It is so good to rest," he murmured drowsily.

"Should we make a little fire?" she asked suddenly. "To keep all the varmints away?"

Charl' opened his eyes. "I don't think we should, Tez. The shrimpers could see us . . . and we'd better not take the chance. Don't worry," he consoled her. "I've scared the daylights out of anything in the rushes.

And I've learned to sleep light, you know, when I've been out trapping. You just sleep, petit Tez."

The affectionate buzz of her pet name lulled her. "Everything will be fine, won't it, Charl'?"

"It will be *splendide*," he mumbled, and she knew he was almost asleep.

She was tired too, drained from the haste and worry and excitement, all the wild anticipation. And yet, although she closed her eyes, feeling Charl's comforting presence, Therese could not yet fall asleep.

She ran her hands over her still-slender stomach, feeling for the roundness that she knew would soon come. It was so strange to think of a baby inside herself. On the bayou another baby was not always a matter for rejoicing: another baby meant another mattress to make, another bed to build, more food to find. When the baby Elianne had come, so late in Berthe's and Michel's life, Michel had stormed and grumbled, joyless and unwelcoming.

It would be even worse for her, without a husband. She would have to care for the baby, all alone. She couldn't be a burden to Charl' forever; someday he would want to marry.

She glanced at her sleeping brother, who looked so relaxed in the rosy light. He would make someone such a fine husband. He had said he would make money for them all, but Therese had to make money too. Maybe she could learn to sew for the Creole ladies. She would learn everything there was to learn about making clothes. Her baby would not go around in flour sacks, the way Elianne did.

I'll do it, Therese resolved. After all, Charl' had said that this year, 1857, was the richest year there had ever been in the city of New Orleans.

# 2

The early-morning light shone dully on the oily waters of the river when the pirogue bumped against the granite wharf near the French market. Glancing off the water, the sunlight hurt Therese's eyes. She and Charl' had slept by day, traveling by night all the way to New Orleans, and her eyes had grown accustomed to the dark.

The air was different too, cooler and sharper than that of the bayou; the shouting and confusion of voices smote her ears. There were many other boats—barges and skiffs and bumboats, pirogues and dories. Therese scanned the faces of the boatmen unloading their fruit, shrimp, and many-colored vegetables, but she saw no one who was *parenté* to the Pavans.

Charl', who had already tied the boat to one of the great metal rings of the wharf, stooped for their bundles. He caught her surveying the boats. "It is well. I looked too, and there is nobody here who knows us." He held out a hand to assist Therese from the pirogue to the broad planks of the levee.

Charl' took their bundles in one arm and put the other around her waist. He was grinning, and excitement blazed from his dark, kind eyes that were so much like her own. "Noisy, *non*? You will get used to it. It will be quieter on Rampart Street."

It was not the noise that disturbed Therese. She glanced down at her shoes and stockings, still stained with river mud despite all her efforts scraping the shoes and rinsing her stockings in the swamp waters. And the cherry-red dancing dress was most improper for morning; it showed a great deal of her bosom. She clutched her ticking cloak together over her breasts, thanking heaven it was cool enough to wear it and wishing she'd kept the brown dress cleaner.

In the market she had already glimpsed some smartly dressed ladies, followed by servants with laden baskets. Almost everything else, at the moment, was a blur.

"Would you like to look around a little?" Charl' shouted over the hubbub. "It is far too early to wake Odalie. And, Tez . . . smell the *coffee*!"

She had, and her nose quivered like a *lapin*'s. Three whole days without coffee of any kind, in particular Berthe's black, black brew, had almost driven her mad. Sighing, she inhaled deeply, and the city's bouquet of aromas dazzled her senses. The sharp fish and harbor smells were familiar, but the scents of flowers and spicy foods, the pungent odor of cigars, were new and enticing.

She followed Charl's lead over the uneven cobblestones, which chafed her feet through her thin-soled shoes, to an open coffee stall.

"If we do not take a barouche to Odalie's," Charl' said softly, "we can have some of those honey cakes. Can you walk there?"

"Of course! Do let us have the cakes." The smell of the cakes was irresistible after three days of the dried, salty meats and the hard dried fruits.

They sat down on high stools and were served the thick, black, steaming coffee, and with it, the wonderful cakes. Therese drank and ate ravenously, forgetting for the moment her ragamuffin looks, even when a beautiful lady and her escort sat down on stools nearby.

But after she'd satisfied a little of her hunger, and felt the strong black coffee enliven her, Therese found herself looking at the beautiful lady again. She was wearing a gown of dull orange, dark green, and cream-colored stripes, and a cream coat trimmed in the same dark green with dashing mousquetaire sleeves. Most striking of all, on her auburn hair she wore not a bonnet, but a saucy ivory hat with a curving brim.

After the dull cottons and homespun of the bayou, the magnificence of the lady's clothes seemed unreal. Therese had seen such clothes only in drawings, or imagined them in dramas on the stage. And yet this was real life. New Orleans was a "brave new world," like they said in Shakespeare.

"It's like *Godey's* come alive," she whispered to Charl'. "Paris must be like this, no?"

"I've heard it is, a little. But let's have more coffee, Tez. It's glorious."

Therese stared at the passing scene. Crowded under the market's arcade was a great mass of people, buying and selling, more people than she'd ever seen in one place. The market buzzed like a big, colorful cone of bees. Wagons passed, creaking under the burden of orange carrots, carnelian-red tomatoes, and cabbages as green as jade. And the clothes—even those of the servant women were stunning. There were black women in bright *tignons*, vivid turbans of parrot green and peacock blue, an orange brighter than a flame, and a miraculous, startling pink pinker than any rose. A woman at a flower stand offered fresh, varicolored bouquets.

"It is a marvel," Therese murmured to Charl'. "It is better than a play."

"Fu'uf!" he teased her. "When I find work, I will take you to a *real* play, Tez. As to that, I would like to go back to the levee for a minute. I will ask the men there where I can find employment."

They retraced their steps, and while she waited with their bundles at her feet, Charl' approached a big, burly man, questioning him eagerly.

The man threw back his head and laughed. Therese saw Charl's face fall, then brighten as the big man said something else. He returned to Therese, smiling sheepishly.

"I am a bumpkin," he muttered. "The man said very few white men do roustabout work on the levee. But he said there are many other things. I can go out with one of the fishing boats, he said, or I can even learn to be a steamboat captain. The *Sara Belle* is taking on deckhands." He spoke in an enthusiastic rush. "I will come back here to investigate after I have seen you to Rampart Street."

Therese started to say that she could go alone, but she realized she'd seen no unescorted women in the city. Even those who looked a little . . . fast had been accompanied by people walking right behind them, like servants.

Charl' consulted a passing gentleman for the hour. Ignoring the man's contemptuous look, Charl' thanked him civilly and said to Therese, "I think we can safely go to Rampart Street now. It is late enough, for Odalie to be opening her eyes."

She laughed at his dry inflection; for them this was practically midday. Charl' usually rose at five, with Michel, and Therese got up not long after.

The way to Odalie's seemed very long, but Therese was so distracted by the city sights that it didn't matter. She could not get enough of the smartly dressed people passing in their carriages; the pastel houses, mysterious and tall, with their terrace railings casting smoky-gray shadows on the sunny streets; the candlelit interiors of churches, glimpsed through open doors. The churches were prettier than either of the two she had seen in Jeanerette and Cameron.

When they reached a corner, Charl' exclaimed, "There." He pointed out a chapel diagonally across the way. "Our Lady of Guadeloupe. Odalie's house is the yellow one next door."

The butter-colored house had three full stories. "*That?*" Therese demanded. "Odalie has three whole floors *alone*?"

Charl' laughed. "No, not alone. A coachman and a maid live with her too. I am told they sleep up there, at the top. There is another whole floor, below the street, which holds the kitchen. Emile says the cook comes in, and does not live there. But come, you'll see."

Impressed by this new information, Therese crossed the street with Charl' and walked up a brief flight of railed stairs to the door. Charl' rapped the wrought-iron knocker, which was shaped like a smiling moon with a ring in its mouth.

In an instant the door was opened by a tiny, very dark-skinned woman with an impudent face. She was wearing a black dress of excellent material, a white ruffled apron, and a huge white *tignon* with big orange dots.

Once again Therese had the feeling of watching a costumed actor in a play.

"Yes?" the little woman asked crisply.

"We are the Pavans," Charl' said with dignity. "*Mademoiselle* expects us." The woman was looking at their clothes.

"The *Pavans*." The servant's brows shot up and her wide lips parted in patent surprise. "Enter, if you please."

They followed her into a short entrance hall containing two big potted palms. "If you please, wait in the parlor. I will summon *mam'zelle*." She opened a dark door and waved her pudgy hand.

Before they could go in, they heard a call from the top of the stairs. "Zizi! Coffee and *brioche*. At *once*."

Zizi looked up wall-eyed. *"Tout de suite, mam'zelle."* She rushed toward the stairs at the rear of the hall.

Charl' and Therese stood staring upward. Neither of them had seen Odalie for seven years, and Therese could hardly believe that this was the rawboned girl they had played with on the Côte Blanche. Before them was a unique and magnificent woman.

Only the huge black disillusioned eyes were the same; everything else was transformed. Now her posture was stately, and her pale *griffe* complexion, which had once been slightly freckled, was as smooth and rich as gold. Her shapely mouth was coral-colored and her hair, formerly worn in many tight plaits, had been cropped to a small black cap, revealing the fineness of her head. Most of all, her thin figure had bloomed to slender perfection. This was obvious to Therese, despite the fullness of Odalie's elegant morning dress, which was the ringing color of sunflower petals. Fringed gold earrings hung from her ears.

Both the brother and sister were speechless.

Odalie smiled widely, showing her small, even teeth. "That *girl. Bienvenue,* Tez. *Bienvenu,* Charl'."

She came down the stairs in a rush, and in a whisper of silk floated to them, embracing first Therese and then her brother.

Charl' found his voice first. "You are so changed."

"And so are you. It is good to see your faces. But let us not stand here. You have traveled so far, you must be *fatigués* and hungry. Come, come and sit down."

She almost pushed them through the dark, half-open door. When Therese's sun-dazzled eyes adjusted to the shuttered room, she saw how unusual it was.

The walls were whitewashed and the mahogany sofa and chairs were almost like those in the music room at Petite Anse. But they were upholstered not in silk and pastel brocades, but rather in vivid shades of orange, golden yellow, and bright green cotton. Against the background of the white walls, Odalie's sunflower dress was as emphatic and stirring as a beaten drum.

"Please," Odalie said to Therese, indicating a chair. Therese sat, suddenly overwhelmed by the journey, the city, but most of all this new Odalie and her house. Charl' put down their sacks in a corner and took a seat on one end of the gold-covered sofa.

Chagrined, Therese noticed Odalie's swift inventory of her own striped cloak, to which a few seeds of a wild weed still clung; her bedraggled red dress, and her mud-stained stockings and shoes. But there was no scorn in the huge dark eyes, only warm compassion. And Odalie's glance returned at once to Therese's face and hair. "It has been so long, Tez. And you have grown so beautiful."

Therese could feel her cheeks flushing with gratification.

The impish Zizi came in laden with a heavy tray.

Charl', in his easy, matter-of-fact manner, said, "Here, let me help you. You are too small for that." He got up and took the tray from the amazed servant, saying to Odalie, "Where does this go?"

"On this table." Odalie added, *"Merci."* She grinned. After Zizi had gone out, she said to Charl', "You are still the same, *mon ami*. You haven't changed a *sou* since you pulled me out of that 'gator's jaws. But here, let me serve you both." She moved across the black, brightly flowered carpet.

With grace she poured them coffee from a curved porcelain pot, proffering *brioches* that melted on the tongue. Eating and drinking gratefully, Therese remembered what Charl' had said of his interview with old Emile, Odalie's father. "Take your sister to Odalie. None of us will ever forget how you saved the life of our child." Odalie, Therese recalled, was two years older than Charl'; it was difficult to believe that this elegant, sophisticated creature was only nineteen.

More relaxed now, Therese looked around the room again. With pleasure and surprise, she noticed a tall bookcase with glass doors, crammed with volumes that made her mouth water: titles in English and French, two of which caught her eye at once—a green leather book with a gilt title, *Leaves of Grass*, and the name Whitman below it; and *Les Fleurs de Mal*, bound in purple, by someone named Baudelaire.

There were also novels by the few authors she knew.

Odalie caught the look. *"Mon ami,"* she remarked with a wry inflection, "has taught me to be quite a reader. I recall that you were always a reader too, Therese."

"I never saw so many books at once," Therese answered, "even at school."

Charl' smiled. "Only one of the splendors of Rampart Street. I cannot tell you how grateful we are, Odalie. It is no small thing to harbor a runaway Acadien."

Odalie seemed embarrassed. "How can you speak of it, Charl'?" She went on quickly, "You and Therese were always the only ones who treated us like . . . human beings. *Now*. Rolls are all very well, but I judge that both of you could use a meal. I take it that you didn't arrive in the luxury cabin of the *Sara Belle*."

Her sarcastic tone set off their laughter.

Charl' told her something of the trip, making light of their discomforts.

"*Mon Dieu.*" Odalie made a face. "As for me, I miss nothing about the bayou, except, often, my people." She picked up a small glass bell from the table beside her chair and rang it. It had a surprisingly penetrating chime. Almost immediately Zizi poked her turbaned head around the door.

"If you please, luncheon, Zizi, in the dining room."

"Luncheon, *mam'zelle?* But you have not yet had your breakfast!"

Once again Therese was impressed with the luxurious late hours kept in the house.

"*C'est vrai.* Lynelle will make me an omelet. *Vite, donc . . .* and bring a bottle of the good *vin blanc* from the cooling chest."

As before, Zizi fairly leapt to obey. Odalie's eyes twinkled. She murmured, "Zizi believes that I am expert at *voudon.* You have no notion how that belief ensures perfect service."

Charl' and Therese grinned at each other. The intelligent old Emile had never placed any credence in voodoo or *gris-gris*, and had passed on his skepticism to Odalie.

Then all at once, Odalie was asking them a thousand questions about the last seven years. By the time she led them into a small, sunny dining room, where a round table was set with lovely dishes and goblets, Odalie had learned that Therese had made her own ensemble. Soon the women were deep in discussion of dressmaking.

"Tomorrow," Odalie said, "Madame Dufay, the *modiste,* is coming to measure me for a ball gown. You must meet her, Therese, and show her what you have done."

"Oh, but surely . . ." Therese protested.

"But *surely.* Women like me"—once again Therese heard a cool, cynical undertone—"are the Dufay's best patrons. We are not, you understand, so . . . limited in our finery as the respectable ladies." She gave them a one-sided smile. "Therefore, if I recom-

mend she take on a talented student, there is every
reason to believe she will do so. Either that or be
blackballed among the 'protected' women."

Odalie's smile was devilish.

"Take me *on*?" Therese asked. "Do you think she
might? I never thought of that. There is so much I
need to learn."

"I believe she will. I assure you."

Charl' beamed at them. "I was hoping something
like that would turn up. I can only thank you again."
Aware that he had embarrassed their friend, Charl'
said hastily, "I must leave. I want to go back to the
levee and see about getting work on the *Sara Belle*."

He rose and took Odalie's hand. "Would it be better," he asked delicately, "if I came back tomorrow
morning?"

"Feel free, Charl'. *Mon ami*, Raoul de Sevigny, is
taking his fiancée to the opera tonight, and afterward
there is a *fête* for the men, in honor of Raoul's
marriage."

The flat statement shocked Therese. Odalie took it
all so for granted. And yet, when Therese thought of
it, had her own position been so different? With Nicholas, she recalled, she had had even fewer advantages
than Odalie. Neither she nor Odalie was good enough
for the rich to marry. And now, her only family was
Charl'. . . .

Her volatile emotions, heated by the wine, made
her cry out, "Oh, Charl'! When you ship out, I'll
never *see* you!"

"Come, come, *petite*. The wine's gone to your head."
Odalie patted her.

Therese had to admit that it had. Before this, she'd
had only a glass now and then at weddings.

"Charl' must make his way," Odalie said.

"Yes, I must." Charl' patted her much as Odalie
had done. "When I'm making money, I can send you
some, you know."

Therese clung to him. Gently he kissed her on the
top of the head and then he went back to the parlor to
pick up his bundle. After they had seen him out,

Odalie turned to Therese and said softly, "You are all worn out. I will show you to your room. After you have rested, this evening we will see to your clothes."

"Thank you. But first, I simply must . . ." Therese looked down at herself.

"I am *stupide*. Of course you must have a bath. Come. Never mind your bundle; Zizi will bring it." Odalie urged Therese up the stairs to the second floor.

There was a whole separate room for bathing, with a commode and sink and a great white tub on feet like a lion's paws. Next to the tub was a pump. Apparently hot water came right through the pump; Therese had not imagined anything like this. She had assumed that Zizi would be obliged to bring her buckets of water. It was such a luxury, after the big washtub at the cabin, that Therese felt tears fill her eyes as Odalie showed her how to work the pump.

Odalie bustled in and out with fresh, soft towels; a new, still-wrapped bar of soap; and even a bottle of rosewater to scent the bath. Then she went out again and returned with a white cotton wrapper and a pair of white leather heelless slippers. When Odalie had closed the door, Therese pumped out some water and put a few drops of the rosewater in the tub, breathing in the steamy fragrance again and again before she stripped and immersed herself.

The bath was such a marvel that she could hardly bear the thought of emerging from it. She did not know how long she lay back in the warm, sweet-scented water before she heard a sharp tapping on the door.

"Therese, are you all right?" Odalie's voice came through the door.

Therese called out her affirmative.

"*Bon.*" Odalie said. "I was afraid you had shriveled, like a prune . . . or worse, had drowned in your sleep."

Therese laughed. Rejuvenated and tingling, she got out and dried herself, hurrying into the wrapper and flat shoes.

Odalie took her up another flight of stairs. "After Charl' sent me the letter," she explained, "I had a room

prepared. I am sorry that it must be up here, but . . ."
Odalie shrugged, an infinitely Gallic gesture. She
opened the door. "It is, as you see, very plain."

Therese had expected to share a room with someone else. Though this bedroom, tiny as it was, might
seem plain to Odalie, to Therese it was plain delight.
She had never had a room of her own or anticipated
having one. In Côte Blanche a girl went from a room
shared with sisters to one shared with a husband.

"It's the prettiest room I've ever seen." Here, too,
the walls were white and although it was on the shady
side of the house, the room was worlds brighter than
the cabin with its dark, bare wooden walls. The single
window was curtained with red-and-white-checked muslin; the small bed had a coverlet of the same material.

A looking-glass hung above a plain pine table; the
table had a matching pine chair, padded in scarlet, and
there was a red curtain hanging in a corner. "For your
things," Odalie said, drawing the curtain aside to reveal a rod and hangers.

But it was an item on a table directly below the
window that attracted Therese's eyes—a shiny black
machine with curly painted designs of gilt and gray-
green.

"A sewing machine!" she breathed. It was exactly
like one she'd seen in a catalog in Jeanerette. Thrilled,
she fingered the word "Singer" emblazoned on its
side.

"Yes. This used to be the sewing room, you see.
Zizi will show you how to use it." Therese, still exam-
ining the remarkable machine, felt Odalie's bright stare.
"You had better rest now, for a little."

"Rest! Oh, no." The bath had revived Therese, and
the idea of sleep was absurd. There was too much to
absorb, too much to see. She felt as if she would never
want to sleep again, with these new wonders shown
her every moment.

"Very well, then. Come downstairs with me and let
us find you some dresses."

"But, Odalie, you have already done so much.
Dresses?"

"But naturally, Tez. I have already sent your brown dress to the laundress, and the red one is cut too low. If I let you wear it tomorrow morning, I would be a murderess—Madame Dufay would surely expire." Odalie chuckled. "Even the 'bad women' cover their breasts in the mornings. As to the Dufay, I think we must devise a story.

"You are a grieving young widow, no? Who has been left *enceinte* in her bereavement . . . a poor orphan driven away by her husband's cruel family. Will that do?" Odalie looked mischievous.

Therese hadn't even thought of that. "That will do very well," she answered slowly. "It is so near the truth."

"You told the boy's family, then?"

"Oh, *no*. I could never have done that." Therese sank down on the bed, remembering. "He went away to school. He doesn't know either. You see, the last time I went to Petit Anse he . . ." The words died away. Her face felt hot.

"*Mon Dieu*. The son of the Adairs. I *see*. You didn't tell them because you were too proud, is that it?"

Therese nodded, looking at the white rag rug on the floor.

"It is well," Odalie remarked. "There was as much chance they would accept you as the de Sevignys would embrace me." That stung, but Therese could not help smiling a little at Odalie's comical expression.

"Now then," Odalie said briskly. "What on earth shall we call you?" She thought for a moment. "What about Madame Labiche?"

Therese grinned. Emmeline Labiche was the original Evangeline, exiled to Maryland when the Acadiens were driven out of Nova Scotia. From Maryland, Emmeline was taken to the Teche country, where she waited under the Evangeline oak for her lost lover.

"The Dufay is from Paris, and she has never been out of New Orleans. She'll never know," Odalie said, laughing.

Therese could not laugh with her, for Emmeline's
story was too much like her own. She smiled weakly,
saying, "That is perfect," as she rose to follow Odalie
down the stairs.

If her own small room was pretty, Odalie's was like
a bower from paradise, with its silk-covered bed and
filmy draperies hanging from the canopy above. Therese was speechless. At Odalie's invitation, she sat
down on a pink elongated piece of furniture that was
neither couch nor chair, too shy to ask what it was
called, and watched Odalie open the doors of a giant,
intricately carved chifforobe.

Odalie's slender fingers were busy, shoving some
gowns aside, pulling others out for examination. Therese had never seen so many, or such magnificent
items—dimly she recognized the fabrics of silk and
velvet and satin, taffeta and bombazine, which she
had read about but never viewed before.

"Ah!" Odalie pulled out a silk dress with alternate
stripes of brown and ecru plaid and dull orange flowers. There was a little capelet over the shoulders, and
the bell-shaped sleeves were trimmed with fringe of
orange and brown. "This should be nice for you. I am
taller, you know, so it will have to be hemmed. But
other than that, we are very much alike. I will get you
some lingerie. Try it on."

Therese retired behind a screen as Odalie tossed the
lovely lingerie to her, then emerged to try on the dress
in front of a long, very clear cheval glass. She blinked
at her image; she was unrecognizable in her elegance.

"I must be frank," Odalie said. "That dress is two
years old. But you do look nice, no?"

Dazed, Therese nodded and sat while Odalie bequeathed her three more day dresses and two evening
gowns, then looked for the proper shoes and stockings. "The old Dufay says that in Paris, 'the dress is
only the accessory.' We must fit you out so you will be
presentable." Odalie found Therese brown and black
shoes to wear with the day dresses, another pair for
the evening, and some soft felt embroidered house
shoes as well.

"Now, if you will excuse me, *I* am going to *fait do-do*," Odalie said. "I have instructed Zizi to show you how to use the machine, if you wish. I will call her."

Therese went back to her room, carrying her treasures with the help of the silent Zizi, whom Therese feared she had cheated of the garments. After they were put away, she faced the new machine with consternation.

Zizi was not the most patient of teachers. However, after making several false starts with the scraps Zizi had brought for her to practice on, Therese found herself operating the machine with greater and greater ease. She realized after Zizi left her that she worked with far more confidence. Before she knew it, the light in the room was failing, and she lit a lamp, eager to begin hemming the full-skirted striped silk gown, and at least one of the evening dresses.

Triumphant, she finished them both, and by the time Charl' arrived for dinner at eight o'clock, Therese went proudly to the door in her new gown.

He goggled at the modestly cut dress of black rep silk, with its undersleeves and filled-in corsage of white chiffon. "You have already become a lady of fashion, Tez."

Dinner was very gay, and even the news that Charl' would be shipping out the very next day as a deckhand could not oppress her spirits. She would find her strength in learning a skill to support herself; she had already made so much progress in just her first day.

That at last, when Charl' had gone, fatigue overcame Therese. All of a sudden, she was so tired she could hardly climb the stairs.

For New Orleans, she supposed, it was still very early: from her bed she could hear the voice of the watchman cry out the hour of ten, a twang of guitars from somewhere, a woman's voice singing, and the rhythmic clopping and squeak of horse-drawn barouches and cabriolets.

Her eyes were as heavy as cypress logs, and yet she could not quite let go, for the moment, of her new surroundings—the cheerful checked curtains at the window, the shadow of the wondrous black machine, and her drawings, which she had stuck in the soft white-washed wall with sewing pins.

As she drifted in half-sleep, her thoughts were random, names and faces floating in her consciousness like phantoms—her mother's, Amelie's; her father's and the boys'. What would they be saying now, or doing, back on Côte Blanche?

Her father, no doubt, had gone to sleep, just as on any other night. So would Amelie and her brothers. But Berthe—Therese pictured her lying awake in the dark, and her heart ached for her mother. She had wanted to leave Berthe a letter, but Charl' said they could not take the chance. Michel could find it and blame their mother for their escape.

The baby, Elianne. Elianne would cry for Therese, and miss her. Therese had been the only one with time to play with her; Berthe was too tired from her responsibilities, and Amelie, too wrapped up in her own concerns.

The baby.

A swift thought, like a blade of light, pierced Therese's hazy reflections. She had not thought of her own baby for all that day. Even when Odalie had referred to her as *enceinte*, the word had had no true meaning in the day's exciting jumble of new sensations.

In the spring, her baby would be born.

By that time, she must have money and a place of her own to stay. Raoul de Sevigny, the rich "*ami*" of her friend, would never tolerate a crying baby in his house.

But tomorrow, tomorrow was her shining hope. If she could prove herself to this Madame Dufay, she might be able to work for her, to make some money for herself and the child.

She must be strong. Berthe had always said, "You are an Acadien, Therese. An the Acadiens are strong. We've had to be."

There was truth to that. All the Acadien children along the bayous knew the story of their people; Berthe had told it to Therese when she was still quite small.

More than two hundred years ago their ancestors from France had come to a place far up north called Newfoundland, to a land they named Acadia. The people in Acadia fished and traded furs with red Indians, and bothered no one. But the cruel English, Berthe said, fought with the Acadiens over their boats and furs, and took many of the French trading posts away.

Much later, after a terrible war, the Acadiens were driven out. Some went to Maryland and other places; others, who had heard of the country just like France, to the south, in the state of Louisiana, kept going. One of these was the ancestor of Therese Pavan; others were forebears of her friends and relatives.

And so the settlement of Acadiens along the swamps was born. Berthe said that the Anglos called Acadiens "Cajuns," a name they hated, a term of contempt in the slurred, soft, Southern tongue. Among themselves they were forever and proudly Acadiens, named for the lost paradise from which they had been driven.

Therese learned early in life that Acadiens did not mingle with others; the swamp people kept to themselves because, as her father always said, an Acadien could not trust outsiders.

Well, that, like so many other things Michel had told her, was a lie. Odalie, for example, could be trusted utterly. And there might be many others like her.

The bayou, beautiful as it was, was desolate, like a prison for the likes of Odalie, Therese, and Charl'.

Yet the bayou, and Petit Anse, had brought her Nicholas, had brought her glory for a little while.

But he had been faithless and uncaring. He had left her with a child she would have to bring up alone.

"I must forget him," Therese whispered.

Yes, she must forget her brief time of happiness, and the traitorous paradise from which she'd been driven as her ancestors had been expelled from Acadia. She must not remember the taste of his mouth, or how his arms felt, or his hair that smelled like lemons in the sun.

Her last waking thought came: I am an Acadien. And Acadiens are strong.

I will be strong enough to become someone. I will show Nicholas Adair.

# 3

Therese's nighttime bravado began to fail her the next morning as the time for Madame Dufay's arrival loomed near. She was expected at eleven, so Therese was faced with hours of anxiety before Odalie would open an eye.

But she spent the time as well as she could, calculating what she could do with the small store of money Charl' had left her, dressing in the black bombazine day dress, and braiding her hair, winding the braids in a coronet around her head, so she would look older. She was glad to see that the dress was the proper length—it must have been short on Odalie, and the heels of the dainty black shoes helped. Therese was satisfied that she looked demure and neat, as a young "widow" should, and hoped she could carry out the masquerade.

To pass the time, she went quietly downstairs to the parlor and chose one of the books from the glass-doored cabinet. It was a novel called *Madame Bovary*, and Therese became so absorbed in it that she forgot how much she wanted some coffee. She hated to ask the pert Zizi to serve her, because the girl seemed to resent her so much.

After a while, though, the tantalizing smells of bacon and coffee drifted upward through the open parlor door, beckoning her down to the kitchen.

After replacing the book, Therese descended the stairs to the basement level of the house. Through an open archway she saw a fat dark-skinned woman in a brilliant red *tignon* turning bacon in a skillet. The

woman turned, surprised, when she heard Therese's
footstep.

"*Bonjour*," Therese said, smiling.

The woman's face was good-natured, her small black
eyes as bright and observant as a monkey's. "*Zur,
ma'zelle. Zizi fek al labutik, i pâkor returne.*"

Therese could barely understand, but the word that
sounded like "*boutique*" cleared up the mystery a
little; evidently Zizi had gone to the market, and was
not back yet. The woman seemed to be awaiting Therese's orders, smiling and bewildered. Odalie had probably never set foot in the kitchen, she thought with
amusement.

"*Café, ma'zelle?*"

Therese nodded fervently, and sat down at the
scrubbed wooden table. It was obvious the cook didn't
know what to make of her, but she served Therese a
cup of coffee and offered her the sugar.

Remembering the cook's name, Therese thanked
her. "*Merci*, Lynelle. *Merci bien.*"

Lynelle beamed and indicated the skillet. Therese
shook her head. She wondered what dialect it was
Lynelle spoke; she must be one of the island people. It
was not going to be easy to communicate, except by
smiles and nods and shakings of the head; nevertheless
she could feel a friendly warmth emanating from the
broad Lynelle as she returned to her cooking. The
cook watched her finish her coffee and replenished
Therese's cup.

Just as she was finishing the second cup, Zizi came
in from the street entrance, laden with a huge basket.
Her scandalized greeting to Therese said more plainly
than words that the kitchen was no place for a lady,
even a spurious lady such as Therese Pavan. Therese
did not know whether she was amused or irritated.
She rose and went to the stairs, listening to Zizi and
Lynelle chatter in that strange *patois*. Apparently Therese did not belong anywhere—she was not elegant
enough to be on a par with Odalie, but neither was
she a servant. And she had belonged with neither the
Acadiens nor the Adairs.

She saw Odalie peeking over the banisters. "Therese? What are you up to?" she asked. She was resplendent in a morning dress the shade of new cream, almost the color of her skin; and in contrast her great black eyes were striking. Oval gold earrings set with coral dangled from her dainty ears and a matching brooch was pinned to the bodice of her dress. The jewelry, even more than the dress, aroused Therese's deep desire, and Odalie's quick glance registered Therese's hungry stare.

"Getting some coffee."

*"Pauvr' petit!"* The affectionate Acadien term warmed Therese. Odalie put an arm around her waist and they walked into the dining room. "I will have to teach you—all this *égalité* with the servants confuses them. They won't know where they are, you comprehend."

As they sat at the table, Therese said, "I know it, Odalie, but it is too much for my sense of humor. My mother, my sisters, and I waited hand and foot on my father and the boys . . . the kitchen corner was the center of the cabin. We sat there all the time. It makes me laugh to think that I am now too good to go into the kitchen."

"Don't laugh, *ma petite*." Odalie raised her brows. "If I never saw another kitchen, it would be too soon for me. In this world there are those who go into kitchens and those who do not. You must become one who does not." She grinned. "When Zizi is at the market, ring for Lynelle, or Jean-Jean. I will speak to them today about more sensible arrangements."

They fell silent as Zizi brought in their coffee and covered dishes. Today the maid's hair was hidden in a *tignon* of brilliant peacock blue.

When she had gone, Odalie asked, "How did you sleep?"

"Like the dead." Therese served herself and began eating hungrily. "I must say, I can't understand Lynelle at all."

"She is an *émigrée*." Odalie shrugged. "She speaks a *jambalaya* of African, Creole, and a kind of English.

So do Zizi and Jean-Jean, but I had to teach them some kind of plain French or we would be grunting at each other, waving our hands." Odalie's rich laugh bubbled out.

Therese thought how Odalie's own speech had changed. Seeming to read that thought, Odalie offered, "Yes, I had to be taught too. Do you remember when I left the bayou seven years ago?" Therese nodded. "My Aunt Cletie turned me over to the famous Victorine. Her establishment is the best-known brothel in New Orleans."

Therese blushed, saying nothing.

Odalie went on matter-of-factly, "She taught me everything—how to speak, how to walk, sit, and stand. Even how to eat elegantly at the table. What clothes to choose and how to wear them, with *tournure*, with style. La Victorine was for years the most pampered courtesan in Paris. There is nothing about style or elegance . . . or men . . . she doesn't know. I began as her personal maid. And graduated, still a virgin, to become the *amie* of Raoul." She smiled crookedly.

How strange it was, Therese thought. Odalie took her position utterly for granted. Therese couldn't see how she could bear it; she herself still smarted from Nicholas' rejection. "Tell me," she said impulsively, "are you happy?"

"Happy?" Odalie said the word as if it were a foreign one she was just learning to pronounce. "Do you think I would be happier in rags and pigtails on the bayou . . . or serving as a lady's maid, or one of the girls at Victorine's? Tez, the life I have is the best a *griffe* can have. When Raoul marries in December, he'll give me the deed to this house and some money and bonds. I'll find myself a proper man of mixed blood, and we'll start ourselves a business."

"But what about . . . love, Odalie?"

*"L'amour,"* Odalie mocked. "My dear Tez, it is 'love' that has brought you to this pass." She took Therese's hand. "I am sorry to be cruel, but it is true. Now, enough of these gloomy subjects. We must prepare you for la Dufay. First of all, I must prepare you

for her looks. She is for all the world like a wicked
*épouvantail*, a veritable scarecrow. A spinster of painful respectability."

Beholden to a "wicked" *griffe*, Therese thought,
giggling.

"And, to speak of preparations, there is something
else you need. Remain where you are. I will be right
back."

Puzzled, Therese waited until Odalie returned. Her
friend handed her a small cameo brooch ringed with
seed pearls. The head of Madame Pompadour, delicately carved, stood out against its onyx ground. With
her other hand, Odalie put a pair of matching eardrops of seed pearl and onyx by Therese's plate.

"They were given to me by Victorine when I left her
house. Now they must go to you, *ma protégée*."

Therese looked at the delicate pieces. "But you
must not—"

"If you please. No Acadien was ever kind to me but
you, and Charl'. Do you think I would ever forget
that? Come, put them on, quickly. The scarecrow will
be flapping in at any moment."

Therese took her treasures to a gilt-framed mirror
and removed the tiny gold hoop earrings that her
mother had passed on to her at her First Communion.
She slipped the wires of the eardrops in her ears;
turning her head this way and that, she watched the
jewels dance. The ornaments gave her a spirited air,
and she saw that the light pearls, the onyx, gave her
eyes and skin and hair new definition.

When she had pinned the cameo to the throat of her
dress, she turned to thank Odalie, but they heard the
tap of the knocker, and Zizi went to answer the door.

Odalie went to the hall, followed by Therese.
"*Bonjour, madame*. Come into the parlor."

Her friend's description had been apt, Therese decided. Dressed from head to toe in black, Madame
Dufay was as thin as a cornstalk, with a long thin nose
and flinty gray eyes that leapt curiously at Therese.

Once again she had the feeling of being out of step
with the world—a white woman in the house of a

*griffe*—and yet she interpreted Madame Dufay's almost imperceptible shrug: "The patron is rich, and New Orleans is a strange city, after all."

"Ah. We are fitting you in the parlor today, *mademoiselle?*" Madame Dufay asked in what Therese supposed must be Parisian French. The woman's tight-pursed lips pronounced each word with great precision.

"No, no." Odalie waved Dufay into the parlor. "There is something I wish to discuss with you. Be seated. I wish to present my guest, Madame Labiche."

Dufay inclined her head, which was covered by a stylish black bonnet, and Therese smiled at her hopefully. She noticed that the rest of Dufay's attire was even smarter than the bonnet; her gown and jacket fit her to perfection.

Odalie chatted easily with the dressmaker, insisting that she enjoy some pastries and coffee. As she served Madame Dufay, Odalie began to tell her something of Therese's story. In her nervousness, Therese hardly followed, conscious only of random phrases.

"Your drawings, my dear Therese. Perhaps you will show them to Hortense, with your burnoose."

Therese got to her feet. "Of course." She raced upstairs and returned with the drawings, handing them to Hortense Dufay. The striped cloak was over her arm.

The woman's gimlet survey took in the sketches rapidly. "Remarkable," she pronounced, looking up at Therese with curious interest. "And that?" Therese handed her the cloak, which had been brushed and cleaned. "Amazing," Dufay pronounced. "Such stitching. A most original translation of the burnoose." Something approaching a smile trembled on the stingy lips. "I see no reason not to employ you, *madame.*"

Therese's heart hammered. She was actually going to get a place in the salon of the Dufay.

"However, I fear I cannot oblige even you, *mademoiselle*," Madame Dufay said, attempting a twinkle which emerged more like a tic, "by making Madame Labiche an instant *midinette*. It took me five full years to become a seamstress in Paris. But I am sure that there are many other tasks that Madame Labiche can do."

"I'll be most happy to do anything," Therese blurted out, ignoring Odalie's slight frown.

"Well, then, one of my girls has run off to be married, and I could use you at once. When can you begin?"

"Tod—" Therese started, but a quick, fearsome frown from Odalie made her revise it to, "Tomorrow, *madame*."

Exultant, she watched Madame Dufay stalk out after Odalie for the fitting in her bedroom. Her excitement carried Therese through the rest of the afternoon and even through the solitary evening in her little room upstairs. Raoul de Sevigny was visiting Odalie that night, and it was tacitly understood that everyone in the house would remain invisible.

Zizi seemed to take it as a matter of course that Therese would be served dinner in her room, and the evening passed quickly as Therese read the adventures of *Madame Bovary*.

She understood Emma so well, sympathized completely with her longing for romance, and the life of elegance.

Why, it was almost like Therese's own life—the contrast between Emma's husband and her noble lover reminded Therese of the awesome difference between Hector Rocaille and Nicholas. Those two were as unlike as . . . a monkey and a human.

Therese marked the place in her book and put it aside, remembering. . . .

Summer was at its height then—the damp, dragging heat so intense that Therese felt enclosed in it. She walked slowly toward the yellow-green meadow of Petit Anse, afraid that at any moment she would lose her careful freshness.

Just a little while before, she had washed her hair again, dried it in the sun, put on the pink dress she had ironed that morning, and rubbed vanilla on her skin, telling the inquisitive Berthe that the vanilla made her feel cool. No one ever took such trouble with herself on Côte Blanche during the week. Special primping was for dances or for church on Sundays.

Therese looked forward with a high heart to meeting Nicholas again; they would walk, as always, in the cool rose garden, and he would say to her the sweet things he had before. She knew he would like the dress, a new one she had made, because it was cool and thin and dainty, with simple lines and a ruffled hem; and it was just the color of his mother's "prize" roses.

Her secret visits to Petit Anse had become the high point of her life; while she was there, she could be sure that someday she and Nicholas would marry, that she would be the mistress of all that splendor.

This was only the fourth time she'd gone, of course. She hadn't met Nicholas' parents yet, nor had they gone into the house. He always said it was nicer outside in the summer. Soon, though, she knew that he would introduce her to his mother and father. And he would ask her to marry him.

She was sure of that. Otherwise he wouldn't look at her with such loving eyes, kiss her hand, and say the wonderful things he said to her. He was such a gentleman, he hadn't even kissed her yet, not on the lips. Perhaps today . . .

Therese was so deep in dreamy thoughts, looking down absently at the ground, that she almost collided with Hector Rocaille.

"Well, *well*." He reached out and grabbed her by the shoulders, his rough hands wet with perspiration. Therese slipped out of his grasp, defeating his slick, damp fingers.

"Get out of my way, Hector."

He stepped in front of her again, holding out his massive hairy arms to block her way. "Where are you going in such a hurry?"

Therese could smell his musky scent, compounded of rank sweat and fish. Hector dropped his arms then, grabbing her around the waist with one hand; with the other, he turned her chin upward roughly.

She was forced to look into his small black eyes, glittering under their shaggy roofs of brows. His hair grew low on his forehead, giving him a bullish, threatening air. She shrank back; she was close enough to count the stubbly hairs on his chin, and his thick mouth, with its silly grin, was near her own.

"Why do you tease me, Therese?" Still holding her face in his viselike grip, he opened his lips and clamped them over hers. She could feel his heart hammer through his dampened shirt. Pressing against her breasts, bruising them, his wide chest felt like a block of cypress.

She struggled in his hold, unable to breathe, sickened by the smell and taste of him. He would not let go.

Then she remembered what Charl' had taught her; summoning all her strength, she bent her knee and brought it sharply upward, driving it as hard as she could into Hector's groin.

He bellowed in pain, loosing her abruptly and bending over to grasp his injured center. "Bitch!" he grunted. "Bitch!"

She wasted no time: in a few seconds she was racing toward the meadow, running up the hill of waving grass. Her heart was beating so hard she was afraid it would leap right up into her throat and out of her body.

At the top of the hill, in the sun, she saw Nicholas. He started down to meet her.

"Therese! What is it—what's the matter?"

Chagrined, she felt the perspiration stream down her back, the lovely dress sticking to her skin; the moisture around the edges of her hair. It was horrible . . . humiliating. Nicholas was always so clean and cool, smelling of lemons.

"What is it?" he repeated, bewildered.

She was about to blurt it out when she was suddenly filled with shame. How could she tell him? He might think she had encouraged Hector. "Something . . . frightened me . . ." She faltered.

"A 'gator?" He was smiling at her now, as if she were a foolish child. She felt all hot and ruined and

. . . disgusting. He didn't touch her and she was glad.
She couldn't have stood it, couldn't have stood him
feeling her damp skin. His crisp white shirt, his faultless trousers shamed her. "Well, you shouldn't run
like that in this weather . . . in the sun. Shame on
you."

He offered her an immaculate handkerchief. Embarrassed, she wiped her face and neck with it. "I'll
wash it for you," she said diffidently.

"Don't be silly," he said lightly, taking the handkerchief from her. "Come along. Let's go get you something cool to drink."

At last, at last, she thought, he's going to invite me
into the house. She hoped her dress would be all right.
Looking down at it, she pulled the skirt away from her
warm body, shaking out the ruffle.

"We'll go to my little house," Nicholas said. "My
own little *garçonnière*. You haven't even seen it yet,
have you?"

Her heart sank: he wasn't going to invite her into
the big house. His *garçonnière* was a whole house . . .
at home, Charl's and César's was an attic. That seemed
to widen the distance between her and Nicholas even
more.

Then she thought of something else, something even
worse. Charl' had told her that the rich boys in New
Orleans had their own little houses to "sow their wild
oats in," away from the sacred precincts of their family mansions.

But no—Nicholas was not like that. He was such a
gentleman. He was not like Hector Rocaille. He was
inviting her to the little house just so she could cool
off and feel good again.

Reassured, she walked with him through the rose
garden toward the edge of a wood. There, gleaming
white in the sun, was a wonderful small house, a
replica of the big one at Petit Anse.

"Why, it's beautiful," she said softly. Smiling, Nicholas took her hand. He led her up the two front steps
and opened the door, gesturing for her to enter.

Inside, the house was dark and cool, and full of the

smell of roses. Nicholas led the way into a little sitting
room off the tiny hall. "Make yourself comfortable."

She sat down on a shiny loveseat as he went to a
cabinet. "I think you could use a glass of wine."

Therese had rarely tasted wine, but she did not
protest. She was shy of letting him know how inexperi-
enced she was in the ways of the elegant world. He
poured two thin goblets of pale golden wine and handed
one to her. Sipping from his goblet, he sat down
beside her and set his glass on a side table.

Nervously she drank nearly the whole goblet of
wine.

He chuckled. "May I give you some more?"

She hesitated. Her head felt strange; her body was
becoming very lazy. Then she nodded. Smiling broadly,
he went to the cabinet again and brought back the
decanter, filled her glass again, and set the decanter
on the table.

Conscious of his regard, Therese drank as quickly as
before. When she set her goblet on the other table, she
nearly let the glass drop over the edge.

"Pretty Therese," Nicholas murmured, stroking her
hair. "So dark . . . like the night." His hand wandered
from her head down her cheek, over her neck. She
raised her face to him, admiring his sleepy blue-gray
eyes and his smooth, lightly tanned skin, so different
from the brutish Hector's. Before she realized it, she
was stroking his cheek. He lowered his face to hers
and began to kiss her, sweetly and gently. Then the
kiss was not so gentle anymore.

His hands were fondling her shoulders and arms,
then her breasts. "Oh, Nicholas. No, no," she said
weakly.

"Yes. *Yes*," he murmured against her mouth, and
then everything began to change very quickly. Before
she knew what was happening, Nicholas' hands had
become rougher, almost savage; he was touching her
all over her body, through her clothes, and she was
trying to stop him, trying to resist, but he was too
strong for her.

And she knew hazily that she loved him too much to

stop him. If this was what he wanted, it was what she wanted too. He picked her up in his arms, carrying her into the little hall again, and into the bedroom of the *garçonnière*.

It was meant to be, she thought, submitting to his urgent hands as they undressed her and stroked her bare flesh. It would be wonderful, with Nicholas.

She saw that he was naked too, and he was beautiful, more beautiful than she had ever imagined a man could be. He threw himself upon her, and she was aware of a tearing pain, protesting silently: This is not the way love should be . . . this is not the way it was in the stories of love.

And it was over almost instantly: he gasped and lay upon her while she felt only bewilderment and a slight cessation of the awful pain.

Nicholas raised his body and lay beside her, not touching her. Timidly she looked at him; he was staring at nothing, with a slight smile on his mouth.

"Oh, Nicholas," she whispered, touching his arm. "I love you."

He leaned over and kissed her on the nose. "And I love *you*," he said lightly. "Right now I'd also love another glass of wine."

She was dismayed: the way he'd said he loved her was so . . . strange, so careless. She watched him walk, still naked, from the room, and return with the decanter and two glasses. He held up an empty glass to her.

Therese shook her head. Nicholas poured the wine and drank off a goblet, still standing; then poured another, which he sipped from and set on a table with the decanter.

He threw himself down beside her and kissed her bare skin. "Lovely, lovely Therese," he murmured, squeezing her flesh.

"Nicholas . . ." she said, raising her hand and stroking his cheek. "We'll . . . we'll be married now."

He smiled down at her. "Of course we will. After a while."

She felt a chill run over her body. "A while?" she repeated uncertainly.

"Of course, my dear. You see, I have to go away to college this autumn. I must finish school. But we'll see each other during the holidays . . . and next summer, and—"

"But that will be four *years*," she whispered, stricken.

"It may not have to be that long," he murmured. His persuasive hands caressed her. "I'll speak to my father soon. But you see, I'll have to . . . prepare him. I'm only seventeen."

Under his stroking hands she relaxed—he touched her with such soft skill, erasing the terrible memory of Hector Rocaille. Therese began to feel a new ease, a new excitement.

"We are here now, Therese, together. Be with me . . . let's not worry about the future."

He lowered his mouth to hers again in that delicate kiss that turned, so gradually and sweetly, strong, and she responded, eager and uncaring now. He'd said that they would marry, so it was all right. In her heart, he was already her husband.

Therese did not go back to the cabin until sunset, thanking God that her father had not yet returned. But her mother observed her with curious, anxious eyes.

The following summer weeks were like a lovely dream, as she went back again and again to the little *garçonnière*. However, when the high heat began to slope away and autumn drew near, Therese began to feel apprehension. Whenever she asked Nicholas if he had spoken to his father, he answered her sharply, saying that she was ruining things for them.

And he still had not asked her to come into the big house. She was beginning to feel furtive and unclean; what had been an enticing secret, like the "fatal loves" she had read about, was now a dark shame in her mind.

Yet she could not deny him: when his mood was good, the lovely, clever things he said melted her resistance, erased her doubts. She had become en-

slaved to the knowing touch of his fine, long-fingered
hands, the feel of his lightly muscled body with its
smooth, golden skin. He and his world were everything that Hector and the bayou were not, and never
could be.

One morning near the end of summer, she crossed
the meadow to Petit Anse, in an anxious frame of
mind. Surely now, when she told Nicholas what had
happened, he would have to speak to his father and
arrange their marriage. Surely, if he loved her, he
would be glad to know that they were going to have a
baby. But maybe he wouldn't be glad. Her father
hadn't been glad when her mother told him Elianne
was coming.

Therese took the back way Nicholas had shown her
and emerged from the little wood.

From the *garçonnière* she heard a woman's laughter.

Her heart almost stopped beating: could he be there
with someone else? But no, that was monstrous. That
was impossible. She paused at the edge of the wood,
listening.

The woman laughed again. This time the laugh was
echoed by another woman's; it sounded like a black
woman. And Therese did not hear Nicholas' voice at
all.

She crept nearer to the little house.

"That boy is something," a woman was saying. Now
Therese was sure they were servants. They must be
cleaning the house. But she wondered where Nicholas
was, why he had not met her, as he always did.

Therese moved closer, until she was near the bedroom window. She peeped in. Two servants were at
work, one stripping the postered bed of its coverings,
the other removing garments from a chest.

The one at the chest grumbled, "He sure is one
selfish boy. How come he didn't pack these things
before?"

Therese's heart lurched. Nicholas must have gone
off somewhere already. He had told her nothing about
that; it wasn't time for him to go to school yet, and he

hadn't even given her an address where she could
write to him.

"Lord knows," the other woman said. "He never
did care how much trouble he gave folks. His mama
acts like he was Jesus."

"Whooo," her companion ejaculated, and broke into
laughter again. "You are *bad*. That boy sure don't act
like Jesus in this here house."

"Who you reckon he had coming here *this* summer,
Lou?" The woman put a pile of folded clothes on a
chair and took a dust cloth from her apron.

The other, busy with smoothing on fresh linen, shook
her head. "Another one of them little bayou trash, I
figure. Maybe something nearer than Jeanerette, like
last summer."

Therese felt sick; she leaned against the outside of
the house.

"Well, this last one must of got too serious, I reckon.
That boy seems mighty anxious to get out of here."

"He sure does, that's a fact. Well, I figure we're
done here, don't you?"

"Looks like it. I'll take these things on up to the
house—Miz Adair's been deviling me for 'em—then
I'll come back and help you with the rest."

Therese came to her senses. The woman would be
coming out of the house, and would see her, Therese
Pavan, crouching like a rabbit against the wall. She
had to get away, fast.

"Lou? Goddammit! Where in the hell are those
shirts?"

Therese froze at the sound of Nicholas' voice.

It was a hundred times worse than she had feared.
Now he was going to catch her there, right in front of
the servants. But there was no way out. He was bound
to see her.

Nicholas came running toward the *garçonnière*; Therese was trapped, pressed against the outside wall. He
slowed to a walk and sauntered toward her with his
hands on his narrow hips. "Therese! Good God, what
are you doing . . . spying on me?"

She stood there wretchedly, tongue-tied, feeling the

nervous sweat gather on her brow and trickle down her face, in sharp contrast to his immaculate coolness. She felt like one of the muskrats struggling in a trap of mud.

Just then, the servant came out of the little house with an armful of ruffled shirts. "Right here, Mr. Nicholas. I'm takin' 'em right to your mama." The woman stared at Therese.

"Well, hurry up. I've got to leave," Nicholas snapped.

The woman rushed off toward the big house.

Therese found her voice. His face, his whole manner told her that what she had overheard was true, but she had to hear it from his own mouth. "Why were you going away without even telling me good-bye?"

His gray, contemptuous gaze swept her like a winter wind.

It was as if an evil spell had been placed upon him. "You said you'd speak to your father," she persisted, "that we'd get married."

"You stupid bitch! I'm an Adair. Do you think I'd marry *you*?"

"But you *said* so!" she cried out.

His face twisted. "Of course. It was the only way to get you on your back. *Marry* you—and find crawfish heads in my bed? Now, get out of here and leave me alone." He turned on his heel and stalked into the *garçonnière*.

*Crawfish heads*. The words stung like blows, those laughing words from the Acadien song *"Cribisse, Cribisse."* When Acadiens sang the song, they were not making fun of themselves, but of the high-toned French who considered them inferior; those French who called Acadiens "nèg 'méricains." But when an Anglo like Nicholas referred to the song, it was the bitterest insult, as if Therese actually smelled like *cribisse*.

Therese raced into the wood and then doubled back across the meadow; she could not stop running until she was safely back on the bayou. At last, in the shelter of the great kindly oaks, she threw herself full-length upon the spongy ground, taking great, gasp-

ing breaths. Her heart was pounding so hard she thought
she would break apart. Finally that terrible pounding
began to slow, and a deep, raging ache stole over her
whole body.

All Therese Pavan had been to Nicholas was "bayou
trash," a convenience for a summer. She hated him
now . . . she hated him more than she had ever hated
anyone or anything in her life, even her father. . . .

In her bedroom on Rampart Street, Therese awoke
to the lonely present. She would not read any more
about the poor, foolish Madame Bovary that night.
Tomorrow was her hope, tomorrow.

Madame Dufay had told her to appear at nine o'clock,
at the salon, which was only four blocks away.

The next morning, after breakfast had been served
to her in her room, Therese put on her black dress
again, instinctively omitting the treasured jewelry.

She crept quietly downstairs past Odalie's closed
door and out of the house, walking toward the salon
with quick, light steps.

When she saw the tall white house that was Madame Dufay's, she thought: This is the beginning of
my *bonne chance*, this is the answer to Nicholas and
all the damned Adairs.

Her driving hope, her stubborn resolve, sustained
her through her first reencounter with the intimidating
Madame Dufay and kept her spirits high throughout
that first long day, which lasted until nearly seven in
the evening.

Therese approached each task she was given with
the utmost solemnity, even though Madame Dufay
assigned her to the most menial and tiring occupations, from sweeping up cuttings to pulling bastings
and running errands for the patrons.

There was no maid to do those things; the thrifty
Madame Dufay cut corners the way she cut the cloth
for gowns. Therese was awed by her instinctive skill.
Madame could usually calculate a lady's measurement
by sight, and the tape measure invariably agreed.

In the rare moments when she and the other girls

were idle, Therese found herself keeping a civil distance from them; their chatter of beaux and *fêtes* and
other amusements seemed alien to her. They seemed
to take the work very lightly, as an obvious stopgap
until they married or moved on to better things.

Therese was amazed at that. For her there could be
no better thing than to learn all there was to know
about the fascinating business of making clothes, the
matter that had absorbed her since she had sewn her
first crude dress for a corncob doll when she was six
years old.

She noticed that some of the girls smiled when she
rushed to do Madame's slightest bidding, but she didn't
care. At lunch, when the others gathered to take their
food from baskets, Therese realized she had not even
thought of bringing her own; she had been too preoccupied with getting started. She had remembered to
bring a little money, so she hurried out to a small café
she had passed on the way to the salon that morning
and spent a few of Charl's coins for a bowl of gumbo
and a cup of coffee.

The next day, she resolved, she would bring her
own food; she certainly couldn't afford to eat in a café
daily. But for the moment, she relished the privacy
and her release from the company of the twittering
girls. Most of them were far older than Therese, but to
her they were as silly as children. She, Therese Pavan,
had a mission that they could not possibly understand.

Quickly, before she could forget them, she scribbled
in a little notebook the many new and exciting terms
she had heard Madame Dufay use—oiled silk and
ottoman, sarcenet for linings, panne and crushed and
mirror velvets, and best of all, the heavy satin *peau de
soie*, which meant "skin of silk."

Therese would write down everything and at the
very first opportunity find out what it all meant.

Afraid to be late returning—she was told she had
only a half-hour to eat—Therese left half her gumbo
and put her precious notebook and pencil in her worn
purse before dashing back to the salon.

She had given careful thought to the purchase of

those two items, and she knew they would be very necessary. The notebook had been only a nickel; it was the pencil that had been the greatest extravagance. It had cost fifty cents. But the shopkeeper had assured her that it would last "forever"; it was one of the new, fine Thoreau pencils from up north. Therese judged it was soft enough to sketch with too, so she willingly parted with the precious fifty cents.

At the end of the day, she was still too excited to know how tired she was. All afternoon, the others had complained of aching backs and heads and other small maladies, but Therese's strong young body was used to the rigors of the bayou. She felt she would never tire of the work at the salon.

It was not until she was having dinner with Odalie that Therese realized that her muscles pained her from the endless kneeling at the salon.

"What's the matter?" Odalie asked her in a rather absent way. Her friend had appeared somber, and even somewhat indifferent to Therese's excited reports.

When Therese told her, Odalie said with distant gentleness, "We will fix that." Taking Therese to her room, she ordered her to undress and be rubbed with an aromatic *baume* from a little jar that smelled like peppermint. "Since you are not receiving a lover, you should rub yourself again with this after a long, hot bath." She laughed sardonically. "I may as well smell of peppermint myself tonight."

That must mean that Raoul was not coming, Therese thought. She wondered fleetingly about Odalie's gloomy manner, but her sudden tiredness, her utter preoccupation with all that had happened at the salon, did not allow Therese much time for wondering. After the luxury of a bath, and another rub with the *baume*, Therese lay in her own small bed and thought back over the day. She felt off-center as though she were two or three people. Here in Odalie's house she was a guest, waited upon; this afternoon she had acted like a maid for a rich patron, slipping on the woman's shoes so the hem of her gown could be adjusted to the height of her heels.

Several of the patrons had complained of the fatigue of standing and of returning for fitting after fitting. Surely, Therese decided, there must be a way around that. In fact, during the few hours she had been at the salon today, she had noticed the grim, parsimonious air of the place. It seemed to Therese that such beautiful clothes should be selected in a more charming atmosphere. She also thought that Madame Dufay's methods seemed a bit haphazard. If Therese Pavan ran such a salon . . .

Therese began to laugh softly. She, a fifteen-year-old runaway, who'd never even seen a length of velvet, was ready to take over Madame Dufay's. She was still smiling when she fell asleep.

The following day, and the one after that, went more smoothly. Therese, always adaptable, was already becoming used to the routine. She could tell, also, that the Dufay was pleased with her eagerness and her quiet, respectful demeanor. Once, when Therese had been making her copious notes, Madame called out sharply, "Labiche! Come pull these bastings!" Therese rushed over, slipping her notebook into her apron pocket. In her haste she dropped her pencil.

After the patron had gone, Madame Dufay watched Therese pick it up. "What were you doing there?"

"Making notes, *madame*."

"Of what?"

"Of everything you say," Therese confessed. She reddened.

"What do you mean? I talk no scandal." Madame Dufay frowned.

"Oh, no, no! Of the kinds of cloths, the methods you use in pinning, fitting, and draping."

Madame Dufay studied her. "That is most interesting. Excellent. You are *très sérieuse*. Not like these other featherheads, whose brains would do to stuff a pillow. It is good to be serious. We are creating beauty," Madame said grandly.

Therese was very gratified. Then she heard one of the girls, who must have been listening, mock her to the others, calling her a "serious novice," as if she were a nun. Therese gathered that praise from Madame Dufay was rare, and they were envious.

But none of that mattered. Even the continuing absence of Charl', and Odalie's glumness, troubled her less. All that concerned her now was the salon of Hortense Dufay.

# 4

One morning during her second week, Therese heard one of the girls say excitedly, "Mademoiselle du Lac is coming *in*, imagine! Madame always goes to *her*."

Odalie's rival. Therese was afire with curiosity about the woman, but glad she would not have to fit her; that honor would likely fall on the senior *midinette*, Marie Lanou. When the time came, however, Madame Dufay called out, "Labiche. That fool Lanou has burnt her hand. You will fill in with du Lac."

Therese felt a guilty pleasure; it was obliquely disloyal to Odalie to wait upon Mademoiselle du Lac, and yet Therese was very excited to have been given an assignment of this importance.

She followed Madame into the fitting room. A slender young woman was already standing on the platform in her petticoats and chemise. A cloud of carefully arranged black hair overwhelmed her pretty, petulant face. It was the face of a pampered kitten.

A fearsome and magnificently dressed older woman, a positive grenadier, sat in one of the chairs by the platform, and behind her stood a dark-skinned woman who wore a black dress, white apron, and brilliant flowered *tignon*. By the chair a rich leather case rested, open to reveal a riot of gloves, purses, and shoes.

"Madame du Lac . . . *mademoiselle*." Madame Dufay smirked.

"Labiche, bring the rose grenadine, with the black silk mantle. After that we will go to the green glacé. And don't forget the bonnet."

With enormous care, Therese brought in the items,

56

carrying the heavy clothes spread over one of her slender arms. In her other hand, she delicately held a fragile bonnet of crepe and blonde, with an attached silk blush rose.

The grenadier mother critically examined the bonnet. Apparently it passed muster, for Madame Dufay relaxed a trifle. "You will find these things very useful in Italy this winter, *mademoiselle*, on your tour of the southern countries."

"Yes, she will need a few little ensembles like this," the grenadier declaimed in her deep voice. "But naturally, there will be Paris for the more important items."

"But naturally, *madame*," Dufay agreed, as if any other course would be unthinkable.

"*Maman!* I need my rose slippers with this," the girl on the platform demanded. Even her voice was thin and high and pettish, Therese thought, repressing a smile.

Her amusement quickly vanished, however, when Madame Dufay ordered, "Labiche, assist *mademoiselle* into the gown." Trembling with nervousness, Therese laid the mantle over an empty chair and stepped onto the platform to lower the gown delicately over the rich girl's head, careful not to catch her lustrous hair in the neck fastenings.

The stately black maid handed Therese the tiny rose-colored shoes, and Therese slipped them on the girl's feet.

"*Voilà!*" Madame Dufay pronounced, holding out her hands. She snapped her fingers at Therese. "The bonnet."

Therese set it expertly on the girl's head.

"How do I look, *maman*?"

"Exquisite, my dear Aimee."

Madame Dufay echoed the mother's judgment. "How does it feel?"

"Just the tiniest bit too loose here." The girl indicated the waist. Madame Dufay sprang forward and felt the waist with expert hands. "Yes, of a certainty. I think you have become a little thinner since last week, *mademoiselle*."

Madame Dufay snapped her fingers again and Therese supplied the pins as the *modiste* adjusted the
seams of the gown. "There now. Better?"

The girl nodded. After the mantle had been tried
on, the ritual was repeated with the green glacé, its
black silk negligé jacket and its harmonizing *châpeau*,
which had a transparent veil that enhanced the girl's
long-lashed, imperious eyes.

But that was only the beginning; there were endless
conferences in regard to jewels, gloves, and the proper
chemises and petticoats to be worn under the various
garments. Kneeling to adjust the hem of yet another
gown, Therese felt herself quiver with nervousness.
Attending the archrival of her friend was an anxious
business. But she kept her expression blank and
pleasant.

When she was finally released and Dufay told her
she might get something to eat, Therese had no heart
for the food she had brought in her basket, or the
conversation of the other girls. She decided to spend
some more of her dwindling money at the café.

Rushing out the front door of the salon in her ticking cloak, she almost collided with the du Lacs. She
stepped back with an apology. But the engaged girl
said, "Wait, *maman*."

She reached out her elegantly gloved hand and fingered the material of the cloak. I am no more to her,
Therese thought angrily, than a dress form. "How
amusing! Where did you get this?" Mademoiselle du
Lac demanded rudely.

"I made it." Therese's bluntness was intentional.
She decided she would be damned before adding a
respectful title.

"You will make me one!" Aimee du Lac decreed.

"Really, Aimee . . ." Her mother's fearsome brows
drew together.

"Charge whatever you please," Aimee du Lac said
grandly to Therese. And to her mother, giggling, she
added, "It will amuse Raoul when we take our sylvan
walks abroad. He is charmed by the bizarre."

You just don't know how much, Therese replied in ironic silence. Aloud she said quietly, "I am only an apprentice of Madame Dufay's, *mademoiselle*. I am far from an expert seamstress. In any case, I could not make the cloak for you without her permission."

"Nonsense! *I* give you permission. You may tell her I want the cloak. If she doesn't like it, she can keep the rest of my trousseau, for all I care," Aimee du Lac said, looking more like an angry kitten than ever.

"Enough, Aimee! This is absurd," her mother declared.

Therese rebelled: Aimee had put her back up, handling her like a sack of rice, ordering her around like a maid. Therese Pavan, who carried the child of a man every bit as high as de Sevigny. Aimee, the cause of Odalie's misery. "I regret any inconvenience. I cannot deliver such a message."

Aimee gasped, the picture of fury. Therese was calmly silent. "I'll tell her myself!" Disregarding her mother's objection, Aimee flounced into the salon, wafting a scent of lilac.

Therese waited with Madame du Lac and the impassive servant. No one spoke. Aimee emerged all smiles. "It is arranged. You will make the cloak for me in time to have it sent with the other things."

A liveried black man handed the ladies into their carriage; the dignified maid, after a compassionate look at Therese, took her place beside the coachman.

Piqued, Therese stared after them. She was shaky with hunger, but she had to know Madame Dufay's reaction to Aimee's royal command. She found Madame in her private parlor having coffee and *petits fours*, her long feet resting on a *pouf*. "Sit down, Labiche. Serve yourself."

Therese obeyed, devouring one of the sweet cakes.

Studying her, Madame Dufay murmured, "Aimee du Lac is an overbearing little bitch." Shock crackled through Therese, but it was a delighted shock. "However, like many empty-headed women, she has an eye for style. We will of course execute the commission."

"But, *madame*, she's . . . she's—"

"Your benefactor's rival?" Dufay's scanty brows shot up. "To be sure. It is a situation directly from the dramas of Molière."

Therese could not help making a mental note of the name. For the first time in their acquaintance, Madame Dufay gave her a skeletal grin and spelled the name. "One of the great comic playwrights of the last century. I recommend him."

Therese found herself grinning back, feeling a new ease with her employer.

"You have a very great deal to learn, Labiche. But what you know already . . . through some instinctive knowledge . . . is phenomenal. You have a great gift. A great gift."

Therese listened breathlessly.

"It is a pity that you are going to bear a child," Madame Dufay said bluntly. "When is it due?"

Flabbergasted, Therese flushed, stammering, "In the . . . in May."

"Ah. So by February, let us say, you will have to go into seclusion."

Therese felt her heart plummet. Madame Dufay was leading up to a dismissal.

I can't bear it, she thought. I won't bear it. And an audacious idea occurred to her. "Yes, *madame*. But there is no reason at all that I cannot work at home. I can fill orders there."

"My poor child." Madame Dufay looked kindlier than Therese had ever seen her. "Do you really imagine that the fine ladies of New Orleans would enter the house of a protected woman?"

"The protected women will," Therese retorted. When she saw Madame Dufay's thoughtful look, her heart rose in triumph. All it ever took, she reflected, was audacity . . . audacity and courage.

"You are very clever," Madame responded slowly. "That is true."

Pressing her advantage, Therese said quickly, "And there is no reason that I cannot do other work for you. Jean-Jean—Odalie's man—can deliver the work to me

and return it to you. Oh, *madame,* please . . . I beg of
you, this means everything to me. Everything."

Madame Dufay stared at her. "I believe you, Labiche.
Very well, I will consider it most seriously." She held up
her bony hand to stem Therese's answer. "Enough. *Now.*
Aimee du Lac thinks she wants a cloak like yours. She
does not. Hers must be lined, made of the finest material. I will help you with the cloth: get boys' summer
suiting, in a broader stripe of . . . charcoal gray and
cream. On the rest I will test you. You may choose the
lining and the trim. Go to this warehouse. . ." She
dipped into a litter of papers on another table, immediately finding a small white card.

"Put it to the salon's account. Mademoiselle du Lac
will be charged fifty dollars. *If* I approve the work."

"Fifty *dollars?*" Therese gasped.

"Her ensembles run into the hundreds. Close your
mouth, Labiche. You look as stupid as Colette and
Marianne, not yourself at all. Another thing." Madame Dufay took a banknote from a drawer in the
littered table. "Here is an advance."

The crisp note, elaborate with flowing script, was
inscribed DIX. Therese had never seen ten dollars
before.

"Stop at Holmes's department store, on Chartres
Street, and buy yourself a hat and gloves. I cannot
have you go about like a bumpkin."

Therese performed the errands in a daze, using three
of her dollars to buy a black felt hat with a narrow,
curly brim. A "Eugénie," she was told, named for the
Empress of France.

It was trimmed with a white plume, which trailed in
the back, looking patently absurd with Therese's mattress cloak and plain gown. The plume would have to
go. Therese paid for the hat, then matter-of-factly
requested that the assistant remove the plume and
wrap it separately in tissue paper.

"Remove the plume!" The girl stared at Therese as
if she were a madwoman. "I cannot deface our merchandise, *mademoiselle.* And the plume makes the
hat."

"The merchandise is mine now. And *I* make the hat. If you will hand me some scissors . . ."

Indignantly the assistant handed a pair of scissors to Therese who delicately snipped away the stitching. "If you please." Handing the outraged girl the plume and scissors, Therese waited for her to wrap the plume in tissue and then she put the package into the carryall borrowed from Madame Dufay.

At the glove counter she bought black cotton gloves. Rapidly she walked to the ribbon counter and chose broad grosgrain in several colors. Her "plume," until she had a proper cloak, would be a rosette of ribbon.

Meanwhile, she looked unique and stylish in the untrimmed hat. Walking back to the salon, she admired its reflection in the plate-glass windows of the stores. The assistant, she thought with amusement, had had her first taste of the *originale*, Therese Pavan.

The other girls at the salon, she reflected, even the most experienced, might have kept the plume, unconscious that its stark white muddied the lighter stripe of the cape; that the plume's "gloss" effect would shriek disharmony against the rough ticking.

Therese's gift lay not only in her eye but also in her very nerves; she always felt a *frisson* at observing inappropriateness in materials. For her, the line of a dress or hat, the fabric itself, was a color and a sound. Beauty is harmony with a note of surprise, she thought dreamily as she walked along the street.

Back at the salon, she was amused when one of the girls admired her hat but asked her where the plume was. Answering her only with a smile, Therese resolved: Someday I will teach them all, when I have the House of Pavan. Even the Adairs, then, would not be higher.

To Therese's amazement, the cloak run up for Aimee started to become a craze among the rich young Creole ladies. An acquaintance of Aimee's, a Mademoiselle Broyard, summoned Therese to her house and requested a cloak that was "a little different." The young lady liked to sketch; she wanted something that didn't look too rich for her country rambles abroad. To look too rich in Italy and Spain, Therese gathered, was to invite the attention of robbers.

Therese returned with a sample of children's cotton suiting striped in brown and ecru, which was perfect for Mademoiselle Broyard's ruddy complexion. The serious young lady specified trim and quilling in a "lively color," asking that tassels be omitted. "They're pretty," she said, "but I am sure to catch them on a bramble."

Delighted, Therese remembered her plume. This was the first time a customer had made any reference to comfort and appropriateness. Therese promptly made up the cloak, trimming it in burnt siena, and at Madame Dufay's insistence, charged fifty-five dollars. Madame Dufay reminded Therese that she had called at the lady's house and spent a good deal of time in consultation. The bill was paid without a murmur.

Her own good luck kept Therese in a fever of excitement, driving her to work at an unremitting pace. In addition to filling orders, she worked long hours at the side of Marie Lanou, the senior *midinette*. Marie had no imagination but possessed enormous skill. Therese devoured every scrap of new knowledge, learning how to plumb the mysteries of each fabric's personality, mastering the many different kinds of seams, the subtleties of lining, the perfect fall of a drifting sleeve.

Her sudden rise to prominence caused trouble at the salon, and the notion that she was Madame Dufay's "pet" resulted in unpleasant little incidents. Therese ignored them. Nothing would hold her back. Her energy flamed; she rode the crest of an undreamed-of triumph.

During that intoxicating interval, Therese saw little of Odalie. When Therese left in the mornings, of course, there was deep silence from the *boudoir*, and on her return, she either was told by Zizi that "Mam'selle" had gone out, or a brooding stillness downstairs indicated that Raoul had come. On those nights, Zizi or Lynelle would bring a tray quietly to Therese's room.

Therese barely noticed her confinement; her mind was too full. There always was enough to occupy her, with the books and the newspaper from the parlor, the latest *Godey's* and *Le Follet*. Therese spent hours studying these, drawing her own very different versions of the current mode.

And one night, on the console table in the entrance hall, she found a letter from Charl'. Having expected the return of the *Sara Belle* almost daily, Therese was surprised to see a foreign stamp and postmark. Fifty dollars was enclosed.

"My dear Tez," he wrote, "I regret to say that the boat returned to New Orleans only last week, but before I had the chance to come to see you, a great opportunity came my way and I took it, sure that you would understand. I shipped out at once on a run to Havana, Cuba."

Her heart sank, but she read on as he detailed the strangeness and rigors of his new life as a common hand on the merchant vessel. "I am paid far more," he wrote, "than on the river. And the American dollar goes far abroad. Besides, I could not miss the chance to see the world, Tez, with its great cities."

No one, she thought, could sympathize more than herself with that. Her spirits soared when he concluded that he hoped to be in New Orleans by Christmas.

The mention of the upcoming holiday sent her back to her private sewing, which could be done only in the evenings at home. Christmas was just three weeks away, and she had a mountain of tasks before her.

Therese had set aside some of her new riches to buy Christmas presents and material for heavier winter clothes. The weather had turned sharply colder; the ticking cloak was woefully inadequate.

Her first job was completing her pearl-gray winter cloak and two more black dresses for the salon. Then she would make cravats for Charl' . . . in fine-ribbed rep, *satin façonné* and dull antique satin, lined with the best sarcenet. There would be a less splendid cravat for Jean-Jean, a fluffy petticoat for Zizi, and a black taffeta one faced with red ribbon for Lynelle. Only for Odalie and Madame Dufay would she buy presents. She did not have the temerity to present either with her sewing, good as it was. Both were so worldly.

On the evening Charl's letter came, Therese put the finishing touches on her pale gray cloak. In defiance of the current mode of wasp-waisted mantles, she cut hers full, *à la princesse*, with buttons in front and a floating back. It had a capelet over the shoulders for extra warmth, and was wool, not silk, for it would have to serve her all winter, and she did not have the shelter of a carriage. Odalie had one, of course, but it would not be at Therese's beck and call.

Next, she turned her attention to the dresses: her salon dress was stretched to bursting now. She had tried to ignore the tightness, as if doing so would help dismiss the fact that she would soon be banished from the salon, perhaps without income. Madame Dufay must agree to her plan to work at home, Therese thought. Surely she would.

With renewed hope, Therese pondered the dresses. They would have to *work*. There should be sense to them as well as beauty. The dresses should have deeper armholes, and fuller sleeves enlarged by *godets*, for ease with dash. She would eliminate the pinching set-in waist, and instead sew fine rows of elastic threads into the waistlines, camouflaging them with sashes.

*Bohémien*, perhaps. But she would dare it. She had gotten away with the cloak, had triumphed with it. She would get away with these dresses too.

On Christmas Eve, an elated Therese rushed in and out of several shops in the early dusk.

Hortense Dufay was not the Scrooge Therese had envisioned: she had chosen that afternoon to inform Therese that her request for a working leave would be granted. Madame Dufay advised her that immediately after Twelfth Night, New Orleans began to have many balls, right up until Mardi Gras. The *modiste* said that the extra orders for ball gowns sometimes so overwhelmed the salon that she frequently gave out the plainer work to outside seamstresses. And she added, "You might start thinking of costumes for Mardi Gras; with your ideas, it would be easy."

Therese was tearful with gratitude, then quickly buoyant. All work ceased at three and the staff was summoned to Madame Dufay's private parlor to partake of minute cakes and sandwiches and a glass of wine. After the meal, each girl was handed an envelope containing a five-dollar banknote. When all the others had gone, Therese had given Madame Dufay, privately, a little coin purse of Russia leather.

After buying wrapping tissue and ribbon, Therese rushed toward Rampart Street. She still had to wrap all the presents she had made—all except Odalie's. She had taken special pains with that one; instead of tying it with the usual ribbon, Therese had expertly enclosed the gift box in bright golden *tignon*-cotton, basting the fabric's folded ends together. Then she stitched on a matching feather rose, which she herself had made.

She eagerly quickened her pace when she saw the glow from the narrow house ahead in the gathering dark. Her heart was high: the *Picayune* had stated that Charl's ship would dock this very evening, and she was wild to see him.

Odalie herself opened the entrance door. She was resplendent in an evening gown of deep brown taffeta, displaying her jewels of coral and gold. *"Joyeux Noël."* She smiled brilliantly at Therese and with a sweeping curtsy invited her in. She was transformed: there was nothing of the somber indifference, the preoccupation Therese had glimpsed in the last few weeks. Odalie was a whole new woman.

"Come into the parlor," she said with an almost feverish gaiety, her voice unsteady and high. "I have seen nothing of you for weeks and weeks, and we must talk. We must celebrate my night of freedom."

Therese looked into her eyes, suddenly noticing that they were red-rimmed. Odalie had been crying.

"Night of freedom?" Therese put her parcels on a table, staring at Odalie.

*"Voilà!"* With a mocking laugh, Odalie handed Therese the *Picayune*, folded open to the society pages.

Therese saw the prominent headline: ANCIENT FAMILIES TO BE UNITED; DU LAC–DE SEVIGNY RITES. Aimee and Raoul were being married that night . . . at the St. Louis Cathedral.

Therese looked up and met Odalie's large, glittering eyes, full of self-reproach. She had completely forgotten. All she had been thinking of, for weeks, was herself and the baby.

And Charl'. All she had looked for in that morning's *Picayune* was the confirmation of his landing.

Therese was chagrined at her own self-absorption. "Odalie," she said softly, putting out her hand.

Her friend eluded her grasp, shrugging. "It is a *blague*, a joke," she remarked in that same metallic tone. "They will be blessed, made over, then go off on their absurd honeymoon. None of it, the ceremony, the blessings, the marriage, will make any difference at all. They will have to return in time for Mardi Gras—Raoul himself has been selected chief of the Mystick Krewe." Odalie raised her brows. "He will be back in my arms before Ash Wednesday."

Therese was not deceived by her blasé manner; Odalie was suffering. But she hesitated to say anything. Her friend was too proud for sympathy.

"And now," Odalie resumed brightly, "shall we have our own small *Noël*? I am going out to a splendid *fête* of my own—and later, I shall ride by St. Louis, laughing and singing, making mock of the whole *grotesquerie*!"

"Odalie, please. Don't . . ."

"You say to me don't?" For an instant the blaze of anger in Odalie's eyes intimidated Therese; she looked wild, almost mad.

"I'm sorry."

"So you should be. I have told you, this is my night of freedom! For two whole months I shall do exactly as I please, and the great de Sevigny can say *nothing*.

But come," she added with that disconcerting change
of mood that worried Therese. "Let us go to the tree
and open our presents. When Charl' comes, I shall be
gone, and I do not know what time I shall return, or in
what condition. Meanwhile I have arranged an early
dinner for the two of you, so that if you choose to go
to the theater you will be on time. Or Mass . . .
although I do not imagine you will rush to *that*."

Therese laughed. It was true enough. Therese hadn't
once gone to Mass since she had come to New Orleans. Never devout, as a child she had been attracted
only by the church's pageantry, scarce enough in Cameron and Jeanerette. But now, freed of the Sunday
prodding of Berthe and the command of Michel to go
to church, it was too delicious to lie in bed late on
Sundays, even though Guadeloupe was just next door.

"I have a few little parcels for you under the tree,"
Odalie said as she led the way. The tree, Therese
thought, was beautiful, with its globes of colored glass
and a star on top. At the cabin, there had been only
boughs of pine tied with red ribbons.

"And yours is here too," Therese said, handing
Odalie the golden package.

Declaring the package *très belle, très originale*, Odalie
ripped the thread carefully to leave the rose intact,
and exclaimed, "But this is marvelous, *petiote*. I will
carry it this very night." It was a dainty purse, fortu-
itously coral appliqué velvet on leather. "La Dufay
must be doing you well. I am so glad."

Therese reddened. "As to that, Odalie, I have been
wishing to discuss it with you. Now that I am earning
money, it would make me feel . . . I would like to be
able to contribute toward my board. You have been
so—"

"What folly!' Odalie frowned and waved her hand.
"Do not offend me, Therese. Open your little *cadeaux*."

Therese fell silent. She knew how Odalie hated to
be caught out in generosity, much like Charl'. "All
these?" she cried, diverted, when her friend gave her
three packages.

Opening them eagerly, she uncovered a dainty little

evening reticule of fine black silk, and two remarkable
pairs of gloves. She was speechless: the first pair was
of satin-soft black kid, for day. The other was splendid
beyond anything she had ever seen. The same pearl
gray as her cloak, they were evening gloves of even
finer kid, sparkling over the wrists with beads of iridescent black and beads the shades of abalone: gun-
metal, rose-lavender, and bluish-green. "How can I
thank you?" she murmured.

"By enjoying yourself, *petit*." Odalie rose from her
kneeling position in a rustle of flounces, saying, "Now
I must go."

Before Therese could speak, Odalie was in the hall,
calling out, "Zizi, bring me my brown mantle and
cream gloves, and put my things in the new bag on the
table. Jean-Jean, call a *cabriolet*. I will not need you
tonight."

Therese wanted to go after her; she was frightened
by Odalie's feverish, wild look, but she hesitated. Odalie
would not thank her for interfering. Therese listened
to the flurry, then the closing door and Zizi's footsteps
on the kitchen stairs.

Charl' might be there at any moment. She had to
hurry. Therese ran upstairs to bathe and dress and
wrap the presents.

It was not yet six when she put Charl's gift below
the tree and took the others to the kitchen. When she
came back to the parlor to wait, she looked at herself
in one of the numerous mirrors. Her abundant hair
was plaited into a coronet on top of her head, and the
let-out evening gown was a success. Removing the
white corsage from the neck and the undersleeves, she
had substituted sleeves of pearl gray, achieving a mock
redingote effect with the insertion of gray and black
striped satin into the bodice and down the front of the
skirt. With her cameo jewelry, the result was very
pleasing.

Therese smiled at her image, concluding that hard
work agreed with her. Her eyes and skin had a vital
glow. The knocker interrupted her reflections, and she
dashed to open the door.

*"Joyeux Noël!"* Charl' stood there hatless, tall and smiling; his face was even more deeply tanned and his usually disordered hair was barbered.

She threw her arms around his neck. He hugged her to him and his arms had the feel of home; she had not known until now just how much she had missed him. "Come in, come in!"

"Let me look at you, *petit*." He stood back, observing her fine appearance. "You have made another gown."

"Not exactly. But you . . . you are so grand." He was wearing a black swallowtail coat and trousers the color of butterscotch, his dark cloak tossed back over his shoulders.

"Well, what would you have?" He laughed. "Did you think I would call on my sister dressed as an able seaman?" Charl' glanced toward the stairs. "Where is our *marraine de fée*?"

Odalie was a kind of fairy godmother, but Therese could not smile at Charl's fancy; the memory of those eyes haunted her.

"What's the matter?"

"Nothing." Therese did not want to be gloomy. Not now. "Odalie's gone to a *fête* of her own, that's all. And the house is ours tonight. Think of it . . . and she has ordered our dinner here, if you wish to have it."

"Wish to have it! For weeks on the ship I have had my choice of soup or stew—for soup, the cook ladled from the top of the pot; for stew, from the bottom."

His new air of confidence impressed her. In just weeks he seemed to have grown stronger, older. "First, though," she insisted, "come into the parlor. I will give you a glass of wine, and we will have our Christmas."

When they had toasted each other, she found his package under the tree. "What is this? How pretty it is," he remarked, tearing away the tissue. Examining the handsome cravats, he said wonderingly, "Tez, these are magnificent. I am sure there is nothing finer, even in Paris. I must put one on." He strode to the mirror and, snatching off his plain black cravat, replaced it with the one of antique satin, a *mélange* of dark red and gray and gold.

"Thank you, little Tez." He reached into the tail-pocket of his coat and brought out two minute boxes. "I have brought something too, for you and Odalie." He placed one of the boxes under the tree and handed the other to Therese. Inside, she found a pair of seed-pearl earrings with dancing fringes.

"Charl', they are beautiful." As eagerly as he had put on his cravat, Therese exchanged her eardrops for the new ones. Grinning, she asked him, "What have you done . . . become a robber?"

His dark eyes gleamed, and a smile twitched at his mouth. "Not directly. But our captain was up to something, of a certainty—there were many mysterious landings that were not logged. When I happened to discover that, I implied that my secrecy would cost him something. And he was very generous. In addition to my pay, he gave me two hundred dollars."

She gasped.

Charl' nodded. "When we put in at the last port of call, I sent our mother something, for herself and the girls. I thought it best that my envelope not be post-marked New Orleans."

"But, Charl', will it not be dangerous when you go back to sea . . . because of the captain, I mean?"

"I will not sail with him again, Tez. Something is up and I do not want to be in the middle of it, you see. I have already signed on with another ship that leaves in a few more days, for . . ." He stopped abruptly. "But let us have dinner! We must not be late for the St. Charles Theater, at eight o'clock. And I want to hear everything that's happened."

He listened to Therese with smiling lips and bright eyes as she told him about the Labiche alias and Madame Dufay, with her steely exterior and soft heart, laughing when Therese imitated the high-nosed patrons.

"I've always known, since you were no bigger than a minute, that you were meant to be outstanding. Someday you'll have your own salon, Therese. I know it."

"The House of Pavan," she said dreamily.

"That has quite a ring to it. You will. I believe it."
After an instant's silence he said, "But see here, you've
done nothing but work, from morning till night. You've
seen nothing of New Orleans, I wager. Of course
there's been no one to escort you."

"No. And naturally I couldn't go to the theater and
the opera with Odalie." The "protected women" were
restricted to one special balcony, where white women
were not admitted.

"I know." Charl' shrugged. Then he asked abruptly,
"What age did you give Madame Dufay?"

Therese grinned. "Eighteen. And you?"

"Twenty. They always believed me; you know any
fellow from Côte Blanche is bigger and stronger than
these city types." They laughed at each other's devices. He sobered. "I must confess now—I've signed
on for a longer voyage, to Liverpool and Calais. Think
of it, Tez—I'll be able to see the splendors of London
and Paris. When I was on the steamboat, going up and
down the old brown river, I knew I had to go to sea."

"Of course. But . . . how long will you be gone?"

"Until the spring." Noticing her expression, he
stroked her hand. "The time will go fast, busy as you
are. And you'll have Odalie, and the others, when the
baby comes."

She was afraid to look ahead that far, right now.
Quickly she asked him about his life on the merchant
ship, and what it was like in Cuba. Sooner than they
knew, it was time to leave.

"Let's walk," Therese said when they were outside.
On their way, they passed the mighty St. Louis Cathedral. A smiling bride in voluminous white and a tall
Creole man with a haughty face were emerging, followed by a stream of richly dressed people.

*"Mon Dieu,"* she said softly. "De Sevigny." Suddenly she forgot Odalie's pain, overcome with her
own. She should have married Nicholas Adair; she
should have worn such a wedding gown.

"Oh, Lord," Charl' said. "And there's Odalie, in

that carriage." Therese looked: Odalie was driving with two other mulatto women. "I think she intends to make a scene."

They heard Odalie's voice raised in a bawdy song, and noticed the uneasy glances of some of the wedding party. The groom, however, had not appeared to notice. That was fortunate. If he did, Therese thought, it would be a calamity. She had sensed already, from the frequent doldrums of Odalie, and from the capriciousness of his visits, that Raoul was a cruel and arrogant bastard. If he saw Odalie now, trying to disgrace his mighty family name . . .

"Stay here," Charl' ordered. "It will not do for you to be seen in this."

That was all too true: Therese had glimpsed Mademoiselle Broyard and other patrons of the salon. She stepped back in the shadows, watching Charl' stride toward Odalie's carriage.

When Odalie saw him, she broke off her risqué singing; Therese could see her face change. Smiling as if it were the most ordinary meeting in the world, her brother held out his hand, exchanging pleasantries with her companions. By now the bride and groom were safely driving away in a large closed carriage. Therese almost wept with relief. She saw Odalie sit up proudly in her carriage; in a moment, it too drove away.

Therese waited in the shadow for Charl' to return.

"You have saved her," she said in a low, uneven voice.

He took her arm and squeezed it. "And you, Tez," he said with Gallic practicality. "If Odalie goes, so do you. I cannot have you living here alone."

It turned her cold to recognize that she, too, depended on de Sevigny for the home she had come to know. She had not seen it before in that light. "What on earth did you say to her, Charl'?"

"I appealed to her pride." Charl' whistled for a *cabriolet* and handed her in. Directing the coachman to the St. Charles, he added, "If there is anything we have plenty of in the bayou—Acadien or *griffe*—it is pride. And I am too proud to have you go on living there. Yet, until we can afford a proper place for you, Tez . . . and then, Odalie is our friend. She will know how to look out for you. But we have arrived."

Therese was surprised at the plainness of the famous theater's facade. When they went in, however, she knew why everyone talked of it: it was titanic, the largest place she'd ever seen in her life. The seats seemed to rise to heaven, among pristine columns and friezes and chandeliers. She was glad that they were sitting on the ground floor.

But when the velvet curtains parted on the first act of Shakespeare's *Hamlet*, Therese dismissed everything but the scene before her. It was a revelation to hear spoken the words she had only read, to watch the actors move through brilliant light in their splendid antique clothes. Perhaps she would even design such clothes someday.

Afterward Charl' took her to the famous Begue's for a late supper. They made plans for the rest of his visit, which would extend through New Year's Day.

Odalie had not returned when Charl' took Therese back to Rampart Street, nor was she there at noon the next day, the hour set for Charl' to call for Therese. The servants seemed to take it as a matter of course, so they assumed it had happened before.

One night Therese and Charl' came upon a tumble-down cottage on a side street. "*Smell*, Charl'! Only our food has that *lagniappe*." She caught the aromas of crawfish *étoufée* and filé gumbo. "Let's go in!"

"If someone from our parish is there, Tez . . ."

Her heart sank. They were still fugitives, so easy to forget in that big, varied city. "We'd better go."

They started to walk away. A family was coming out of the homely restaurant. "My Lord." Charl' pulled at Therese's arm. "*Vite*. I know that woman. She's looking at us. Come."

He guided Therese around the corner. Unfortunately the family was going that way too.

"Who is she?" Therese half-turned to look.

"Don't look back," Charl' warned, hurrying The-

rese along. "The woman has the look of a Rocaille,
Tez. Perhaps she is the cousin who married the man
with the fishing boats."

When they turned the corner, Therese asked him
fearfully, "Do you suppose she recognized us?"

"Maybe not. Maybe in our fine clothes, she didn't."

Therese was not much comforted; Charl' did not
sound confident. He spoke like a grown-up lying to a
child. "But she could have."

Charl' stopped and faced her. "Yes. Maybe in New
Orleans we'll always have to be looking back over our
shoulders."

The idea turned her cold: this was the city that had
become her new world, her *bonne chance*. To have to
leave it now . . . and how could she leave now, in her
condition?

"Come, Tez, we can't stand here all evening. Let's
find a place to eat, where we can talk."

When they had found a modest restaurant and were
seated, Charl' spoke with great seriousness. "I think
you should consider leaving, Tez, after the baby comes.
There are plenty of other places, and I can come visit
you anywhere."

She listened, silent, struggling not to cry, thinking of
having to leave the pretty house on Rampart Street,
but most of all Madame Dufay's, where she was just
beginning to learn, where she had already gotten recognition. "Where should I go?"

"When I was on the steamboat, I heard a lot about
Cincinnati. So I looked around there when the boat
landed. It is nothing like New Orleans. It's almost like
the West. There is a great bare landing, plain and kind
of ugly. But people seem to be . . . freer there, Tez.
Nice women walk about alone all the time. There's
money there. It's so centrally located, you see, and
people are streaming in. Germans, mostly. It's a place
where nobody cares much who your father was, and
all that."

"Or if you have no husband," Therese said dryly.
"No one would know who I am."

"That's right. Except you yourself. And that should

be good enough for anybody." Charl' smiled at her. She took his hand.

"A place to start all over," she said thoughtfully. "Where we wouldn't have to look back over our shoulders . . . too far away for Michel to find us."

"We couldn't go back again, Tez. In just this little time, we've learned so many things. We're free to be ourselves. We've got to go ahead, wherever it takes us. And pray that word does not get back to the bayou for a while."

# 5

On a sunny afternoon in May, Therese sat on a bench in Lafayette Square with the baby in her lap, thinking about what Charl' had said. Several times, back in January, she thought she saw the bayou woman again, once near Madame Dufay's, another time coming out of the Guadeloupe chapel.

But Therese decided she had been wrong. Otherwise Michel would have learned where she was. He would have come to New Orleans.

Therese looked around the square, elated to be out-of-doors again, after the long months of isolation. Lafayette Square was a great resort for respectable people, and on fine days like this one, it had a lively air about it. The gentle sun picked up a watery gleam from ladies' silken flounces, and turned the tall hats of their escorts to dark satin.

Therese saw a nursemaid in a white *tignon* pass, wheeling an infant girl in a cart like a toy *cabriolet*, followed by a little girl in a ruffled dress and flowered hat rolling her hoop.

It felt so good to be in the world again, and it was even all right to be alone; no one accosted a woman with a baby, even if Therese had noticed curious stares. She supposed it was unusual for a well-dressed young woman to carry her baby, unaccompanied by a nursemaid.

A handsome young pair strolled by Therese's bench, looking only at each other. The young woman carried her gloves; her bare left hand had a broad gold ring on the wedding finger.

Some of Therese's pleasure evaporated: the woman looked so carefree and secure.

Charles made a fretful sound and Therese moved him so that his face would be in the shade. The sun shone at its warmest now. She regarded the fuzz of golden hair emerging from the baby's cap, and his eyes that, after three weeks, were still blue. Already it seemed to her that his tiny features were like Nicholas Adair's, that nothing of her had been bequeathed him.

She sighed. Her body was light again, but there was a heaviness in her heart: the sense of responsibility she had felt, carrying the baby, was nothing to what she felt now, with this small human life in her arms.

A human life with an uncertain future, alive because of her childish fascination with Nicholas Adair and his splendid world. Therese knew that now, surely; she had had hours to think about it during the lonely months of her confinement. And Nicholas had never loved her at all. He had used her for his amusement. Whatever soft thing she had once felt for him had hardened now into bitter anger.

Therese looked down at the sleeping baby. She called him Charles, for the only good man she had ever known. It occurred to her now that her brother might think it a dubious honor, to have the son of the man who had betrayed her named after him.

If only Charl' were here, so she could talk to him. But he had been delayed, and his ship would not land until next month.

Next month would be June; Therese's flagging spirits rose. She would be able to go back to the salon. She would be strong enough by then, and Rubine would be nursing the baby.

Right after *ti* Charles was born, the midwife had been mystified by Therese's inability to nurse him. Odalie had called a doctor in, and the doctor, after examining and questioning Therese, had told her she would never be able to nurse him. Therefore the task had been delegated to a hired nursemaid, the stately and patient Rubine. The baby took to her at once, and seemed content with the arrangement.

It was just as well, Therese thought. Otherwise she couldn't have gone back to the salon until the baby was weaned. All the same, it made her feel strange, as if she were not a proper mother.

When she said that to Odalie, she retorted, "You are very fortunate. Nursing destroys the figure."

Odalie would never understand. She had changed so much in the last few months; she was detached and hard now.

On the night of Mardi Gras Odalie had arrayed herself in a costume Therese had designed, and rushed out to a quadroon ball without a word to anyone. Remembering Odalie's boast that Raoul would be with her by Ash Wednesday, Therese was careful to stay in her room the next day. But she had sensed an odd, funereal quiet from below. At twilight Odalie had come to her, her mouth stiff with despair. "He saw me that night, Therese. We are finished."

Then she had turned and walked away.

Throughout the rest of the brief winter, and the swift-arriving spring, Odalie had been listless and quiet. There wasn't much gaiety in the house anymore.

But there was still a lot to be thankful for, Therese decided, caressing the baby's tiny hand. At least she could take care of Charles, with the earnings still to come, and the money in the bank. And he was perfect, and strong.

Feeling better, she let her gaze wander around the park.

Two familiar figures caught her attention: a man and a boy. They were standing with their backs to her, but their rough clothes, their heavy, muscular bodies and aggressive stance were pure Acadien. The man turned his head slightly.

The man was her father.

The boy was Hector Rocaille.

Therese froze, immobile with shock. Then her whole body began to quiver, the weakness of convalescence aggravated by terror. They hadn't seen her, thank God. She scrambled awkwardly to her feet, her arms so shaky she was afraid she would drop the baby. She

started to run; in the voluminous skirt it felt like trying
to run through sand or water. Her legs began to ache,
and the baby felt as heavy as a stone.

Gasping, Therese held the baby tighter, and slowed
to a fast walk, realizing that she was attracting attention. If others noticed, Michel and Hector might notice too. She looked back; she was not being pursued.
But one of them could turn and see her at any moment.

She hailed a passing *cabriolet* and after the kindly
driver had helped her in, lay back against the cushions, gasping out the address on Rampart Street.

Charles, fractious after his rude awakening, began
to whimper. Therese joggled him to make him stop,
raw and quivering in every nerve. She could not forget
the look in Michel's eyes as he scanned the square; she
had seen that look before, when he had drawn a bead
on a hunted animal or prepared to hit her or one of
the other children.

Agonizingly she wondered why he had waited so
long to come. The answer offered itself to her: the
Rocaille *cousine* had not been sure, at first, that she
had recognized Therese. Later, perhaps the third time,
coming out of Guadeloupe, the woman had been sure.
And then it had taken weeks, perhaps, for the word to
reach Michel; more weeks for him to decide what to
do, then find the time to make the long journey.

And Therese could guess why Hector was with him.
Stupid as Hector was, he was sly and conniving. He
had always wanted Therese. Probably he had told
Michel that Therese was carrying his baby, that he had
asked her to marry him and she had refused and run
away.

That must be it. Michel would be determined to
make his daughter do the right thing.

The tears streamed down her face. To marry the
brutal Hector—compared with that, death itself would
be a *fête*.

Surely Michel would trace her to Odalie's. She was
the only person the Pavans knew in New Orleans,
except for that Rocaille woman. What a fool she had
been to think that nothing would come of that encoun-

ter. The passage of months, without disturbance, had lulled Therese into a false complacency.

She would have to leave New Orleans, and leave today. Thank God it was Monday; the steamboat left on Mondays, Wednesdays, and Fridays. If she missed it, there would be two more days of terror.

There was nothing to do but to go.

Go away from everything she had come to know, all that she had worked so hard to grasp, just when she was getting started. She was heartsick, but resigned.

When the *cabriolet* stopped on Rampart Street, she fumbled blindly for coins, and without waiting to be assisted, struggled to the ground and ran up the steps. The jouncing baby began to scream.

Too frantic to look for her key, Therese banged with the knocker, crying out for Odalie. Odalie herself snatched open the door.

Before she could speak, Therese sobbed, "Michel has come. I saw him in the square . . . with Hector."

Odalie moaned and pulled Therese into the hall, slamming the door.

Zizi and Lynelle stood at the top of the kitchen stairs, gazing with stupefaction.

"Where will you go?" Odalie asked with amazing calm.

"To Cincinnati," Therese gasped.

Odalie turned. "Zizi, take the baby down to Rubine. Tell Jean-Jean to bring one of my trunks from the box room to Ma'am Tez's room. Start packing. I will be up directly to help you. Have Jean-Jean hitch up the carriage and have it ready to go. *Move*," she added sharply.

Galvanized, the women hurried downstairs, Zizi calling out to Jean-Jean.

Therese swayed; her stomach felt sick.

"You need brandy," Odalie said succinctly. "Go in the parlor and get it." Therese obeyed. After she drank some of the burning liquid, she felt restored.

She heard Odalie run up to the second floor. After a moment, there were servants' outcries, a confusion of running feet up and down, excited exclamations.

In hardly any time at all, the unruffled Odalie was back, in a broad-brimmed summer hat, holding out a bundle of greenbacks to Therese. "This will hold you for a while. When you get to Cincinnati, write to the bank and ask them to send you your money. There's no time to get it now. We must hurry."

Therese followed her unthinkingly, hearing the thump of the trunk on the stairs, the confused voices of Lynelle and Rubine downstairs. Odalie shouted, "Bring the baby, Rubine! *Vite!*"

Jean-Jean led the way, carrying the trunk to the waiting carriage, and the three women crowded in. Jean-Jean cracked his whip over the horse's head, and they rattled away at high speed toward the levee.

The noise of the jouncing carriage made speech impossible; Therese was still too dazed, anyway, to say what she wanted to say to Odalie. She felt overcome with gratitude and admiration: Odalie was remarkable. She had accomplished Therese's escape in less than a quarter of an hour.

The carriage joined the chaos of the levee as Jean-Jean drove them toward one of the steamboats lining the pier, skillfully wending his way among the burdened roustabouts, the hurrying passengers, the wagons piled high with barrels and with boxes.

A big clock on the outside of a storage shed marked twenty minutes to four.

They had made it.

Waves of relief washed over Therese. Then, with the relief, came a delayed hysteria: her teeth began to chatter.

Odalie squeezed her arm. "We can't stop now. They'll be lifting the plank soon. You can rest when you're on the boat."

Therese nodded, clenching her teeth as Jean-Jean helped her out of the carriage. A roustabout hauled down the trunk. Therese fumbled for a bill to give to Jean-Jean. He had done so much for her on Rampart Street, bringing her unfinished work from the salon, taking it back, always refusing to be paid. "Thank you, Jean-Jean," was all she could find to say.

*"Bonne chance, m'zelle."*

Odalie pulled her up the ramp.

"The baby!" Therese stared at Odalie. "I can't—"

"Rubine is coming with you," Odalie said calmly. She walked away to buy their tickets. The whistle sounded; the deck began to vibrate below their feet.

Odalie returned, hugging Therese and handing her the tickets.

"Now I must hurry. I have to erase every sign of Therese Pavan from Rampart Street. Good luck." Odalie rushed off, down the ramp to the landing.

She turned back once to wave, and then she and Jean-Jean were lost in the tangle of carriages and wagons along the levee.

Ponderously the boat moved out into the river's muddy stream.

"Ma'am?" Therese jumped. A smiling roustabout touched her elbow. "I show you to the ladies' cabin."

Disoriented, she gave him a nod and followed him up a flight of stairs with white-painted banisters. The boat was something like a house; for the first time she really saw its fancy wood and scrollwork.

When the man opened Therese's cabin door and she entered, trailed by the stately Rubine holding Charles, Therese said, surprised, "Why, this is what a hotel must be like."

The roustabout set the trunk down in a corner, grinning. "Yes, ma'am, this is a mighty fine boat." He started to leave.

"Wait." Therese found a coin for him. "Please, could you tell me when we'll get to Cincinnati?"

"Well, ma'am, I heard about two years ago they made the trip in just over five days. But our captain takes it easier; he don't want to heat her up too much, 'cause she might blow."

There was a moan from Rubine.

"So I calculate about a week. We got to stop five or six times on the way, to take on goods and passengers."

A week, Therese thought in dismay. Seeing her expression, the man consoled her, "It won't be so bad, ma'am. You can sit on the deck and look at things.

An' we'll be stopping at Natchez and Vicksburg, then at Greenville and Memphis. Right after Evansville, you'll be in Cincinnati. Now, did they tell you there's two servings in the saloon—at six and seven?"

He said to Rubine, "Generally us folks eat down below, but since you're taking care of the little baby, you just go right along with the lady to the dining saloon, down the one flight of stairs."

Therese thanked him again and he went out.

Taking off her hat, she looked around the cabin. The accommodations were fit for an aristocrat. The windows had colored glass, a figured carpet covered the floor, and there were two mirrors and a brass chandelier, and a washstand in a corner. Two bunks and two chairs completed the furnishings. Therese was amazed at the roominess of it.

Rubine stood in the middle of the cabin holding the baby and gazing around. "This sure is fine."

"Sit down, Rubine. I want to talk to you." The woman sat down on one of the beds. "I feel so bad about this," Therese said gently. "I didn't realize you were coming with me until we were on the boat. Everything went so fast."

Rubine smiled. "*Mam'zelle* know how to move."

"She sure does." Therese grinned back. "You see, my daddy was coming after me, and—"

"I know about all that," Rubine said calmly.

There was nothing the servants didn't know, Therese had discovered. "Look, Rubine, if you don't want to stay in Cincinnati, I can find another nurse, and send you right back.''

"Oh, no, ma'am. I'll be glad to stay. I've never been anywhere much, you see. And there's nothing to keep me in New Orleans anymore."

That was true. Rubine had lost her husband and baby in a boating accident a few months before. Maybe she wanted to try to forget, and leaving New Orleans would help her.

"Besides," Rubine added, "I love to take care of this sweet little boy. Even after my baby was gone, the good Lord provided me with ample milk, and kept on providing."

"That's wonderful, Rubine. I'll be so glad to have you with me. Why don't you go out on deck, if you want to, and look around? I'll take care of the baby. There's a lot to see."

"There sure is." Rubine sounded eager. "I think I'll do that, then."

When the slow days on the river merged into one endless waiting, Therese discovered that there was less and less to see. She felt that there would never be anything but the monotony of the muddy waters, flowing on forever, and unchanging landscape slipping past. Time itself took on a new dimension; she could see why Charl' had abandoned the river life.

The only change was the comparative excitement of a landing; their meals were the big events of the day. The rest of the time, passengers spent hours sitting on deck, staring somnolently at the churning water or the uninspiring land, talking and talking.

Therese rarely had the desire to join them. After the first night in the dining saloon, where she had sat at a family table, the friendly questions of the ladies discouraged her. They wanted to know everything about her—where she came from, who her family and her "late" husband were. Therese was hard put to make up the proper answers, and she was especially anxious to avoid the people who were going back to Cincinnati. The less they knew about her, the better; that was the city where she would make her new start.

She was glad she had happened to be wearing black and white when she boarded; it bolstered the widow charade. She was certainly tired enough of black, which was required for work at the salon, and had almost put on a pink dress that morning. In the free-and-easy atmosphere of Rampart Street, Therese had totally forgotten that a "nice" woman wore mourning for three full years after her husband's death, and the baby's age made her a "new" widow.

Therese and Rubine fell into a companionable routine. Except to feed the baby and to sleep, Rubine spent most of her time on the lower decks with her own people, who shared that space with the crew.

Sometimes on the higher decks Therese could hear their singing and laughter. She envied Rubine their easygoing company. There were times when the friendly racket made Therese positively homesick for the *fêtes* of Côte Blanche, in the days before her father had turned so mean.

At those times she ached with a deep, sore longing for Berthe and Elianne and for the exuberant *fait do-dos*, despite the fact that life on the Côte Blanche had become untenable. She always reminded herself of that—the bayou had been shadowed by the dark presence of Michel, the maddening attentions of Hector Rocaille, and the treachery of Nicholas Adair.

And the lack of any change, or chance.

She missed New Orleans so much that thinking of it could make her cry: the pretty house on Rampart Street, Odalie in her days of happiness. Most of all, Therese missed the tempo of Madame Dufay's salon, where she had been most fulfilled, absorbed to the exclusion of everything else.

The first night, after dinner, Therese had written a long letter to Odalie, enclosing a letter for Madame Dufay. She had not yet written to Charl'; his would be the longest of all, and she wanted to gather her thoughts and impressions.

She sorely lacked for books. Sometimes passengers would leave newspapers on the deck chairs, and she eagerly devoured those, but they were full of things she had no interest in. Some place called Minnesota had been admitted as a state; they had started to build a church in New York, called St. Patrick's. And some man named Abraham Lincoln was running for the Senate in Illinois, talking against slavery.

The days and nights began to quicken on the journey north. When the Cincinnati landing at last slid into view, Therese could see the justice of Charl's description. It was a bare, ugly landing; compared with the levee, it looked like a prairie. There were fewer boats in the water, fewer vehicles on the land. And instead of the jumble of sheds of New Orleans, there was a long row of brick buildings set back from the piers, neat and uniform, but sterile-looking.

The air was different too—sharper, cool for May. Therese found that stimulating, and liked the brisk, serious look of the people on shore, a look that answered something in her own hard-driven nature.

Charl' had been right about that too. It looked like a place where people didn't notice each other. And well-dressed, respectable women walked matter-of-factly alone.

Yes, even if there were no bright colors, no singing or laughter, Therese liked the look of Cincinnati. Perhaps it was a place where she could be accepted.

Feeling optimistic and excited, she walked quickly down to the landing, with Rubine and Charles in her wake.

"Buggy, lady?" The sharp question startled her. A young white man in rough clothes was waiting in a battered vehicle. Therese realized she had no idea where to go.

"Could you take us to a boardinghouse?"

"Sure. Plenty of 'em, side by side, on Second Street. Get in." The driver didn't help the roustabout with their trunk; he seemed impatient to start.

The buggy rattled down the long promenade and onto a busy thoroughfare whose signs read "Main Street." The buildings were neat and low, and Therese saw very few church spires. It wasn't exactly pretty, she thought. A drunk man stumbled in front of the buggy, and the driver swore at him. He made no apology, as a Southerner would have done.

"I wonder where the gardens are," Therese said to Rubine.

Overhearing, the driver answered her. "This is right downtown. Lots of folks live outside of town."

They turned a corner. The driver volunteered, "This here's Second. They say Miz Prickett keeps a clean house. It's that one, right there." He pointed to one of

the narrow brick houses, identical to the others except
for its number.

When they stopped, Therese asked, "Can you wait
a minute?"

The driver's small blue eyes squinted at Therese
with a blend of admiration and suspicion. "I reckon.
Just so you come back."

When Therese understood what he implied, she was
indignant. "I'm certainly not going to leave my baby,"
she retorted, and hurried up the steps of the house.
She used the knocker next to a neat sign that read,
MALVINA PRICKETT, ROOMS.

A rotund white-haired woman opened the door.
Her sharp green eyes examined Therese from a ruddy,
uncompromising face. "Yes?" Her voice was harsh
and squeaky. Therese stated her business. "Are you
Mrs. Prickett?" The woman nodded and let her in.

The hall was dimly lit, its walls a dingy brown
trimmed with somber wood. Mrs. Prickett led Therese
into a stiff parlor.

"Have a seat." Therese sat gingerly on a slick sofa;
it was very hard, like Mrs. Prickett's voice.

"And who do you want the rooms for, Miss . . . ?"

"Mrs. Pavan. I am a widow."

Mrs. Prickett's green eyes softened. "My land, so
young. You look younger than my own daughter. Is it
just you alone?"

"I have a baby, and the nursemaid. We would need
two rooms, if you have them."

The woman's sharp scrutiny made Therese nervous.
"How is it you are out looking for rooms, Mrs. . . .
Parvang?"

Taking a deep breath, Therese looked straight into
Mrs. Prickett's eyes; she was going to have to come up
with a good story, or there was no telling what the
woman might conclude.

"I must confess, Mrs. Prickett, I have . . . run away."

The fat woman frowned. "Run *away*!" She shook
her head.

"From my in-laws. You see, I have no mother and
father of my own anymore. They are dead. Only a

brother who has gone to sea. And after my husband
died, my in-laws were so cruel—"

"Why?" Mrs. Prickett demanded.

On the edge of her vision, Therese saw a familiar
item—a statue of the Virgin Mary on the mantel.
"Because I am a Catholic," Therese answered, letting
her voice quiver slightly.

"Why, that does beat all!" The landlady looked
indignant. "And so you have had to run off. Where
was that?"

"Kentucky," Therese lied. "And now, you see, I
have to . . . make my own way, and support my baby.
I hope to get a position, perhaps with a dressmaking
establishment."

"Well, that is a mighty sad thing. You say you're
from Kentucky. You don't talk like folks from there."

"My husband was," Therese said quickly. "I was
born in Louisiana."

"Well, now, that explains it. I'll tell you what, Mrs.
Parvang, I have two real nice rooms on the second
floor. One little and one big. I can let you have them
for five dollars a week, and I give the boarders breakfast and supper."

Therese was overjoyed. It seemed very cheap. She
accepted the landlady's offer and rushed out to the
buggy to get the baby and Rubine. The sullen driver
was persuaded to take her trunk upstairs for an extra
dollar.

Both rooms were ugly and sparsely furnished, but
also very clean. There was a strong smell of wax and
polish, and the soap on the washstand was pungent,
without fragrance. Mrs. Prickett said Therese would
share the bath with the two single ladies living on the
other side of the hall.

While Rubine stowed her meager possessions in the
smaller room next door, Therese took off her hat and,
shaking her hair free of its pins, stared at herself in the
spotty mirror. She had won the first victory, persuad-
ing a proper, suspicious landlady that she was decent
enough to deserve a room. The rest might be more
difficult.

Therese studied the reflection of her black, tilted eyes, impudent nose, and narrow features. Looking French, she supposed, made her seem inherently disreputable to the plain people of this northern city. In New Orleans she had looked like everyone else.

But here, she imagined, most folks would not even know what an Acadien was.

Smiling to herself, Therese washed her face and hands, tidied her hair and put it up again. She shook out the wrinkles from one of her modest black dresses, removed her travel-stained ensemble, and changed into the black dress. Satisfied of her neatness, she opened the door and stepped into the hall.

The smell of unflavored meat and boiling cabbage drifted up from below.

She started down the stairs and raised her head high. She would not live here forever. And she and the baby were safe now. Tomorrow she would start looking for a position.

She was going to make Cincinnati sit up and pay attention to Therese Pavan.

# 6

At the bottom of the stairs Therese noticed that there were people already seated in a gloomy dining room. Besides Mrs. Prickett, there were two women, an amiable-looking older man, and a painfully-thin younger one. It was surprising how hungry the unexciting odors of food made her. She was suddenly ravenous.

"Here is our new boarder, Mrs. Pavang," Mrs. Prickett said brightly from her place at the table's head. Therese took the empty chair next to the thin young man while the landlady introduced the others. The dowdily clad women facing Therese were Miss Nell Jamison and Miss Letitia Park. The old man was Mr. Reid, the young one Mr. Quentin. Mrs. Prickett pronounced their names indifferently, as if it were improper for Therese to have any interest in them at all.

Mr. Reid smiled kindly at Therese as he helped her to dry slices of meat, then potatoes and cabbage. He had muttonchop whiskers that made him look a little like a walrus, but his faded eyes were intelligent. "What an interesting name you have, Mrs. Pavang."

Smiling in thanks, Therese corrected mildly, "It is Pavan, actually." She spelled it.

"That's French," Miss Park said accusingly from across the table. She had a narrow face very much like a hen's, with no perceptible eyelashes or lips. There was a look about her that was both stingy and aggrieved and her dress was too fussy for her grim features and skinny body.

Feeling sorry for the woman, Therese answered her

calmly. "My late husband was of French ancestry and so am I."

"Do you come from New Orleans?" Miss Jamison asked Therese. She was the only one, Therese decided, who did not look like one of the animal kingdom. Even the silent young man next to Therese reminded her of a weasel. Miss Jamison had a low, pleasing voice, less harsh than the others', and her gray eyes were friendly. She wore her dark blond hair more loosely than Miss Park's. Therese reevaluated her unusual dress. It was an agreeable dark red, with loose sleeves and bodice, like the "hygienic" dresses ridiculed in modish magazines.

Therese had never seen such a dress, and she liked the look of it. Perhaps there could be a compromise between . . .

She flushed. She had waited so long, in her distraction, to reply that Miss Jamison repeated her question, and the others were looking at her. Therese hastily answered, "Originally. But my husband's family was from Kentucky."

"What a wonderful city New Orleans is," Miss Jamison said. "I visited it once, and enjoyed it so much."

Therese only smiled, thinking what a lot of questions these people asked. Old Mr. Reid seemed to sense her discomfiture and turned to Mr. Quentin.

"Well, I see Governor Cumming has set that Colonel Johnston straight."

The weasellike Mr. Quentin only nodded, eating stolidly.

Therese asked politely, "Is he the governor of Ohio?"

Quentin and Miss Park looked shocked. The latter chirped, "He is the governor of Utah, where the Mormons were holding that awful rebellion."

Therese was chagrined at her own ignorance. Old Mr. Reid appeared anxious to put her at her ease. "This has been an eventful month, has it not?" he said to Miss Jamison. "What with that Kansas bill, and John Brown acting up. And then of course, Miss Anthony's convention in New York." His eyes twinkled

at Miss Jamison before he added to Therese, "Our
Miss Jamison is the Independent Woman of our little
group, Mrs. Pavan. All het up about women's rights
and reason. As befits a teacher of mathematics."

His comment was without malice, almost affectionate. Therese saw from the way Miss Jamison smiled
that she took his teasing good-naturedly and that they
were friends. "Indeed I am, Mrs. Pavan." She countered,
"I still think it shocks Mr. Reid that a woman should
teach mathematics."

Therese looked at Miss Jamison admiringly. Here
was a woman with a brain, she decided.

"Well, it *is* most unusual." Miss Park bridled and
bobbed her head, looking more than ever like a peck-
ing chicken. "I myself teach English grammar and
literature. I have always felt that more suitable for a
lady." She darted a glance at Quentin, but he was
helping himself to the sinewy roast as if no one else in
the room existed.

Poor woman, Therese reflected. She flirts like that
string bean is a figure out of a romance. From sheer
courtesy she offered, "That must be very rewarding,
Miss Park. I myself have always gotten so much pleasure from reading."

Miss Park brightened. "How nice. Who are your
favorite authors?"

"I love the poems of Walt Whitman . . . and
Baudelaire. The novels of Flaubert, too."

"Whitman. Baudelaire. Oh, mercy." Miss Park
looked mortally offended. "I am afraid that both would
be highly improper for me to teach."

As Mr. Reid grinned with amusement, Miss Jamison
impatiently intervened. "After a cosmopolitan city like
New Orleans, Cincinnati must seem strange to you.
We are not all barbarians, Mrs. Pavan." She smiled
her agreeable smile. "As a matter of fact, we have
several theaters now, and the showboat will be coming
this week. Perhaps you would like to go with me. I
understand that you are a newcomer, and before you
have made friends . . ."

The hospitable invitation warmed Therese. "Oh, I

would! I've never . . ." She stopped abruptly. It would be difficult to explain why a New Orlean had never been on a showboat. Not without giving her suspect past away. "I've never been to the theater much, especially since I've been in mourning," she amended.

"That is a difficult thing," Mr. Reid said gently. "I myself am a widower, of many years. But even now, I feel it."

There was an uneasy silence at the table. Therese wondered if Reid had ever expressed himself so frankly before the group. Evidently not. All of them were gazing at him in surprise.

Miss Park was the only one who seemed annoyed. Therese had a feeling that she did not like attention directed away from herself. "There are other diversions besides the theater, Mrs. Pavan. We have some excellent lectures at the meeting hall. For instance, this very week there is going to be a program on phrenology."

Quentin made a restless movement, and Reid exclaimed, "Pshaw." Miss Jamison appeared bored.

"I'm afraid I don't know what that is," Therese admitted.

"And well you shouldn't," Reid declared. "It's all stuff and nonsense—reading a man's character from the shape of the back of his head."

"But you should go to the lectures, Mrs. Pavang." Mrs. Prickett had been so silent, Therese had almost forgotten she was there. "The ladies all dress up, just like they do, I hear, at the opera in New York. It's the place to see the fashions." Her round face was redder and more porcine than ever. "But before you all claim Mrs. Pavang's time, I want to get ahead of you with Sundays. It will be so nice to have company at Mass. I've sure missed that since Hettie—that's my daughter," she explained to Therese, "moved away."

Therese's heart sank in dismay: why hadn't she made up another story about herself? Now she'd never be able to sleep late on Sundays again.

She noticed Miss Jamison and Mr. Reid observing her compassionately.

"You see," Mrs. Prickett went on, "there's not another Catholic in the house. Miss Park is a Presbyterian, Mr. Quentin's a Methodist, and Miss Jamison's an Episcopalian. That naughty Mr. Reid, I fear, is absolutely godless."

"I confess to it, ma'am, without shame." Reid was undisturbed; his intelligent eyes twinkled. Therese found herself liking him more than ever.

"You are all very kind," she said tactfully. "But before I do anything else, I must get settled in some employment. Maybe you could tell me," she asked Miss Jamison, "where I could find a list of dressmakers."

"Why, certainly. In the *Cincinnati Directory*. They have it right at the counter in all the newspaper offices. I'll write the addresses down for you, right after dinner."

Miss Jamison's friendliness was heartening. And after dinner, when Therese excused herself to look in on the baby, the teacher was good as her word.

That night Therese went to sleep in an optimistic frame of mind. She had two friends already—Miss Jamison and, she felt, the kind and irreverent Mr. Reid.

The next morning she got up early and dressed with care, feeling a great resurgence of energy. She hadn't felt so good since she had worked for Madame Dufay in the early days in New Orleans.

The sun was shining and from her window Therese saw that the day looked pleasantly mild. She put on one of her best black day dresses, and over the neckline set an accessory of her own invention, a sparkling white Pilgrim collar so large that it looked like a tiny cape. She pinned on her treasured cameo. Instead of a coronet of braids, she arranged her hair softly around her face to offset the severity of her black brimmed hat, and added long white cotton gloves. Over the gloves, her *godet* sleeves looked graceful and pretty.

The newspaper offices, Miss Jamison had told her, were only blocks away, so she would walk. Two of the offices were right on Main Street. Therese headed out of the house with an intoxicating sense of freedom; to be free, outdoors, and alone made her almost giddy. Apparently there was no "restricted" area in Cincinnati. She saw many refined-looking women walking alone. Some were nicely dressed, but none, it seemed to her, in the height of fashion. She was aware of the admiring and curious glances people gave her; one rather racy fellow in fine clothes tipped his hat to her, muttering, "Ain't you a dolly."

Ignoring him, Therese sighted a big market. It was nothing like the market in New Orleans, with its vari-colored fruits and flowers, and the lazy chatter of many types of people. Instead, it was subdued, with somber-colored vegetables and ugly sides of meat. To her amazement, there were many men in business clothes there, filling market baskets. There were things about Cincinnati that were very strange.

But just like the day before, she responded to the busy, serious tempo; these people seemed to know what they were about, seemed to take the business of making money seriously, just as she did.

In one of the newspaper offices an eager young male clerk led her to the Cincinnati directory. She scribbled down the addresses of the dressmakers, finding to her surprise there were only four. The obliging clerk told her how to find them.

By lunchtime her mood of optimism had become one of despair. Every one of the dressmakers operated from poky houses with gloomy, stingy interiors. But she would have been happy to work in any of them, except for the grim fact that none of them could use her.

Two had received her with impatience, one with that suspicion Therese was getting so used to, and the last with pure hostility.

At that house, a fat man had opened the door. His unpleasant little eyes lit up at the sight of Therese.

"Who is it, Herman?" A plain, harried woman with pins stuck over her broad bosom came into the hall.

When Therese explained her business, the fat man lingered. "I'll take care of this," the woman said crabbily, and the man, after another greedy glimpse of Therese, went off down the hall.

"I certainly can't use *your* services," the woman snapped, "and I don't like you making up to my husband."

Therese gasped. Before she could defend herself, the door slammed in her face.

She flounced off, boiling with fury. It was so unjust, so unfair. She wouldn't have that woman's husband on a tray. And it was not as if she looked . . . fast.

Therese glanced at her reflection in a shop window. Maybe in Cincinnati she did. In New Orleans she had been almost invisible.

The ugly little incident rankled, and depressed her all the afternoon. At dinner, she was hardly able to be civil to the inquisitive Miss Park or the awful Quentin, but she made an effort with Reid and Miss Jamison.

Declining the women's offer to sit with them in the parlor, Therese went to her room as soon as the meal was over. Anxiety kept her awake: if there were no employment here, she would have to move on again . . . learn about another city, adjust to new acquaintances. If she went to an even larger city, it might be daunting, alone; people might not be as friendly as Miss Jamison and Reid.

But this had been only her first day. There had to be something for someone as determined as she was.

She remembered the motto she had adopted in her association with Madame Dufay: audacity and courage. It had served her then and would serve her now.

The next morning she was more determined than ever. Recalling people's reactions to the way she looked, she took care to dress at her most austere. Surely no one could find fault with her today: she was a positive crow, in unrelieved black, without a single ornament.

Once again she approached the helpful clerk at the *Globe*. This time, she decided, she would read about every business in Cincinnati. Finally, nearing the end of the alphabetical listing, she came across "Tailoring Establishments."

That was it. Well aware that tailors generally hired only men, she was sure that one could be persuaded to hire a woman. Ignoring the gaze of the curious, interested clerk, Therese wrote another list of addresses. And once again, as he had yesterday, the boy told her how to find the places.

She knew the first was hopeless as soon as she went in. There was only one flabbergasted old man and an overworked assistant, so intent that he did not even look up when Therese made her startling proposal in his hearing.

The second was not much better, and at the third and fourth the proprietors seemed almost outraged.

At the fifth, the tailor made an indecent suggestion, and Therese rushed out, her face flaming.

But at least, she thought dolefully, it was going faster. Since yesterday she had learned to state her business succinctly, without hesitation.

Feeling that her last visit would be as futile as the rest, she nonetheless made herself apply to the sixth tailor. The directory had advertised Madison and Company as "fashionable tailors" offering "fine ready-made clothes for men and boys." She had never heard of ready-made clothes, but the advertisement sounded promising.

When she saw the big establishment's neat windows, her hopes soared like the morning birds from the bayou. Surely a business like this would have more room for many workers.

A frock-coated man opened the door to her and bowed. "Good afternoon, madam. May I assist you?"

She got a swift impression of the tone of the place. Out of the corner of her eye she caught glimpses of tailors' dummies in finely sewn coats, mirrors and chairs, tasteful displays of fabric. "Yes. I have come about employment."

The young man's respectful manner subtly changed. "If you will take a chair, I'll get Mr. Madison." Even

his elegant accent, she thought, amused, had become
more like regular Cincinnati.

She sat down in one of the softly upholstered chairs,
free now to observe her surroundings. In contrast to
the poverty of the other establishments she had visited, the luxury of this receiving room was intimidating. This, she thought, was how she would decorate
her own salon, only much more femininely.

The man returned. "Would you follow me, please?"

He opened a mahogany door at the end of the
receiving area and gestured her into a big corner office.

A well-dressed man in his thirties stood up from a
rolltop desk. "Will you sit down, miss?" His voice was
deep and drawling, and his face, while not handsome,
was pleasant.

When she was seated, he took a creaking chair
before the desk. The appointments of this room were
simple, in stark contrast to the splendor outside. "You
are looking for employment, Miss—"

"Mrs. Pavan."

His blue gaze, keener than she had perceived at
first, dropped, taking inventory of her face and hair
and figure.

"Well, Mrs. Pavan, what kind of work are you
seeking?"

"I am an excellent seamstress," she said boldly.

Mr. Madison leaned back and stroked his light brown
mustache. "I'm afraid we employ only men."

"At higher wages," she retorted. Surprise stiffened
his face; then he began to smile. "You can get my
services for less, Mr. Madison."

"You are a very enterprising person, Mrs. Pavan."
His smile had reached his eyes now, and there was a
gentleness about him that reminded her abruptly of
Charl'. "I suggest that you apply to the local dressmakers."

"I have, Mr. Madison, without success. And I must
get something to do. I am a widow with a baby to
support."

Something flickered in his mild blue eyes. "I see."
After a pause he said, "We do employ female clerks in

our office. If you write a neat hand and can cipher, I believe we could use you in the office. With the increase in our trade, there is more work than the present staff can efficiently handle. If you are willing to do that, I will take you to our head bookkeeper."

Therese's heart sank. This was not what she had envisioned—serving as a clerk in a stuffy office, her gift, her precious gift, wasted. But it was a position, and a position in the clothing business. "Yes, Mr. Madison. I am willing."

Mr. Madison smiled, and she could not help warming toward him. He looked like such a nice man. "Good. Then I'll take you to Mr. Mundey."

He led her through the handsome receiving room and up two flights of stairs. Passing the second floor, she heard the great hum of a number of sewing machines, smelled the good smell of their oil and the unmistakable, crisp aroma of fine cloth. Her nostrils quivered.

The smells in the third-floor office were like those from another world—the pungent, musty odors of buckram and leather, the acid smell of paper and stale air.

Mr. Mundey was a small, bowed man with a crabby face and defeated eyes. There was apparently only one other clerk, a nondescript lady of uncertain years, who did not look up from her copying when Madison and Therese came in.

"This is Mrs. Pavan, James. We'll want to try her out for a bit, to see how she will do. I hope she will be able to give you some assistance."

Mundey nodded, unsmiling, and Therese observed the litter of paper and the piles of what appeared to be bills with consternation. There certainly seemed to be a good deal of work to do.

For the time being, it was settled that she would share a desk with "Miss Amanda," the nondescript lady. Therese hung her hat and reticule on a hook and waited for instructions.

When Madison had gone, Mundey removed some ledgers from a dusty chair and pulled it up to Miss Amanda's desk. The woman's only acknowledgment

was a curt nod; she stared at Therese from her color-
less eyes, then went on working.

Mundey gave Therese an account to cipher, asking
her to write up a bill, from an accompanying sample.
Apparently her clear, graceful hand and her figures'
tally earned his grudging approval, because he awarded
her an encouraging grunt before he handed her another pile of accounts.

The afternoon passed in silent misery; Therese wondered if Mundey and Miss Amanda ever said a word
to each other aside from business. When she was
leaving at six o'clock, she encountered Mr. Madison
again downstairs.

"Well, Mrs. Pavan, Mr. Mundey tells me that you
gave good account of yourself. We can take you on."

"Thank you, Mr. Madison. I am grateful for the
position."

He looked embarrassed, and she wondered why.
"He has told you about the hours, I believe, and your
wage."

"Yes." She was to work from eight until five-thirty,
or six if need be, during the week, and until three on
Saturdays, for a wage of eight dollars a week. There
would be very little left over after she paid Mrs. Prickett.

"I am glad you've joined us, Mrs. Pavan." She
couldn't understand the uncertainty of his manner,
this man who was the head of such a thriving enterprise.

All she could think of in reply was "Thank you, Mr.
Madison." He touched his hat to her and walked
away.

She was late for dinner at the boardinghouse, but
the boarders were still at the table. They received her
news with surprise, Miss Jamison congratulating her
warmly, and old Mr. Reid declaring that it was "phenomenal" that she had found employment on the second day of searching. Therese hid her deep disappointment from them.

At the end of her first dreary week she was surprised to discover eight dollars in her envelope, and
not the smaller amount she had anticipated for a short
week. Mr. Mundey remarked a little dryly that Mr.

Madison had said to make it eight. Therese caught an
aggrieved expression on Miss Amanda's face. She was
moved by Madison's generosity and wanted to thank
him, but when the employees were leaving on Saturday, he was not in evidence.

That night, she was glad enough to lie down in her
room and rest; she had never had such a sedentary
job, and her body found the adjustment difficult. At
the salon, she had been in constant motion, keeping the
tendons and muscles stimulated, and she now found
the hours of sitting still awful. But she had moved
about as much as she could, volunteering to run up
and down stairs for Mr. Mundey and Miss Amanda.

On Sunday she endured Mass with Mrs. Prickett,
and spent the afternoon outdoors with Charles and
Rubine. It disturbed Therese to hear the baby grum-
ble when she took him from the nurse's arms; the
same thing had happened before. But she could not
dwell on that problem now. She was able to pay for
the rent, and their food. And she had to save all her
energy for the business of survival.

The second week, and the third, passed in much the
same way, despondency robbed Therese of her usual
vitality, and she felt like a middle-aged woman instead
of a healthy girl. She had no heart for the entertainments suggested by Miss Jamison. After her first two
refusals, the agreeable woman stopped asking her.

Therese knew she would go mad if something didn't
change. But she was the one who would have to change
it. That was when she got her outrageous notion.

During her fourth week at Madison and Company,
when the summer heat began to oppress the city,
Therese set her plan in motion. When she helped
make up the payroll she learned that all the employees
were on the same schedule that she was. The other
floors emptied out each evening at the same time she
left. And from the advertisements and handbills kept
in her office, she had become acquainted with Madison's clothes.

On the Tuesday evening, she found her opportunity. Saying good-night to her coworkers, she lingered

on the pretext of finishing some work. She smiled to herself when Mundey warned her not to get "locked in," saying that she could get out the back if she did. After the place quieted, she stole down into the workroom and surveyed it.

The machines were Singers, like the ones at Madame Dufay's, but bigger. It would just be a matter of getting used to the larger proportions. She fished in a box of remnants and brought a fragment to one of the machines to practice on. It was easier to use than she had expected.

Encouraged, she chose an unfinished coat and inserted one of the shoulders into the machine. The noise, in the after-hours quiet, was horrendous. She knew, from scanning the roster of employees, that Madison's had no watchman, but she was terrified of attracting a passing policeman, and more frightened still of ruining the coat.

Nevertheless she went doggedly on; she had to take her chance. The stitching of the sleeve proved the most difficult; positioning and sewing the material at the shoulder took the greatest skill of all. But Therese had learned well at Madame Dufay's, where she had worked with ladies' jackets and on occasion made jackets for the patrons' little boys.

When she was done, both shoulders were perfect. She consulted the little chatelaine watch she had bought cheaply at a pawnbroker's shop; it was not yet seven. And all the coat needed was the buttonholes and buttons. She was determined to finish those tonight.

Not trusting her ability with the buttonhole device on the machine, she was forced to sew them by hand. The buttons went faster; she could sew buttons on perfectly, like lightning.

When the coat was done, Therese sat back for an instant to get her breath. But not for long; her lateness to the boardinghouse was already going to create a scandal. And she might be discovered at any second.

Hastily she put out the lights and ran back upstairs to the office. On a blank statement she wrote in her clear, bold hand, "This is what I can do. Therese Pavan."

She took a pin she had thrust into her dress and
pinned the note on the coat's lapel. Turning out the
office lights, she went downstairs and into Mr. Madison's unlocked office. Carefully she laid the coat over
his chair.

The surprised boarders were sitting in the parlor
when she passed on the way to her room. Making no
excuse for her lateness, she hurried on. Later, she fell
asleep with her stomach rumbling from hunger. It had
not occurred to her before that she had had no dinner.

The next morning, she entered Madison and Company in fear and trembling. Perhaps her daring action
would result in her discharge. Only a few minutes
after she had taken off her hat, one of the frock-
coated young men from below appeared in the office.
"Mr. Madison wishes to see you in his office, Mrs.
Pavan."

She felt the surprised glances of Miss Amanda and
Mundey, and imagined that the messenger's tone had
been severe. Quivering inwardly, she followed him
downstairs and into Mr. Madison's sanctum. Darting a
glance around, she saw that the coat had disappeared.

"Thank you, Harry." The young man went out and
closed the door. Madison stood by his desk, the trace
of a smile on his amiable mouth.

"Am I . . . discharged?" She faltered.

"Discharged? No, Mrs. Pavan. On the contrary. I
see I did you an injustice. Sit down."

She was so amazed she could only stare. Finally she
sank down on the chair next to his desk.

His smile broadened. "I must confess, nothing like
this has ever happened to me in my life."

Therese was silent, but as his smile broadened, she
felt an answering smile on her own lips.

"As a matter of fact," he said in a companionable
tone, "I laughed out loud. My employees thought that
I'd gone crazy. It's been too long since I have really
laughed," he added in a low, confidential voice.

She wondered why, wondered what heaviness lay on
him that made laughter so unusual. But she was too

elated with the turn things had taken to consider that puzzle for long.

He spoke again in a more businesslike manner. "I am going to put you on in the workroom, Mrs. Pavan."

Her heart thudded with excitement and triumph.

"Your wage will be ten dollars a week, and for a time your position will be that of tailor's apprentice. Of course, in the matter of, er, fittings, naturally your work will be restricted." A faint redness touched his cheekbones.

Therese's own cheeks felt warm; this was an aspect she hadn't thought of.

He seemed glad to change the subject. "You are very skilled for someone so young."

"I've been sewing since I was a little girl," she answered quietly.

"I see." Their eyes met again and she smiled.

Suddenly Madison sat up again in his chair, shifting his shoulders under his finely tailored coat. "Well, then," he said briskly, and scribbled on a sheet of paper, "take this to the workroom and give it to Mr. Steinman, the supervisor. I will advise Mr. Mundey that you will be working there."

Therese got up and took the sheet from his hands; he was careful not to brush her fingers, and that struck her as peculiar. Full of anticipation, however, she dismissed the thought.

Her reception in the workroom was nothing like that at Madame Dufay's. The men resented her from the start, and she knew she would have to work harder than they did to be accepted. But she was prepared for that. It was enough to be busy again at the work she loved.

The shocked faces of the men in the workroom gave Therese a clue as to how her news would be received at the boardinghouse. There was no way in the world she could keep it a secret; she had learned already that Cincinnati was just a big little town, and almost everybody knew somebody who would know her business.

At dinner that evening she quietly told Miss Jamison and Reid what had happened.

"What's that?" Mrs. Prickett cried. "In the *tailoring* rooms? Why, I never heard the like, in forty years."

Quentin's persimmon face registered his disapproval. The genial Reid only chuckled. And Miss Jamison said, with spirit, "It's time women were given some opportunities."

"Well." Miss Park raised her invisible brows, surveying Therese with the look she probably reserved for fallen women.

Annoyed at this public scrutiny of her private business, Therese avoided the parlor again and went upstairs to spend a little time with Charles before he went to sleep.

She was in a wrapper, brushing her hair, when there came a soft tap at her door. "Come in," she called over her shoulder.

Miss Jamison entered, looking relaxed and pretty in a voluminous monklike robe, her shining dark blond hair streaming down over her shoulders. "I hope I'm not disturbing you."

"Oh, no. Please come in and sit down." It seemed so long since Therese had had a woman friend to talk to. She smiled at Miss Jamison in the mirror as she plaited her hair for the night.

"I just wanted to tell you . . . don't pay any attention to the others. This can be such a stuffy town. It's all money and convention and religious revivals."

The face Miss Jamison made in the mirror started Therese laughing. "I won't. Don't worry." She turned and faced her visitor, asking curiously, "What made you settle here, Miss Jamison?"

"Please, won't you call me Nell?" Therese nodded. "I come from a very small town near here, one you've probably never heard of. And I thought that when Letitia . . . Miss Park . . . and I came here, there would be more freedom. But it's not like that at all. Good heavens, being a schoolteacher is worse than living in a convent!"

Therese could not conceal her delight. Here was a woman who thought like her, who wanted the same things she wanted—to be free to run her life, to be private and unobserved.

"Why, you think the way *I* do," she said.

"Yes, I do. You are very wise, by the way, to go to Mass with Prickett. It'll keep her quiet. I pretend to go to the Episcopal Church, but usually I just take a walk, with a book."

Therese giggled.

"I have a strong feeling," Nell remarked, "that you're not exactly devout." They grinned at each other.

"I'm not. My father always made me go; he said it was good for women."

"He sounds like mine." Nell made a face. "Father thought the world was ending when I decided to move here. Only the 'piety' of the place saved me. And my brother." Therese heard a soft, gentle note in her voice. "He's always understood me, taken up for me."

"We have a lot in common," Therese said. "My older brother is my idol."

"We're fortunate. Also, being Episcopalian and Catholic, we're spared the *revivals*."

"What are they?" Therese asked.

"Some awful preacher comes to town and holds huge meetings. People get hysterical and *see* God." Therese smiled at Nell's wry tone. "Women dress up like they're going to the opera. Letitia loves them, I'm afraid . . . like séances and spiritualism and phrenology."

"You two came here together? You seem totally . . . seem so . . . unlike each other," Therese said with slow tact, "to be such friends."

"You Southerners put things very delicately." Nell smiled. "That is nice. We're not close friends at all. She's older than I am, for one thing, but back home our parents were neighbors. And Father thought Letitia would be my guardian from perdition, she's so *very* proper.

"You know, I'm actually sorry for her," Nell added confidentially. "In some ways I almost take care of her. She is very innocent, and terribly susceptible to gentlemen's attentions."

"Such as Mr. Quentin's?" Therese hazarded.

"Isn't that pathetic? In that case, it's a lack of attention."

"Oh, Nell, this is so nice. Talking with you like this."

"It is for me too." Nell stared at her with her heavy-lidded gray eyes. How pretty they are, Therese thought, and said so. Nell blushed; she seemed unaccustomed to compliments. "Frankly, I was afraid you didn't like me, when you kept refusing to go to the showboat and the theater."

Therese quickly disabused her. "I was just so depressed and worried . . . about not getting a position, and then having to work in that horrible office."

"How on earth did you get hired in the workroom?" Nell demanded.

Therese told her.

Nell gasped, her expression a blend of astonishment and admiration. "That's the most wonderful thing I've ever heard of. Mr. Madison must be a very nice man, a very unusual man, not to send you packing."

"I suppose he is. I hadn't really thought about it."

Nell rose. "I'd better go and let you get some rest. Look here, now that things are going better for you . . . how about coming to the theater with me Saturday night? Letitia's *such* a dreary companion."

"I would love to."

The new work, and her conversation with Nell Jamison, were the turning point. Therese was sure, from that day on, that her zest for life was back again.

A few days later she received the long-awaited letter from Charl', saying that her letter had missed him. He had gone to New Orleans to see her, and Odalie had told him everything. He wrote of his sorrow in missing her, but he had had to ship right out again, and asked her to write him about everything in Cincinnati. In the same mail, her funds arrived from New Orleans, and she took great pleasure in returning Odalie's loan and writing her about what had happened.

Therese had received only a brief letter from Odalie, describing Michel's and Hector's visit to the house on Rampart Street, their rage at not finding a trace of

Therese, and Odalie's calm declaration that she would call the police if they did not leave. Therese felt happier than ever to be so far from her father's reach.

On that Saturday evening, when she accompanied Nell to the theater, she enjoyed the performance of the actors. But the theater was disappointingly small and the manners of the patrons unbelievable. Having been to the New Orleans opera, the splendid St. Charles, Therese could hardly credit the casualness of the Cincinnati people's dress and the rudeness of their manners.

"I know what you must be thinking," Nell said dryly as they emerged. "It's so different in New Orleans. I dream of going to the theater in New York."

Therese noticed that people were staring at her now more than usual; she had left off her dowdy widow's weeds, for the evening, to wear a tightly fitting gown of brown and pink stripes, and a neat brown fedora on her softly dressed hair. She was glad Mrs. Prickett had not seen them leave the boardinghouse; what she would think about this dress on a "widow," Therese could only imagine.

She glimpsed a quietly dressed gentleman, better-mannered than the others, stepping back to let a trio of women pass.

It was Mr. Madison.

He saw Therese.

"Why, it's Mrs. Pavan!" He looked so stupefied that Therese had to stifle a rising laugh. "I didn't recognize you." He snatched off his hat.

That was no wonder. He had never seen her as anything other than the silent raven of the office and the workroom.

"Did you enjoy the play?"

"Very much," she said warmly, and introduced Nell.

All the time he chatted with her friend, his eyes kept returning to Therese. At last, when he could find no further pretext of lingering, he touched his hat to them and said good night.

Nell was silent and smiling as they walked back to

the boardinghouse. "I think Mr. Madison admires you," she said softly.

Therese flushed. "Not at all. I think he just likes to observe me, like some funny new animal in a menagerie. He says he never had an employee like me before."

Nell gave Therese a skeptical glance and began to talk of something else.

When she returned to work on Monday, Therese thought of what Nell had said. All that week she noticed that Mr. Madison appeared more and more frequently in the workroom. It was evidently unusual, because Therese caught snatches of muttered comment from one of the other men. ". . . never checks up. No, he's . . . special interest."

The man's coworker said something inaudible and they laughed, stopping in embarrassment when they saw Therese listening.

After that, she didn't even look up when Mr. Madison came in the workroom. She fervently hoped he *didn't* admire her. All she wanted now was to be left alone to work in peace, to learn all she could about tailoring. Already she had absorbed valuable knowledge of several things that could be put to use in her salon. Ready-made clothes, for instance.

Therese had a half-formed idea of applying uniform sizes to women's clothes, making proper patterns to avoid some of the torturous hours of fitting. And she had a notion that Nell, with her knowledge of mathematics, could work out very accurate charts of sizes.

Also, Therese had resolved that she wouldn't use the headless dress forms for display. She would find some kind of . . . statue that looked like a person.

These were the things preoccupying her now. There was no room for anything else in her life. She was still bent on attaining such a stature that she could outshine the world's Adairs.

## 7

Raising his voice over the racket of the band, Mr. Reid asked Therese, "What do you think of our Fourth of July?"

"It is very interesting," she shouted, in competition with a rattle of drums, a blare of brasses. Actually she thought it was dull, compared with Mardi Gras processions—just a parade of volunteers from the military corps marching stiffly in the broiling sun with members of the commercial societies and pompous-looking officials.

The heat had a brutal quality, unrelieved by the rich vegetation and the languorous pace of New Orleans.

"What I cannot fathom," Reid said when the band had passed, "is how you ladies stay so cool."

The old man removed his panama hat and mopped his face with a huge white handkerchief. Replacing his hat, he peered at Nell Jamison, then at Therese.

Nell was wearing a powder-blue muslin dress of no great style but obvious comfort; her face was shadowed by an untrimmed hat the hue of cocoa.

"But then you're our tropical flower," Reid said fancifully to Therese. He admired her embroidered gown of white cambric muslin, the matching hat with its wreath of silken daisies. The yellow and white complimented her skin and emphasized the startling blackness of her eyes and hair.

"And how are my other ladies?" Mr. Reid called out gallantly to Mrs. Prickett and Miss Park. He was serving the four as escort. Much to Miss Park's dismay, Mr. Quentin had declined to come along, saying that he was going to visit his mother.

Miss Park looked hot and fractious in her unbecoming high-necked dress. Her bonnet gave little protection from the glaring sun. Mrs. Prickett, similarly dressed, fared no better. Her broad, ruddy face was wet with perspiration.

"I'm much too warm," she panted to Mr. Reid. "Are you really going to wait for the orations, Letitia?"

Letitia Park paused, indecisive. "It seems a shame to miss them."

When the band reached the end of its march at the First Presbyterian Church, there would be prayers and then addresses—which Nell had confided to Therese would be "endless"—by some prominent citizens.

"I think not," Miss Park quavered. "I am feeling somewhat faint. Perhaps you would escort us back to the boardinghouse, Mr. Reid."

"Drat it," the old man said under his breath. Therese turned away to hide her smile. "I would be most happy to," Reid said to the two sweating women.

Raising his hat to the others, Mr. Reid moved off with the landlady and Letitia Park, who cast a resentful backward glance at Therese's floating, fragile dress.

It was one Odalie had given her. Its collarless corsage was scalloped to correspond to the scalloped overskirt, which was embroidered in an elegant arabesque design. The demilong sleeves were worn without undersleeves, and gave Therese's ungloved arms a delicious freedom.

"Oh, dear." Nell grinned at Therese. "I'm afraid that Letitia resents our friendship very much, and resents you for being so beautiful. As if you could help that." She gazed at Therese's white gown. "That really is an exquisite dress. You have the gift of looking elegant and being comfortable at the same time, and I never thought that was possible. It is beyond *my* powers."

Nell looked down at her "hygienic" dress, unquestionably comfortable but unattractive of line. "I am obliged to wear conventional dresses to school," she said, "and then I am in a constant state of unease. On the other hand, these clothes make people raise their brows. I suppose when I am as old as Mrs. Bloomer, that won't matter. But I confess it matters to me now."

Therese laughed. The emancipated Amelia Bloomer had invented ankle-length, baggy trousers worn beneath a loose tunic that reached to a little below the knee, and her creation had not been received kindly. It was scolded by modish magazines and denounced from pulpits as sinful.

"Of course it does," Therese said. "It's all a matter of compromise." She added, with sudden inspiration, "You know, I think I could design a dress for you that would fulfill both functions. Why don't I try?"

From her savings she had bought a sewing machine, hungry to resume her own sewing, and was already at work on heavier garments for the cool Ohio fall. Sewing for Nell was a project that interested her greatly. Besides, she wanted to show her appreciation for Nell's kindness. In only a few months Nell Jamison had educated Therese in a variety of matters. She had what Mr. Reid referred to as a "man's brain." While Nell received that as a dubious compliment, it was true that her mathematical gift made it easier for Nell to comprehend business and finances than most women.

"Oh, could you?" Nell seemed delighted. "But you have your own sewing, and the baby's," she protested. "And so little leisure time."

"You have as little," Therese insisted. "You worked out my size charts on Sundays and in the evenings. I insist. It will be a challenge, and help me keep my hand in design until there is a House of Pavan." Early in their acquaintance, Therese had confided her goal. "Who knows? Someday you may even work for me. You would make a magnificent businesswoman."

"It's a wonderful notion," Nell said thoughtfully. "Heaven knows, there isn't much excitement in teaching these little porkpackers to cipher."

Therese grinned at Nell's mordant humor, but all the same, she had been quite serious about working together. It was a pleasant dream to hold onto.

"They've arrived," Nell said, indicating the massed

paraders at the end of Main Street. "You don't want to hear the orations, do you? They'll go on for more than an hour."

"What an idea! The very thought gives me a *migraine*. Let us go to one of the museums."

"I'd like that. There won't be any crowd until this evening."

They strolled slowly away from the gathering masses, the hundreds of people who were walking toward the church.

One of the pedestrians was Mr. Madison.

When he caught sight of the two women, he swept his panama hat from his head and smiled. He looked neat and faultless in a swallowtail coat of dark broadcloth and cream-colored trousers.

He walked toward them eagerly. "Mrs. Pavan. Miss Jamison." He stood with his straw hat pressed to his chest in an attitude of respect, asking with mock reproach, "You are not going to listen to the pillars of the community?"

Therese saw a twitch at the corner of his mouth; below the neat mustache his half-smile was most attractive.

"No, alas," Nell retorted, parodying an eighteenth-century lady, "we fear that our ears are too fragile, and the heat too great."

Madison laughed. "I may say you do not seem much affected by the weather." The remark was meant for them both but he was staring at Therese with a new light in his mild eyes. He surveyed her face; wandering downward, his look encompassed the flowerlike dress, with its embroidered overskirt falling from her bosom to her knees.

Then, to cover the brief, awkward pause, he asked quickly, "May I drive you ladies to your destination? My buggy's right down there." He indicated a vehicle down the street, where a horse was tethered in insufficient shade. "I must get my horse to a cooler spot. He'd be glad of the change."

Madison's concern for the animal touched Therese.

"We were going to one of the museums—the one with the wax figures. If that's all right with you, Nell."

Her companion murmured in agreement.

Therese was eager to look at the figures again. Ever since she had conceived of using a more attractive substitute for the headless dress forms, an idea had haunted her.

"May I escort you?" Madison asked gently.

"Of course," Nell said in her open way. Then she glanced at Therese, as if uncertain.

Politely Therese echoed her friend's agreement, but inside she was mildly irritated. She had looked forward to a quiet visit to the museum with no other company than Nell's. When they were alone they were so much freer to converse, and there was a lot she wanted to ask Nell about the figures. Her friend was an encyclopedia of information. Therese really didn't need a third on their expedition.

Still, she had to admire the gentle way Madison treated the horse—like Charl'. For some reason she suddenly remembered how indifferent Nicholas had been to animals. Dogs and horses, to him, were only hunting tools.

And Therese also liked the well-bred way Madison included both of them in his conversation. It was obvious he valued their intelligence. But there was a subtle difference in his tone when he spoke to Therese.

He had handed her into the buggy first, so she was seated close to him. She was uncomfortably aware of his physical nearness. As they drove along Third Street, she grasped at something to talk about.

"I've been meaning to ask you, Nell, what *is* that peculiar building?"

She indicated a four-story structure whose front was formed of three big arabesque windows with arches, supported by four huge pilasters. Over those was a wall that ended in battlements, each one supporting a stone sphere.

Therese heard Madison chuckle. Nell answered, "I don't know. All I know is what it's called— 'Trollope's Folly.' "

"But what on earth *is* it?" Therese persisted. "It's like nothing else in the city . . . like a . . . foreign temple or something."

"I can tell you about it," Madison volunteered in his deep, pleasant voice. "Thirty years ago, it was one of the most heroic failures in Cincinnati."

"Failures?" Therese was fascinated now.

"A failed department store," Madison answered. "It was once called the Bazaar. And as 'Trollope's Folly' it's named for a rather haughty English lady who attempted—mistakenly—to foist European elegance on our plain pioneers." Madison grinned. "She stocked the Bazaar with thousands of dollars' worth of merchandise, far beyond the purses of Cincinnati. Far beyond our rather plain imaginations."

His voice was good-humoredly contemptuous, and Therese was surprised at his sudden talkativeness. "Poor Mrs. Trollope," he went on, "sank about twenty-three thousand dollars into the building, and five thousand more into merchandise. She even offered entertainments there, trying to recoup some of her investment, but the Bazaar finally went bankrupt."

"What a shame," Therese commented, looking back. "Surely it hasn't been empty all these years. What happened after that?"

"It fell into receivership, and is now one of the white elephants owned by a bank. Various enterprises tried to make a go of it, but I heard none of them succeeded. Good Lord, let me see—they say it's been an inn, a church, a theater, even a military hospital at one time. But the structure is such that it doesn't seem good for anything." Madison chuckled again. "The last I heard, the owner said he wouldn't even charge rent. I believe some quack doctor, some cult or something, partially occupies the first floor."

"Good heavens!" Nell's sudden exclamation caused the others to turn and look at her. "Why, that must be where Letitia goes to her 'spiritual classes on Third Street.'"

Therese laughed merrily. "Do you really think so?"

"It must be. And to think that all this time I never knew." Nell smiled to herself.

"I take it, then, that neither of you ladies subscribes to spiritualism?" Madison looked at them both, but again Therese felt his gaze linger on her profile.

She shook her head, smiling, as Nell responded, "You take it correctly. Does that make us inappropriately hardheaded and unfeminine, Mr. Madison?"

From any other woman, Therese thought, the question would sound coquettish, but she knew Nell asked as a provocative feminist. Therese was well-acquainted with her free, boyish manners.

Madison evidently knew little about coquettes, either. He took the question at face value, answering lightly, "On the contrary. I find you both admirable."

Therese was still hard put to understand Northerners' almost sexless banter. She noticed, though, that when Madison spoke, his voice had a warm resonance that made her feel abruptly shy with him.

While they waited for him to find a water trough and some good shade for his horse, Therese thought: At times like this he reminds me more than ever of Charl'.

That thought, too, made her feel self-conscious, and kept her silent as he walked with them around the museum. But all that changed when they reached the exhibit of wax figures.

He almost led the women past it before he saw that Therese had stopped and was staring with inordinate interest at the rather gruesome figures of criminals and their victims.

"I didn't think that ladies would like such an exhibit," he remarked.

"I am *most* interested." Therese felt him staring. "Where are these figures made, do you suppose?"

"Made?" he asked in real surprise. "Why, some of them come from New York and Chicago, I believe. Others are made here, by a local sculptor, Harold Mead."

"I see." Therese stared at the figures thoughtfully, reflecting that all her figure would need would be a head, arms, and feet. The rest of the display figure could be padded wire. "They must be expensive to make." She glanced at Madison. He smiled at her, puzzled.

"They probably are. I understand it's an intricate process. Takes a lot of time."

Maybe, she thought, wax wasn't the right material. Maybe plaster of paris would work better.

As they strolled on to the picture display, Therese was so absorbed in the problem she didn't pay much attention to what her companions were saying, until Nell exclaimed, "I really must go. I have lessons to prepare for tomorrow."

Madison consulted his watch. "The time has gone so quickly," he agreed, with another warm look at Therese.

"I have to go too," she said. She wanted to spend some time with the baby on her free day. It had been too hot to bring him out in the blazing sun, with his delicate skin. She looked forward to holding him and playing with him now.

Mr. Madison drove them back to the boardinghouse. When he assisted Nell to the sidewalk, she thanked him and paused an instant to wait for Therese.

But she must have noticed something in Madison's expression, because she then gave him a pleasant smile and walked on toward the house.

"Mrs. Pavan." Madison put his hand on Therese's arm. "Could I speak with you?"

"Of course."

"I was wondering if . . . you would give me the pleasure of taking you to the theater next Saturday." He spoke as hesitantly as a young boy, and his eagerness touched her.

She answered impulsively, "Why, yes, Mr. Madison. That would be very pleasant."

His eyes lit up. He helped Therese down to the curb. When she was going into the house, she did not hear the buggy driving off. Glancing back, she saw him staring after her.

She did not see him in the workroom all the next week, or run into him when she was leaving.

He called for her immediately after dinner on the next Saturday night, but didn't linger in the boarding-house for much more than a civil good-evening to the other boarders.

Therese enjoyed the evening thoroughly. He was very pleasant company, and his presence gave her a new sense of security, a feeling she hadn't had since she had last seen Charl'. As free as women were to go unescorted in the evenings, it was still gratifying not to have to endure the remarks of insolent fellows who had occasionally spoken to her and Nell.

And he was so respectful, so attentive to her wants, that he made her feel enormously valued, not only as a woman but also as a companion. Besides, his man-ners were far superior to those of the other men she noticed, and the greetings of his acquaintances were deferential.

When the occasion was repeated the next week, and the week after that, she found herself liking him more and more. By then, at his diffident request, she was calling him George. He addressed her still as "Miss Therese."

In the workroom he took pains to avoid her assidu-ously. It amused Therese that this avoidance seemed to increase her coworkers' respect for her. She de-cided that they believed he had made advances to her and had been rebuffed. Everything went easier at work because of that.

One Sunday afternoon, when she was pushing the baby's carriage down Main Street, Therese saw George approaching. As soon as he caught sight of her, his face lit up, and he swept off his hat, holding it to his chest.

"Miss Therese! This is a pleasant surprise."

She paused and he hurried to join her. "And look who's here." George smiled down at the baby.

"This is Charles." Watching him lean over and touch the baby's cheek delicately with one finger, Therese was moved by the tender expression on George Madi-son's face.

Charles made a pleased chortling sound and waved his small fists. "How do you *do*," George said softly.

"Very well indeed," Therese answered with a smile. "I think he likes you."

Immensely pleased, George made a silly face at the baby. Charles stared back at him, apparently fascinated with the muscular voice and touch. Therese had never seen a man so naturally tender with a child.

As the weeks passed and her relationship with George Madison began to attract notice, Therese ignored the whisperings of Letitia and Mrs. Prickett, evading even the friendly interest of Nell and Mr. Reid. She knew that soon George Madison would propose to her. And it came to her, with surprise, that she would accept. She did not love him; he did not exercise that treacherous magic that Nicholas had, but she was warmly fond of him now. His presence was pleasing. He was a fine, gentle, intelligent man.

With fondness, she could also feel respect. He was universally liked and admired, for all his reticence and aloofness. And he would make a wonderful father. Sometimes they had taken the baby with them on their outings, and he had been tender and merry with Charles. He confided to Therese that he had always wanted a son of his own. The baby would have a father and a name. She would be protected and secure. The honor of marriage was a better lot than "magic" that had left her abandoned.

Best of all, George understood her; he'd listened with interest to her dreams of the House of Pavan.

Late one evening near the summer's end, he drove them to a wooded area just outside town.

She knew what would come next when he tied the reins and turned to her with a serious expression. "You must know by now that I love you, Therese." Mistaking her silence, he said, "I know you can't love me. I'm so much older . . . and I'm not exactly a romantic hero. And I can't ask you to become my wife until I tell you my secret."

She looked at him in silence, waiting.

"I never thought I could propose to any woman . . .

with my disability." He swallowed and went on, "When
my mother was carrying me, she was severely afflicted
with German measles. I was born imperfect. The doc-
tors told my parents that I would probably never be
able to sire children. When I grew up I sought out
medical advice on my own. To my sorrow, the fact
was confirmed."

He pressed her hand and she returned the pressure,
thinking: How sad it is for such a man not to be able
to pass on his goodness and fineness. She felt extremely tender toward him.

"But you," he said softly, "already have a child, so
I thought . . . oh, Therese, I love you so dearly. I
have from the first time we met. Tell me—is it possible that you could consider becoming my wife? I realize that what I've told you—"

"Yes, George. It *is* possible." She smiled.

He was too overjoyed to speak. His whole face
shone with happiness.

She thought: He has honored me with a truth he's
deeply ashamed of. Suddenly she knew she must honor
him likewise, no matter what it cost. She must tell him
the whole truth about Therese Pavan. Her stubborn
pride, her sense of honor, demanded it. It was one
thing to lie to a judgmental world, another to deceive
this good and gentle man who had risked her scorn
with his secret.

"You are not the only one with a secret," she began. "Before you renew your offer, you are entitled to
know what my life has been. Pavan is not my married
name. I have never had one."

She was surprised at his neutral expression and the
twinkle in his eyes. But she went on rapidly until he
had heard it all.

"Don't you think I knew it was something like that?"
he questioned gently. "Do you imagine that I care? I
love you, Therese. I love you and even more for what
you have suffered . . . and achieved, through your
own brave efforts. I've traveled a good deal, you know,
and have some knowledge of the world. You never
struck me as a pampered society lady. There is some-

thing stubborn and wild in you that is consistent with all I have heard of the Acadians. Maybe it's that itself that made me love you."

"Then I will be happy to be your wife."

If his kiss brought none of the hot sensations she had read in her novels of desire, it aroused her to tenderness. She did not shrink from him when his mouth covered hers.

Therese Madison clutched her husband's arm, moving carefully in her dainty boots down the planking to the New York pier. She could hardly believe that she was in the famous city, on her honeymoon.

The harbor was a mass of ships and tugs and ferries, the docks a milling scene of horse cars and drays, wagons and cargo. "Good heavens! This is like another country," she said breathlessly to George as he pulled her back from the path of a rumbling wagon.

"What are *those*?" They crossed a row of metal tracks, after several vehicles, each drawn by two horses, had rattled by.

"Those are the horse cars. I think we'd better take a public stage; they have places for our baggage."

Therese could not stop staring; there was so much activity, so many people. It was so different from the prairielike landing at Cincinnati.

George hailed one of the stages. A man beside the driver leapt down and secured George's grip and Therese's trunk to the rear of the stage with a rope as the two were getting in.

"This one will take us right to the Irving House." George smiled down at Therese. There had been no seat for him; he stood, hanging onto a strap attached to the ceiling, with his knees pressed close to hers. The aisle was narrow, and other gentlemen, she noticed, were standing as he was, one right behind him.

As the stage gathered speed, she discovered that conversation was difficult, so she contented herself with glimpses from the opposite window of the big, exciting city of New York. George surely could see little from his standing position, but it didn't seem to bother him. In fact, she had found in the last two months that very little bothered George Madison. That was one of his most lovable qualities. She looked up at him again and smiled.

He smiled back, a whole new warmth in his eyes. He is enjoying my enjoyment, she thought. When the stage jerked to a sudden halt, she started to rise, but he pushed gently on her shoulder, shaking his head. Apparently the stage was discharging passengers and taking on more, and she and George had not reached their destination.

When the stage started again, Therese could barely see out at all; there were too many people. She glanced at the other women, proud that she looked as elegant as any and even more so than most. Her full-skirted dress of woolen rep was the new shade, *tan d'or*, "golden bark," a rich, autumnal golden-brown. She had made her own *pardessus* cloak of dark brown velvet, with deep, pointed, flowing sleeves and a pelerine hardly deeper than a big collar. Her hat, instead of the bonnets she deplored, was the saucy old Eugénie deftly covered with velvet that matched the cloak, trimmed with an ecru plume.

Therese's color scheme was unlike the others'; it was a season of black, pearl gray, and plum. But she had had her fill of black and gray during her term of "widowhood" and hand-me-downs, and plum was a terrible color for her complexion.

She noticed other women returning her glances; some were plainly envious, partly, she concluded, because of the devoted attitude of her husband. When Therese looked up at him she saw him staring down at her fixedly, with utter adoration.

That adoration had made it so easy, she reflected, to submit to the act of love. George's very ardor softened her long-chaste body, aroused her not to desire but to an overwhelming tenderness. He had been grateful, astonished with her submissive ease, confessing to her that he had not dared expect so much. Making him so happy gave her a whole new value in her own eyes.

She thought back over the full, happy months that had preceded the wedding. His first action, after she had accepted him, was to call on her at the boarding-house the next day with a huge bouquet of flowers and a beautiful engagement ring of honey topaz surrounded by diamonds. The ring, he said, had belonged to his mother: a rectangular stone, horizontally set, it was like none Therese had ever seen.

The parlor, that hour, was blessedly empty. Soon, however, the others began returning from church and the godless ones came down for midday dinner. Seeing the flowers and the new ring on Therese's hand and observing George's flushed and smiling face, they grasped the news before a word was said, and there was a clamor of congratulations.

Mrs. Prickett brought out an ancient half-bottle of wine for toasting; old Mr. Reid declared that George was the most fortunate man alive. The landlady, in awe of George's fine appearance and prominent position, positively gibbered, while Nell Jamison offered her good wishes more quietly, with probing glances at Therese.

Quentin and Letitia Park were the quietest of all; the sour Quentin muttered conventional words, and Miss Park seemed on the verge of apoplexy.

George amiably endured midday dinner with the group and quickly thereafter took Therese driving.

Therese smiled to herself in the crowded stage, re-calling Rubine's pleasure in the news, her eager offer to "keep on maiding" for Therese when Charles no longer needed her as a wet nurse. Rubine worshiped George, who had spoken with her genially, assuring her that she would live with them as a matter of course.

Another sharp memory was overhearing Letitia's comment to Nell, from the room down the hall: "It isn't fair! I tell you, it just isn't fair! This nobody comes from nowhere and snatches up the most eligible bachelor in Cincinnati . . . in three months. I tell you, Nell, she's no better than she should be."

Therese heard the door close and caught the sound

of Nell's low, indignant reply. That same evening, Nell had come to Therese's room. "Therese, are you sure that you love Mr. Madison? Do anything rather than marry a man you don't love. This has all happened so fast . . . and you never gave any indication of caring for him."

Therese reassured the innocent and romantic Nell, who had told her once that she would wait "forever" until she found the man of her heart. "I *do* care for him, Nell." And that was true. She cared warmly and deeply, and would do everything in her power to make George happy.

"Chambers Street! Chambers Street!" The outcry, and George's light touch on her shoulder, broke into Therese's reflections. He took her hand, assisting her up, and then handed her down onto the stone-paved street in front of the fashionable hotel. An attendant came rushing out of the hotel to take their baggage.

When they were alone in their room, George took her in his arms and gave her a lingering kiss. She responded with affection: he was so good, so fine-looking, and he was doing so much for her, bringing her to this splendid city, full of ideas for her pleasure.

Releasing her, he stood there still wearing his hat. "I thought perhaps you might want to rest. It's still early enough for me to take care of some business a few blocks from here. I'll hurry right back."

"*Rest*?" She laughed at him, patting his face. "I'm not going to rest for a minute."

"That's wonderful." He took off his hat and tossed it onto a table. "Maybe you'll come with me, then. My business won't take long, and I can show you some of the sights before dinner. I'll wait for you to get unpacked."

After the unpacking was done, their garments properly hung and Therese refreshed, they went out together with a sense of holiday. She observed with interest the two businesses they called on—both manufacturers of sewing-machine parts on Duane Street. While she waited for George in the receiving areas of the cluttered enterprises, Therese examined the devices that spilled over into the alcoves she occupied.

She realized it hadn't occurred to George that she would be as interested as he in the new devices; there were certainly no other female patrons in the place. It was as if he took for granted her new state—a married woman, with a baby of her own, who had no further need to think of such matters.

For the first time since his proposal, she felt an odd little coldness in her depths. During the month of their engagement, they had not discussed the prospect of "Pavan" again. When George rejoined her, she gave him such an uncertain smile that he asked anxiously, "Are you all right? Perhaps you're too tired, after all . . . or bored with all these ugly attachments. Let's look at something pretty."

He was so concerned that she was eager to reassure him, passing over the reference to "something pretty," a thing a man would say to any empty-headed little wife.

She responded gaily, "I am perfectly fine. And let's do look at pretty things. I'm dying to see the fashion displays. And everything else."

Responsive to her bright mood, George beamed and squeezed her arm. "Well, I've placed my orders, and the parts will be delivered to the hotel before we leave. I'm at your disposal, Mrs. Madison."

Explaining to her that a good many fashion houses were now located around Madison Square, uptown near Twenty-third Street, George asked her how she preferred to travel.

"Let's walk," she suggested.

He laughed at her fondly. "This isn't Cincinnati. 'Uptown' is a good many blocks up, and long, long blocks across. Would you be more comfortable in a private carriage?"

Therese opted for one of the horse cars, enjoying the novelty of the wheels' sound on the tracks and the mildness of the sunny October day.

She felt like a child at the circus as George led her in and out of one stylish store and salon, then into another. He urged her to let him buy her something, but she gently ridiculed the idea of buying clothing, saying it would be like "carrying pigs to Cincinnati." That aroused more good-humored laughter; there were still sections of the western city where roaming pigs acted as refuse collectors. But he persisted, and she finally accepted a pretty new purse and several pairs of fine gloves.

They also visited some tailoring emporiums where, George said, he could pick up some new ideas for Madison and Company.

Therese had been making mental notes at every ladies' establishment they visited, so interested in methods of display and floor arrangements that she had hardly seen the merchandise. There were one or two places she would like to emulate if she had a salon of her own, but in many of them, errors glared—a sameness, a lack of daring and imagination.

Her good mood lasted throughout dinner and the beginning of the play *Camille*, which starred the noted actress Matilda Heron. Therese had read Dumas's great novel, but enacted, the story was a hundred times more moving. She had never seen such a realistic portrayal of a tragic heroine.

And the scenes with her lover, Armand, and his cruel father, brought back all over memories of Petit Anse and of the arrogance of Nicholas and the Adairs.

"You are very thoughtful," George remarked gently when they came out of Wallack's Lyceum at the end of the play.

"It was so sad. And beautiful."

"Yes. But Miss Heron looked much too hefty to be dying of consumption." George grinned at Therese. "Someone like you would have played it better."

His jocular mood grated on her nerves. When he asked her if she would enjoy a late supper, she shook her head. "What's the matter, darling?"

"Oh, nothing. Nothing at all." She squeezed his arm. "I guess I was so wrapped up in the play I hardly noticed how much she weighed. Though I *could* have

improved on her dresses," Therese added in her usual
style.

Back in their hotel rooms, she caught him studying
her and realized he had looked at her like that once or
twice during the play, when Camille had expressed her
passion for her lover. Therese felt a tentativeness in
her husband's embrace, as if he were measuring himself against a ghostly predecessor.

"Therese . . ." he asked slowly, "did the play remind you of . . . the South?"

"A little. But only in a way that made me glad of
the way things are now." She saw him brighten.

With pitying tenderness, she showed him more affection than usual that night. Later, before they slept,
he murmured. "This is too good to be true, my love.
Too good to be true."

I will make it true, she reflected. I won't cheat him.
I will not be haunted forever by the past.

# 8

As soon as they came back from New York, George moved Therese, the baby, and Rubine into the family house he had occupied alone since his parents' death.

"I'm afraid it's not very cheerful," he remarked to Therese. "But you will know more about these things."

She repressed a shudder. The house was positively funereal; it obviously hadn't changed for many years. And the servants had apparently taken advantage of George's bachelor state, because everywhere there were small signs of carelessness and neglect.

"I want you to change it," he said grandly, "any way you like. I want you to be happy here." He kissed her. "Now I'd better get back to the office."

He added hurriedly, "Don't worry too much about expense. I've got such a frugal wife that we spent next to nothing in New York."

George had been surprised when she refused to let him buy her a fur—she said truthfully she hated fur; she would never forget the agony of the animals trapped on the Côte Blanche—or jewelry other than a good but modest little collar of pearls. She gathered that her husband was very well-off, having also inherited properties of his father's. But always at the back of her mind was the possibility that he might someday back her own enterprise, and she was not eager to squander his money.

"I do have a few small changes in mind," she said tactfully, "but I don't think they'll be expensive." George embraced her again and hurried out.

Therese accomplished a great deal on the first day;

she hired some small boys, released from school on Saturday, to help her and Rubine move some of the parlor clutter to the attic, and then helped the reluctant maid and Rubine do a thorough cleaning of the first floor of the house.

George was very pleased with the gleaming look of the place when he returned. Remarking on the parlor, he confessed that he had never cared for "all the knickknacks," and was always knocking something over. "You seem to know just what to keep," he went on admiringly.

Therese had removed none of the family photographs; the frames had been dusted and polished, and they were all arranged attractively together on a table.

The next week she brought in painters and, taking a leaf from Odalie's book, had the dark hall, the dining room, and the parlor painted creamy white. While the painters were at work, Therese and Rubine cleaned the dingy upholstery of the dining-room chairs, which emerged a rich claret red. They had the same experience with the parlor furniture. There was one parlor chair that was beyond renewal, and Therese had a sudden inspiration.

Carefully she cut a pattern from heavy paper and sewed a cover that completely hid the chair. She made the cover out of painted cotton calico, with a glazed finish appropriate to the formal room. The fabric was striped in subdued blue, gold, and apple red, picking up the colors of the oil painting over the mantel.

Therese wisely left George's small office alone, so he would have a haven, she told him, during the upset. After the downstairs was improved to her satisfaction, she attacked the bedroom floor and then the servants' quarters, changing a small room into a nursery and another into a sewing and dressing room for herself.

By Thanksgiving, the house was almost completely renewed and George constantly expressed his satisfaction with it. When Therese presented him with the bills he was amazed. "I had no idea you were such a businesswoman," he said thoughtfully.

She only smiled, thinking of how much she longed to use that talent in her own enterprise. But George seemed to be taking it more and more for granted that her housekeeping, care of the baby, and private sewing would keep her content. They still had not discussed the ambitions she had confided to him before they were married.

What he didn't realize, she reflected, was that now that the house was refurbished, she would have a great deal of empty time on her hands. At first, it was true, she had seen to the redecoration with huge enjoyment: it was the first home, the only home, she had ever had.

But the baby still seemed to prefer Rubine's company, or George's. When her husband came home in the evenings, he always went up to play with Charles, often bringing him little surprises. Therese was touched by George's affection, but it seemed to her the baby hardly needed her at all.

The maintenance of the house, of course, was left to the servants. Therefore Therese had long hours to spend studying new fashion directions in *Godey's* and *Le Follet*, gathering ideas for her own original designs; and visiting Cincinnati's rather backward shops, not to buy, but to look over merchandise and arrangements. She was convinced that a good salon should also deal in accessories; she never forgot Madame Dufay's pronouncement that in Paris the dress itself was only an accessory.

At first, Nell Jamison had delicately refrained from dropping in, knowing that Therese was busy with the house, and not wanting to "intrude on the honeymooners." But as the domestic chores lessened after Thanksgiving, Therese began to seek Nell out more and more.

On Saturday mornings and early afternoons, when Nell's schoolday was over and George was still at work, Therese pressed her friend to visit. After giving only half their attention to Christmas preparations, Therese and Nell found themselves becoming absorbed in plans for a dressmaking business. Nell was more and more excited about the idea of working with Therese, glad to apply her hardheaded intelligence to matters of prices and expenses, and the accuracy of size charts and patterns.

One Saturday afternoon when George returned from Madison's earlier than usual, he found the two women in the dining room in a welter of sample tissue patterns, papers covered with columns of figures, and intricate-looking charts.

"What's all this?" he asked genially. He liked and respected Nell and was always happy to see her, knowing that Therese took great pleasure in her company.

"Just a few inventions of Madame Therese," Nell answered gaily.

Curious, George sat down at the table and looked at the charts and patterns.

"I had no idea it was so late," Nell said, and rose to go.

"Please don't run away." George smiled at her. "Stay and have some refreshment with us."

Nell hesitated, but his invitation was so sincere, she couldn't help accepting. Therese went off to get them all some cake and coffee, wondering what George would really think if he realized the scope of her plans.

As she served them, George said speculatively, "This is very interesting, very original."

Therese held her breath. George had been so open-handed, so indulgent, that she still didn't have the nerve, on top of everything else, to ask him outright to invest in her.

"I would like to study this some more," he commented.

Nell and Therese exchanged excited glances. And then the talk drifted to other matters.

After Nell had gone, Therese noticed that George was observing her with fond, still-speculative glances. And when she tidied up the papers in the dining room, starting to take them upstairs, he said, "Leave those in my office, would you? I was quite serious about want-

ing to study them some more . . . my inventive little
Madame Therese."

She did as he suggested. Late that night, when she
found that he had not come up to bed yet, Therese
stole downstairs. The door of his office was open, and
she saw him scribbling in a notebook, looking intent
and thoughtful. Without disturbing him, she went soundlessly back upstairs to bed.

It mystified her that in the following days he made
no further mention of the matter, she wondered if he
had forgotten. For some reason, she was hesitant to
bring the subject up; he seemed unusually preoccupied
and she assumed that business matters were pressing
him.

In any case, as Christmas approached, she was diverted by holiday plans and obligations. George had
asked her to give a small holiday party, saying he was
eager to show off his beautiful wife and house; in
addition, there were all the other Christmas chores.
This would be Charles's first Christmas, as well.

On the afternoon of Christmas Eve, it began to
snow, big, drifting flakes that gave the Cincinnati scene
an uncharacteristic beauty.

Therese, in a pensive mood, was sitting by the fire
looking through the latest *Harper's Weekly*. She came
across a drawing by the famed painter Winslow Homer,
entitled "The Christmas Tree." The drawing showed a
happy family gathering in a warm-looking, richly furnished parlor. The room reminded Therese of their
own, except that their own was prettier, she thought
with satisfaction.

One young man in the drawing was adding a finishing
touch to the Christmas tree while children frolicked
about; two pairs of lovers looked on. Something about
one of the men reminded Therese sharply of Charl'.
She had not heard from him lately, and suddenly she
was overwhelmed with longing for his familiar presence.

In the rush of events, she had had little time to miss
him, or to think of past Christmases with Berthe and
Elianne. Now, though, her nostalgia overcame her; she

thought of the small sacrifices her mother had made so that she, Therese, might have some joy of the season. And she remembered her last Christmas in New Orleans.

Sighing, she studied the drawing again. But then she looked around the cheerful parlor and reminded herself of how much she had—a tender and considerate husband, and a life that was comfortable and secure. The baby was well and taken care of.

When she heard George's key in the lock, she ran to open the door.

"How beautiful you are!" He held her at arm's length, admiring her scarlet dress. There was a gay, almost conspiratorial look about his eyes and mouth.

"We have plenty of time before our guests arrive. I want you to come with me and see your Christmas present."

He went to the hall closet and took out her hooded cloak. "Come on!"

Laughing, bewildered, she obeyed him. Outside she held up her face to the pure falling snow; this was the first time in her life she had ever felt snow or tasted it on her lips.

He handed her into the closed carriage he had exchanged for his old buggy, and they drove away. Soon she saw that they were going in the direction of Madison's.

"But what *is* it?"

"You'll see." He grinned at her as they pulled up before the establishment. The snow was thickening, and it was hard to see the facade through the white, swirling mist.

In silence he tethered the horse and helped Therese down to the street. Mystified, she allowed him to lead her to a narrow building next to Madison's. George fumbled in his pocket for the key.

When they were nearer, she saw the sign over the doorway of the building.

In swirling gilt script, on a purple ground, were the words "Madame Therese."

George opened the door and hurried her in.

Speechless, she looked around. The room was spacious; beyond it she caught a glimpse of uncurtained cubicles.

"There was a tailoring shop here a good while ago," he said, smiling. "This is where Madison's began. I own the building now."

She was still incoherent; all she could do was stare at him, a smile breaking out on her face. "Come upstairs," he urged her.

On the second floor was another spacious room; on the third, there were long tables, and on each table stood a fine industrial-size sewing machine.

"Oh, George."

"The rest is up to you. I'm sure there's plenty to be done, to make it the place you want. Merry Christmas . . . Madame Therese."

She ran into his arms.


On a rainy April morning in 1861, Therese unlocked the door to the salon. She liked to come in before the day was started and walk around her small empire alone.

It was always spring there; the salon bloomed with silken lilac and wisteria. The elongated blossoms cascaded from random corners, the lilacs were "potted" in pale gray containers. With the dearth of fresh flowers in Cincinnati, the millinery flowers were a godsend. And they didn't die.

Therese had used the colors of the bayou for the interior, drawing from memories of brilliant flamingos, flying cranes dyed rose by the sunrise, long carpets of lavender-blue water hyacinths, and the glimmering wings of dragonflies. The stair runners and carpet were as green as new grass, like the lawns of Petit Anse.

When George had presented her with a check for starting capital, Therese determined that she would be as stringent as Madame Dufay herself. The main outlay would be for stock and wages; for the rest she relied on imaginative makeshift.

With George's full approval, she raided the attic at the house, finding pieces that were better than anything in the furniture stores. When refinishing was futile, she and Nell enameled old wood with gray-tinted white, adding narrow touches of gilding. The result was pleasing, and reminded Therese of what Dufay had called "provincial French."

The fitting cubicles she curtained in the "dragonfly" material. She chose iridescent *avignon* for linings, and each drapery was either lavender, blue, green, or rose. All shimmered like abalone through overcurtains of white gossamer.

To recover the cushions of the waiting-room chairs, and the fitting-room *poufs*, she had chosen inexpensive sarcenet in a high-gloss medium gray. The *poufs* were dear to her heart: she had never quite forgotten the discomfort of kneeling on hard floors or wooden stools to adjust the hems of dresses. But *poufs* had to be ordered from out of town, and were expensive. Nell came up with the idea of using peach baskets; they had filled them with fragrant cedar shavings, reinforced and padded the strong lids, and covered the whole with gray sarcenet.

Therese smiled to herself, thinking about those early days. Nell, wary of giving up her position until they saw which way the wind would blow, had volunteered in late afternoons on Saturdays and on Sundays. Therese enlisted Rubine, whom she had taught to perfect her already competent sewing, turning over Charles's care to a gentle woman named Savannah. At first Rubine and Therese had done all the sewing, working long hours on both tailor-made and ready-made dresses. The latter, a great innovation, sold at prices any woman could afford. And it amused Therese that her penchant for simple designs appealed to the puritanical tastes of the pious Cincinnati women. Therese often remarked to Nell that the women were becoming elegant without knowing it.

"Your secret is safe with me," Nell retorted. After a few months as a "volunteer," she decided to throw in her lot with Madame Therese. She quickly became invaluable, not only managing the books but also handling a number of other areas. Therese was gratified to be able, after a time, to pay Nell a higher salary than she had received as a teacher, and to give Rubine an hourly stipend that far exceeded her nursemaid's wages.

Nell was Therese's partner and therefore would have a percentage of any profit, in addition to a wage.

They had come a long way in two years, Therese reflected, looking up at the framed article from that historic *Leslie's Weekly*. The article had been printed at the end of last year, calling Madame Therese the "Western Madame Demorest," "a truly American *modiste*." The article cited the fact that Therese Madison had even gone into the paper-pattern business ahead of the famous Demorests of New York. It was George, bursting with pride, who had had the article framed.

Now Therese glanced at the display window. It was time to change "Miss Sally," as they called their plaster-of-paris lady devised by Harold Mead, a local painter and sculptor. Therese had traced him as the sculptor who made some of the wax-museum figures. He had made Miss Sally with a skill and rapidity that amazed them, he was also able to mix special shades of paint, which saved them a great deal of time and money.

In Cincinnati, barns were red; the walls of houses were ecru, ivory, or washed-out pastels. Paint for the wealthy, who requested richer colors, was ordered from out of town at great expense. Harold laughed at that, telling Nell and Therese that "pigment was pigment, no matter how you looked at it," and that he could mix any shade they wanted by adding his own colors to cheap local paints.

The lilac-pink he created for a single wall in the display room and the hyacinth shade he made for the second-floor office were unique. Cincinnati had never seen anything like them and freely said so.

It was Harold, too, who suggested varying Miss Sally's appearance by using theatrical wigs ordered from Chicago, so the figure could have golden, black, or auburn hair to harmonize with the dress of the moment.

Therese removed Miss Sally's golden wig and put it away in one of the raided pieces, a capacious bureau. She undressed the bald figure and slipped on her new grass-green silk gown. The dress was strikingly simple by the standards of the day, with a single flounce over the shoulders of a tight bodice, three big flounces forming the skirt, and a narrower crinoline in accordance with more conservative Ohio tastes.

Therese squinted at the gown, thinking: I'm better than Worth. The famous Englishman, who had opened his own house on the Rue de la Paix three years ago, had taken Paris and America by storm. But to Therese, most of his dresses looked pompous and fussy; they were for Europe, not America.

She arranged a black wig on Miss Sally, then rolled up the muslin curtain that hid the display window from the street. George had devised the clever device; rolled up, the curtain was invisible behind the window frame.

Therese stepped outside to view the effect. To the left of the vivid figure, in the background, a silken lilac bloomed on a long marble-topped side table. It was all very pleasing.

Satisfied, and feeling like a tour, Therese went back in and up to the third-floor workroom, which she decorated completely differently from the dingy and depressing one at Madame Dufay's. Here in the cheerful white-walled room, sturdy plants grew from hanging baskets. The windows were curtained in theatrical costume fabric of a startlingly bright checked design. Therese's draper, Levitsky, almost gave the material away; he had received it by mistake, he said, when his order had been confused with a theatrical order in Chicago. Never able to correct the error to his satisfaction, the draper had finally resigned himself to "taking the loss." Therefore the workroom profited from the exuberant color.

There was a gas ring in the corner, and a painted cabinet holding the necessities for making coffee and tea. The gray-painted fabric shelves had been edged in bright paints by the interested Harold, to go with the curtains. He confided to Therese that as much as he needed money, the aesthetic adventure of the salon motivated him even more.

Therese descended to the hyacinth-colored office she shared with Nell. Harold had enameled an eyesore secretary, handy with numerous shelves and cubby-holes, the same hue as the wall. She glanced up at the framed opening announcement: "Presenting Madame Therese, the last word in Cincinnati fashion."

How she had fretted that day, afraid no one would come. But the women of Cincinnati had come, in droves; some out of sheer curiosity, the more fashionable determined to keep up with all that was new, some scenting scandal.

The unknown Therese Madison had appeared from nowhere, snapped up one of their most respected citizens and most eligible single men, and then proceeded to open up a business of her own. Instead of staying at home, where she belonged, to attend to her baby, the stranger—of French extraction, too, they said, with all the naughtiness that implied—was pursuing an unwomanly course, when there was not the slightest need for her to make her own living.

Therese grinned at the memory, and hung up her waterproof cloak. She had had no need, like Mrs. Demorest, to assume the title "Madame" to sound French. And the salon, with its exotic look of New Orleans, carried with it overtones of Paris, the fashion capital of the world.

Demure and stately in a pearl-gray gown, with her proud husband at her side, Therese had won them over. Even if there was something a little . . . fast about Madame Therese, she did have the cheapest and prettiest clothes, said the ladies. And George Madison, no fool, *had* married her.

From downstairs now the usual morning noises drifted upward; the others were coming in. Therese heard the chirpy greetings of the dressmakers, the dignified voice of Rubine, and the harsh good morning of Mrs. Reich.

Therese could still hardly believe that she now employed the same four dressmakers who had refused to
hire her . . . including the sour Mrs. Reich, who had
once accused Therese of "making up" to Horrible
Herman. Mrs. Reich had been the last to surrender to
the rising tide—the banditry of patrons by Madame
Therese. Even now their association wasn't cordial,
but Therese recognized the woman's artistry with a
needle. Another asset was her total lack of imagination; she could only follow directions, not invent. Usually when Therese gave her orders, Mrs. Reich assumed
they were the patron's and was not averse to carrying
them out, a situation which highly amused Therese
and Nell.

Therese sat down at the desk with a feeling of
anticipation. Today she would write out a check that
would make Madame Therese truly hers—a check to
George Madison, the original investor.

George would balk, of course. But she must make
him understand that this was something she had to do;
it signified her personal victory. He was unfailingly
openhanded, yet it galled her to be dependent on him.
She wanted her own funds, for Charles. And someday, somehow, she would be in touch with her mother
and Elianne again. There were a thousand things she
wanted to do for them on her own.

"Good morning!"

Therese jumped. Nell had come in so silently Therese hadn't heard her; her tall, full-bodied friend moved
as lightly as a sylph.

"*Voilà!*" Therese held out the check. Scanning it,
Nell looked up and smiled.

Handing it back to Therese, she said, "Congratulations. 'Independence Day.' You must feel wonderful."

"I do. But you know, I couldn't have done it without you, Nell." She took her friend's hand. "By the
way, did you bring the corsets?"

Nell looked chagrined. Slipping her hand from Therese's, she put it to her face, reddening. "Oh, Therese,
I'm so *sorry*. I was so intent on stopping by the telegraph office . . ."

She had been anxious over the situation down at Fort Sumter in South Carolina, where a small force of Union troops was holding off a large group of Confederates. "Any news?"

"Not yet." Nell's expression was worried. "Therese, I'm frantic about Joe. If anything happens down there, it'll mean war. And then he'll have to go."

This was the first time the reticent, calm Nell had voiced her fear outright. Therese knew that all the rumors of war had made Nell constantly anxious about her brother, but she had kept a good face on it until now.

"There can't be war," Therese protested. "It's too horrible to think of. They've got to settle it in an amicable manner. There's just no other way." She tidied the desk, got up, and hugged Nell to her.

"You'll get your lovely dress all damp," Nell said, backing off. The dress, put on new just that morning, was soft and simple, in an intense rose color that flattered Therese's complexion and rang a bright note in the dismal day.

"Nonsense. Look here, I'll get the corsets. You hate this weather and I don't mind it at all."

Before Nell could object further, Therese had wrapped herself in her waterproof cloak again and was walking toward the door. "Just look after things a little while downstairs. There shouldn't be much business today, what with—" She stopped abruptly. She had been about to say: "with all this war talk," but Nell's tense look prevented her.

"What with the rain," she amended. She paused a moment to glance in the hall mirror. Her hair was smooth, its heavy, gleaming braids gathered into a soft chignon effect behind her ears, a new French mode that had just come out.

She raised her hood and, calling out to Nell that she'd be back soon, hurried out of the salon.

The moist air and the soft rain felt agreeable on her face. As she walked toward the department store, she thought intently of the new Thomson's corsets. They

were quite revolutionary, with no bones at all—just
front snaps and a latch to keep the garment from
popping open. Her best patron, the redoubtable ma-
tron Agnes McKay, would love the Thomson's corset.
And she'd be coming at ten.

Therese smiled to herself, recalling that Mrs. McKay
often said she was too old to suffer for beauty in
corsets. Therese rarely wore one herself—she hated
the things—being too slender to need one except under the most extreme fashions.

Skirting a mud puddle, Therese mused that, Mrs.
McKay had really been her Princess de Conti. Just as
the noted princess had "adopted" the dressmaker Rose
Bertin a hundred years ago, Mrs. McKay had fallen
instantly in love with the salon, and bullied her wide
circle into patronizing Madame Therese.

Therese went on dreaming, hardly aware that she
was perilously close to the curb, as she recalled that
Rose Bertin wound up as court milliner to Marie
Antoinette.

*Versailles*: it occurred abruptly to Therese. The very
architecture of that lovely, wicked place suggested certain dress designs. . . .

Therese drifted off into the world of her imagination, far from the Cincinnati street.

Then, in an instant, she was splashed from head to
toe and looked up in utter shock.

She was cheek-by-jowl with an expensive open
carriage. Glancing at the driver's seat, she saw a strikingly handsome young man, not much older than herself. He was staring back at her, appalled.

"Oh, good Lord, I *am* sorry, miss." He touched his
hat, then tied the horse's reins and leapt down from
the carriage, striding toward her.

Therese looked down at her cloak; its pale gray
watered-silk surface with its dragonfly sheen was black
with ugly stains of muddy water. And where the breeze
had blown the cape back slightly from her dress, black
mud also defaced the rose-colored fabric. She was so
annoyed that before she knew it, a stream of indignant
Acadian issued from her mouth.

The young man, who now stood with his hat in his hand, stared down at her. A slight smile creased the edges of his well-shaped mouth, but he sternly repressed it. "I recognized 'careless' and 'inconsiderate,' " he said in flawless Parisian French. "But the other was beyond me. A thousand apologies; I was . . . watching you, but I thought you'd surely move away when I passed."

Abruptly indignation faded and she began to see the comical side of it all—she had been dreaming so hard of dresses, and he, apparently, had been looking so hard at her that he hadn't minded his driving. He said he'd been "watching" her. In spite of the situation, she couldn't help being flattered.

He was dressed in flawlessly tailored English clothes and was obviously a man of refined taste. At the same time, there was a bold, unashamed masculinity about him. He had none of the languid softness of the rich dandies she had seen in New Orleans and New York.

As he stood there towering over her, staring at her face and hair, she realized that he was also the handsomest man she had ever seen.

"It's nothing," she said in French. "Please do not regard it." She turned to walk away.

"Please. Wait!" His English, she noticed, did not have the harsh accent of Ohio at all. "At least take my handkerchief and clean yourself up a little." He took out a large immaculate square of fine linen.

She shook her head.

"Then, *mademoiselle,* allow me to compensate you for the damage." He drew out his pocketbook. "You might have to buy another cloak, and it's all my fault."

Therese repressed her laughter. *Buy* another cloak. There was not another one like hers anywhere; she had designed and made it herself. Why, he must take her for a shopgirl. The whole affair, now, was more and more amusing. "I assure you that's not necessary."

"But let me drive you to your destination."

He was certainly persistent, she thought. "I don't think that would be possible. That's my destination."

She nodded toward the door of the department store just a few yards away.

The young man laughed and reddened. "I see. You're sure you won't . . . accept some compensation?"

"No, thank you. Absolutely not. Good morning." Therese walked off then, still half-amused, half-annoyed, wondering why she had wasted so much time talking to the beautiful young man.

Anthony McKay steered the carriage across the street and waited for her to come out.

She had aroused his curiosity; she was the prettiest woman he had ever seen in his life. There was a mischievous kind of *hauteur* about her that he had seen only in Paris, and that *patois* she had cursed him in was fascinating. Yet she had followed that with perfect French.

He wondered if she were a local *midinette*.

In a short time his patience was rewarded; he saw her emerge from the store, more impressed than ever by her grace and beauty. The cloak seemed mysteriously cleaner; of course she must have seen to herself in the store. He still felt like a fool.

He had been so intent on her, wandering along with that dreamy air, that he hadn't realized he was driving practically onto the curb.

Anthony wondered how far she was going.

Not far, he discovered—she was entering the salon of Madame Therese.

Too bad he had been there already, with his aunt's message for the respected *couturière* the locals were always going on about. Anthony could imagine what Madame Therese was like; his mother and sister had dragged him to enough dressmakers in Paris and New York.

She would be skinny as a rail; probably with a wart on her chin. The *midinettes* were always the pretty ones.

Anthony chuckled. Well, he was damned sure going to escort his aunt on her next visit to Madame Therese's establishment. There was one little *midinette* he was determined to know.

"Good heavens, Therese! What happened to your *cloak*?" Nell exclaimed when Therese walked into the salon.

"Somebody splashed me," Therese answered briefly. For some reason, she didn't want to go into the incident with Nell. The meeting with the strange young man had affected her more than she cared to admit. "Rubine can clean it; she's a wizard at that. But I'd better change my dress. Here are the corsets."

She handed Nell the tissue-wrapped bundle and went to the ready-made section to find a dress to wear. "Would you put one in the dressing room for Mrs. McKay? You know her size."

"She may not be coming. While you were out, her nephew came with a message from her." Nell handed Therese a small creamy envelope.

"My dear," Therese read, "I have a slight cold and my worrisome caretakers thought I shouldn't come out this morning. However, I am eagerly expecting you and George at my *soirée* tonight. Affectionately, Agnes McKay."

Therese smiled and handed the note to Nell. "It seems you're right. Perhaps I'd better look for something else to wear tonight, too. If the rain goes on, the pale pink will be a disaster. Every speck of dust shows up on that."

She began to look among the evening gowns. Nell disposed of the corsets and went back to the office.

The day went as Therese expected; there were very few clients because of the rainy weather and because of the tension about a possible war gripping the city as well. At the department store, she had heard people talk of almost nothing else.

That afternoon she was surprised to see George coming into the salon. He generally did not come until closing time, when he arrived to escort her home.

He looked extraordinarily solemn and anxious.

"What's happened?"

"You haven't heard, then," he said quietly. "Early this morning the Confederates fired on Fort Sumter. The news just came in at the telegraph office."

"Oh, my God." Thank God Charl' is in France, Therese thought. But César was eighteen now; he might be considered old enough to fight. And Joe, Nell's brother . . . "It's bad, isn't it?"

George nodded. "The Union will have to surrender the fort. It'll have to. It's only got eighty-five officers, against four thousand Confederates. And when that happens, war will be inevitable between the North and South."

"And Madison's will be making uniforms. Thank God for that. It is true, what you told me . . . that you'll be 'essential' to the war effort. You *won't* have to go to war?"

He gave her an odd little look, almost as if he didn't know her. She realized he had been thinking of the wider picture, the greater horror, not of himself. "I'm thinking like a woman," she said. "Thinking of my own small world."

George smiled at her forgivingly and took her in his arms. "Of course you are. That is only natural, darling, and I'm glad your first thought was of me. But you don't have to worry. First of all, I'm too old."

She thought he sounded a bit wistful and sad. Guiltily she remembered her reaction to the beautiful young man in the carriage.

"I suppose Mrs. McKay will cancel her *soirée* tonight," she murmured.

"Good Lord, is that tonight?" George frowned. "No, I don't suppose she'll have time. It's probably all arranged. But it's a bad night for me, Therese. That's what I came to tell you. I'm going to be late. I've set up a meeting with an Army man." At her look of surprise, he explained, "Yes, they're sure the war is coming.

"Anyway, I've set up a meeting with him and my foreman. We want to get going as soon as possible. Look here, do you think you'd mind going alone to Mrs. McKay's?"

"I wouldn't *mind* . . . but why don't I just stay at home, George? I hate to go without you."

"Nonsense, sweetheart. I wager you've already chosen your dress. That one there . . ." He grinned, indicating the apricot-colored silk gown hanging apart from the others. "It's lovely. Go and enjoy yourself. Mrs. McKay always has such fine music. And you can dance, for a change. I'm such a terrible dancer."

His consideration and generosity moved her. More than ever, she regretted her flirtation that morning with the stranger.

"Do go, darling," he urged her. "This may be the last celebration for a long, long time."

# 9

"Therese, my dear. You look exquisite in that color."

Agnes McKay, standing in the doorway of her drawing room, held out bejeweled hands and clasped Therese's. She was the nearest thing there was, Therese thought, to royalty in Cincinnati, whose open, free-wheeling society was composed mostly of rich merchants, simple-hearted people. She smiled. "You're feeling better."

"Yes." Mrs. McKay looked splendid in a lavender creation from Madame Therese, her imposing bosom, arms, and fingers glittering with fine amethysts set in white gold. Her silvery hair was beautifully coiffed, but her *grande dame* air was offset by her unaffected manners and her look of humor and intelligence. "But where is your fine husband?"

Therese explained George's absence. A shadow fell over Mrs. McKay's sculptured features. "I cannot believe it. But everyone says the war will come. Well, I could not let this horrible war fever stop me from giving this *soirée*. We'll have little enough gaiety when it happens."

"That's exactly what George said. He urged me to come anyway."

"He is a very wise man; I've always thought so. And I am so delighted you did. As you see, we are a rather small party tonight. Others had grimmer business. But enough of that. It's almost time for the music . . . and I want you to meet my favorite nephew." Mrs. McKay hurried out of the room.

As Therese went about greeting other acquaintances,

the musicians began to tune their instruments. She took a chair, accepting a glass of sherry from a passing servant, glad that Agnes McKay wasn't "temperance."

She looked toward the door. Mrs. McKay was coming back. Just behind her, in evening clothes, walked the young man with the offending carriage.

Therese almost laughed aloud at his look of shock. If anything, his surprise was greater than hers.

Mrs. McKay led him to Therese's chair. "Mrs. Madison, this is my nephew Anthony McKay, who's visiting me from New York. And this, my dear boy, is the lady I've been telling you about—Mrs. George Madison, our Madame Therese."

Therese acknowledged the introduction with proper cordiality, but Anthony McKay struggled with surprise. "Mrs. Madison," he said at last, with a faultless bow.

"Are you enjoying your visit, Mr. McKay?"

"Very much." A bright gleam lit his pale gray eyes, eyes so light they contrasted starkly with his tanned face. "Cincinnati is full of surprises." His well-shaped mouth twitched a little at the corners; his keen gaze took in her face and hair, and her bare shoulders above the décolletage of her gown.

"Now take a seat, boy, and be quiet," Mrs. McKay reproved him. "The music's about to start."

With another long look at Therese, Anthony McKay walked across the room and deliberately took a chair directly facing her. Disturbed by his intent stare, she looked away.

The quintet of musicians began to play. Therese was agreeably surprised: instead of the customary chamber music, they played instrumental versions of operatic arias. It was an uncommon choice. Only the original Agnes McKay would have asked for such music.

Therese recognized love music from *Rigoletto* and *Il Trovatore*, and then the passionate "*Un dì felice*," from *La Traviata,* an opera she'd enjoyed in New York. "*Un dì felice,*" the rapturous song of Alfredo and Violetta.

The strong emotion of opera had always moved

Therese; tonight, at that moment, it stirred her more than ever. Unwillingly, yet unable to help herself, she glanced at Anthony McKay. His bright, pale gaze was fixed on her; his face held naked admiration.

Chagrined, Therese looked quickly away and, when the music ended, turned to the woman next to her and began to chatter. Yet all the while, she was aware of Anthony McKay's unswerving observation.

And later, when Mrs. McKay announced that there would be dancing in her little ballroom, Therese knew instinctively that he would approach her, asking, "May I have the honor?"

Although he held her at the proper distance during the waltz, she was sharply aware of the warmth of the big fingers barely touching her waist; her hand lay submissively in his. He looked down at her in silence.

She cast about for something to say: it would look strange if they didn't talk.

But he spoke first. "Madame Therese. I never imagined someone so . . . young could be the head of a business."

"I've planned it all my life." The polite conversation was even stranger than their silence, belying the passionate intensity of his eyes and her sharp uneasiness.

"My aunt says you are from New Orleans." His words were heavy, as if he found it hard to speak, unlike that afternoon.

"I lived there. I'm from a place called Côte Blanche, in Acadian country."

"Acadian." A bright glint appeared in his pale gray eyes. "That's what you were speaking this afternoon when you reproached me so colorfully." His brilliant smile softened the noble austerity of his features, making him look more like the mischievous cavalier she had first seen. "I do apologize."

"Please." Therese dismissed the incident with her tone.

Suddenly lowering his voice, he confessed, "I waited for you. I saw you go into the salon."

"And you thought I was a *midinette*."

"How on earth did you know that?"

"You spoke Parisian French," she said, finding it hard to look away from his magnetic eyes. "And *midinettes* are required study, are they not, for young men who take the Tour?"

He laughed. "You've been to Paris?"

"No. Not yet. But I've read a great deal about it."

"You should go to Paris. You belong there." A faint red flush touched his cheekbones: he seemed to realize that he was holding her too closely, speaking in too intimate a tone. He drew back a little.

They waltzed once more in silence, and she felt that she was floating, that her feet touched the flowering grass of meadow, not the polished floor of a Cincinnati ballroom. For an instant, she became the tragic Violetta, whirling in the arms of the young patrician Alfredo.

The sensation was overwhelming: she had never known what it was to feel like this, just from being near a man. Not even Nicholas, at the height of her adolescent infatuation, had affected her so strongly. Remembering George, she was hot with guilt.

As they circled, she glimpsed Mrs. McKay sitting in a chair against the wall, watching them.

I must break this inappropriate silence, she thought. "I'd like to hear more about Paris," she said calmly. "My husband and I plan to travel there when we can get away."

At the word "husband" there was the faintest movement at the corner of her partner's sculptured mouth. He gave her a tight smile, and obediently detailed some of the beauties of the City of Light, its libraries and museums.

Watching him as he spoke, she found herself comparing him with George. She felt so close to this man, so distant from her husband; time had not yet worn away the new-minted look of these classic features, slackened the muscular body, or weakened the powerful hands, one grasping her waist, the other pressing her fingers. All of a sudden, George seemed so old.

And Anthony's gaiety, his impudent cast of mind, were so akin to her own. He was a man from a wider world than George's, a man who had never been bowed down with responsibilities that made him solemn and sober. Yet, for all his merriness and elegance, Anthony McKay was thoughtful and intelligent; intelligence blazed from his remarkable eyes.

He is a man who sees the poetry in the world, as I do, while George merely gropes to comprehend, she thought. How wonderful it would be to visit Paris with a man like this . . .

Therese caught herself, chagrined. She must not think like this. She had the best and kindest husband in the world. So when the music ended, she replied coolly to Anthony McKay's fervent thanks and excused herself. She fled upstairs to the bedroom Agnes McKay had set aside for the use of guests. Looking in the mirror, she smoothed her hair. Her reflected eyes were huge with excitement, her cheeks vivid with color. She felt the way she had at her first *fait do-do*, as if a new world full of unknown delights was opening to her.

But the woman in the mirror was not an untouched girl at her first dance; the glass reflected soigné hair, a fine pearl collar, and the inimitable lines of an exquisite dress of her own devising.

She was Therese Pavan Madison, a married woman who was someone in this city. And she could not risk all that she had struggled for, and gamble her reputation, on a silly flirtation with a charming man. Most of all, she couldn't do this to George.

Therese went back downstairs, feeling more in command.

Anthony McKay was in the hall, waiting. He looked up at her.

She gave him a cool smile and saw that she was to be rescued as her old friend Mr. Reid made a belated entrance.

"Therese!" Mr. Reid came to her, holding out his hands. "You're just in time to waltz with this feeble old admirer. The music sounds very inviting. Will you?"

"Of course. I would be delighted." Therese smiled brilliantly at Mr. Reid and went with him into the ballroom.

The rest of the evening she avoided Anthony McKay.

At home, when George asked her if she had enjoyed herself, she answered him with calm indifference.

And yet, trying to fall asleep, she still remembered the touch of Anthony McKay, the look and sound of him, and the fantastic sensation, in his arms, that she was waltzing in a field of flowers.

The next morning at the salon, Therese found herself in a state of heightened nerves. Abnormal excitement possessed the whole city, and the very weather conspired to increase tension: there was a weak, hazy sun, and the air was charged with an approaching rainstorm.

Therese felt raw from lack of sleep. All night long she had lain next to George listening to his regular breathing, knowing that her marriage to him had been a grievous and irreversible error.

There was not enough to occupy her in the salon, and she missed the soothing presence of Nell, who had joined the crowds waiting outside the telegraph office for the latest news from the South.

No one had come in yet; she supposed women had other things to think of today. On the other hand, upstairs the machines hummed steadily. Therese wished she could do some sewing—anything to occupy her hands and her mind.

She was feeling too jumpy to sketch out the Versailles designs that had inspired her yesterday. Wandering to the display window, she made superfluous adjustments to the skirt of Miss Sally's gown and to the glowing silk vines.

She heard a carriage stop outside and looked up.

Anthony McKay got out and handed his aunt to the sidewalk.

Therese's heart lurched: she had not expected Mrs. McKay this morning, and the effect of seeing Anthony again unnerved her. A casual flirtation should not make her feel like this, with thudding heart, her hands turned suddenly cold.

She opened the door.

"Good morning, my dear." Agnes McKay kissed

Therese on the cheek, observing her sharply. "You look worried too, as we all are. I couldn't bear the suspense any longer. I thought I might as well come along for my fittings."

"I'm glad to see you're feeling better." Therese turned to Anthony McKay. "Good morning," she said neutrally.

"Madame Therese." His bow was very correct, but his eyes seemed to penetrate her soul. He extended his hand. Taking it, she felt a shock, a dart of mysterious heat along the veins of her arm. The very air between them seemed to vibrate. He took a quick, sharp breath.

Therese released her hand, saying quickly, "Please sit down. I'll get Rubine."

She was glad to escape upstairs. A few minutes later she returned with Rubine, who gathered Mrs. McKay's dresses and took them to a cubicle.

"You needn't wait, Anthony. I know you'll be bored to distraction," the old lady said. "Why don't you go to the telegraph office with the others . . . and call for me in about an hour?"

"I assure you I won't be bored at all." He glanced at Therese. "There's no point in going to the office, anyway. The very racket will announce the news. Anyway, I thought I'd pick up some gifts for Mother and Marian. Perhaps Mrs. Madison would help me."

"Of course," Therese murmured, wishing fervently he would go away. His presence filled the room: his disturbing masculinity was more apparent than ever among all the feminine knickknacks.

"Very well," Mrs. McKay followed Rubine into the fitting room.

"Please call if you need me," Therese said nervously. She felt those penetrating eyes again, and turned to Anthony McKay. "What sort of gift did you have in mind?" she asked him briskly.

"I'm not sure. I'll just look at everything." His piercing gaze swept the room, taking in its flowerlike colors. "This is beautiful," he said softly. "And most original. It's better than anything I've seen in New York."

He smiled at her, wandering toward the massive china cabinet she had converted into a display case for accessories. He leaned down, peering into the case.

"Earmuffs . . . in April?" he asked, looking at a hair ornament with silk carnations in shades of rose and red.

Therese eased a little and smiled. The carnations, sewn on a velvet headband, did look like earmuffs. "An ornament for the hair."

"Fascinating." He examined a Victoria tie of bright silk with black lace. "The eternal feminine."

He gave her a mischievous side glance that brought back the events of yesterday, their innocent and comical first meeting.

"Help me pick out something."

She questioned him about the size and coloring of his sister and mother. His answers were so vague that she was certain his gift-buying was a device to detain her.

Remembering the Thomson's corset, she excused herself to take one of the tissue-wrapped garments from a cabinet into Agnes McKay's fitting room.

When she came back she found him staring dreamily at the silken flowers. "Did you . . . find anything?"

"I'm afraid not. What would you suggest?"

Desperately she opted for gloves. He leaned close beside her as she took several pairs from the case, and once again she felt that astonishing heat, that electric reaction. At last he chose four pairs, and she wrapped them for him.

To her relief she was called into the fitting room.

When the fittings were concluded and the McKays were preparing to leave, there was a sudden startling clamor of bells and shouting from the street.

"Surrender! They've surrendered!"

Mrs. McKay turned white. She swayed on her feet. Therese and Anthony moved toward her. "Sit down," he said gently.

"I will get her a glass of wine," Therese offered, and brought it from a corner cabinet.

She glanced at Anthony; his face was grim and set, and his bright eyes bored into hers.

"You will be rejoining your regiment," Mrs. McKay said to Anthony in a broken voice. She struggled to her feet, leaning against him.

He led her toward the door. Anthony touched his hat to Therese and she watched him help his aunt into the carriage. But he did not get in after her.

Therese saw him coming back into the salon as the carriage drove off.

They stood there staring at each other. He must see it, she thought, he must see it in my eyes, the feeling that he has aroused so suddenly, in just this little time.

"I will be leaving this afternoon," he said. "I wanted to tell you . . . to tell you good-bye.

She offered her hand to him. "Good-bye, Mr. McKay. And Godspeed."

An expression of pain crossed his features. He raised her hand to his mouth and pressed a kiss on her fingers.

Then, in one swift motion, he put on his hat again, touched it to her, and walked through the door.

She could not tell how long she remained there staring after him, stunned by the swiftness of events, by the sudden terrible power of his farewell. She had met him only yesterday; they had danced one dance, exchanged a few dozen words. And yet she felt as if her whole life had changed; in just a day and night and this gray morning, she had been touched by him as she had never been touched by another man.

And now he might be going off to die, in all his strength and youth and manly beauty. The tears gathered in her eyes and slid down her cheeks.

Through a blur, she saw George coming in. When he saw her crying, he took her in his arms and soothed her. "Don't cry, darling. We must all face this with courage. It can't last long."

A rumble of thunder rolled across the sky like the roar of cannon. Beyond her husband's shoulder Therese saw the sudden onset of a drenching rain.

The Northern states mobilized with amazing speed: by late May, Union forces had crossed the Potomac and were occupying Alexandria, Virginia. Most of the fighting seemed to be taking place south of the Mason-Dixon line.

Added to Therese's constant anxiety for her family she worried about Anthony McKay. George assured her that the war would never reach the bayou. Following closely the newspaper accounts of the war, Therese saw no sign of fighting in that area.

All the same, she was terrified when, late in the summer, she received a letter from Hortense Dufay describing the "war fever" in Louisiana. "I have decided," Madame Dufay wrote, "to sell my house and go north. I read with pleasure, in the *Leslie's Weekly*, of your astounding success. I wonder whether you can use my services."

Therese read the letter with astonishment and sadness: her proud mentor, Hortense Dufay, was seeking employment with her former student. Therese could not see how it would be possible for Madame Dufay to adjust to such a position. But she wrote and told her to come. Nell could see to her living quarters until she could choose her own.

Graver than Madame Dufay's dilemma was the wider threat to Louisiana: the loveliness of New Orleans faced destruction. And the peace of the bayous could be invaded.

Therese knew that she must write to Berthe, and pray that Michel would not find the letter and punish Berthe for keeping a secret. That was why Therese had never felt free to write to her mother before. But now she had to. She must know that they were safe, or she would go mad.

After many anxious weeks, Therese received her mother's loving reply. "I think of you all the time," she wrote, "but I understand your silence, dearest daughter. Your father has not forgiven you. I have never ceased to. Thanks to the good God, we are all safe and well. We have never seen a sign of the fighting. Charl' has written to me from Calais, France. He is married, and happy. And he told me of your own marriage, and that you now have a little boy. Someday I will be so happy to see my grandson."

Bless Charl', Therese thought. He must have told Berthe that the child was George's.

"Amelie has married Hector Rocaille, and they have gone to the West with César. Many of the bayou families are sending sons to the West. Your father says they must not fight the rich Anglos' war."

That was so like Michel. But Amelie—her own sister—married to Hector Rocaille!

"I wish you could see Elianne, Therese. She is the most beautiful little girl you could imagine; she reminds me so much of you.

"I pray each night that we will be reunited, that time will soften your father's heart. My love goes to you, *petiote*, and my blessing."

The tears gushed from Therese's eyes. She missed her mother and Elianne so sorely. For days afterward, her heart was heavy with longing.

The indomitable Agnes McKay had resumed her visits to the salon, saying, "We can't let down. We must go on with our lives." Triumphantly she told Therese that her brother had "maneuvered" an office position in Washington for Anthony. The maneuver had taken place without her nephew's knowledge or consent, but he was bound to follow orders. "The foolish boy is still trying to get to the front," Mrs. McKay declared. "I think all men are mad, especially young ones. But the general who arranged the appointment will see to it that he stays alive in spite of himself.

"I declare, any woman has more sense at birth than a boy of twenty-two. When his father tried to buy Anthony's way out of the war, he threatened to go off and fight for the South. As a West Pointer, though, he was obliged to take a commission."

Therese listened hungrily to the childless woman's news of Anthony, who was as dear as a son to Mrs. McKay. Therese was shamed by her relief that he was not in battle, when so many men were dying, but she was savagely glad that he was safe. His leaves, Mrs. McKay said, would not be long enough for him to journey to Cincinnati. So Therese had to content herself only with the word of him.

Her very hunger for that news flayed her; every dream of Anthony McKay was a betrayal of George.

George's business was overwhelmed with orders for uniforms, and he worked long, hard hours to fill the military orders while maintaining the civilian business. Guilt-ridden, Therese treated him with special consideration, trying to make up with affection what she lacked in desire.

There was much to occupy her mind, to help crowd out the daydreams—the salon was busy again, and she worried about her little boy. At three, Charles was at his most raucous and demanding. He was as spoiled as a little prince from George's indulgence and the attentions of all the grown-ups in the household. Accustomed to Therese's absence, he would hardly obey her at all. It was saddening, and humiliating.

His resemblance to Nicholas was striking; he also had Nicholas' arrogant manner. Sometimes he did not seem hers at all. But she was determined to win him over. Now that George was working so late, Therese was always the first one home, and she began to spend more time with the child. Yet time after time, despite all her affection, the boy would pause in their play or say abruptly, when she was reading to him, "I wish Daddy would come home." Therese wondered darkly if her attentions had come too late. The child was too young to understand that all her absences, all her apparent neglect, had sprung from her desire not only to fulfill herself but also to ensure his future. She made plans for him, for sending him to college, giving him undreamed luxuries beyond the moderate expectations of George Madison.

Pressed by her anxieties about Charles and burdened by her treacherous memories, Therese was overjoyed by the arrival of Madame Dufay in early October. She brought new distraction to Therese's life.

Unable to conclude her business quickly enough, Madame Dufay had landed in Cincinnati a mere week before the Confederates began attacking Union shipping on the river. Therese was moved by the woman's haggard look and exaggerated thinness, yet Madame had kept her proud carriage and her mordant humor. Her clothes were last year's style, but were marked by her habitual elegance.

For the time being, she settled in Mrs. Prickett's boardinghouse, where, she confided to Therese, she was "saved" by Nell and the civilized Mr. Reid.

On her first visit to the salon, she said simply, "*Magnifique*." The patrons loved her. Madame Dufay worked like a madwoman among the other seamstresses, declaring that Therese had saved her life and sanity, so it was proper for her to return the favor. She seemed more than glad to remain in the background.

However, as the autumn became winter, and spring approached again, Hortense Dufay had made herself so invaluable that Therese knew it was wasteful to keep her in the sewing-room. Madame Dufay and Nell took sole charge of business matters, presenting regular and meticulous financial reports to Therese and George, who had always offered his advice when asked, and took a proprietary interest.

If Therese thought she was adept at cutting corners, she had forgotten the full extent of Madame Dufay's business acumen. With certain minor adjustments in the operation, Madame Therese began to realize higher profit.

In April 1862, the unfortified city of New Orleans fell to the Union invaders. Most of its men were to the north fighting for the Confederacy, and Admiral Farragut's fleet, passing blockades and the two inadequate forts below the city, took New Orleans without a struggle.

But mob madness seized the old city: more than ten thousand bales of precious cotton were carted to the levee and set on fire. To keep them from falling into enemy hands, tobacco and sugar warehouses were soon aflame, then the ships at the wharves, and steamboats. Looters emptied warehouses. The city was sacked by its own people.

Therese was heartsick, terrified again for the safety of the Pavans and grieving at the death of the beautiful city. Madame Dufay kept saying, "All that cotton . . . all that splendid cotton."

For months, cotton had been almost impossible to obtain—the beleaguered South could not get cotton through the Union blockades, for sale to England. Therese could picture other Confederates burning cotton so that it would not fall into "Yankee" hands, or letting it rot in its bolls, now that the slaves had been conscripted by the Confederate Army.

The war dragged on into its third year and its fourth. The country was becoming weary of destruction and death. Therese read, horrified, of Sherman's ruthless march through Georgia.

The wartime dress of women became more utilitarian, and there was a greater need for mourning veils and of black cloaks and dresses. Bonnets were smothered in crepe or *lisse*; the mourning cloak was passementerie and jet trimming had been ubiquitous for as long as Therese could remember. Nell wore black now, for her brother, and went about with a stony face.

In the middle of January 1865, Therese heard from Mrs. McKay that Anthony had contrived to join his regiment in active duty eight months before, but had not written to her about it until that very month.

"He is safe, thank God," the shaken old lady told Therese. "He was with Colonel Lamb in North Carolina when they captured Fort Fisher. Men died all around him . . . but through some miracle he survived."

This latest news brought Anthony alive again vividly for Therese. After all these years of his absence, he had become someone she had dreamed of once but would probably never see again. Now, listening to Agnes McKay, she could see him clearly in her mind's eye—tall and stalwart, with his powerful shoulders and graceful form, his keen silvery eyes twinkling with humor and intelligence, gazing at her longingly across Mrs. McKay's drawing room.

And she could feel him near again, dancing with her, touching her hand, arousing her astonished body to that swift, electric heat, that treacherous excitement.

No, she had not forgotten, although she told herself so often that she had. She began to suffer agonies of apprehension for his safety. The war was not over. Only one Confederate army had surrendered, Lee's army of Virginia. The others were still fighting.

However, the rebels were reduced to desperate holding actions; the end was in sight.

In April, as the whole nation reeled from Lincoln's assassination only eleven days before, the second major Confederate army surrendered to the Union; the others followed.

A month later, the new President, Johnson, declared the armed resistance virtually at an end.

George burst into the salon and, picking up Therese by the waist, whirled her around in a frenetic waltz. "It's over, Therese! It's over!" When he set her down he embraced the astonished Madame Dufay.

Therese and George ran out into the street, where there was a scene of wild jubilation. All the church bells were ringing; from the landing the steamboats' few horns and whistles added to the clamor.

The destruction, the death, are at an end, Therese exulted. The bayou is safe.

And Anthony.

She could not prevent the sudden leap of her heart; perhaps he would be coming home to see Agnes McKay.

But as the summer wore on, and gradually her world resumed its former tempo, she learned from Mrs. McKay that Anthony had been posted with the military government of Louisiana. It would be a long time before he obtained leave. The scene of his assignment struck Therese with its bitter irony. Perhaps fate was warning her to forget.

She would try to heed that warning, with all her might.

Perhaps, in time, forgetfulness would come.

And she would fill that vast emptiness with her husband and her child . . . with Madame Therese.

# 10

## *1866*

During that first year of the peace, Therese was dismayed to learn that political battles had begun where military conflict left off; the embittered South, which had fought against such overwhelming odds, was now resisting Reconstruction with the same obdurate spirit.

Yet she gave the new conflict small attention. The Pavans were safe in the sequestered world of the bayou. Therese's Gallic practicality did not allow her to dwell on things she could do nothing about. Women would certainly never have a voice in government, despite all the furor caused by Elizabeth Cady Stanton in the winter, or the big women's-rights convention that May in New York.

There was enough to occupy her in the worlds she could control—her home circle, and above all, Madame Therese.

The Empress Eugénie had given understated dress a lift when she took up linsey-woolsey, which delighted Therese. Real Aberdeen linsey or wool linsey-woolsey was the best possible material for winter gowns. Its simplicity, combined with the *panache* of Madame Therese designs, set the fashion world on its ear.

This and a hundred other matters preoccupied Therese; in August she had added a girls' department to the salon, inspired by thoughts of Elianne, who was now twelve. She was already gathering a collection of dresses to send to the Côte Blanche, together with gowns for her mother.

On a mild afternoon in September, a telegraph messenger came into the salon. He handed her a wire.

Tearing it open, she read: "MICHEL IS DEAD. WAITING FOR YOU TO HOLD FUNERAL. CHARL'." There was a request to reply to the Hotel deVille in New Orleans.

Therese stared at the flimsy paper, stunned by all that it implied.

Her father was dead. And she was truly free.

Charl' . . . in America . . . in New Orleans.

Where Anthony McKay was.

"Therese?" Nell touched her shoulder and repeated her name. When Therese didn't answer, Nell gently took the wire from her hand. "What can I do?"

Therese shook off her stupor. "I must leave at once. "Please look up the boat schedules and call Rubine."

Nell complied. As she was checking the newspaper's shipping schedules, Therese said rapidly to Rubine, "Please help me find a mourning dress and accessories for a twelve-year-old girl. I will find the things for my mother. When I'm through, pack them in boxes with the other clothes and take them home in a public carriage. Have two trunks brought down from the attic and pack these things in one of them, with Charles's lighter clothes . . . for a week."

While Therese was choosing dresses for Berthe among the ready-made women's clothes, Rubine hurried back with a pearl-gray dress trimmed in black, underwear, gray cotton stockings, and a black velvet hat.

Therese nodded approvingly, laying aside a handsome black mourning dress in her mother's size.

"The *Dictator* leaves at four," Nell informed her. "It is a fast boat and will get you there in three days. Shall I go to the steamship office and book a double stateroom?"

Therese nodded. "I am beholden to you, Nell." But her friend was already halfway out the door.

Therese snatched a jet brooch and earrings and a small string of artificial pearls from the accessory cabinet and was on her way. Calling out to Madame Dufay to watch the showroom, she ran next door with the wire in her hand. She found George in his office, and handed him the telegraph message.

Scanning it, he looked up and said bluntly, "I will not say that I am sorry, Therese. I cannot. I hope that does not offend you."

"How could you ever offend me?" she asked gently. "My father never even knew me, George. He never saw me, unless I was doing wrong. I am free now, and so are my mother and sister."

George frowned. "It will be very difficult for me to leave now, Therese. But I cannot let you go alone."

"I'll be taking Charles, and Savannah."

His face cleared. "When will you be going?"

She told him of her arrangements.

"That does not give you much time." He went to the safe and opened it, taking out a thick stack of greenbacks. "You will need this. You might want to do something extra for your mother."

His generosity shamed her; guiltily she remembered that one of her first thoughts had been of Anthony McKay.

"Come, darling." He put on his jacket. "I'll drive you home. When you are ready, I'll take you to the landing."

On the way to the house, she thought: I must put Anthony out of my mind for good. It was all too likely she would not even get a glimpse of him in the conquered city.

Rubine had prepared for them so well that there was little left for Therese to do. They reached the landing with time to spare.

Charles was dancing with excitement; the war had brought new commerce to the landing, and there were more steamboats there than Therese had ever seen before. Savannah was smiling with anticipation. "It's been a long time since I been on a steamboat."

"This is a fine one," George said, but his heartiness sounded false to Therese, and she saw that he looked inordinately tired.

"Please," she said softly, "try to get more rest while

I am gone. You've worked so hard all through the war."

"I'm fine," he protested. Yet she still caught that note of falseness in his assurance. He drew her aside. "How long do you think you'll have to stay?"

"Just a few days after the funeral," she said.

"It will be pleasant for you to see all your old . . . friends." His comment seemed to be asking her something. He was thinking of Nicholas.

"All that is over, George. I am your wife. I belong to you."

The whistle began to blow. Unashamedly, George gathered her into his arms and kissed her savagely. "Hurry back, my dear. It will be so lonely without you."

Charles began to cry. He grabbed George around the knees. "I wish you were going, Father!"

"Now, now." George took out his handkerchief and wiped the boy's face. "You are getting to be a man, Charles. You will be taking care of your mother and Savannah."

The boy stood straighter, with all the pride of his eight years. "Let's shake on it," he said.

Smiling, George shook hands with the child, and then stooped down to kiss him.

When the three were on board, George left with a great reluctance.

Therese stood waving to him until the Cincinnati landing was out of sight.


"Is that enough, Mother?"

"Yes, that's fine. You read that very well."

The eight-year-old closed his primer with a sigh of relief. Therese smiled at Charles and ruffled his fine golden hair. At her insistence, they had brought his schoolbooks along on the journey so she could hear his lessons. It was important that he not fall behind during his absence. The boy had balked at first, but George had supported Therese; Charles idolized him, so that settled the matter.

Now, on the steamboat deck, she relieved the child

of his book, and he got up and went to the rail, staring with fascination at the passing landscape. He loved being on the boat and, apart from a few high jinks, such as trying to sit on the rail, had behaved remarkably well.

Therese regarded his sturdy but slender body, his small fine head with its wealth of blond hair. He stood in half-profile; his aristocratic little nose, his heavy-lidded blue eyes and eager, narrow lips were so much like Nicholas', it was startling.

Oh, I hope' he turns out to have George's temper, she thought, not his natural father's. The boy's beauty moved her to a whole new tenderness. She gloried in these private days with him, feeling that they had already grown closer to each other.

What a mysterious bond there was between a mother and her child, she reflected. She had felt a physical jealousy of Rubine, then Savannah, during his baby years, when she had been forced to leave him with one of them all day. Now that he was in school, it was different, somehow. He had other idols—his schoolmates and teachers. Therese smiled.

"Look, Mother! What is this place?"

"It's . . . it's Vicksburg," she said wonderingly. She had hardly recognized it. The Battle of Vicksburg had been one of the worst of the war. She had read about it, but seeing the result was far worse; the city was devastated.

Charles turned to her with a serious face. "This place was in the war, wasn't it? That's terrible. Why didn't these people's mother keep them from tearing up those houses? Savannah spanked me that time . . . you know . . . when I stamped on my wooden horse."

Out of the mouths of babes, Therese commented in silence. "Well, grown-ups don't listen to their mothers anymore. War is a very bad thing."

He looked so doleful that she was eager to distract him. "You know, I think it's about time for midday dinner. Are you hungry?"

"Yes!" He clapped his hands, looking more cheerful already. "The food on this boat is the best thing of all.

They have so many things on that big . . ." He measured with his hands.

". . . menu," she supplied. "They certainly do." The menus these days were even more elaborate than they had been eight years ago, when she had taken her first trip upriver. "Think of it, darling," she said, hugging him to her, "when you came to Cincinnati."

Therese stopped, appalled. She had been about to say, "you were just a little baby." And Charles thought he'd been born in Cincinnati, that George was his real father. Good God, she'd almost given the whole thing away.

He looked at her, puzzled. "What do you mean, Mother?"

She amended quickly, "I mean when *I* first came to Cincinnati . . . before you were even born . . . the boats were very different."

Therese felt a dew of nervous moisture break out on her forehead. She wondered if she'd ever have the courage to tell him about his real father.

"How?" the boy asked curiously, diverted.

Gathering her wits, Therese dredged up the memories of that trip, pointing out the differences in the old boats and the new ones.

"Well, I'm glad I *wasn't* born then," Charles said, giggling. "I don't think I'd want to be on this boat a whole *week*. Why, that's as long as school and Saturday and Sunday put together!"

"Very clever," she teased him. Taking him in her arms again, she kissed his face and hair. He squirmed restlessly in her embrace.

"I'm too old to kiss now, Mother," he reproved her, and she let him go.

"I wish you had some playmates on this trip," she said. "Maybe on the trip back there'll be some boys to play with."

"It's all right, Mother," he said generously. "I've had a good time playing ball with you and Savannah. And the sailors told me a lot of interesting things."

She grinned at him. For the past few days he had

haunted the lower decks and made friends with a number of deckhands.

"Aren't there any children on the bye . . . the bye . . ."

"The bayou? Lots of children. Where we'll be staying, though, at my mother's house, there'll just be us, your grandma, and your aunt and uncle. Your Aunt Elianne will play with you. Do you know she's just four years older than you are?"

"My aunt's only twelve years old?" Charles laughed merrily. "Gee. Everybody's aunt is *old*. That's funny."

Everybody's mother is older too, she thought dryly. "Come on. Let's go and wash our hands and get ready for dinner. I'm starving."

"So am I!" The boy seemed to have forgotten everything else now, and she was glad.

If she had been saddened by the ruins they had passed, her sorrow was nothing compared with what she felt as they landed at New Orleans. So much was gone—the grace, the laughter, the good-humored tenor of the levee. The people looked disoriented and bitter, and no one sang. Surveying the crowd along the shore, she saw numerous soldiers in blue, and proud-looking men and women in patched and ugly clothes. Women who were not wearing homespun were dressed in the styles of five or six years before.

But Charl' was there, somewhere, she thought, and her heart lifted. She peered among the waiting people, and at last focused on his beloved face. She started waving wildly. It was a moment before he saw her; his face broke out into a wide smile, the sweet smile she had never forgotten, and he returned her wave.

She rushed down the ramp into his waiting arms.

"Oh, Charl'! Charl'!"

He laughed with pleasure. "Tez, Tez, it is so good to see you!"

She turned to Savannah and Charles, and introduced them. Gently Charl' shook the little boy's hand. "So this is my namesake." But when he stood up again, his smile was a little stiff. And Therese's spirits sank.

When Charl' looked at the child, he looked at Nicholas Adair. She was quiet while Charl' arranged for the unloading of their trunks and hailed a public carriage.

"I'm afraid we must go right to the train," he said apologetically.

"The *train*?"

"Oh, we have progressed mightily since the war," he answered dryly. "Wonder of wonders, there is a train that stops right at Jeanerette and Cameron."

She marveled at that; such an amenity had been unheard-of eight years ago. George had mentioned to her that the railroad was the "coming thing," that since the war, trains were springing up everywhere. Now she wished she had paid more attention. "It is hard to believe," she murmured. "But tell me, Charl', how did you come to be back? Is your wife with you . . . is she at Côte Blanche?"

His face stiffened. Then he said slowly, "You didn't get my letter."

She shook her head.

"She died in childbirth, Therese."

Silently Therese pressed his hand.

"And then, when our mother wrote me that Michel was ill, I knew I had to come back. I could not leave her there to manage it all alone, without César." He smiled at her forgivingly. "I should have known the letters would go astray. Our isolation in the bayou is even more complete . . . despite the new iron horses. But that very isolation saved us. That, and the fact," he added bitterly, "there is nothing that was worth taking."

Therese glanced at the boy and Savannah. They were intent on looking out the windows at the passing city.

"But what of Petit Anse?" she asked in a low voice.

Charl' glanced at her with consternation.

Reading his look, she shook her head. "All that is dead and buried, my dear. I meant that Petit Anse, and the salt mine, must have been considered valuable. I was always afraid that a raid on it would spill over into the Côte Blanche."

"Remember that old man Adair was always a Union sympathizer. Well, he was very canny with the Yankees, advertising his loyalties loud and clear. He even passed off his slaves as freedmen." Charl' grinned. "Therefore Adair's Island remained untouched, and the salt mine is in full operation now. Nicholas," he volunteered, "was sent to Europe during the conflict."

"But Mother, Charl' . . . and Elianne. How are they?"

"They are both well," Charl' said affectionately. "But Mother misses Michel sorely. She keeps harking back to their early days together."

Unspoken between them was their own patent lack of grief, their puzzlement over Berthe's mourning the tyrant Michel to such a degree.

"We're here," Charl' said, as if glad to change the subject.

Outside the busy railroad depot, Charl' put their trunks in the charge of a surly black man and hurried inside to buy the tickets.

When they were on the train, it seemed natural for Charles to sit with Savannah and for Therese and Charl' to take a seat together. She hoped the trip would be long; she and Charl' had years to catch up with, and had not even gotten started.

He let out a loud breath. "I'm glad to be leaving New Orleans," he muttered. "It is no place for a woman nowadays."

"You mean the Butler order?" In 1862, the Union general Butler had enforced an order that outraged even the North, and was censured as far away as the British Parliament—the dictum that any Southern woman who failed to treat Union soldiers with respect would be treated as "a woman of the streets plying her trade."

"Yes. I've stayed out of New Orleans as much as I could," Charl' said grimly. "I would have shot someone, for sure, and Southern men are not 'allowed' to carry guns these days." He gave her a tigerish grin, lightly touching a bulge in his inside breast pocket.

"My God, my dear. Be careful," she whispered.

Then, to lighten his dark mood, she began to chatter
about life in Cincinnati. He listened with great interest, beaming when she told him how well the salon
was doing, fascinated with the circumstances of her
hiring Madame Dufay.

"This Nell you keep talking about . . . she must be
a very managing sort of woman," Charl' remarked.

"Not at all. She is beautiful, and gentle. You would
love her." Therese's face heated. Not a tactful comment to a recent widower, she thought. Gradually,
gently, she began to draw him out about his late wife,
who had died the year before.

"She was very young and pretty," he told her, "and
very French . . . very practical. Nothing like us, Tez,
with our adventurous natures. She was . . . solid. Just
what I needed." He smiled a little sadly, and they
began to speak of other things—his fishing boat in
Calais, the prosperity he had enjoyed there, the city of
Paris.

"I saw Odalie," he said, "and her husband. They
are very happy. They run a small café called Raoul's,
frequented by students and other disreputable types."

Therese laughed. "Raoul's"—for de Sevigny.

The train rattled onward; she could hear little Charles
asking Savannah numerous questions about the empty
wooded area through which they passed.

She heard the call "Jeanerette! Jeanerette!" before
she had even begun to tell Charl' all that she wanted
to tell.

Disembarking, they took a swaying wagon to the
narrow river that led to Côte Blanche. An amiable
Acadian stowed the trunks into a huge dory, balancing
one at each end and leaving little room for the
passengers.

"Can you handle it, *ami*?" The Acadian cocked a
skeptical eyebrow at Charl' in his city clothes. Both
Therese and Charl' burst out laughing.

"Since I was six years old, *cousin*," Charl' retorted.
The man studied him and Therese, then the golden-
haired boy in his well-tailored jacket, and stately Savannah, with burning curiosity.

"*Bonne chance, cousin.*"

As Charl' poled them out into the stream, a dream-like feeling possessed Therese. It was as if the bayou itself had been a dream of her childhood and now she was entering an illusion. The girl who had fled with Charl' nine years ago might never have existed. All that remained of that girl were the relentless ambition, the stony determination. And her love for the brother who was poling them toward the old, familiar cabin.

Charles's questions now came thick and fast: What was the gray stuff on the trees . . . what kind of birds were those . . . and what was that sound like hiccups? Therese and Charl' answered the boy with patience. Soon, wearying, the little boy fell silent and nodded against Savannah.

Therese, who was sitting nearer to Charl', asked softly in the plashing quiet, "Is our father . . . is the . . . ?"

"He is laid out in the chapel in Jeanerette, Tez. He was . . . at home until yesterday. I thought, since you might be bringing the boy . . . and it was terrible for Elianne."

She blessed his sensitive consideration. Looking up, she saw the redness of the sunset steal across the sky. To her surprise, a kind of peace enveloped her in this swamp she had longed so to escape.

There was the familiar bend to the willow-veiled shore, the great oaks thick with Spanish mosses . . . and then, the cabin.

Berthe and Elianne were sitting on the porch staring toward the water. When they saw the dory, they got up and ran down the steps, crying out, "Therese! Therese!"

The dory landed, and Therese scrambled out. Charl' assisted Savannah and the half-awakened boy, hoisting their trunks to the ground as Therese raced to her mother and sister. She drew them both into her arms at once, crying and kissing their faces while Elianne sobbed, "Tez, oh, Tez," and Berthe smiled shakily through her tears.

When they were inside the cabin, Therese took the

sleepy child's hand and drew him forward to Berthe. "This is your grandson, Charles Madison," she said softly. To the boy she murmured, "This is your *grandmaman* Pavan, and your *tant'* Elianne," reverting without thought to the old way of speaking.

She saw Berthe's sweet smile fade and her eyes narrow. In a flash of recognition, Therese saw that her mother knew the boy was an Adair. Yet even more surely, Therese knew that Berthe would never admit that fact, either to herself or to another living soul. Berthe's children, Therese realized wryly, were incapable of sin.

It all happened in less than a second; Berthe's kindly face was wreathed again in smiles, and she stooped to kiss the boy.

Charl' said, "Tez, you take the old room, with Elianne. *Ti* Charles can sleep in the little bed. And Savannah can go up to the *garçonnière*. I'll bed down here on a mattress." He ignored Savannah's protests.

"Now," he said, "let's get all of us something to eat." Charl' smiled at the boy. "Then I'll show this young man around the bayou."

It was clear to Therese that Charl' had totally taken charge of things from the still-dazed Berthe and the willing but young, unschooled Elianne. Berthe seemed overjoyed to see Therese; her eyes returned again and again to her daughter, but her worn face bore the marks of long weeping. It saddened Therese to see how old she looked at forty-two.

Therese turned to Elianne. Now that the blind excitement had subsided, she felt as if she were looking at herself as a child. Elianne, as Berthe had written, was almost her twin. The girl was staring at Therese in fascination, taking in her plain but fine black dress and elegant hat, the cameo at her throat, and the glittering rings on her fingers.

It tore Therese's heart to notice the somber crudity of their homespun dresses. She anticipated their pleasure when she unpacked the trunks.

"Let us wait on Mother," she suggested to Elianne,

taking off her hat and gloves and tying on an apron. Berthe protested, but feebly; she looked exhausted.

Their supper was a subdued affair; out of deference to Berthe, Therese, Charl', and Elianne reined in the gaiety bubbling within them. It was apparent to Therese that Elianne mourned her father as little as her older sister and brother.

After they had sat together for a while, Therese went off to unpack the trunks. She said to Elianne, "Your dress for tomorrow is on the bed, *petiote*." Elianne raced off to see, and Therese displayed her mother's funeral dress. From the bedroom she heard a gasp. She could picture her sister's face and longed to go to her.

Berthe stared at the dress and fingered the material. "*Mon Dieu*," she breathed. "You are so good, daughter."

Therese took the rest of the things into her parents' old room and put them away. Berthe would not want to look at them tonight. Even now, she seemed asleep on her feet; between them, Charl' and Therese supported her to her room. When her brother had gone, Therese helped get her mother ready for bed, touched by her helpless, childlike manner.

Going to Elianne, Therese saw that her dresses were all spread out on the bed. The girl was stroking one with her hand. She turned, her eyes glowing. "Tez, they're . . . they're beautiful." She rubbed the string of pearls against her cheek. Therese's throat closed up as she was seized with a whole new passion—to do everything for Elianne. To take her sister away.

Later, when they lay side by side in the bed she had once shared with Amelie, Elianne whispered, "You even brought me shoes. It's been so long since we've had shoes, Tez. During the war, paper shoes, even, cost eighty dollars. Father made our shoes from hides, but they always hurt my feet. And oh, Tez, they smelled so awful."

Therese tasted a salty wetness at the corner of her mouth as her silent tears slid down her face.

"You will never have to wear them again, Elianne."

She thought of the greenbacks George had given her, which she had carried under her chemise. "Never," she repeated strongly.

"Well, a lot of people did him honor, Tez. I'm glad . . . for her sake." Charl' spoke lazily, stretching his legs.

"So am I."

Lounging on the cabin porch, they reveled in the quiet. Berthe was lying down; Charles played in the yard. Through the open door, the soft murmurs of Elianne and the nurse wafted to Therese and Charl'; they were tidying up the main room after the departed visitors.

"You're more than a designer, you know. You're an artist, Tez."

She smiled; it seemed like they had last spoken only yesterday, not years before. They were so in tune they could jump from one topic to another without confusion, understanding each other's train of thought. "The mourning dresses?"

"Of course. I know less than nothing about these things . . . but they were so *plain* that they didn't seem out of place. At the same time, Elianne looked like a Parisienne. How do you *do* that?"

"With painful effort. It's so funny—Nell says I tricked the pious ladies up North into elegance with my devious simplicity. It is the same in the bayou; the dresses have no 'side' to offend our neighbors. All my day things are like that. It's only in evening dresses that I can go really *fou.*"

"It's Elianne that worries me, Tez."

She nodded, knowing what he was thinking. He must have been recalling, as she had, the picture of their younger sister in the dory. Charl' had stood at the pole, steering the *famille* at the head of the twenty-boat procession winding toward Jeanerette. Therese and Berthe occupied the stern, Berthe leaning docilely against her; in the middle Elianne sat, straight and proud, shy in the discovery of her new beauty. "I know. She must be given her chance, as we were."

"We took ours, *petit*. But Elianne is still so young. When César comes back, you know, Hector and Amelie will come too. I don't want Elianne in the house with that lout. She is too beautiful. She is too much like you."

Therese's skin crawled at the implication.

"Yes, I want to take her away," Charl' said. "And Mother too. She's never liked Hector, you know that."

"I was thinking last night . . . do you suppose Mother would come to Cincinnati? With both of you?"

Smiling, he pulled a letter from his pocket. "I wasn't going to mention it before. I didn't want to get your hopes up before I was sure." He handed her the letter. It was from a steamship company in Cincinnati, stating that it was considering Charl's employment. Therese looked at him, excited.

"By this time, there's damned little I don't know about boats and cargo, Tez. That's all I've been doing with my life. The day's coming when the steamboats will be used mainly for cargo; the trains are already grabbing off the passengers.

"I'm hoping against hope. It'll be the most perfect arrangement there could be, for everybody. The cabin would be absolutely spacious—with César by himself in the *garçonnière*, the extra room filling up with little Rocailles."

Charl's grimace made Therese laugh.

"Miz Madison, Miz Madison."

Savannah stood in the doorway, her coppery face frightened. "I can't find our little boy nowhere."

Charl' scrambled to his feet. "He couldn't be upstairs; he'd have had to go by us." He soothed Therese, "It's all right, honey. I'll go look for him by the dory . . . he's been interested in the boats."

She knew he was not as calm as he sounded: there was a multitude of dangers for a child who didn't know the bayou. "I'll go in the other direction."

She headed toward the meadow. Sighting the distant chimneys of Petit Anse, it occurred to her that he might have gone there. Only that morning he had asked her if it was a castle.

Therese ran to the edge of the meadow and began to climb the hill, her fragile shoes sinking into the waving grass. Halfway up, she saw a man silhouetted, his back to the sun.

It was Nicholas Adair.

He stared at her in amazement, then descended toward her. "Therese? Is it *you*?"

She called out sharply, "Have you seen a little boy? My son is lost."

"He's in the kitchen, eating gingerbread."

Her relief shook her body. Her voice shook too when she snapped, "Well, call him! I have to go back at once and let my brother know. He'll be worried to death."

They were standing level with each other now. Nicholas asked in that languid drawl she had always remembered, "Is that all you have to say . . . after all these years? Not even hello? Living up North has not improved your manners, Therese."

His comment infuriated her. "Possibly not. But it has surely cleared my brain."

He drew back as if she had slapped him.

Time had cleared her sight, for sure. With maturer eyes, she saw him for the first time exactly as he was—a boy the chronological age of a man. That's all he would ever be. Even now, in the midst of her agitation, all he could think of was his wounded vanity. She marveled that she could have been so utterly stupid, even as a fifteen-year-old girl.

"Please," she said more politely, "go get my boy."

Maddeningly, Nicholas ignored her. "He's a very handsome child. So very fair. Apparently you *didn't* forget me"—he smiled— "because his father must look a good deal like me."

"His father's *nothing* like you," she blurted out. "In any way at all."

Nicholas raised his golden eyebrows. His sleepy eyes were alert and gleaming. "Oh? Now isn't that amazing."

She wished she had bitten off her tongue. She could fairly see the wheels turning in Nicholas' head.

"Amazing," he repeated softly. "He has my nose

and mouth and eyes . . . his hair is the same color. Even the shape of his hands." She was stubbornly silent. "Good God. He's *my* son . . . isn't he, Therese?"

What a fool I was, she agonized, to let that slip out. He knows. He *knows.* Therese cursed her own honesty, the transparency of her face. Her very expression must have told him, because he looked triumphant.

"So that handsome boy is mine."

"No, he's *mine.* I carried him, and bore him, and have been responsible for him all these years. He's never been yours, Nicholas."

"Why didn't you let me know?" he asked softly.

She lost control; there was no point in trying to protest anymore. "How could I—when I didn't even know where you had gone? When you abandoned me. Abandoned *us.*"

"Well, things are different now."

"Indeed they are. I'm no longer a swamp girl with bare feet, creeping into your music room," she retorted.

"You certainly are not," he murmured, observing her smart dress, her carefully coiffed hair. "You are the noted Madame Therese . . . married to a Yankee merchant."

She was flabbergasted. "You know that?"

"Really, my dear, even here in the wilds my mother manages to get the *Leslie's Weekly* and the other periodicals. When the boy introduced himself as Charles Madison, I put that together with the gossip of 'foreign' visitors for the funeral . . . and there you are. My condolences, by the way."

The last was brutally ironic; he had always known how much she disliked her father. Everyone on the bayou was acquainted with Michel Pavan's savage temper. She didn't deign to answer.

"We're different people now, Therese. I wish you could stay awhile . . . so we could get reacquainted."

He was perfectly serious; she could see that from the look in his eyes. His insolence was so incredible she was at a loss for words.

"And now, you see, we have an indissoluble bond, Therese. We have a son."

At last she found her voice. "My husband and I have a son, Nicholas."

"But he has my blood, the blood of the Adairs. Do you really think I'll step aside now—even with the *suspicion* that that boy is my son—and let him be raised by some crude shopkeeper in the North?"

*Shopkeeper.* Therese saw the wise, kind face of George Madison, heard him speaking with love to the boy. Vindictively she thought: I wish George were with me now. He'd see how little he ever had to fear.

Therese loosed the full force of her anger. "That 'shopkeeper,' Nicholas, is a *man*, one of the few real men I've ever known. Now, will you call my son, or shall I go get him myself . . . and pollute the sacred halls of Petit Anse?"

Still smiling his superior smile, Nicholas looked down at her, impervious to her sarcasm. "He's asked me if he can stay here for a while. He calls the house a 'castle.' "

"Stay *here*? You must be insane. What have you said to him? Have you insulted his father, have you . . ."

She broke off at the sound of her son's call. He was running down the hill. "Mother! You've met my friend Mr. Adair."

Therese put her arms around the boy and pulled him close. "You were very naughty, darling, to run away like that . . . what made you go off, without a word to anybody to say where you were going?"

"I'm sorry," he said lightly. "But I have been with my new friend." He grinned up at Nicholas. When Nicholas smiled back, their resemblance was startling. They both had the self-confident look of those who believe their charm will get them anything.

Controlling herself, Therese said, "That's nice. But we have to go now."

"Why?" Charles's blue eyes were mutinous, and he dug in his heels. "Mr. Adair's going to show me the animals and his little house. He had a whole little house of his own, when he was a boy. Why don't *I* have a house, Mother?"

She hated Nicholas' look of triumph, and was hard put not to answer sharply.

"You do have a house, darling. With me and your father. Come, we've got to go back right now. Your uncle will be worried. He's looking for you."

With one of his abrupt changes of mood, the boy said equably, "All right. I'll run down and find him."

"No," she said sharply. "Wait for me."

But the child was already racing down the incline toward the cabin.

"You cannot fight both of us, Therese."

"Don't be too sure," she countered, meeting his victorious smile with rising ire.

"Our son wants to stay in his castle, Therese. And someday he'll bear the rightful name of Adair."

"You will never see him again," she promised grimly.

She cursed the thinness of her city shoes, which made a dignified exit impossible as she struggled downward through the meadow grass.

By the time she reached the cabin she felt drained.

She found Charl' trying to interest her son in a game, but the little boy was in tears.

"I want to go back to the castle. I told Mr. Adair I would," he sobbed.

Therese held him, caressing his hair. "You can't go back right now," she said. Over his head she caught Charl's frown.

"Why not? We're not doing anything else."

"You must hush crying, Charles," she evaded. "You will disturb your granny."

"I hate my granny, and I hate this ugly house," he shouted.

Therese and Charles looked at each other; his eyes were wretched.

Savannah intervened. "Now, that's no way to talk to your mama, honey. You'll be going to the castle another day. Why don't you come inside with me now. You're too big a boy to make all this fuss. You come on now." Savannah rubbed his golden head.

Miraculously, he succumbed. He seemed tired out

from excitement and from crying. He went along with
the nurse into the house.

"I should have killed Nicholas, Tez, years ago."

"And brought down the wrath of the Adairs on the
whole bayou? Besides, you shrank even from clubbing
the animals, Charl'. You hated it as much as I did."

"But this is different." He sounded hard and
determined.

"Charl', promise me. Promise me," she pleaded
with desperation, "that you will not do anything . . .
foolish after we go away. If I thought you would, I
couldn't bear it. I'd never sleep a wink again. Charl',
if you did . . . and they hanged you, I would die."

"I know that, little sister. Don't worry. I promise."
He hugged her, trying to soothe her fears.

"Besides, we'll probably never come back here again,
Charl'. Nicholas will never see the boy after this.
Charles is just a little boy, and he'll forget."

Her brother did not answer. He was probably thinking what she was thinking, in spite of her brave words:
Nicholas Adair knew now that he had a son, and he
would know where to find him.

But during the remainder of the visit, Therese forced
herself to thrust aside the frightening notion.


At last she was standing on the deck of the upriver
boat, and the whistle was blowing. As much as it hurt
her to leave Charl' and Elianne, it was a blessed
release, after all.

She wanted nothing so much as to go to the stateroom and sleep until they reached Cincinnati, to forget it all—the hurtful parting from Berthe and Elianne,
her anxiety about Nicholas Adair. But that was too
fantastic to consider.

It would be impossible to walk away now, while
Charl' stood down there on the levee and they were
having their last sight of each other. As for the journey, now more than ever she needed to regain her
slight, hard-won closeness to the boy. On the bayou
he had been more receptive. Now he was sullen and
withdrawn.

Moreover, she had work to do, plans to make, work that she had abandoned for the journey south. Fortunately, she had had enough sense to pack her sketchbook and notepad and the recent magazines.

She couldn't even let herself consider the thought that Charl' could break his solemn promise not to hurt Nicholas; there was enough to bear now without that.

"Wave to your uncle, darling," she prompted Charles.

The boy complied with ill grace. "Why didn't Mr. Adair come to wave good-bye at us?"

She was appalled at his tenaciousness; he could cling like a bulldog to one idea. He had always been that way, she thought. She had been overoptimistic to say he would forget.

"I'm sure he was too busy."

"That's not true, Mother. He said he had plenty of time for me. I didn't even say good-bye. I didn't act like a . . . like a 'ristocrat." He looked up at her.

"Where did you get that word?"

"From Mr. Adair. He said that I'm a 'ristocrat, just like him, and that's why we look the same. Why do I look like him, and not like my father?"

Therese glanced at the impassive Savannah. The nurse looking down at the levee, but it was obvious that she only pretended not to hear.

"Look, Charles," she said desperately, "there are two other boys getting on, just about as old as you. Won't that be fun, having playmates?"

But her son was not to be diverted. "Yes, Mother. But why? Why don't I?"

Mercifully, the last great blast of the whistle and the vibration below their feet drowned out all conversation.

But she knew Charles would question her again.

The ramp was about to be lifted.

Charles and Savannah waved to Charl', and Therese kissed her fingers to him.

Then, just before the raising of the gangway, a Union officer dashed toward the boat.

There was a shout and a flurry, and the gangway was arrested in place.

Something about the tardy passenger struck Therese, something most familiar in the set of his shoulders and his strong, lithe form. He was still too far away for her to see his face, which was shadowed under the brim of a black slouch hat. He wore the insignia of a major, decorations she had become versed in when George was making uniforms.

When the officer raised his head and smiled, awarding a grateful salute to the crewman who had made it possible for him to board, Therese's heart lurched in her body.

Anthony McKay stepped onto the lower deck, disappearing under the roof below her.

In his hasty boarding, he hadn't looked up, so he couldn't have seen her.

But he was there, on the same boat, entering her life again.

She stood there stiffly on the deck, waving to Charl', who was still on the levee straining for a last look at her face.

When Charl' became a faceless figure on the shore, Therese said to Savannah, "I'm going to the stateroom. Stay here with Charles, if you like."

Before the woman had a chance to answer, Therese hurried off to their cabin.

## 11

Therese meant just to close her eyes a little. When she opened them again, she knew she had slept for hours. Darkness had taken the color from the cabin windows; one dim lamp was alight.

On the other side of the stateroom, Savannah snored. Charles was sound asleep in the trundle bed beside her.

Therese's chatelaine marked the hour of ten. Feeling pent-up, alive in every nerve, she got out of bed. When she drew the wardrobe curtain back, she saw her dresses neatly hung and shaken out.

Passing over the black ones, she chose a thin gray wool skirt and her Garibaldi blouse of the new "magenta" color.

Its brightness exhilarated Therese after her recent return to mourning. Slipping into gray boots, she buttoned them with her small metal hook; impatiently she surveyed her hair. The heavy rolls of her chignon were loose. Rather than take them down and start all over, she stuck some hair pins into the rolls and covered the whole chignon with a fragile black silk net and drew it tight. A quick brush of the waves of hair at the top sufficed. She need not be perfect in the shadow of night; no one would see her.

Certainly not Anthony—men passengers were prohibited from the ladies' deck.

She stepped into the darkness, rhythmic with the engine hum. Her nostrils quivered: the air was crisp, with the dank, familiar smell of the river. Reflections of the steamboat's lights rippled on the sliding water. Therese was quite alone. From below, she heard the raucous voices of the gambling men, the faint sound of poignant music.

The music struck her nerves. She felt a nameless longing, a hunger for some bright thing that eluded her. It had nothing at all to do with her own ambitions, her battle to secure a good life for Elianne, or even with the "salon of spring" that was the first step toward Pavan.

A deep oppression crushed her spirit. The last few days had dragged her down—the sight of her mother's devastation, her own grief over not being able to grieve, and her worries about Elianne . . . and now about Charles.

Yet it was more than that. Seeing Anthony again had made her recognize the emptiness in the very heart of her. Perhaps the romantic maxim of the novelists—one she'd always scoffed at—was true after all. Perhaps a woman was only half-alive until she had known profound love for one man.

Certainly with Nicholas she had known nothing; she had been a child. For George she felt almost what she felt for Charl'. Only with Anthony had she experienced deep excitement, tumultuous emotion. For that brief time she had been truly alive. In those few days, something had been born.

She had been a fool to believe that the past few years had changed her. If there was nothing left to fear, she would not have wanted to run away and hide when he boarded. And there were three more days to the journey; they were bound to meet.

The band was playing the melodies of operatic arias, a practice more common now than in 1861, when she had first heard them at Agnes McKay's. And there it was—the "*Un dì felice*," from *La Traviata*, bringing back the rainy April night and Anthony's passionate steel-gray eyes. Therese moved toward the rail to watch the light-dappled river.

Glancing down, she saw a solitary man in evening clothes emerge from under the roof below. Now that the war was over, steamboat passengers dressed for dinner like guests in a fine hotel. The man's elegance harmonized with her poignant mood, with her memory of long-lost beauty of that night years ago.

Therese grasped the rail, leaning forward.

The shape of the man's head, the set of his shoulders, were so familiar.

It was Anthony.

Standing there alone, like her, staring out over the water. He was wreathed in the smoke of a cigar.

Suddenly he turned and looked up, peering as she moved back into the shadows.

He tossed his cigar into the river and walked toward the stairs.

She started toward her cabin. But before she was halfway there, he was standing level with her on the ladies' deck. He called out softly, "Wait! Wait, Therese."

Her name seemed so natural on his mouth. She waited, half-unwilling, but convinced there was no escape.

He hurried to her. The war had changed him: the planes of his fine face had hardened and an aura of strong command had replaced the merry, carefree look he had had before. Yet with it all, there were a boundless gentleness.

Even the sparse light gave back the glow in his piercing gray eyes. "This can't be true." He sounded incredulous. He made no move to touch her. "You are traveling alone."

"How did you know that?"

"I felt it, Therese. I have called you by your first name, like that, for the last five years; called you that in my mind. I kept your picture there too, every detail of your face and your form and your hair."

"You must not say these things." She felt as if she were struggling to wake up, and her protest was feeble.

"I must say them. Don't you see . . . I was down there thinking of you. Then I looked up . . . and you were here."

Her traitorous flesh responded to his closeness; her own pulse sounded like the sea in her ears.

"Oh, please," he begged her, "come to the rail. I

want to see your face again, see it clearly." He touched her arm. Even through the woolen fabric of her blouse, the slight contact almost burned.

Like someone walking in her sleep, she let him lead her to the rail, where the ship's lights flickered in his eyes.

He stared at her in utter silence. She was dismayed by the power he exercised over her will and reason, and yet she could not withstand it. With a fateful motion she raised her face, her mouth consenting to his lowered mouth. The kiss ignited her body.

One of his hands caressed the softness of her face and her throat where the pulse wildly fluttered. She gave in to the liquid burning, sliding her arms around his neck.

When he raised his head, he rested his chin against her hair. "I love you, Therese. I love you. I felt it since the day I saw you on the street in the rain. And you felt something too. I know it. Otherwise I could not have made it through the war. You did care. You do."

Her every bone was warm and lazy water; reason, resistance, melted away like a sunlit stream in eternal summer, under the hum of dragonflies. She did not know how long she felt that strange enchantment. "I did. I do." She heard her answer, as if through the dream.

Then a cold alarm rang in her brain. She drew back, and with such pain that it took all the force of her will to withdraw.

Shaking her head, feeling the hot tears gather, she said hoarsely, "No. I am going, and you must not follow."

Astonished at her suddenness, he involuntarily dropped his arms. When she started to walk away, he pleadingly called her name.

She tried to shut her ears to the sound as finally as she closed her door.

Charles and Savannah were undisturbed. Therese sank down on her bed, drained by the dark encounter. It was futile to protest that loneliness and the moving music had made her susceptible so soon after the affecting visit to Côte Blanche. The bald truth was that she had felt the same toward him on the very first day of the war. She had wanted him to embrace her, to say every passionate word that he had said.

She loved him. Resistance had been the illusion.

But they could never be together. If she abandoned George, she would never be able to live with herself again. She might lose her son, as well, just as he was beginning to warm to her a little, because she would be branded an "unfit" mother.

Too numb to cry, she went to bed, lying wakeful until the stained-glass windows sprang to pallid color with the early light.

When she heard Savannah stir, she kept her eyes closed, pretending sleep. She listened to Charles's piping questions, the sounds of dressing, and then the closing of the door. Her watch indicated that it was still very early. She shut her eyes again and drowsed.

"Miz Madison, Miz Madison. Wake up. They're calling the last breakfast." Savannah was shaking her gently.

"Thank you." Therese managed a smile for her and the boy as she got up.

"You didn't get your dinner last night," Savannah scolded. "You've got to go down and eat now." The nurse examined her. "Are you sick?"

Therese shook her head.

"I thought you'd sleep *forever*," Charles declared, "like the lady in the fairy tale. Can I go play?"

Savannah smiled. "The little Harmon boys, down the way, are bustin' for him to come."

Therese heard them shouting just outside the door. "Of course. Go ahead, Savannah. I'll go right down to breakfast."

When they left, she looked at herself in the mirror. No wonder Savannah was puzzled. Nobody who had slept so much would look like such an *épouvantail*. Her eyes were deeply shadowed, her face more pale than usual.

To bolster her flagging courage, she put on a rose-colored dress that would give her skin more color, applied faint rouge and even some mascara, that lash darkener that was scandalizing Saratoga. More confident, she made her way to the dining saloon.

The strong black coffee helped revive her, but she ate without appetite, despite her long fast.

When she was drinking a second cup of coffee, Anthony came into the saloon. He was in uniform; the somber blue and the gilt trimming emphasized his sun-darkened skin and light brown hair, with its streaks of gold. As always, his pale gray eyes contrasted starkly with his tanned face. They seemed to penetrate her secrets.

But his voice, when he approached her, was gentle. "May I sit down?"

Seeing her nod, he took the empty chair next to hers. There was no one else at the table, but across the saloon, Therese thought she recognized one of her Cincinnati patrons. She felt vulnerable, on display. And still his nearness pulled at her. She could not move her arm away from his.

"I ask your forgiveness," he murmured, "for last night. I could not help myself, Therese. I had thought of you so constantly for so long. And then to . . ."

He broke off, shaking his head at a hovering waiter. The man moved away.

"Please, speak to me," he pressed her. "At least tell me that I am forgiven."

"I cannot forgive myself." She set down her cup slowly, not looking at him. "We cannot be alone again. You must leave me now."

She glanced sidelong at him and saw his face contract with pain. "Leave me," she repeated.

"As you wish," he answered softly. "But I will never give you up now, Therese. Never."

He got up and, giving her a slight bow, walked away.

She was in turmoil, newly aware of the dangers in his proximity. There could be no peace in his presence —or in his absence, if it came to that.

She decided to get to work. If she did not stop

thinking about him she would go mad. Work was the only thing that could make her forget. She wouldn't come out again today until time for early dinner. Perhaps he would dine at the later service.

Charles was still on the ladies' deck, playing with the other boys. Savannah sat a ways apart from a group of ladies, two of whom looked familiar. They stared at Therese curiously as she went into her stateroom.

Hoping that in her agitation she hadn't snubbed one of her patrons, Therese took out her sketchbook and sat down at the writing table. Immediately she felt calmer, more in command.

She looked over her drawings for spring 1867. It had always been her habit to work in advance of the current season; this was considered an innovation, even by Madame Dufay. For spring, Therese foresaw the return of narrower dresses and the abandonment of the crinoline's absurdities with the emergence of the "walking costume" this year.

The rich, with their bigger houses, that had wider doors and their more capacious carriages, had been able to wear the most exaggerated hoops. Cincinnati ladies wore them mostly for the evening. When metals became scarce during the war, dressmakers made hoops of cane and reed. Therese, who had used vines to stiffen her petticoats in the bayou, still ran cane into the casings of petticoats for her "more unassuming" patrons. She and Mrs. McKay and Nell had never used anything else.

She smiled, remembering Charl's approval of the simple but elegant mourning dresses. She tried to picture a crinoline at Côte Blanche . . . in a dory, or better still, a pirogue. The idea made her laugh, and raised her spirits.

Narrower gowns would be more economical, too, she thought. Aimee Du Lac's plainest day dresses had required thirty yards of goods; Therese's new ready-mades used ten. It was all in the lines, the draping. Her spring designs, especially for slenderer women, would call for even less material.

The war had brought about a subtle change in clothes; they had become more practical, more utilitarian. Therese's daytime gowns had the look of traveling and riding clothes. The simple lines were compensated for by a richness of fabric. With the dearth of cotton, she had been looking to many other materials.

Therese finished her sketch of a *paletot* over a harmonizing dress. The cone shape of the crinoline, which needed tiny hats and purses to balance it, had been replaced with a gentler line, like that of an upended flower. The *paletot* was long, almost reaching the hem of the dress, and belted at the waist. After the waistless *sacque*, it was an interesting new look. She smiled, thinking how she had invented the waistless cloak in 1857, when she was pregnant, three years before it became fashionable in 1860.

The modest flare, she exulted, could carry a wide-brimmed hat, her favorite kind. A *mousquetaire,* for instance. She sketched some hats, calculated purse sizes and lengths of gloves, and considered shoes. These outfits could stand more elaborate ones. She ran over colors in her mind's eye, accepting and rejecting. Leaning back, she rubbed her eyes.

The door opened; Savannah glanced in, then closed it. Used to Therese's ways, she hadn't said a word. Presumably she would be taking Charles to midday dinner.

Resuming her work, Therese sketched more new designs of dresses with a faintly martial style. The war was over, but the war of politics raged on, she thought dryly, and martial dresses were still well-received. What with all the country had suffered from the war, the irony of that did not escape Therese. And yet the trim lines, the gleaming buttons, caught the eye. The clothes were neat, demure, and jaunty, in one package.

She was surprised when Savannah came back, announcing it would soon be time for early dinner. Therese looked at her almost without recognition. With a pang, she realized she had forgotten Charles completely. On the other hand, she had also been able to dis-

miss her thoughts of Nicholas and Elianne, not to
mention her disloyalty to George.

She shook off her gloom and hugged Charles. "Did
you have a good time?"

"Oh, yes! Tommy and Jim's daddy is a real Union
nawficer!"

"That's wonderful." She was glad he did not draw
back this time, with the reproof that he was "too old"
for hugs. In her sensitive state, she would have cried.

Therese changed into an unobtrusive dress of light
brown silk, omitting jewelry, and accompanied the
nurse and Charles to the saloon.

Mrs. Harmon and her two boys were already seated
at a table with three other women. Therese recognized
one as a Mrs. Reynolds, who had patronized the salon—
the woman, she thought, chagrined, that she had
snubbed in her preoccupation that morning.

Therese apologized for her lapse, saying, "I'm afraid
I was very absentminded . . . thinking of business."

"I understand there was a death in your family,
down South," Mrs. Reynolds remarked. "Please accept
my condolences." The way she said it commented on
Therese's hardheartedness at thinking of business at
such a time. Mrs. Reynolds glanced at Therese's light
brown dress.

I'm creating a scandal, Therese thought with annoyance. Of course I should be wearing black.

"Thank you. A distant relative." That should excuse her lack of mourning.

Mrs. Harmon leaned toward her. "It is very thrill-
ing," she chimed in, "to meet Madame Therese."

The woman scrutinized her with thinly veiled suspicion, as if she were a bit fast. Therese recalled what
the easygoing George had said to her once, when she
worried that Cincinnati's wariness of her might hurt
both their businesses. "You're not a parson's or a
politician's wife," he'd said with a smile. "We offer
something good, so 'disapproval' be damned."

All of the women were very chatty, giving Therese
little chance to participate even if she had had a mind
to, and were full of themselves and their business,

which was fine with Therese. Mrs. Harmon said her
husband's tour of duty in New Orleans was drawing to
a close, and she was returning to Cairo, Illinois, in
advance of him to get their house reopened.

"I believe one of his junior officers is on this very
boat," Mrs. Harmon simpered. "Young Major McKay.
I know he is going to visit his aunt in Cincinnati." She
glanced at Therese, who wondered what she had seen
. . . or heard.

"Why, yes," she said calmly. "As a matter of fact I
ran into Major McKay this morning at breakfast. He
stopped to pay his respects. Agnes and I are such good
friends."

Mrs. Reynolds seemed nettled, but she looked at
Therese with grudging respect and some envy. Agnes
McKay was quite a force in the town; using her first
name inspired awe.

That should hold them for a while, Therese thought.
Now, if she were seen talking with Anthony, there
would be some apparent reason for it. Little as she
cared what the women thought, she hated the thought
of gossip reaching George, perhaps causing him pain.
She couldn't bear that; he had been worried enough
about her seeing Nicholas.

There was a rather awkward silence. To fill the gap,
the lady from Evansville said to Therese in her well-
bred manner, "You must have found New Orleans
sadly changed."

"I certainly did." The change of topic, even to a sad
one, seemed to lighten the atmosphere at the table.
Nevertheless, during her conversation with the pleasant woman, Therese felt she was being closely observed by Mrs. Reynolds and the Harmon boys' mother.

She declined the ladies' invitation to join them on
deck, saying she must write some urgent letters, and
returned to the stateroom. It was a partial truth: she
had thought of a good many questions she wanted to
ask Elianne about things she could send her from
Cincinnati. And she was anxious to repeat to Charl'
her request that he hold onto his temper with Nicholas
Adair. She dispensed with that first, so she could

enjoy writing a long letter to her younger sister, then one to Berthe.

To Elianne she could open her heart and write endless descriptions of pretty treasures the girl might choose. Therese got quite lost in the pleasure of writing. By the time she had finished and had done some more drawing, she realized she would be late for the early dinner service.

She found her luck was excellent: Mrs. Harmon and her retinue were already sitting with Charles and Savannah at a full table. Charles, enjoying himself with the other boys, wouldn't miss her, so she took a seat at another table with elderly couples. Anthony did not appear.

Neither he nor the others were at early breakfast the next morning, and at the midday meal she contrived what luck had accomplished the evening before —to sit with her son and the nurse at a table apart from the curious women.

At last, on the final evening of the journey, her patience was at an end. She was weary of acting the fugitive again—she had had enough of that in New Orleans—and wearing her dullest dresses. She decided to risk the late dinner service and put on the one rich gown she had brought along. It was modestly cut, with a minimum of ornament, but its color, the dark golden orange of a nasturtium, was austerely splendid. Smiling, she remembered that Harold Mead had told her she had a "painter's eye for color."

She dined without conversation at a table of elderly strangers, and then went into the music room. Seeing Mrs. Harmon in the first row, she sat in a far rear corner. The orchestra began with Foster airs and sentimental tunes of the day. Then came the melodies of operatic arias, love songs from *Rigoletto* and *Il Trovatore*: and at last, once more, the "*Un dì felice*."

The passionate aria wrung her heart: it had been playing when she had seen Anthony standing at the head of the stairs and had looked on his face again after five years of separation.

Her dreamy gaze wandered over the music room and came to rest.

He stood under the open archway, staring at her, his wild emotions plain on his fine, hard face.

She looked away, but out of the corner of her eye she saw him approach. Leaning down from behind her, he murmured, "Come with me. Please. I must speak with you."

Therese hesitated. Half-unwilling, she rose and walked before him out of the resounding hall.

She knew why she had come to the concert, why she had worn the dress. She had wanted this to happen. She felt assent in every part of her body; his slight touch on the small of her back, vital and elated, set off a warm thrill along her nerves.

A full moon silvered the water; the aria faded to a distant, plaintive cry as they moved on deck. But there was no friendly darkness or isolation. Couples and pairs of men walked past and around them or stood at the rail; randy laughter sounded from the gambling room.

Anthony led Therese to a quieter corner. "I've tried to respect your wishes," he said in a low, unsteady voice, "and it is killing me, Therese. I can't believe you want me to stay away. I saw it in your eyes . . . just as I saw it when we danced that night."

She could not protest now. His voice, his physical closeness, exercised their mesmerism. I once imagined Nicholas made magic, she thought. It had been nothing compared with this. She had been a shallow slip of a child then. She was a woman now, hollowed out by struggle and loneliness and ancient fears so that her spirit could contain this vast desire.

Her will had turned to vapor.

Sensing her new complaisance, he urged her, "Come with me, Therese . . . where we can speak in quiet."

She knew that he meant his cabin. He pressed her hand pleadingly, and she felt her fingers relax in his.

He took a quick, jagged breath and led her slowly around the end of the deck. As soon as they had entered his stateroom and he closed the door and turned to her, Therese knew that there could be no turning back.

There would be no talk between them, not now.

He took her in his arms and kissed her hair, saying her name in a voice so drunk with feeling she hardly recognized it. At his touch, a solemn fire devoured her. She slid her hands up to his cheeks and pulled his face to hers. His kiss was savage and long: it shook her to her core.

Her body became a fluid ache as he raised his mouth and pressed soft kisses on her neck and in the throbbing space below her ear. His hard hands stroked her sides, tracing her curves and softness. He leaned to kiss her naked arms, and a quiver raced along her frame. She felt weightless, like a plume in the wind, as he caressed her through the voluminous silk of her clothes, his proud head lowering to hers again.

She felt the heat of his breath, heard his inchoate murmur. Suddenly she moved closer, and some barbaric impulse made her touch the skin of his neck with the tip of her tongue.

He gave a guttural groan, and his hold on her tightened. She melted to his hardness, flowing to him and around him.

*We cannot let each other go,* she thought with exultation. He raised his mouth and looked down at her. His eyes glittered. Holding her close by his side, he led her to the dim-lit corner that contained his bed.

Nothing was real for her anymore; she moved with the watery motions of someone in a dream, half-closing her eyes. He began to unfasten her dress. Rustling, it fell into a fiery pool on the carpet, looking like a huge blown flower. She stepped from the silk like a dancer; his breath caught at the sight of her slender body in its thin cambric and foaming lace.

He bared her body, and kneeling down, kissed her all over her hips, belly, and thighs, giving her that exotic caress that had been hinted at in the novels of desire. From the center of her, a small flame sprang up like candlelight and spread into a wide, consuming

fire. She cried out with pleasure, her body all amazement, quivering as his mouth lingered on her skin.

Through half-closed lids she watched him stand and
rid his splendid body of his clothes. She gloried in the
sight of his lean, hard-tendoned frame, in the power of
his muscular torso and arms.

Then he invited her to lie in his embrace, and their
bare flesh melded together in the rhythm of profound
fulfillment. Pounded by pleasure waves, she heard her
outcry follow his. She floated . . . and descended on
the breaking wave to the deepest peace she had ever
known in all her life.

They parted gently; he pulled her to him, kissing
her tumbled hair. Silent, he stroked her head, her
neck and shoulder, sliding his fingers down her arm.

She looked up at his face. It was serene and ecstatic,
smoothed out. When he turned his head to look at
her, his eyes were naked with devotion.

"If you knew," he whispered, "of the hours and
years I've dreamed of this." He smiled. "I was already
half in love with you five minutes after I saw you.
That's how the accident happened. I couldn't take my
eyes off you; I hardly knew where I was going."

Overwhelmed, she burrowed into his shoulder.

"Therese." He took her gently by the chin and turned
her face upward. "You *did* feel something that night
. . . and the day I said good-bye. I know you did."

"Yes. I felt something I had never known, with
anyone."

He squeezed her head against his chest. "I knew. I
*knew.*"

"But I tried so hard to forget you," she murmured.
"I had almost given you up. Until I saw you getting on
the boat."

"We were destined to be here together. It is a sign
from fate that we have been given these days. We
belong to each other now, Therese. For always."

She thrilled to his words, and yet she could not
prevent the small ache of betrayal she felt when she
remembered George. "I am married to another man."

Anthony's fingers tightened on her arm. "You do

not love him. I know you do not. Otherwise you would never have come to me."

"No," she admitted. "I don't love him, not as I love you. But I am bound to him. No one has ever been so kind to me, or given me so much."

"But don't you see?" He moved and took her by the shoulders. "If you don't love him, then the marriage itself is a betrayal. Of yourself and of him."

Anthony spoke the thought that she had so often had—she had cheated George, in a way, by marrying him. Her resistance to Anthony's pleas began to weaken.

He felt her yielding, and said in a victorious tone, "You know that too, don't you? Therese, you must divorce him now. We are meant to be together. You are meant to be my wife. Anything else would be . . . impossible."

"I know, I know. I cannot imagine ever being without you again. I would . . . die."

He held her close, covering her face with kisses. "Then say it, say it, Therese. Say that you will divorce him and marry me."

His kiss was dizzying; for a long, blind moment, she was overpowered. And yet deep within her, something obdurate protested.

"I cannot, Anthony. Not now. This has all happened too quickly. I can't even think." Agitated tears began to form in her eyes and spilled down over her face.

"Oh, Therese. Forgive me." He kissed her moist cheeks and wiped away the tears as if she were a child. "Come here." He pulled her to his body again, stroking her tenderly. "Don't cry, don't cry."

She lay with her head on his chest, fondling its hair-roughened expanse with quivering fingers.

Then, astonished, she felt in both of them the abrupt renewal of their gnawing desire. He turned her soft, submissive body until, once more, it met his own.

Afterward they lay side by side, clasping hands.

"Anthony?" She spoke in a drowsy tone.

He answered in the same bemused way. "Yes, my darling."

"Just for tonight, just now . . ." she began slowly, "let us pretend that this is all the time there will ever be. Just this once, I want to imagine there are no other obligations, that I have no life apart from you. When the time comes, we will . . . talk of the other matters."

He smiled and rubbed her arm. "I am at your command."

"Then tell me," she coaxed, moving into his arms again, "tell me about Anthony McKay. Everything your life has been until this moment."

"It was nothing until this moment," he retorted. But then he did as she wished, beginning with his early days as the only son of a powerful New York family. He had a sister who was married to the son of another wealthy clan. He had gone to the fine schools she had read about, and to West Point, at his father's urging. It was thought that he had a "gift" for the military.

"I thought so too, at one time," Anthony remarked dryly. "I certainly had no gift for banking, or a settled life. But now," he added soberly, "everything is different."

When she did not answer, he went on with his story. For years his father had been trying to match him with a "suitable" young woman. He pronounced the word with contempt, saying the young ladies he had met at Newport and Saratoga, at functions in the city, had all been patterned after one model, born to spend money and pour out tea.

"And now," he murmured, caressing her, "I have found a wild Acadian. You were so charming that day, putting me in my place in that strange *patois*."

She smiled at that, and started telling him about her life on Côte Blanche.

And then she described what had happened because of Nicholas. She poured out the story of their last meeting.

Anthony's face stiffened. "He will never take your boy, Therese. No one will ever make you suffer again, I swear it. Your life has been so hard. From now on, I am going to make it easy."

She was deeply moved. Yet she had violated her own dictum that they not speak of anything outside this sequestered world on this one night of their own.

She noticed that the quality of light through the colored window had subtly changed. "Oh, Anthony, I must leave you."

"Therese, I can't endure it." As he held her close, she thought: I can't endure it either. To be separated from him now was an almost physical pain.

She told him so, speaking against his body. "But I must, I must."

"I know." He sounded as pained as she felt, heavily resigned. "It would never do for you to be seen coming out of this cabin in daylight. Oh, God, I *hate* this, Therese. I want you to be known as mine. Honorably, before the whole world."

"I want that too, Anthony." She gave him a final kiss and, timid in her nakedness, withdrew to put on her clothes. When she came out from behind the screen, he was dressed. He took her in his arms and pressed her against him, giving her one more long, impassioned kiss.

"I'll see you to your cabin."

Softly, they took the stairs to the ladies' deck. Anthony raised her hand to his lips and kissed it.

Just as he was walking away, and Therese turned the knob of her cabin door, another door opened farther down the deck.

Therese stepped quickly into her cabin. Closing the door, she leaned against it.

Thank God she had not been seen. If she had, the scandal would surely reach George, and Therese shrank more from the agony it would cause him than the trouble it would cause her. It would break his heart.

Therese's throat ached—the loveliest moment of her whole existence had been shadowed by so much remorse.

As she undressed behind the screen, preparing for bed, she longed for Anthony again already, wishing they could fall asleep in each other's arms. But that could never happen. Unless she divorced her husband. Even now, she could not bear the thought of telling him. She pictured the desolation it would bring him.

Once again she lay wide-eyed in her bed, unable to fall asleep until the stained-glass windows had regained their color.


She slept so late that only a few hours remained until landing.

Savannah was full of anxious questions; she insisted on bringing food to Therese from the saloon, standing over her until she forced down some of the meal.

Listless, Therese stayed in bed until it was time to dress. She responded with difficulty when Savannah asked her what she would wear.

The golden interval was over. There would be no chance for a private word with Anthony. And George would be waiting for her on the landing. How she would face him after what had happened, she could not fathom.

She got up and prepared herself grimly but with care. She must look perfect, with not a hair astray. That would stiffen her backbone for the encounter with her husband.

When the steamboat slid into the Cincinnati landing, Therese stood proudly on deck, ignoring the knot of curious women farther down the rail. She scanned the deck below for Anthony, and then the shore for George. There was no sign of either.

But as the plank went down, she saw the lower deck empty first. Anthony, in uniform, strode with the others onto the landing. She also glimpsed Nell and Agnes McKay, standing together. They looked unusually solemn.

When she recognized Anthony, Mrs. McKay's withered face broke into a smile; he hurried to embrace her.

Nell looked up and saw Therese. Nell did not look like herself at all. Therese wondered where George was. Nell waved without smiling, and Therese was puzzled. Something must be wrong.

When she was at last on shore, Nell and Mrs. McKay hurried toward her. Anthony swept off his hat and stood waiting.

"Oh, my dear," Agnes McKay cried out, putting her arms around Therese.

"Nell, what is it?" Therese pleaded.

"George is very ill," Nell answered sorrowfully. "He has had a stroke."

Therese's shock left her speechless.

In a swift glance at Anthony, she saw the terror in his eyes, the fear that her sense of obligation would be so heavy now that all their hopes and dreams would come to an end.

## 12

Therese ran up the curving stairs to the hospital's second floor, with Nell walking quickly behind her. She was cold with apprehension and remorse, thinking: It's a punishment, retribution for my betrayal.

And her first concern, when she heard, had not been her suffering husband, but Anthony.

Reaching the landing, Therese faced a stocky, solemn figure, a gray-haired man with a small goatee, in black, rumpled clothes. "Mrs. Madison? I am Dr. Statler."

"Where is my husband? Please take me to him."

The doctor grasped her firmly by the elbow. "I wish to speak with you first, before you see him. You are extremely agitated, madam. Sit down here, if you please."

Irrelevantly, she was aware of his strong Germanic accent, his firmness. He pushed her gently into a chair. "I want to prepare you," the doctor said bluntly.

"Prepare me?" Her voice quavered. Two nuns passed by almost soundlessly, their great white headdresses looking like pale preying birds.

"He is paralyzed on his right side, Mrs. Madison. And you must expect a certain . . . contortion of the face, an enormous difficulty in speaking."

She digested that for an instant, with a sense of freezing horror. Then she blurted out, "But how is he? Is he going to . . . die?"

"No, no."

"But will he get better?" she persisted.

The old man's somber eyes met hers levelly. "No, Mrs. Madison," he answered bluntly. "I am afraid, in my opinion, he will never be other than he is now."

She reeled from shock at his finality, and heard a little moan from Nell, who was standing apart from them. In the next moment, though, all that was obdurate in Therese denied it. "You said 'in my opinion,' " she countered.

He observed her compassionately. "Yes, Mrs. Madison. I encourage you to consult another physician . . . as many as you wish. But I fear that their judgment would concur with mine."

Therese bent her head, trying not to break down. But the tears gushed down her cheeks; she could no longer control them.

"Sister. Please bring the lady a glass of port." Statler directed. In a short time, she had drunk some of the wine and felt somewhat restored.

"Would you like to see your husband now?" the doctor asked gently. She nodded, wiping away her tears.

When she entered the room, where another white-coiffed nun sat on a chair by the wall, Therese admitted the kindness Statler had done her by his frankness.

The man on the bed was not George.

But girded with her knowledge, she was able to smile, to take his hand with some degree of composure.

"Therese." Her name, on his contorted mouth, sounded grotesque. He could not form the R, and her name came out almost like the "Tez" of her childhood. Trying to hold back her tears, she realized George had been *famille* for so long, almost from the very first. Now his right eye was drawn down, like his mouth; but the other side of his face was perfectly normal, giving him a horribly clownish appearance.

She spoke his name tenderly, and stooped to kiss his ruined mouth. He grasped at her pathetically with his good arm, yet turned slightly away from her caress, as if he feared to offend her.

He gave her a dreadful grimace.

"Oh, my dear, are you in pain?"

She was horrified at her mistake. He shook his head and his eyes looked like a wounded animal's. She knew then that the grimace had been an attempted smile.

Her control broke; deep sobs racked her body, and she learned her head on his insensate shoulder.

"Don't . . . cry," he labored. "Glad . . . see you."

Ashamed, she sat up, dabbing her face with her balled handkerchief, and forced a smile. He met it with his grimace.

". . . Charles?" he grunted.

"He's fine. But indignant that he could not come to see you." She contrived a cheerful, almost merry tone, and his demeanor brightened.

She saw Statler at the door. "I think that is enough excitement for today," he said indulgently. "You may come back in the morning," he told Therese.

She bent to kiss George's undamaged cheek and squeezed his shoulder.

When he followed her with his eyes, she turned to blow him a kiss, her heart aching. His eyes swept her face and form, despairing. She could hear his silent cry as clearly as if he had voiced it aloud: I will never be a husband to you anymore.

If he felt like that, how much more awful it would be to be alone. She could never leave him.

The knowledge weighed on her like a stone. In the hall, where it didn't matter, she let her body slump, her mouth relax from that hideous smile.

Out of the corner of her eye she saw Nell waiting patiently. Nell got up and put her arms around Therese. "Are you all right?"

I'm splendid, she retorted in bitter silence. George's life is over, and so is mine. "The doctor said it was time to leave."

"Let me go home with you."

Home, with its quiet. The room she shared with George. "Oh, Nell, not now. I can't face it yet. I don't know what to say to Charles. Let's go to the salon."

Nell colored. "But, Therese, it would seem so . . ."

"Unfeeling," Therese finished for her. "I don't care. No one knows how I feel." Not even Anthony. "It's the only place I can stand, just now."

"Let's go, then."

A little later, surrounded by the silent beauty of the

salon, Therese felt immeasurably calmer. Soon she would be able to lose herself in the work again. Right now, it was enough just to be there.

That one brief night with Anthony was over, and there could never be another one. But at least, for a time, she had known what love was. Tomorrow she would shoulder her burdens again, the old along with the new one which she would have to carry as long as her husband was alive.

This was where her heart was, and would be, as far ahead as she could possibly envision.

"I was being foolish, Nell. I was acting like a coward. I had better go home and talk to my son."

Slowly the women turned out the lights and locked the door.

Therese did not come back to the salon until the end of the week. That night she comforted her son as well as she could, and was moved when he asked to sleep in her bed. The next morning, and the morning after, she dressed with particular care in the clothes George liked most and arrived early at the hospital. She did not let herself think of Anthony at all, immersing herself in reading to George and devising small treats for him to raise his spirits.

Returning home from the hospital on the third afternoon, she found Agnes McKay's calling card on the hall table. On the card, written in a bold masculine hand, she read, "and Major McKay."

Hiding her agitation, she listened to Rubine's admiring comments about "that fine lady, and the fine young gentleman," regarding the flowers they had left with a blind gaze. If there were any mercy left at all, Therese decided, Anthony would soon go back to New Orleans.

The next morning, it took all her strength to present a cheerful face to George. She found him in labored conversation with Mr. Mundey, his accountant, Mr. Steinman, his workroom foreman, and another man she'd did not know.

Therese went to George's bed and kissed him lightly.

Mundey and Steinman greeted her courteously and the third man introduced himself as Gregory Morris, George's attorney. He was a thin, sharp-featured man with observant eyes and a smooth, amiable manner.

"Could I speak with you a moment, privately?" he asked Therese. She went with him into the corridor. "I would prefer to do this in the privacy of my office, but since you are here . . . George wants you to have his power of attorney. That way, you'll have the authority to act for him in all business matters, to withdraw his funds from the bank and the like. I . . . had thought such a decision premature, but after talking with Dr. Statler . . ."

Mr. Morris paused, as if he feared to upset her. She sank down into a chair and said evenly, "I know. Do whatever he thinks best."

He looked relieved, then admiring. "Very well, then, I will bring the documents by your home. This evening, if it is convenient."

She named a time and shook his hand. Steinman and Mundey came out of George's room, touching their hats to her as they passed.

When she went back in, George's dull eyes brightened. She told him what had transpired with Morris, and he handed her a sheet of paper. She saw that it was a note from him, written with dreadful awkwardness by his left hand.

"Can't talk . . . well." He struggled to push the words out and she pressed his hand. Then she read the letter, which was a telegraphic expression of his thoughts and plans and his desire to make everything as easy for her as possible. It concluded, "Sell Madison's. Better all round."

"Sell Madison's!" she cried out, shaking her head. "No, George! It's been yours so long . . . and your father's before you. No. *I'll* run Madison's if I have to . . . until you're well enough to run it yourself. They'll all help me—Mr. Steinman and Mr. Mundey, and Mr. Morris. Surely you don't want to let it go. It's meant so much to you. Tell me, George. Tell me you'll let me try."

She saw a tender light in his eyes, and the slow beginning of the grimace she had come to know as a smile.

"Terese . . . wild 'cadian. Yes," he got out with excruciating slowness. "Love you."

"And I love you, George. I love you."

She refused to look on George's homecoming as an admission of defeat, a concession to the idea that a longer hospital stay would be futile in his hopeless condition. She had to believe that someday he would be himself again; it was the only thing, besides Madame Therese, that kept her going.

Statler had referred her, without much hope, to a physician in Chicago and another in New York. She resolved when George was stronger, to travel with him to both places.

Meanwhile she turned the house upside down, having a smaller dining table and four chairs moved down from the attic into a corner of the parlor, and converting the dining room into a bedroom for herself and George. She made the office into a bedroom for the male nurse hired to care for him.

When George was carried into the new bedroom, he caught sight of Therese's dressing table, and his eyes moistened. With an ache, she realized that he had expected to be alone there, that the signs of her intention to share his room overwhelmed him. The pity of it was so great, it locked her heart like a manacle she would never be able to remove.

Between 1866 and 1868, Therese no longer recognized herself as the woman on the river, the one who had felt those nameless longings.

Aside from the one conventional call with Mrs. McKay, Anthony had made no move toward her. She knew that he avoided her out of delicacy of feeling, and learned from Agnes McKay that he had returned to duty. A week later, Therese received his impassioned letter, which ended: "We are meant to be

together, and someday we will be again." He pleaded
with her to write to him.

She wept over the letter, but she knew she would
not answer. It was futile for either of them to hope.
Even when his letters continued to arrive through the
winter and the spring, she still did not answer. That
summer, the letters stopped coming. At last, it was
truly over.

More than ever, her work became the antidote for
her crippling sense of loss; it filled her emptiness, as it
had so long ago in New Orleans. Madame Therese
helped blot out her loneliness, blurring the images of
Anthony, the helpless George, and her increasingly
distant son.

She had prepared Charles as gently as she knew how
for the first encounter with George, but the boy shrank
from the stranger in the bed. It was a perfectly natural
reaction for such a little boy; both Therese and George
understood, and forgave him. But gradually Charles
began to act less and less like a typical child of eight.
Therese knew he was keeping secrets from her. She
was dismayed when she discovered what those secrets
were—letters from Nicholas Adair. Therese found them
hidden under the boy's underclothing one morning
after he had gone to school, when she was putting
fresh laundry in his bureau drawer.

Ashamed, but ridden by anxiety, Therese read them:
every one indicated that Charles should hide them
from his mother, and described the pleasures of Adair's
Island. Therese knew she should talk to Charles about
it, but concluded she must let it be. She would only
arouse his resentment; and he was so young, she believed that he would ultimately lose interest in the
correspondence, the same way he had suddenly lost
the interest he had acquired in boats during their stay
on Côte Blanche. He never played any more with the
miniature pirogue Charl' had made for him. Therese
told herself it was idiotic to place so much importance
in the letters.

Besides, she was so pressed with other responsibilities that she had to put aside her worry over Charles.

She was obliged to meet each week with the lawyer and the banker, and with Mundey and Steinman, to go over George's business. Begrudging every minute that Madison's took her away from Madame Therese, she learned to delegate more and more, discovering new talents in the accountant and the workroom supervisor. George was not strong enough during the first year to participate much, although Therese tried to involve him as much as she could. It was becoming clear to all of them that Madison's must expand to meet the competition of ready-made factories springing up everywhere since the war.

The salon also needed to expand. Madame Therese was becoming well-known all the way to the East. In an issue of 1867, the new magazine *Harper's Bazar* called Therese "America's first native designer," reproducing one of her dresses on its cover. Therese was overwhelmed—it was one of the greatest moments in her life. She sent copies of the magazine to Berthe and Elianne and even to Odalie, whose Paris address she had obtained from Charl'. It was a painful irony, however, that her triumph was overshadowed by the perpetual burden of her responsibilities, and her anxiety about Charles. She gave him as much time as she could, and yet he seemed to withdraw from her more and more, and he totally avoided George.

But a month after the article was published in the *Bazar,* Therese was buoyed by the arrival of Charl', Berthe, and Elianne in Cincinnati. She gladly assumed another task—the direction of her younger sister's future. Charl' had done the rest, finding a nice house for the three of them and helping Berthe adjust to city living. Elianne took to the city at once. And when she was enrolled in one of its fine free schools, her extraordinary talents came to light. Her English teacher discovered that Elianne had a natural gift for authorship. Therese began to plot and plan for her education. Charl', of course, was eager to share the cost of Elianne's schooling, but Therese sidestepped that issue. The income she and George had was so much larger than her brother's, and he was still supporting

Berthe. Besides, Therese suspected he would soon have new responsibilities: he and Nell had been instantly attracted to each other, and Therese hoped against hope they would marry.

That autumn, to her delight, they did. Berthe also was overjoyed. But Charles still cast his small shadow on Therese's happiness. It had been more than a year since he had seen Nicholas Adair, but Therese discovered that Nicholas' letters were still arriving. And to her dismay, Charles had begun comparing the house, and their riches, with those of Petit Anse. She had a gloomy feeling that at any day, Nicholas Adair might come to Cincinnati.

She hated Nicholas now, for giving her this added worry. Charles was too young to be blamed. But Therese thought sometimes she would absolutely break under all the burdens—George's condition, the businesses, the guidance of Elianne. It was unbearable to fear, on top of that, the alienation of her own child.

She had to remind herself of all the things that were going right—Berthe was ecstatic to be near her favorite children; the house that Charl' had found for her seemed like a palace after the cabin on Côte Blanche.

And Elianne was healthy and content, remarkably independent for a girl of her age. It was an ever-pleasant distraction, too, for Therese to have the joy of dressing her.

Still, Madame Dufay and Steinman kept pressing her for the expansion. Ever since the Duke of Windsor had introduced to America the "suit"—the new concept of a matching coat and trousers, with the shorter, easier-to-produce jacket—more factories were turning out the revolutionary ensemble.

"We've got to have more room and more men, Mrs. Madison," Steinman said repeatedly. And Madame Dufay was eager for the salon to produce "suits" for women; they would be ideal, she said, for travel and the needs of the daring women who every day were beginning to go into "business."

"Therese, we must not let that false Frenchwoman" —that was Madame Dufay's favored epithet for "Ma-

dame" Demorest of New York—"get ahead of us.
Madame Therese must introduce the suit for women.
And with the tailoring required, it is possible that a
women's section at Madison's could be the answer.
*Closely* supervised, of course, by us," she added se-
verely, eliciting a chuckle from Therese.

It could no longer be postponed. The business had
to expand. But where?

As usual Therese's inspiration came to her when
she was doing something not directly related to her
enterprise. She was looking over *Harper's Bazar*, simply with a woman's eye, dreaming for once of a life
without responsibility, one dedicated to enjoyment,
like that of the beauties pictured in the magazine.

It is 1868, she thought, and I am only twenty-six
years old. Yet I am carrying the burdens of a man of
fifty. The old, almost forgotten longing for Anthony
resurfaced; she ached with nostalgia and regret.

Still, in the very midst of her unusual mood, something nagged at her consciousness. What was it? She
stared at the cover of the magazine.

Bazar. Bazaar.

Mrs. Trollope's Bazaar, the enterprise that had failed
forty years ago, and was still dubbed Trollope's Folly
by a contemptuous Cincinnati, flashed into her mind.

And the outrageous old building was empty to this
day.

Therese's maxim of "audacity and courage" echoed
in her memory. If she had been audacious enough to
carry off all that she had, and with such a measure of
success, she could tackle even that—converting the
useless Bazaar into an expanded Madison-Pavan.

That's what she would call it: in deference to George,
his name would be foremost. She liked the ring of
Madison-Pavan. And on the spot, she resolved that
she would do it, no matter what anyone said.

And a great deal was said, she was to discover in the
next hectic months. Morris, the lawyer, and Benson,
whose bank handled George's account and owned the
ancient white elephant, could hardly conceal their
amusement. Benson and Morris exchanged condescend-

ing glances that irritated Therese beyond endurance; it was clear that the men did not think highly of women's business acumen.

"Now, Mrs. Madison," Benson began, "a number of enterprises have abandoned that building, one after the other. No one found it practicable, or habitable for any . . . reasonable purpose."

"I think you will find this reasonable, Mr. Benson." Therese handed him her carefully thought-out plans. He seemed taken aback at the unwomanly demeanor, an attitude that she had noticed before. "The building is structurally sound; when the hospital occupied it, the gas pipes were thoroughly repaired. All it will take to carry out my plans is a little imagination and effort."

"But how on earth will you get all that new machinery up four flights of stairs? You have designated the fourth-floor ballroom for your factory. Really, Mrs. Madison . . ."

"Hoisting, of course," she said bluntly. "The windows are wide enough to admit a piano . . . or an elephant."

The banker reddened with vexation, and the attorney shifted in his chair. Though the building would not have one of the Otis elevators, which most of the Midwest still called the "vertical railway," when they moved in, Charl' had easily found the solution, being totally conversant with all aspects of the transport of cargo.

Therese was mortified that she had omitted that detail from her report. "In due time, of course, we will install an elevator."

"Vertical railways," Benson said, "are very expensive."

Therese nodded. "But as you see, our initial outlay will not be prohibitive. I intend to realize a profit on rentals of the present Madison building and from Madame Therese."

"Rentals?" Benson raised his brows. "It might be more profitable to sell."

"There is no question of that at present." She had no intention of selling the building that housed Madame Therese; it was the site of the Madison family's first business, and also of the first "Pavan." "Both premises can be easily converted; I already have interested tenants."

Benson seemed annoyed at her temerity. "Then I take it you have not come to us for advice. Why have you come to us, Mrs. Madison?"

"To make you an offer for the Folly."

"An offer!" Morris exploded. "Why, the owners don't even charge rental! The place is a local . . . jest." His manner changed from shock to amusement. "Why don't you just move in? I'm sure Mr. Benson would not prevent you."

Therese boiled; he spoke to her as if she were a rather backward child discussing a playhouse. "Because, Mr. Morris, I will be running two good-size businesses. And I can't depend on the whim of the owner. I'm prepared to offer two thousand dollars for the building."

"Good heavens, it cost twenty-five to build!" Benson said huffily.

"And has stood empty for the best part of forty years," she retorted. Her calm was driving them almost to apoplexy. "You'll have an albatross off your hands, Mr. Benson. And I'll be paying the taxes on the property, remember."

The men were silent, flabbergasted. "Do you have George's approval, Mrs. Madison?"

"As a matter of fact, I do. Although, if you remember, I don't need it. I have his power of attorney." The men looked at each other as if regretting that.

"But what makes you think you can make a success of this . . . outlandish location?" Benson demanded.

"This is 1868, not 1828. Cincinnati wasn't ready for the Bazaar then. It is now. Madame Therese has put Cincinnati on a par with Chicago, Philadelphia, and even New York. The very outlandishness of the building will not only arouse the curiosity of local patrons, it will attract national attention, I assure you."

Benson shook his head. "And how much do you propose to gamble on renovation, fixtures, new equipment, and the like?"

"It's in my prospectus," she said brusquely. "At least ten thousand dollars . . . a good deal more"—she smiled dryly—"than the cost of the building."

Morris interjected, "As your business manager, Mrs. Madison, I have to remind you that you have a good deal on your plate already—George's care, your sister's schooling, and the support of your whole family, aside from your brother and his wife."

"I'm aware of that. I am convinced that I can make it succeed. Will you sell me the building, Mr. Benson?"

He studied her for a moment. Then, amazingly, he smiled. "Your audacity is admirable, Mrs. Madison. I'll let you have it for a thousand. And, as it happens, I have a cousin who would be able to do a fine job of any alterations you might need. He's sound as a dollar and would be glad to have the business."

*A thousand,* she exulted. "Done, Mr. Benson," she said firmly, extending her hand.

Cincinnati watched goggle-eyed, inquisitive, skeptical, and openly laughing as Trollope's Folly was converted into the new Madison-Pavan. But after the first few months, there was less skepticism and no laughter at all. The few remaining tailors gave up the ghost of their businesses and went to work for Madison-Pavan, which was rapidly turning out tailor-made and ready-made clothes, even before it officially opened.

Jake Steinman had made a trip to Philadelphia, then to New York, to pick up new ideas and to investigate the operation of new factories. Already the news of women's "suits," being created under the eagle eye of Hortense Dufay, had reached the East. Representatives of newspapers and magazines had traveled to Cincinnati to report on the phenomenon.

All the inventiveness and economy that Therese had brought to the creation of the small salon was put to excellent use in the fantastic street level of Pavan. With extraordinary ingenuity and backbreaking work, Therese, Nell, Madame Dufay, and her "right arm," Rubine, made the ground floor into a haven from the Arabian Nights. In keeping with the great rotunda, the Moorish pilasters, and the fairy-tale interior structure, they set up corners piled with huge cushions instead of couches, and found small octagonal tables at secondhand furniture stores, and hung strings of beads in place of curtains.

The ladies' floor, with its fantastic bowers, its capacious seats, and its coffee and tea service, drew women and young girls in droves. It was a respectable and romantic place for young lovers to catch glimpses of each other, providing a benefit formerly possible only at church or the interminable lectures.

On the massive second floor, reached by circular stairs, were the premises of Madison, which had larger fitting rooms, a huge waiting room, and even a small dining room where patrons who had to wait could enjoy sandwiches and nonalcoholic refreshment.

Therese had planned a miniature tavern and billiard room, but the horrified attorney stopped her just in time: cards and billiards were illegal in Cincinnati, and those who engaged in those games were subject to fines. As to wine and ale being served, Morris warned Therese, the temperance factions were capable of practically putting her out of business. Exasperated, she contented herself with the dining room.

By June of 1868, Madison-Pavan had become an honored tradition. Many said it had put Cincinnati on the map, and its elegance and innovation were in keeping with the expanding city's new names—the Queen City, the Athens of America.

At twenty-six, Therese was at the height of her beauty, stimulated by the astounding success of Madison-Pavan. Now that the rest of her family was flourishing, the enterprise preoccupied her every waking moment.

Even if the journeys to Chicago and New York, with George, had resulted in the same gloomy prognosis as Dr. Statler's, George had benefited from his examination in New York. A radical doctor there had insisted that he begin a course of grueling arm and torso exercises; eagerly George complied, and by now had regained some of the use of his right arm. Though still confined to a bath chair, he could speak more clearly. His face was less distorted, too. After the elevator was installed in Madison-Pavan, Therese thought happily, George might even be able to resume some of its management.

Elianne was prospering too, her free-school classes supplemented by a private tutor. Her teachers said that by the time she was sixteen she would be prepared to enter Mount Holyoke College in Massachusetts, the country's first college for women. Next to the business, Elianne was Therese's greatest triumph. She gloried in the fact that her sister was living like a young princess in comparison with her life at Côte Blanche, and was determined that nothing would ever change that.

Charl' and Nell were expecting a child—it was, as Charl' said happily, his way of perpetuating the name Pavan—and Berthe, to their affectionate amusement, had a suitor. He was none other than the gentle widower Mr. Levitsky, who had been Therese's draper for years. The draper had been immediately struck with Berthe, who was still only forty-three to his fifty-five, and who had regained much of her old beauty in the ease of her new life.

If only, Therese pondered, she could be as certain of her boy. He was strangely mature for a child of ten. Despite his lucid gray-blue eyes and golden hair, there was a darkness in him, a secret shadowiness. On Sundays, when the family gathered, sometimes enjoying themselves in the old Acadian ways, singing the old songs, Charles did not take much part. He would observe them with a coolness that disturbed Therese.

He sulked if he had to go on family outings, and was regularly invited to Sunday dinner by his friends' parents, usually the richest and stuffiest in Cincinnati. Therese noticed that he favored the richer boys at the free school, which was attended by children of moneyed as well as the poor because it was one of the best schools in the North.

Charles went to the Episcopal church because his friends did, he said. Berthe once remarked that it was a pity the boy did not go to Mass with his own grandmother, his "flesh and blood," but Therese made it clear that she was not going to force any religion on her son, thinking privately that she'd had enough of that from Michel. And if Charles's friends were always the richer boys, it was no surprise; after all, the Madisons were rich themselves by Cincinnati standards.

Nevertheless, it bothered Therese that the Episcopal faith happened to be the faith of the Adairs. She recalled Nicholas mentioning that in one of the letters she had read. And always, there was an undercurrent of uneasiness between her and her son, as if Nicholas were influencing him from a distance, despite everything Therese tried to do to bind him to her and to the Pavans. She still hadn't mentioned finding the letters.

In May, when an elaborate birthday present had arrived for Charles from Adair's Island, Therese asked her son how "Mr. Adair" had known of his birthday. "I wrote to him, of course," Charles said at once. Then the child flushed.

"What's the matter, darling?" She touched his hair. "Why do you look like that?"

He remained sulky, not answering.

"Charles," she said firmly. "Tell me."

Not looking at her, the boy mumbled, "It was supposed to be a secret."

"What, the letters?" He nodded. "A secret, from your own mother?" She was still hurt that Charles hadn't volunteered something about the correspondence.

"Yes. Mr. Adair says you're so busy you 'shouldn't be bothered.' " She could hear the quotes. "He says he has lots of time to write to me . . . and that you might not like it if you found out."

"If it was all right, then why would he ask you to keep it secret?" she demanded.

Charles looked confused and rebellious. "I don't know. But he did. And now I've broken my word."

Therese gathered him to her and hugged him. "It's all right to break your word when someone has asked you to make a bad promise," she assured him.

"Is it, Mother?"

"Yes. Besides, you know that your daddy and I . . .

and your grandmother and aunt and uncle . . . love
you the best of all."

It pained her that he looked so unconvinced. But at
least, she thought, the matter was out in the open.
And in the main, their lives were good. So good.

Except for the times, more frequent now, when she
began to long for Anthony. She was not at all the
innocent she had been in the years during the war.
She had been so young then, untouched, unacquainted
with the splendors of his body. Now that he had awakened her to real love, her yearning had a new dimension when she remembered him, a burning physical
ache.

She contemplated the future without him, as 1868
drew to an end.


"Happy New Year, darling." Therese sat on the
edge of the bed and kissed George lightly on the
mouth. He smiled and squeezed her hand, already
half-asleep. She had made it a tradition to be alone
with him at midnight, when the church bells and the
harbor whistles heralded another year. She heard guests
leaving.

Quietly she got up and went out, closing the door.
The New Year's Eve reception had dwindled to her
favorite four—her brother and Nell, Elianne, and Madame Dufay. Charles had gotten too drowsy to see the
year come in.

"George is fast asleep," Therese said, smiling at them.
"He loves these parties, but they make him so tired."
She glanced at their dishes. "Can I get you anything?"

"I am replete," Madame Dufay said with amiable
precision, and the other refused too. Therese had succeeded in making Madame Dufay feel like one of the
family, and she was glad, recalling how alone she
herself had first felt in New Orleans.

"Sit down, *petit*." Charl's voice was lazy. "We were
just making our predictions for the year 1869. And
one of them was especially interesting." He hugged
Nell to him, and she laid her head on his shoulder,
languid in her early pregnancy.

Therese sat down in the chair next to their love seat and put her feet on a hassock, regarding them fondly through half-closed lids. "That could only be the event of next August," she teased him.

"Inexact," Madame Dufay said with one of her scarecrow grins. "We were speaking of an expedition to Paris."

"Paris!"

"Yes. Your brother agrees with me entirely. No *modiste* worthy of the name can fail to visit Paris. And this new year is the time. I'm afraid this will be the last peaceful summer in France."

"Hortense is right, you know. Napoleon's been having his troubles for the last two years, and the Prussians are circling," Charl' said soberly.

It was true, Therese conceded. Napoleon's failure to intervene in a quarrel between Austria and Prussia in 1866 diminished his support in France, and Bismarck's power was increasing. She remembered her own naive assumption that America's Civil War would be somehow averted, and Madame Dufay's sixth sense about approaching catastrophe.

"And who is to go on this expedition?" she asked lightly.

"You are, Madame Therese . . . and Elianne," Charl' said.

Therese glanced at Elianne, reflecting how lovely she looked in her first long evening dress of ecru grosgrain and lace, her coral ornaments. The girl's black eyes were sparkling, expectant.

"How can we?" Therese demanded. "Elianne's studies . . . and all that I must—"

"Do you think Jacob and I cannot manage for a month or two?" Madame Dufay broke in. "It is a pity you have hired such incompetents."

Therese grinned. "That's all very well, Madame, but it doesn't answer my other questions . . . about Elianne, and Charles. And George."

"It was George's idea," Charl' countered.

"George's?"

"Yes," Madame Dufay said. "When I happened to

mention that the false Frenchwoman is going in July, your clever husband said that you should go in May. As to the boy, you told me he was invited to a resort by the Hammills. They have been planning the visit ever since last summer."

"Of course." Therese had been putting Charles off in the hope that he would change his mind and go to an Illinois resort with Berthe and Elianne, to be joined later for a short time by Therese. Of course, she thought guiltily, he probably wants to be around his friends in a real family—not with a preoccupied mother, with George back in Cincinnati. Maybe it would be best for Charles to let him go with the Hammills.

Elianne said eagerly, "Tez . . . I can study every morning. My tutor can set a course for me."

The girl's eyes shone; she waited with parted lips for Therese to answer.

More than anything else, it was impossible to deny Elianne, Therese decided. She was more like her own child than a younger sister. More, Therese reproached herself, than Charles sometimes. But it was so much easier, so human to love someone who loved you back. And Elianne tried so hard in every way to please her, even to emulate her.

All at once Therese remembered that rainy day in the spring of 1861 when she had first met Anthony on the street. He had mistaken her for a *midinette;* that evening, dancing with her, he had said she "belonged" in Paris.

Oh, yes, there were so many reasons to go. She smiled at Elianne and said, "Very well, then. We will go to Paris."

# 13

On a mild afternoon in June 1869, Anthony McKay lounged at one of the outdoor tables in front of his favorite café on the Left Bank of the Seine. He had found the place some years ago, and liked to come there alone when he had had his fill of business and the dandified society of Second Empire Paris.

Today he was surfeited on both, between the sense of impending disaster among the circle he frequented as the bank's New York representative, and the terrible sameness of his mistress's plans. She was in her element in the salons and jewelers of the Rue de la Paix, and the weary round of restaurants.

The only reason he had gotten involved with her in the first place was that at the time she reminded him a little of Therese. It hadn't been long before he discovered that she was only a heartless, vapid copy. Their association had continued from sheer apathy on his part.

Anthony leaned back and stretched out his legs; it was pleasant at Raoul's. One could sit for hours as the easygoing waiter piled up saucer after saucer under a coffee cup—the Parisian style of calculating the number of cups served, without hurrying the lounger.

Funny, he thought, how much easier it was to forget in the winter. In the spring, and on the early-summer days like this, he kept harking back to the drowsy days of New Orleans. That was one of the main reasons he had adopted Raoul's: the proprietors, Victor and Odalie Deplis, were from New Orleans, which also reminded him of Therese.

Madame Deplis was a beautiful mulatto. He liked

the mordant and down-to-earth humor of her and her husband. The first time he had asked for "Raoul," Madame Deplis told him there was no Raoul, that the name of the café was a family joke. Anthony had never bothered to ask what the joke was; he respected their privacy as they apparently respected his, never remarking on his extravagant drinking when he had first become their patron, or on how much he had changed since then.

He had been half-crazed with loss when he had come to Paris to handle some international banking business in the City of Light.

Well, he had exorcised some of his demons in a way—those first wild years had offered plenty of distraction. Only this year had he "settled" into a more rational arrangement, with Mariette Saint-Jacques. But she was no shopgirl, he thought dryly. Her socially conscious, "rising" family kept hinting that she should marry.

Anthony raised his head lazily to the waiter, who brought another cup of coffee.

He would never marry anyone, Anthony knew very well. It was time he did the decent thing and broke off with Mariette completely.

Sipping his coffee, Anthony reviewed the stages he had undergone: the initial, tearing grief when Therese would not answer his letters, the angry resentment. Then the painful realization that she still possessed his heart. That had been the worst of all, the months he had been powerless to seek the company of any other woman. Afterward, slowly, he had come back to a kind of life.

And still, through it all, on afternoons like this, he was visited by her ghost, by the passionate images of that one glorious night on the river.

The hope of that had carried him through the worst of the war.

The reminder of war brought his attention back to the newspaper on his table. He glanced at it. These fools, these greedy Prussians and idiotic French, didn't know what they were letting themselves in for.

He read the latest article with a kind of grieving

rage for the stupidity of humankind, no more than
dimly aware of the passersby.

On the edge of his vision he was faintly conscious
that two pretty women had passed.

But he went back to the paper. Paris was famous for
pretty women; they were everywhere. After a while,
one almost ceased to see them anymore.

Therese, with Elianne a step behind, walked up to
the handsome golden-skinned woman intently counting money in a far corner of that café.

Absently the woman murmured, "A moment, please,
*madame.*"

When she had finished counting, Odalie looked up.
"Therese! It cannot be *Therese.* And . . . ?" The huge
eyes surveyed Elianne.

"And Elianne," the girl said, smiling.

Odalie jumped up, embracing them both. "But let
me look at you both. You look as good as the empress." Odalie took Therese's hands and held them
out, examining the elegance of her bronze street dress.

"Better," Odalie declared, making them both laugh.
"You have omitted all the froufrou and the bows, and
the grotesqueness over the *derrière.*"

Just as she had modified the crinoline, Therese had
cavalierly rejected the current trend of wadding fabric
over women's hips, which made them look like hippo-
potamuses from the rear.

Odalie turned to Elianne. "And *you, petit.* I would
never have known you." She took in Elianne's mauve-
pink walking dress, her tiny feathered hat and parasol.
"You know, Tez, this reminds me of when you first
came to New Orleans. You are just that age now, are
you not?" Odalie asked Elianne.

"Yes. Fifteen."

"But oh, my dears, sit down. I will bring us all a
glass of wine—not this vinegar I keep for students and
travelers. I will get a bottle from the cellar."

She hurried off as Therese and Elianne pulled out
the chairs from a nearby table. A small gray tiger-
striped cat wound its way among the other tables,

heading straight for Elianne. The girl stroked the cat, murmuring to it, as Odalie returned, carrying a bottle and three thin goblets on a tray.

Serving them, she smiled at Elianne. "I see you have been honored by Minou. She never goes to strangers like that—only to a Pavan. Did you know that there is actually a street in Paris named for a cat . . . the Street of the Cat That Fishes? You must go there while you are here."

Elianne smiled at her with delight, wide-eyed.

"Which reminds me, how is the dear Charl' . . . and everyone else?"

"They are all splendid," Therese said, not wanting to bring up Charles and her uneasiness over leaving him. It would darken the happy reunion.

"But I was so thrilled when you sent me the *Harper's*," Odalie rushed on. "At last you have become the famous Pavan, as I always knew you would. You are, of course, doing all the salons in Paris, I take it."

"Three this morning," Therese admitted, grinning.

"*Mon Dieu*! Always the workhorse, Tez."

Yes, Therese thought. And Paris was made for romance and gaiety. "But we are going to the opera tonight," she said. "Why don't you and Victor join us?"

"It sounds enchanting. I wish he were here—he has gone to the market. Yes, Tez, I would love that." Odalie chuckled. "It is possible here . . . not like the old days in New Orleans." She sobered. "But these are not good new days, altogether, in Paris. You may have come for our last summer."

"That's just what Charl' and Hortense Dufay told me. Odalie, what will you and Victor do if a war should come?"

"I fear there is no 'if,' Tez. As a matter of fact, we are planning to go to America. To New York, after the summer is over," Odalie said. "It is the next best thing to Paris—and there will be no war there."

"Oh, I'm so happy," Therese exclaimed, grabbing her friend's hand. "Then we will not be so far away from each other, and—"

"Ah! But here is Victor! Now you must meet my husband."

In the flurry of greetings and introductions to the handsome, amiable mulatto, no one noticed that the elegant-looking foreigner at a table outside had paid his bill and walked away.

From their box at the Théâtre Lyrique, Therese looked down on the glittering company below.

Elianne murmured, "I think I am in fairyland, Tez."

"So do I." Therese thought back to her first visit to the opera and her own excited response to the theater's pageantry and glamour. She was glad to give her young sister such pleasure, resolving that on the way back they would spend a few days in New York, so the girl could enjoy the delights of the city.

"I have never seen so many flowers in a city," Elianne confided to Odalie, who was sitting with Victor slightly behind them. "And the air is *silver* . . . it is amazing!"

"That is true," Odalie said. "It is the result of the sunlight, and the twilight, on these ancient gray buildings." She studied Elianne with her great dark eyes, probably unaware that she herself was the object of many stares. She still wore her hair like a brief, startling black helmet, striking with her pale golden skin, her simple gown the color of a blue-green peacock's wing.

Their whole party, Therese supposed, was noticeable—the two "foreign" women in company with Odalie and Victor; Elianne vivid in her golden dress, and Therese herself stunning in a coral-pink evening gown of silk grosgrain with a narrow overskirt of misty ivory lace. Aside from the brilliance of their gowns, the women of their party were dressed with almost scandalous austerity, in contrast to the flounced and bowed, the blossomed and ornamented company around them. Their comparative starkness was likely the cause of whispers behind fans in the other boxes.

Therese smiled broadly, glancing at the clothes of other women. The overintricate designs of Worth were very evident. She felt a greater pride than ever in her own new Pavan, distinctive and very modern in its departure from the current mode. The overskirt scorned the *en panier* draping, showing more of the true shape of her body, and the *basque* corsage was composed entirely of the vivid grosgrain, being merely edged with lace and unconfined by the usual cluster of flowers. Below her pearl collar, she wore a single strand of pearl beads, with a coral medallion; her hair was unornamented, and in her ears, instead of the customary chandelier earrings, she wore coral buttons ringed with seed pearls.

"You have not heard this opera before, then," Odalie remarked to Therese.

"No. It has been sung only in New York." Gounod's new *Roméo et Juliette* had debuted in Paris two years before, and Therese was looking forward to it eagerly; it combined her two favorite pleasures—opera and the plays of William Shakespeare. Even more she anticipated seeing and hearing the matchless Geraldine Farrar.

"I have heard it called 'a love duet with occasional interruptions,' " Odalie commented. "It is indeed beautiful."

The orchestra was tuning up. Therese leaned forward expectantly. She glanced at Elianne; the girl was dazzled, perfectly still, with wide, bright eyes. For an instant Therese was so caught up in enjoying her sister's enjoyment that she almost missed the music, but soon she forgot everything else in the delight of the exquisite melody of Juliet's Waltz; the *Ange Adorable* of the great Madame Farrar.

When, at the end of the second act, Elianne went out with Victor and Odalie for intermission, Therese kept her seat. She liked to spend the intervals quiet and alone; watching the brilliant swirl of people helped her keep the sublime mood of the music, and enabled her to review the costumes she had seen. With all her success, there was still one fashion world closed to her—the costuming for opera. Someday, she resolved, that world would also be open to Pavan.

Her gaze wandered over the chattering, milling operagoers in the other boxes and below. And in an empty box opposite, which had been unoccupied before, she saw a man and woman enter. The woman was quite pretty but so overwhelmed by her flowers, jewels, and ruffles that her small features, Therese thought critically, became insignificant. Therese glanced idly at her escort, who was still half-obscured by the shadow of the box. When he stepped into the light, she recognized Anthony McKay.

Her heart gave such a thud she was afraid it would pound its way through her flesh, that her breast would rend. She took a gasping breath. Her ears rang with the sudden shock, and her head swam. She had rarely in her life felt faint, but she did now, and the whole scene blurred before her eyes.

She took a deep, shuddering breath and hung on to the edge of the box. Her hands were cold, even in their gloves. Trembling, she took up her opera glass and trained it on Anthony's box. His face, abruptly close and clear, made her heart flutter again. He looked so different—cynical, impervious. And yet there was still the faint gleam she remembered in those pale gray eyes restlessly scanning the house, a ghost of the old Anthony.

The woman could be his wife.

Therese lowered the glass. Then she saw Anthony raise his own glass to his eyes, pointing it at her box. At her.

She saw the reflexive tightening of his fingers. Slowly he lowered the glass. Therese watched him bend to the woman, say something to her briefly, and disappear into the shadows.

He had recognized her.

He was coming to her.

Good God, she couldn't bear it—Anthony, in Paris. Agnes McKay had complained, in the last two years, that her nephew had become a very poor correspondent, that she hardly knew where to find him these days. As far as Agnes knew, he was with his father's bank in New York, and sometimes traveled on its behalf.

Therese's nervousness increased a hundredfold until she could barely get her breath. If the others should return just as Anthony stepped into the box, she was not at all sure that she could control her expression. And what she could say to Elianne, she could not fathom.

She sat there rigidly, turning hot, then cold.

She heard the velvet curtain behind her being pulled aside; there was a sudden mew from its sliding rings.

And then Anthony was sitting in Elianne's chair, beside Therese, looking at her in silence. His face no longer seemed cynical and weary; the restless indifference she had seen through her glass was gone. His very heart was in his brilliant eyes.

Below, the orchestra began to make its tentative noises—the ascending and descending scales of brass and woodwind, the squeaking scrape of strings.

"We have been given another chance," he said abruptly, holding out his hand and grasping hers. She did not withdraw her hand, but she could not speak.

It was true: they were being given a second chance by destiny. It was no accident that both were there tonight.

"Are you alone?"

"No . . . my sister, and friends . . . will soon be coming back." At last she found her voice, and her words sounded breathless and alien in her own ears.

"I will leave you. Please—say that I may come to you to your hotel, Therese."

She hesitated for a timeless instant, then nodded. She gave him the name of her hotel. "I will meet you in the lobby, at midnight."

Anthony raised her hand to his lips and kissed it. Then he got up and hurried away.

It seemed only seconds later that the others rushed into the box and the third-act overture began.

All through the rest of the act, Therese was barely conscious of the music; she kept stealing glances at Anthony, in the opposite box, and at his angry-looking companion.

Surely she had seen, Therese thought. And it hadn't

even mattered to Anthony. The woman could not be
his wife. Her spirits sang.

She could feel Anthony's eyes on her even when she
looked away.

It was not until the fourth act of the opera that the
music reached her again: the exquisite duet, *O douce
nuit d'amour,* sweet night of love, struck her to the
heart. The perilous secret meeting of the star-crossed
lovers might have been that one brief intimacy of hers
with Anthony, that single night on the light-dappled
river in his dim stateroom.

She knew that across the great space of the Théâtre
Lyrique Anthony McKay was lost in the same reflections; the music soared and gathered power, culminat-
ing in the last duet—"Oh, heaven grant us thy grace."

Triumphant and certain, Therese met his look again
for the last time before that brief, expectant parting,
knowing that they would seize this sign from fate and
never let each other go again, no matter what had
parted them, no matter what obstacles still remained.

"Therese."

Hearing her name repeated softly, she opened her
eyes: the first thing she saw was Anthony's face. The
tenderness in it, the gentle stroking of his hands, struck
her nerves like little bells. She quivered pleasurably,
moving nearer to his sleep-warm body.

His half-parted mouth closed on hers; she stroked
his muscular neck, his wide shoulders, glorying in this
morning revel, the whole night they had spent in each
other's arms, the first of their whole lives.

And amazed, she knew that even after the ecstasy
of that last wild night, they still felt this sweet and
urgent longing. He held her closer; her flesh tingled,
and her veins ran with fire. Her body almost sang with
the hectic coursing of her blood.

He moaned and let his hands slide upward along her
trembling sides, playing with her loosened hair, and
then his fervent mouth abandoned hers to explore
the soft whiteness of her neck, her naked shoulder.

Moving ever nearer, at last they came together: the

throb of pleasure was so sharp she felt as if butterflies
with fiery wings beat at her senses and she teetered on
an aching edge, nothing existing but that velvet ache;
and then she was stabbed with a sweeter ache, tipped
with fire like a flaming arrow; she heard her pleasure-
cry, and his, which seemed torn from the depths of
him.

She tightened her arms around him with a sense of
absoluteness and coming home. Lying in his tight embrace, she marveled at how the face of the whole
world had changed, because their love had been
unchanging.

"You are so lovely in the morning," Anthony said
softly. He sat on the edge of the bed, watching Therese enjoy her first sip of coffee from a fragile Sèvres
cup. The late-morning sun, slanting through a wide
bedroom window of his flat, revealed the golden lights
in his tousled pale brown hair.

His sharp gray eyes looked blue and drowsy and
tender, accentuated by his slate-colored dressing gown
and the summer sky behind him.

"So lovely," he repeated, playing with her loosened
hair.

"Even in your robe?"

"Especially in my robe." Smiling, he took the cup
from her and rolled up each sleeve of his red dressing
gown a little higher. "There." He gave her back the
cup. "And especially on our first morning. I am in
Odalie's debt for her arrangements."

This was the first full night and morning they had
contrived; Odalie, with her intuitive knowledge of these
matters, had invited Elianne to stay with her and
Victor for a few days so that she might "get acquainted
with the Left Bank" of the Seine.

"Paris is wonderful and strange," Therese murmured.
"Love is treated with fine tolerance."

After the restrictions of New Orleans, and Cincinnati, she had been astonished at how matter-of-factly
Parisians took her comings and goings. For Elianne's
sake, after the first evenings of their reunion, Therese

had insisted on going back to her hotel in the late-night hours, observed indifferently by the hotel's attendants.

"New York will be the same, Therese. It is an immense place, where no one minds another's business." Anthony took up her free hand and kissed it.

"I can't wait, I can't wait," she said eagerly. She set her cup down and took his face between her hands, drawing it down to hers, planting a multitude of light kisses on his cheeks and nose and closed eyelids. "It will take a little time, but I am going to make it happen."

"It makes utter sense, my darling." He held her close, stroking her hair with gentle fingers. "You have reached a point in your career that demands it. Oh, Therese, then everything will be perfect. We will never have to be apart anymore."

"There will be problems, of course," she reminded him softly, thinking of George.

Anthony was still in her embrace for a moment. Then he held her closer, saying, "I know that. But it doesn't matter. We will deal with them. We will deal with everything."

He sounded so confident, so sure and happy, that she let herself believe again.

Anthony murmured against her hair the words that had become a refrain between them during their dream-like week together, the words "When I think how close we came to missing each other . . ."

Therese burrowed against his neck, smiling to remember his amazement that the proprietors of Raoul's were her friends, that he had not even see her and Elianne on the day of her first visit to Odalie.

"We will never be apart again," she whispered. "I promise you."

No, she vowed in silence, never. If their love was a sin, so be it. She knew, now that they had found each other after so many years of absence and hunger, that nothing was going to separate them anymore. "I could not live," she added, "if I had to give you up now."

He turned her face up to his and began to kiss her

with slow gentleness; soon the kiss took fire, and they began roughly undressing each other, until their bare bodies clung together in a new embrace.

Afterward they lay a little apart, with half-closed eyes and clasped hands, lost in the wonder of the joy regained. "I feel that I have come back from the dead," she whispered.

"We have, Therese." His hand slipped up her arm, squeezing her naked shoulder. He raised his body, leaning over her, holding her face between his hands, gazing down at her solemnly.

Suddenly, with a swift change of mood, a smile that made him look like the Anthony she had first met, he said, "It's time for your *petit déjeuner*. I will serve you."

Donning his robe, he went to the round lace-covered table with its centerpiece of roses. Watching him, she thought tenderly: He makes everything lovely, for my delight.

He folded a pristine napkin over his arm like a well-trained waiter and brought her one of the covered dishes. *"Madame."* With a flourish he took off the silver cover.

She gasped. On the empty dish were a wonderful brooch and matching earrings: the brooch was a golden peacock whose outspread wings were paved in topaz, blue-green Australian opals, and pale yellow-green peridots, capturing the peacock's actual hues. The jewelry was so extravagantly beautiful that she was speechless.

"In many languages," he said, "the word for 'peacock' is very like 'Pavan.' It seemed such as apt symbol for you, with its beauty and its pride."

He went to the table again and returned with another covered dish. "The next course," he said lightly. This time the uncovered dish disclosed a glittering brooch of rubies and diamonds spraying out from a central flower, with diamond strands below that danced like a fall of rain, and earrings in a harmonizing design. "This," Anthony said quietly, "commemorates a certain rainy day."

"Oh, my dear." She embraced him. "I have never owned anything so wonderful. No one has ever . . ."

"From now on, someone will, always." He gathered her to him. "You have had little, most of your life, but work and sacrifice and effort. From now on, I am going to indulge you in every possible way. I am going to spoil you for the rest of our lives, as you deserve."

Delighted, she slipped the peacock earrings into her ears, and he led her to the table for the dishes "with food on them," and served her *petit déjeuner*.

She had never known what it was to be so happy. When she was dressed again in her blue-green gown, she pinned the peacock brooch on her *basque*, admiring it. Anthony accompanied her back to her hotel.

They had had five glorious, bewitching nights and days, wandering everywhere from the Louvre to the glittering marts of the Rue de la Paix. Anthony had "run into" her and Elianne again and again—at Nôtre Dame, at the *Folies Bergère*—cleverly devising their sacred time alone, the sweet ritual that ended the evening and began the day.

One morning as they returned to the hotel, the attendant at the desk called out, *"Madame,* a cable has arrived for you."

Therese tore the message open. It was from Charl'. "COME HOME," she read. "CHARLES HAS RUN AWAY."

There was only one place he could have gone—to Petit Anse.

Wordlessly she handed the cable to Anthony. Below her pain was an undercurrent of resentment. Anthony had been right the day he gave her the brooches. All her life, she had been burdened with some damned responsibility or another. And now, having had so few days of happiness for the first time in her life, she had to take up the burdens again.

Reading the cable, Anthony looked grim. All the joy had fled from his eyes.

Consoling them both, she said, "It doesn't matter, my beloved. This time it will only be *au revoir*. In a few months we'll be together in New York."

And she saw her own hope shining again from his eyes.

\*       \*       \*

Climbing the familiar hill toward Petit Anse with the silent Charl', Therese was overwhelmed. Ever since the clamorous arrival in New York, her life had had the unreal quality of a terrible dream, with no hope of waking. In Paris, Anthony had aroused her from years of emotional sleep; abruptly she had been enclosed again in the lurid succession of events—the encounter with the remorseful Hammills in Cincinnati, haggard with guilt over their inadequate guardianship of Charles at the resort; George's worsening condition; and then the beginning of another tiring journey, with no time to rest from the first.

Finally Charl' broke his grim silence. "Are you all right? You look so pale."

Ignoring his question, Therese asked him for the hundredth time, "What if he is not here?"

"He must be here, Tez. I know your first instinct was right."

She glanced at her brother. "Please, Charl' . . . you have promised. You will hold onto your temper."

He nodded, but his expression did not reassure her. He had the same look he had always had as a boy when he was ready to fight. "How the fool thinks he can get away with this . . ." Charl' muttered. "Don't worry, Tez. I have promised I won't kill him. And I won't."

They walked up the familiar stairs to the veranda of Petit Anse, toward the imposing entrance Therese had never crossed.

She raised her head, straightening her shoulders. Charl' sounded the gleaming knocker in the form of an eagle with outspread wings, and Therese felt the bitter irony of their visit. All their lives they had been consumed with curiosity about the splendors of Petit Anse. Now that nothing could have been less important, they were to cross its threshold.

A neat, dark-faced butler opened the door. When Charl' gave him their names, asking for Nicholas Adair, the man's trained face lapsed into surprise: he had obviously taken the Pavans of the bayou for people of fashion.

"I will see if Mr. Nicholas is at home. Will you wait here, please, in the refusal room?" The butler showed them into a small parlor off the long polished hall with its graceful curving stair.

After the door had closed, Charl' murmured, " 'Refusal room' has an ominous ring." He glanced around the stiffly arranged room, with its eighteenth-century furnishings, its sienna-and-white marble mantel and richly carved friezes.

Almost as Charl' finished speaking, the door opened again and Nicholas Adair sauntered into the room. His narrow face was impassive. "*Therese.* Pavan," he said coldly to Charl'. "To what do I owe this . . . honor?" he drawled the word with the clear inflection of annoyance.

"Is my son here?" Therese asked curtly. Her exhaustion was forgotten as she felt the surge of anger.

"You were always so sudden, my dear." Uneasily Therese sensed Charl's rising ire at the contemptuous term of endearment. "May I offer you some refreshment?"

"Offer us an answer," Charl' snapped, moving toward Nicholas.

Nicholas looked at Charl' with unconcealed distaste, but also with consternation. He is afraid of Charl', Therese thought, and she was savagely glad.

"Yes, Pavan. My son is here at Adair's Island, where he belongs." Therese noticed for the first time the sharp changes in Nicholas Adair: his features were unpleasantly pinched, there was a threading of crimson on the whites of his eyes. He drinks, she realized. And he doesn't look quite sane. He could not be sane, to assume they would hand over her son to him.

Therese saw Charl's hands ball into fists. There was a danger-signal color on his cheekbones. "You have kidnapped an eleven-year-old child, Adair. I suggest you bring him to us now."

" 'Kidnapped'?" Nicholas blustered. "The boy arranged this with me, months ago. He wants to live with me. He is my blood, and he knows it now. He knows I am his father."

*Father.*

The word was a silent cry in Therese's head. Now her son knew it all, her lies, her old shame. And he would sit in judgment on her.

"How could you?" Her voice came out in a hoarse whisper.

"How could I *not*?" Nicholas demanded. "It is the truth, and he has heard the truth for the first time in his life. I have told him how you refused to marry me, preferring to run away . . ." He smiled a terrible smile.

"*Refused*!" Therese was flabbergasted. "And you dare to speak of the 'truth,' when you have piled lie upon lie . . ."

Charl' took a step toward Nicholas. "Call the boy." There was menace in his command, and Therese saw Nicholas draw back. Trying to cover his fear, he gave a nervous laugh.

"Since you put it so . . . violently, Pavan, I must accede to your request. Very well, then, you can hear it from the boy, since you will not listen to me." Nicholas went to the door and called out, "Henry. Ask Master Nicholas to join us."

He called the boy by his own name. Nicholas was even trying to take her son's name away from him. Therese was paralyzed with anger.

Nicholas looked at her, reading her reaction. "It was his idea, Therese."

She did not answer, but there was a muffled oath from Charl'; he looked as if he were at the end of his tether.

They heard the boy's quick footsteps down the stairs, and he ran into the room. He was wearing a small replica of Nicholas' elegant suit; even his hair was cut in the way that Nicholas wore his.

Desperately Therese held onto her control.

"*Mother*." The boy stared at her, ignoring Charl'.

Therese went to her son and knelt down before him, taking him in her arms, kissing him all over his face.

He drew back from her. "I am not going back,

Mother. This is where I belong. My father has told me everything." Charles looked up adoringly at Nicholas Adair, and Therese fairly boiled to see Nicholas' air of triumph.

Therese got up and looked solemnly down at the boy. She was resolved not to cry, not to give in to her pain. Summoning all her control, she told him quietly, "You can't mean that. You can't mean that you want to live away from me . . . and your father."

"George is *not* my father. Nicholas is my father. You told me lies, Mother. You never cared about me. All you care about is your business. I am an Adair," the child declared, sounding so much like Nicholas that Therese was chilled.

"Charles, you must—"

"I'm not Charles," he insisted. "I am Nicholas Adair the Younger." Once again he smiled at Nicholas, so obviously quoting a well-learned lesson that it sickened Therese.

"You are coming home with us," Charl' said firmly. "Now."

"I won't, I won't! I am an aristocrat. I don't belong with bayou people and Yankee merchants. I have my own little house, my *garçonnière* . . . my pony. And when I grow up, this house will belong to me!"

Therese was so overwhelmed by the outburst, by the child's precocious certainty, that she was momentarily speechless. She leaned against a sofa, gripping it with her moist and trembling hand.

"That is enough!" Charl' shouted, and the boy shrank from him as Nicholas had done.

"Please, Charl' . . ." Therese began.

"It is enough," Charl' said more quietly. "Come, Charles, you are going with us now." He went to the boy and took him gently by the arm.

The boy threw off Charl's hand, crying out, "I won't go! I won't. Tell him I'm not going, Father." He turned to Nicholas, beseeching.

Taking the boy's arm again in a firm grip, Charl' reached into his pocket and took out a gun. He pointed it at Nicholas Adair. "We're going now," he said in a hard, level tone. "Don't try to stop us."

Therese, terrified, inhaled a shuddering breath. Nicholas had turned white, and she saw the moisture of fear gather on his narrow face. He did not say a word.

"Let's go, Tez," Charl' said softly.

Still holding the boy by the arm, Charl' walked from the refusal room into the gracious hall. Therese followed, conscious of the goggle-eyed servants gathered there, praying that Nicholas would make no move toward Charl'. If he did, Charl' would surely kill him. She was shaking so that she could barely walk.

Her son was also stiff with fright, walking obediently by his uncle's side. Oh, God, it should not be like this, she agonized. It was unbearable that her own child should have to be terrorized into returning with them. But even now she could not discover another way.

The boy was utterly silent as they got into the dory, and he did not break his stony silence on the train to New Orleans.

When they checked into a hotel to rest before the long return journey north, Therese reluctantly let Charl' lock the boy in his room. "I hate it, Tez," Charl' whispered, his eyes full of pain. "Just as I hated what I had to do at Petit Anse. But I had to. You see that, don't you?"

She agreed, feeling a huge obstruction in her aching throat, the pain of unshed tears.

"He's just a little boy," Charl' went on. "We've got to protect him. That . . . Adair has already begun to change him. You saw that."

"Yes. Every time he opened his mouth, it was Nicholas speaking. But, my God, Charl', he seems to *hate* me. Naturally he puts the worst possible construction on everything Nicholas told him—the things that were true," she added bitterly.

"No, Tez. He doesn't hate you." Charl's voice was gentle. "He's just confused. Have a talk with him. Make him understand. I know you can."

Therese was not so sure. It was natural that the

child should blame her for the fact that he was born without a legal father; natural for him to shrink from a mother who was "bad."

"I hope so," she said.

"I'll have to talk with him too, on the way back," Charl' assured her. "I've got to make him see that his uncle's not some kind of ogre . . . that what happened had to happen." He went on, trying to comfort her. "Adair didn't acquit himself too well, you know. He's not exactly a hero. And that has to weigh heavily with a boy."

"I don't know." Therese frowned. "I'm afraid he'll only look on this as additional evidence . . . that the Pavans are barbarians. Maybe he'll feel closer to Nicholas than ever."

"Tez. You've got to stop looking on the dark side. When we get back, we'll start spending more time with Charles. We'll win him to our side. You'll see."

Therese wished she could agree. But she knew that the battle wasn't over. It had just begun.

Yet soon they would be moving to New York, and she would have Anthony's constant love and support.

In spite of the daunting problem of her son, Therese's irrepressible spirits rose: Dufay would masterfully handle the Cincinnati Pavan, and Therese would have a whole new world to conquer—the mighty city of New York.

# 14

## 1874

Eight years. Eight years.

The words, weighted with their concept, keened in George Madison's brain, the very shape of them a cry. His thoughts were all that was left—thoughts and Therese's visits—so George had become acutely sensitive to his thought-companions.

That such an impotent shell should contain a lucid mind was the worst of ironies. But during this last year he had stopped raging in silence. Now he was only sad. Sad that the greater part of eight years had had to be spent like this.

Therese was the only reason he was still alive. In the early days of his illness, she had been the one to give him hope and determination. And it had looked good for a while—after that first visit to New York, where he had been inspired by the radical doctor, there had been such hope.

George didn't hope anymore. He submitted to the ministrations of the hospital attendants in New York, waited for Therese's visits. And thought.

On this bright October afternoon in 1874, he lay gazing at a blood-red maple tree outside the window. The tree fairly made a sound to his eyes—that brilliant paradox he had discovered once in a book of poems, and understood fully now—the sound of blazing brass instruments in a splendid orchestra.

George was unable to turn his head. The part of the room he could see, the part where Therese sat when she visited, had been adorned with three exquisite

large paintings, one of which she had brought back
from Paris in 1869. She had even had the hospital
furniture replaced with some things from Cincinnati to
make the place less impersonal, less desolate.

Feeling a peculiar elation, George let his memory
range over his picture album, the immense picture
album of his life that his mind looked at again and
again. His eyes filled once more as he recalled his last
bad attack, when he had dimly heard Therese protesting to the doctor that she would not send her husband
away to a hospital. Finally, though, there had been
nothing else to do; if he could have spoken he would
have told her that the doctor was right, that he had to
go. The only way the doctor had been able to persuade her was to tell her that it was better for George,
that they would be able to do more for him here.

George thought about the books she had read to
him, the newspapers she had held up to his eyes so that
he might see and share in her triumphs. She'd had
some of the newspaper and magazine articles framed,
as he had done for her in Cincinnati. She said again
and again, "Pavan was born because of you." It gratified him that Therese was a famous woman now; New
York had made a bold bid to become the fashion
capital of the world, and his own Therese was right
there in the forefront.

She had even had a photographer take pictures of
the new salon, and described the colors to him. The
New York salon was patterned after the old one in
Cincinnati.

And with all she had to do, she was still managing
to keep Madison-Pavan going under Dufay's direction
in Cincinnati; it touched George that she was doing it
more for him than for anything else, because Madison's
had always been so important to him.

On this October day, he remembered pleasurably
the visits of the others, Elianne and Madame Dufay,
Nell and Charl', even Rubine and Berthe Levitsky.
None of them ever failed to come to see him when
they visited New York.

Charles had never come. Therese tried to make

excuses for him; George had no rancor against the boy. But he knew, no matter how good a face Therese tried to put on it, that Charles had grown more and more distant from his mother, ever since he had run off to Louisiana. There was always an undernote of uncertainty and sadness in her voice when she reported on Charles's doings to George. He longed to be able to tell her that it was time to let the boy go.

But now he longed more than anything for her to appear. The pretty clock indicated that it was almost time. There was a different feeling today. He somehow sensed that this would be the last time he would ever see her.

And there she was, at last, smiling, dressed in a wonderful, heartwarming color, a color that was neither orange nor pumpkin nor gold, but all of them. She held a luxuriant bunch of golden and dark red chrysanthemums, his favorite flower.

"Hello, my darling," she said, and kissed his face. What a glory.

She looked into his eyes; he looked, as well as he was able, watching her arrange the flowers, take new books from her reticule, and newspapers. She showed him the books: there was a new one by Mark Twain, *The Adventures of Tom Sawyer*. George blinked once, indicating that she should read that to him, instead of the newspapers. After she had told him about the last few days, Therese began to read.

A remarkable thing began to happen: he was following the sense, the pleasing sound of the words, comforted by the rhythm of her voice, and yet his mind and awareness were growing and growing, voyaging ranging. He was a child again, in the Ohio summer.

And suddenly he was the old brown river that had brought him Therese; he was with her in New York, walking with her through the pristine snow, showing her the first little House of Pavan, a strong and vital man again.

He was surrounded by the strains of mighty music.

Therese's voice had faltered. She was no longer

reading. She leaned to him with terror in her soft black eyes.

He longed to say, "It's all right, my darling." Astounded, he heard a sound from his own throat. For the first time in four years he was going to speak.

The terror in her eyes receded; there was a spark of hope. George had never felt so light: he said, almost without effort, "So good . . . Tez . . . so beautiful . . . made life . . . a glory . . . free now . . . free . . ."

Throwing down the book, she leaned her head against him. He ached to hold her, just to take her once more in his arms. She raised her head and looked into his eyes; he knew it was the last time he would ever speak with his. Summoning all the power of his mind, he brought the years of his devotion into that look: victorious, he knew she heard.

He made his final effort: "You . . . free now, my love . . . free . . ."

The last picture George saw was her beautiful tear-stained face, the bright flowers behind her, and the vivid maple tree . . . before there was the all-encompassing star of huge, pale golden light.

George Madison was dead.

# 15

Therese Pavan McKay smiled at her husband and raised the hood of her waterproof cloak against New York's light April drizzle. She lifted her face to the refreshing moisture.

"You have ordered everything," she said softly. "Even the rain." She slipped her arm through his.

Anthony squeezed her hand. "Of course. I will always have a soft spot for this month and this weather." The day they had first met had been exactly like this, Therese remembered. She had never felt so cherished or so free as she did on this afternoon of gentle rain, emerging from the judge's chambers.

Therese had asked Anthony to arrange everything for their wedding. And he had. It was heavenly; for the first time in her whole life, Therese Pavan was not responsible for anything at all except her wedding clothes and Odalie's.

For her wedding, Therese had devised a revolutionary ensemble, never seen anywhere before, a low-cut dress of rich rose-colored satin—the color she had been wearing when they met—with a snug cuirass, high-collared jacket which she foresaw as the coming shape. Thus the gown served both as a suit and an afternoon dress.

She had written to her family, to Madame Dufay back in Cincinnati, and to Charles at school, about the event, deciding to have no one present except Odalie and Victor. Anthony had fervently agreed. Her family was overjoyed, but Charles . . . She would not think of that now. Not now. Not on this day they had waited for so very long.

Odalie and Victor had disappeared after the ceremony.

Anthony handed her into their newly purchased carriage, and the soft hood of her cloak slipped back. The carriage started off without a stated direction. "Where are we going?" she said, smiling, "And what happened to Victor and Odalie?"

He lifted her gloved hand and kissed it, looking down into her eyes with tenderness. "This will be your first surprise.

"This is only the beginning," Anthony murmured, sliding his arm around her. "I told you in Paris that one day I would make life easy for you. From now on, it's going to be one long pleasure."

Her heart was so full she could not speak; she lifted her face to his and their mouths blended into a gentle, soft caress.

The carriage slowed down. Therese looked out with surprise. "But this is Raoul's!" Odalie's and Victor's elegant, now-famous restaurant which in this year of 1875 surpassed Delmonico's. Therese laughed with pleasure. "So *this* is why they didn't join us for luncheon."

Anthony didn't answer; a mischievous smile played on his mouth.

A smiling attendant opened the gilded entrance door. The great restaurant was utterly empty; all the tables and chairs had been removed from its central space, and only one small round table and two gilded chairs were set there in the dimmed golden light.

From somewhere, behind tall potted palms, an orchestra was softly playing. Playing the waltz the orchestra had played at Agnes McKay's when Therese and Anthony had first danced with each other.

She turned to him, speechless, feeling tears of happiness gather in her eyes. He took her cloak and handed it to the attendant, and they moved into each other's arms, waltzing in wide circles around the polished floor.

The first waltz melded into another, and still another, and once again, as she had so long ago, Therese had the sensation of dancing on a field of flowers, watching the urns of roses, the palms, the pale golden lights whirl past.

When the waltzes ended, she heard the strains of another familiar air—the *Un dì felice*, from *Traviata*. Looking solemnly into her eyes, Anthony held her hand in his, inviting her to the small round table, with a rosy cloth and crystal vase containing one budding flower the color of her gown, among its other glittering appointments.

"This is like a dream," she said as he seated her at the table. He uncorked a dark green bottle of Moët, nested in a silver bucket, and poured the bubbly wine into fragile stems. They lifted the glasses to each other, wordless. She smiled as she recognized the air of "Drink to Me Only with Thine Eyes," and then love music from the opera *Roméo et Juliette*, that souvenir of their reunion in Paris. "*La vie en rose.*"

"In all my life," she added, "I have never known before what happiness was." Anthony reached across the table for her left hand; raising it, he watched the glimmer of light on her circlet of diamonds before he brought her hand to his lips.

"Neither have I, Therese. Not even in Paris. Even there, the shadow of . . . interruption lay over everything. Not anymore," he added in triumph. "Not anymore. Tonight I will fall asleep with my wife in my arms, and wake with her in the morning."

For an instant they merely looked at each other in perfect happiness, enjoying the sound of the music. She recognized the melodies of arias they had heard, so many nights, from separate boxes in New York, during the long years their love had had to remain undeclared.

Anthony seemed to intuit what she was thinking, because he said joyfully, "And from now on, Mr. and Mrs. Anthony McKay will occupy their own box at the opera."

The tears blurred her eyes again. To lighten the great solemnity of the moment, she said, "May I serve you, Mr. McKay?" She indicated the little plates of prettily arranged food.

He laughed. "I have no appetite at all. And you?"

"None whatsoever."

"Then let me take you to the next mysterious destination," he said, sounding as conspiratorial as a child about to show some treasure to an adult. He had never sounded like that before—Therese had always thought of him as a pillar of strength, the one to lean on. Their time together had not been carefree time with much laughter, but snatched, serious hours crammed with all the desperation of their hidden love, and darkened by imminent parting. From now on, she thought with delight, we will have time, so much blessed time; leisure to be easy and light. Finally to be young, gay as children.

"Lead on," she directed. He hustled her into her cloak, then into the carriage, which headed westward to the Hudson River.

She asked no questions as the coachman gave over their luggage to the attendant of a private steam yacht and Anthony led her aboard.

They sat below the roof of a covered deck, where still another table was set with food and wine. Lighter-hearted now, they ate and drank as the boat proceeded upriver. "It won't be long," Anthony promised. "And I think this place will amuse you."

It seemed no time at all before they reached a wooded landing where a smartly dressed black coachman in a tall silk hat waited beside a small carriage on the shore.

When they reached the carriage, the man touched the brim of his hat, saying, "Good evening, madam . . . Mr. McKay."

"Good evening, Jeb." Anthony smiled at the driver. "You're right on the mark."

"Mr. Gould told me I better take good care of you and your new missus." Jeb's eyes twinkled.

Therese smiled at the good-natured driver as he handed her in, and asked Anthony when they were seated, "Who's Mr. Gould?"

"Harold's an old friend of mine. His family owns the house where we'll be staying. They're in Europe

now and we have *carte blanche.* I thought it might be
something a little different for us . . . instead of the
usual hotel."

His casual reference to the house left Therese totally unprepared for what she saw a little later: the
place was a castle from a fairy tale. She was speechless. The gigantic structure was frosted with turrets
and towers, pinnacles and gables and stained-glass windows. Anthony chuckled when he saw her expression.

"This was considered startling when it was built
forty years ago," he said, "in the era of Greek tem-
ples. All it needs is a moat. But I thought you deserved at *least* a castle . . . since we can't go to Europe
now."

Jeb led them through a marble entrance hall replete
with antique motifs—a vaulted ceiling, leaded windows—to
a dramatic flight of curving stairs.

Glancing back, Therese noticed that two men dressed
like footmen—footmen!—trailed behind with their luggage. The men seemed to have materialized from
nowhere.

"You'll be in the State Bedroom, sir," Jeb said to
Anthony.

The footmen placed their luggage gently near a massive chest in an amazing Gothic bedroom. "When you
want to unpack, ma'am, just ring for the maid." Jeb
gestured at a brocade bell-pull near the massive chest.
Then he and the men withdrew.

Therese and Anthony stood gazing at each other in
the gathering dusk, green-tinted by the great trees
outside the leaded windows. He spoke her name in a
whisper, and with great gentleness removed her fragile
hat and put it on a velvet chair.

Then slowly he unfastened her cloak and her satin
jacket, and began to remove her clothes, garment by
garment. Watching him, Therese was astonished once
again by the power of their desire after all the last
years together.

He knelt before her, holding her slender ankles in
his hands, kissing her bare feet. She submitted with
delight to his caresses, fondling his head with her

hands. She looked down into his upturned, worshiping
face, before he lowered it again to continue his ardent
caressing of her excited flesh.

She felt his hot lips on her skin, the stroking of his
strong fingers that traced the shape of her legs and the
slight, bewitching roundness of her hips and narrow
waist; she trembled as he rose and his hands reached
upward to cup her vibrant breasts.

He stood now, holding her nearer and nearer, kissing her so deeply that she almost cried out for breath,
and carrying her to the span of the great Gothic bed.
He rid himself of his clothes; Therese looked up at
him, overcome as she had always been by the sight of
his magnificent body. He was more beautiful than
ever, she thought: ten years ago he had looked like
the classical statue of an ancient youth. Now his mus-
cularity had greater power. He was more than ever a
man.

His brilliant light gray eyes swept over her like
loving hands. He lowered himself to the bed and his
shapely head sought out the center of her body; she
felt the rhythmic beginning of that caress so poignant
that she cried out. The sensation became a tiny point
of burning light within her, a minuscule point of pleasure so acute that it surpassed anything she had ever
felt before. Her mind cried out: It is because we are
free, truly free, at last; then the small burning light
widened into a great circle of fire, rising upward in
shuddering rings to devour her.

And then she felt another new delight as they took
their joy together, and her fires lit narrowly again,
thinned and widened, this time with even more stunning power, into a wide and wheeling flame of broken
light. The world dissolved; she felt, rather than heard,
his glad outcry.

They drifted off together into sleep.

When she opened drowsy eyes, the leaded panes
were dark. She felt the sweet weight of Anthony's
head on her shoulder. He was deeply asleep. She
smiled at the sight of his peaceful face, and she kissed
his forehead, glad to see the lines of strain erased.

Anthony stirred in his sleep, burrowing nearer to her breast.

Holding him, Therese studied the remarkable room with clearer eyes. The vaulted ceiling, shadowy in the dim light, was painted in Gothic patterns of gilt and blue and scarlet. Very gently she removed her arm from below his head and eased herself from under the royal-blue coverlets. Padding barefoot to her trunk, she retrieved a frail wrapper and heelless satin slippers.

She wandered to one of the leaded windows and looked out. In the gathering dark, she could still make out the sweeping view of the Hudson River. She looked back at Anthony, overpowered by a whole new tenderness. He had done so much, planned with such precision, brought her to such a magical place.

She saw him reach out an arm; when it encountered emptiness, a slight frown creased his handsome brow. Smiling to herself, Therese stole back to the bed, kicked off her slippers, and lay down beside him, taking his hand. It touched her heart to see his brow relax again at the feel of her. Lying back on the pillows, she clasped his hand and gave herself up to remembering.

She had never loved him quite so much as she had last autumn. Anthony had delicately refrained from coming to her after George's death, and his sensitivity had extended even to the card that arrived with his exquisite flowers: he had written "Agnes and Anthony McKay." Tears had come to Therese's eyes, reading that; Agnes McKay had died five years before, and Therese still missed her. When she recalled the affection Agnes had had for George, Therese had been overtaken by fresh pity.

George had been cheated of so much—true love of a wife, the respect of the child he had so eagerly adopted as his own, a long full life of friends and of fulfillment. In those early weeks after his death, Therese had suffered horribly from guilt, still pained by Charles's withdrawal from George and saddened by the boy's indifference to his stepfather's passing.

And Anthony, bless him, bless him—Therese withdrew her hand and stroked his ruffled hair—had some-how known what she was going through, because he, too, had shared in her endless guilt; she had always felt that. The only communication he made with her at all was a little note saying, "When you want me to come to you, send for me."

He had not considered his own loneliness and long-ing; he had never even hinted of their hard-won free-dom. The price of that freedom had been too terrible, and Therese knew that Anthony felt that as deeply as she.

After long weeks, she had finally sent for him, but the comfort of their reconciliation was followed by the months of waiting for her mourning to end so they could marry.

Responding to the touch of her fingers on his hair, Anthony stirred, opening his eyes. He pulled her into his arms again, murmuring. "Therese, Therese . . . think of it. You will not have to go home anymore."

"Oh, darling, I know. We are home now. And *we* are home."

Late that night, they sat on a brocade love seat in the castle's art gallery, enjoying the cozy sound of crackling flames in the huge marble cave called a fireplace. The weather had turned wet and wild and colder. It amazed Therese that they had still not seen a servant, all the evening: Anthony had given direc-tions over a speaking tube for dinner in the small dining room and fires in several of the downstairs chambers.

When they went downstairs, dinner was all laid out, with the various dishes on an elaborate carved side-board, and they served themselves. Later, they took a tour of the castle's first floor. "Choose your sitting room," Anthony invited her, smiling. And after a survey of the library and the music room, Therese chose the gallery.

Now Anthony rose and went to a small octagonal table where jewel-colored decanters of wine and frag-ile glasses were set. "I am going to serve you *strega*," he said, with a smile. "There is a myth that those who drink the witch's wine together will love each other always."

He took up a cut-glass flagon of the golden-green liquid and poured them each a tiny glass. They touched glasses and drank, looking at each other with solemn eyes.

Enjoying the new-leaf color of the liqueur, tinged orange by the light of the fire, she whispered, "It looks like a jewel, Anthony. It is so beautiful."

"A *jewel*. Good God!" he exclaimed. "I'd forgotten. Don't move. I'll be right back." Mystified, she waited, hearing him rush along the hall and run up the huge curving stair. In no time at all he was back, holding a big velvet casket in both hands.

Solemnly he put the casket in her hands, with an almost ritual gesture, saying, "These have been in my family for generations. My maternal grandmother told me when I was just a child that someday these would belong to my wife." He smiled. "She was dark-eyed, like you . . . and I adored her. So, happily, these things should look beautiful on you too."

Therese opened the casket, touched beyond words. Inside was a treasure trove—a brooch and earrings of stamped gold set with blood-red rubies, intricate hair ornaments of baroque pearls in unusual colors, combs set with turquoise and coral, bracelet-and-earring sets of diamonds and honey topaz, Australian opals, and unique yellow diamonds.

"It is like a tale from the Arabian Nights," she breathed.

"That's what I want your life to be, Therese."

Deeply moved, she put the casket aside and took his face between her hands. He moved his head so that his mouth could reach her fingers.

"I want to make it up to you," he murmured. "The . . . years apart, the sorrows . . . the difficulties and the . . . longings."

She understood him so well by now that she knew what he meant by the last: he even wanted to make up to her for the deprivation she had suffered as a child,

for the wound to her pride imposed by Nicholas Adair.
For the sake of that very high pride, he used the
gentlest, most oblique means of expressing these things.

"I thought I could not love you more than I did
already. I was wrong," she said tenderly, kissing his
lips.

They held each other for a long moment in happy
silence, and then he said abruptly, with a change of
tone, "And I want you to have *fun!*"

He leaned back and studied her. "My solemn and
responsible Pavan . . . you were never much of a
child, were you, my darling?"

She shook her head.

"Well," he said merrily, "we are going to have a
good time. There are so many things we've never done
together . . . so many places you haven't been. Near
places," he assured her. He had agreed with regret to
her request for a short honeymoon trip—Charles would
be coming home from school soon, and there were
other matters that made a long journey impractical.
"Saratoga, for instance. Do you think you'd like that?"

"I'd love it! Do you know, I've never been to a
horserace in my whole life?" she demanded.

"We'll remedy that, whenever you're bored with the
castle. Tomorrow, the next day, anytime you say. And
then, if you tire of Saratoga, we'll think of something
else." He put his arm around her, and she leaned
against him. "I am going to spoil you . . . and spoil
you."

Therese was moved almost to tears. It was like a
dream.

"Do you know what I want right now?" she asked
him teasingly.

"What? Anything, Mrs. McKay."

"To sit up with you all night." He laughed. "After
all those afternoons," she added wryly, "and the long,
long nights of wanting you . . . it is sheer heaven just
to think of that."

"If it's going to be this easy for me to spoil you, it's
not much of a challenge. But your wish is my command. We will sit here until the dawn."

And he held out his arm, inviting her within its circle. They stared into the orange fire, wordless, ecstatic.

Therese closed her eyes, resolving not to think of Charles or of anything that awaited them beyond this enchanted interval of forgetting.

## 16

Therese and Anthony returned to New York at April's end on a summery afternoon.

When the carriage passed her flat at Eighteenth Street, which they planned to occupy for the time being, she asked in surprise, "Aren't we going home?"

"As a matter of fact, we *are*." Anthony wore his conspirator's look, which signaled a surprise. So she asked no questions as the carriage turned into Gramercy Park. It was an area Therese had always admired, with its pretty houses ornamented with cast-iron porches and balconies surrounding a neat locked park. That private park struck her as the height of luxury, and she had often thought how much it would appeal to Charles.

The carriage drew up before a house on the southwest side of the square, a tall white house with lacy black trim that reminded her of the finer houses in New Orleans.

Handing her down to the sidewalk, Anthony said, "*This* is home . . . if it meets with your approval."

Thrilled, she preceded him up the short flight of stairs and he unlocked the shiny black front door.

The spacious entrance hall led to a parlor of exquisite proportion with a mantel of cloud-gray marble. Therese surveyed the dining room, where the marble was a rich siena color.

"Oh, *Anthony*." She turned to him. "If the rest of it is like this, you may take my 'approval' for granted."

His look of relief touched her to the heart.

"Let's go upstairs!" She pulled at his arm, and he laughed at her childlike impatience. The upstairs was even better, she found: the master bedroom was immense, and there was a dressing room and two more big rooms that would be perfect for Charles and Elianne. "I love it . . . I *love* it," she said, hugging Anthony to her.

"I'm so relieved, so glad. You must have thought I was mad, to buy a house without consulting you first. But the opportunity was so great, I couldn't help myself." Anthony laughed a little, and she grinned at him. "It's been *years* since a Gramercy house has been offered for sale. They're usually passed down from generation to generation."

"I can see why." Therese barely heard his last comment, though; she was already leaping ahead, in her imagination, to the furnished house—the parlor walls would be painted a soft yellow, with pale gray moldings to harmonize with the mantel; she could visualize her treasured French and American Empire pieces, with their glowing russet wood, against the yellow walls.

And Elianne's room would be a bower for a princess, she decided. Its gray-white marble would look exquisite with walls painted the lavender-pink that was her sister's favorite color.

Charles's room would be his favored stormy gray-blue, with touches of brass and scarlet . . . and the master bedroom—oh, that would be the best of all. Therese could see roses and bronze, subtle earth colors.

Anthony's chuckle aroused her from her daydreams. "You are already decorating," he teased her fondly. She nodded, smiling.

"Well, you must put that off for an hour," he remarked with a grin. "Right now, there's this."

He reached into a pocket and brought forth a big golden key, handing it to her with a flourish.

She examined it more closely. "*Anthony* . . . real *gold*?"

"Real gold. All of the fortunate residents of Gramercy Park have them. Would you like to use it now?"

"I'd like nothing better."

They went happily down the graceful stairs and out

of the house, crossing the sidewalk to the eight-foot-high iron fence. Anthony led Therese to the gate and showed her how to unlock it.

After strolling along an immaculate path, they sat down on one of the wooden benches in the shade of a venerable tree. Therese looked around with enormous pleasure—it was an oasis of green peace, right in the heart of the titanic city. At that hour, there were few residents in sight, only one stately old man reading a newspaper and a small girl, accompanied by a nurse-maid, playing with a puppy.

"It's lovely," Therese said quietly. "We are going to be so happy here." She took Anthony's hand. "Once again you have given me a wonderful, wonderful thing." She glanced at the key in her lap. "The golden key," she murmured, smiling, "to peace, to happiness." Looking up into the brilliant light gray eyes, she was impressed as always by their power. "Anthony, you give and give . . . I sometimes wonder what I can ever give you in return."

He looked astonished. "*Therese.*" His voice was tender, reproachful. "Surely you know. You must have always known—you gave my life its first real meaning, the first time I saw you. And now you have brought me back to life, from the death of Paris . . . from the fragment of a life we've had the past five years. 'What can you *give* me,' " he mocked her gently, picking up her hand and holding it against his cheek.

After an instant of silence he added, "As a matter of fact, you gave me a gift in Saratoga . . . and all during our honeymoon."

Therese stared at him, puzzled. "Saratoga?"

"Yes." He leaned back, holding her hand in his. "Do you remember that day we ran into the Lawrences at the races?" She nodded. "I was very annoyed when Hilda Lawrence said, in that feline way, 'But of course you know Marian, Mrs. McKay.' "

"But I do know her, and like her," Therese said calmly.

Anthony pressed her hand. "Yes, from the salon.

But not socially. You must have felt the irony of it, and you never said a word."

"I was too happy," she said. "I didn't care about anyone but us."

"I didn't either . . . and *don't*. But I want to tell you how things are between me and my father. We've been at odds for a long time, more than ever now." Anthony stopped, chagrined. He colored.

Therese thought, His father disapproves of me, but Anthony didn't want to say it. He's trying to save my feelings. She maintained a bland expression and made no comment.

Anthony went on, "I've resigned from the bank. I'm going to be working in a brokerage house. As to visits—I'd rather we didn't visit my mother and sister at the family house."

"Of course not. It goes without saying, if that is your wish."

He raised her hand again and kissed it. "I want to present them to you—in our house, Therese. When I told my sister, Marian, that we were going to be married, she was enormously happy for me. We have always been close. Mother has assured me that she will be very glad to know you. She's already a great admirer of yours, you know."

"Yes." Therese smiled. "I was so delighted when she and Marian came to the salon so many times. It was very difficult, though, to speak of you only in connection with your aunt and Cincinnati." Therese grinned.

Anthony chuckled. "You're a positive Talleyrand in your diplomacy." He sobered quickly. "Something I hated the necessity for, while I couldn't help admiring it. Thank God, Therese . . . that part of our lives is over."

They were both quiet, thinking of the difficult years of their secret association, that "secret" which was an open one to so many people.

"Anyway," he said in a more cheerful tone, "Marian said she'd be writing to you after we came back, so there should be a letter from her any day."

"I look forward to that. I've always liked her, from

the first. To begin with, she looks so much like *you*."
She gave him a quick light kiss; his eyes lit up.

She hated, when he looked so happy, to bring up
the matter of Charles, but it had to be done. "I'm
afraid we might still have other difficulties to face,
Anthony."

"You must mean Charles." He found his answer in
her eyes. "I'm afraid he's never liked me."

"He's never *known* you," she protested. "You see,
he'll never like anyone for a father except . . . Nicholas Adair. Just as I told you after we brought him back
from Petit Anse."

"What happened, darling, when you wrote to him
about us?"

She flushed miserably. "He . . . he didn't even answer my letter. That in itself was an answer."

"I can understand that," Anthony said tolerantly.
"When . . . George died, the boy must have had hopes
that you would marry Adair. That's what I gathered,
although you never put it into words."

"That's exactly what he hoped." To Therese's relief
it was easier than she'd expected to talk about these
unpleasant subjects. But she should have known: it
had always been like that with Anthony. There was
nothing she could not say to him, and very little that
he did not accept calmly, in his matter-of-fact and
worldly way. "Oh, Anthony, I'm so tired of the battle," she admitted. "He's never forgiven me, or Charl',
for bringing him back north. And over the last five
years, he's grown more and more unreachable. He
never mentions Nicholas, but somehow I think he's
more obsessed than ever with living at Petit Anse."

Anthony put his arm around her. "You're his mother,
and I know you can't be expected to agree, or understand fully. But he's sixteen now. He'll be seventeen
in May. In a few years he'd be going away anyway, for
one reason or another."

"I've thought of that. And it helps. But it's so awful
to think that my own child hates me."

Anthony made consoling noises, and she was comforted by his sympathy. But at the same time, she

knew he really could not understand: he had never
had a child of his own. And his relations with his
family were marked by that comparative distance she
had noticed in other Anglo-Saxons.

Nevertheless, responding to a certain wistful look
about his mouth and in his eyes, she said gently, "But
now I have *you* . . . and you are the center of my life.
Just as you have been for fourteen years . . . and will
be, until I die."

"Oh, Therese." His mouth trembled, and he took
both her hands in his and brought them to his lips. "I
am so grateful. I hoped against hope you might say
something like that. If you felt less . . . I couldn't
endure it."

"I know. I know." She smiled up into his eyes.
"Just remember, always, you are the only one who
ever gave me the golden key."

It seemed to Therese in the weeks that followed that
the golden key had symbolically unlocked a whole new
world of happiness: with the marriage, her creativity
had blossomed, and every day was more gratifying
than the one before. She divided her time between the
salon and the new house, astonished at how much she
was able to accomplish. Her vitality surprised even
herself. In less than a month, she had completed the
decoration and furnishing of the house; chosen Charles's
and Elianne's summer wardrobes for their approval;
and gotten a good head start on her new autumn
Pavans.

Marian McKay Sloan had duly written to her a week
after their return, and she and Anthony's mother were
the first guests in their new house. Marian captured
Therese's heart entirely by confiding that she had worn
for years the "unique gloves" Anthony had sent her
from Madame Therese in Cincinnati, and praised Therese's gift to the skies.

Mrs. McKay, while not as forthcoming as her daughter, accepted Therese with warmth and affection; it
was apparent that she so adored her son that anyone
he chose for a wife would be loved as a matter of

course. Therese was more impressed than ever with
the woman's sweet and unaffected manners. And both
the women were sincere in their admiration of the
house, which she had made a haven of rich, lively
color, a blend of the antique and the homely, marked
by an elegant simplicity. The few Acadian rugs and
spreads and other native artifacts that Berthe had
brought to Cincinnati and passed on to Therese were
perfectly at home among the rich austerity of more
formal pieces.

Marian warmed Therese's heart by remarking, "You
are an artist, of course, creating this harmony. I envy
you."

Impulsively, Therese hugged her, reminded suddenly
of her old friendship with Nell.

When the women were in the master bedroom, putting on their bonnets to leave, Mrs. McKay said quietly to Therese, "I have always admired you, my
dear, for the way you . . . conducted yourself. And
now, seeing how happy you have made my son, I am
sure we are going to be friends." She flushed. Therese
kissed her warmly, very moved.

Noticing Anthony's gratification over the visit after
they were gone, Therese thought dryly: If my son has
such a penchant for "aristocrats," I can't wait for him
to meet my mother- and sister-in-law. The McKays
were the real thing, unlike that sham patrician Nicholas Adair.

Then, as May warmed into early June, she found
her attention being focused again on the business of
the salon.

Pavan's outstanding commission, that early summer
of 1875, was the trousseau of Princess Olivia of England, a young woman after Therese's own heart.

She was enormously flattered that the fragile princess, a strongly individual person, had chosen Pavan
over Worth, Demorest, and the noted Messrs. Redfern,
who now had a New York branch on Broadway. The
princess would marry in October, and she and her
husband planned an extensive tour for their honeymoon.

The tour would extend from Austria, where both the bride and groom planned to indulge their enthusiasm for mountaineering, to the sands of Egypt and all the glittering cities of Europe. For some time, Therese had carefully researched the princess's tastes and habits, creating a remarkably small trousseau. From her correspondence with the princess, Therese had concluded that Princess Olivia was impatient with superfluity, demanding clothes that were versatile, comfortable, striking, and unique.

Faced with that challenge, Therese attacked the project with a passionate ingenuity. The ensembles she had created bowed to the current ideal of "the greatest possible flatness and straightness," according to the fashion press; the look of "a pencil covered with raiment," which, happily, the princess's frail figure carried to perfection. With that, Therese blended her own original style and sense of practicality. She hoped Princess Olivia would approve her designs.

There were a hundred matters to take into consideration, among them the fact that royalty carried no money and therefore generally carried no purse. However, on a honeymoon, there might be a scarcity of attendants, Therese decided, so she included some purses with her designs.

Nevertheless, instead of the hundreds of items specified by *Godey's* for a "proper" trousseau, Therese had limited the princess to fifty. The dresses for morning and afternoon were interchangeable, thanks to clever devices for unbuttoning the fillings of necklines for "instant lowering"—the buttons were hidden from view under delicate double foldings, in the grand French manner—and there were several ensembles inspired by Therese's own wedding suit, low-cut gowns with matching jackets that looked like bodices.

Therese was elated beyond measure by the commission—to think that she had bested Worth himself, and the world-famous Messrs. Redfern!

She had stormed those male bastions that dominated fashion and tailoring. Men still dominated costuming, as well; Therese considered the famous Egyptologist, Mariette, who had recreated the Egypt of the pharaohs for the opening of the opera *Aïda* in Cairo in 1871.

During the summer Therese had been in Paris, preparations for *Aïda* were already under way; then the war had intervened in 1870 and the costumes could not be shipped out of Paris. When Therese first heard the name Mariette Bey, she had reacted with envy and surprise. It sounded like a woman's name. She had been devastated to learn that the full name was Auguste-Édouard Mariette, the "Bey" a courtesy title.

But Mariette was no more infallible than Worth and Redfern. Someday Pavan might replace him, too.

At the moment, however, Princess Olivia was the first order of business.

On the morning of the first of June, a few days before Charles was expected to return, Therese nervously waited for the arrival of the princess and her modest retinue of one attendant. She was the salon's first royal patron, and the whole staff was electric with excitement.

Therese was posted at the salon entrance, which was a particular courtesy, as patrons usually were shown into her display room. When she saw a carriage draw up before the entrance and a smart footman hand the princess and her lady-in-waiting down to the sidewalk, Therese's heart thudded. This was the assignment that could make or break Pavan, she thought. It simply must succeed.

The Pavan doorman admitted the women with military precision, touching his hat, and the slender young princess came in. Therese was struck by her natural English beauty: Olivia's skin was flawless, rose-tinted white; her eyes were sapphire and her very curly hair, arranged so that it looked as short as a little girl's, was a rich mahogany brown. She gave Therese an unaffected smile, revealing small, perfect teeth, and extended her hand.

Therese shook it, thinking: She is accustomed to being curtsied to, no doubt. But this is, after all, America. The princess almost seemed to read her mind, because the sapphire eyes twinkled. "Madame Pavan, I am so excited."

The childlike, confidential tone captivated Therese, and she said, "So am I." The interchange turned them, magically, into two women who loved clothes, rather than a royal patron and a *couturière*. And all of a sudden, Therese knew that everything was going to go better than she had ever dreamed.

She led the way to the luxurious display room furnished in the manner of a small Versailles chamber, saw that the princess and her attendant were comfortably seated, and served them tea. She sensed Olivia's admiring glance at her own gown, a rich bronzed gold with severely simple lines and the slightest hint of a train. With it, Therese wore only her peacock brooch.

After the tea things were cleared away, one of Therese's helpers brought in her portfolio of designs, covered for the occasion with an attractive binding of patterned Chinese silk. She noticed Olivia's eyes light up; the princess smiled like a pleased child, and ran her fragile fingers over the silken cover. "How pretty, how pleasant," she remarked. And then she began to look at the drawings.

Therese bowed her head. "Thank you, your highness." sions. Or expression, she corrected in thrilled silence—she had only one, that of unalloyed delight.

"Splendid, perfectly splendid," Olivia murmured, glancing up at Therese with great respect. "I really can't imagine how you managed . . . this is just the kind of thing *I* would have done. If I could," she added with a beguiling modesty, and positively grinned with pleasure.

"I gave the matter a lot of study, your highness."

"I should *say*." Olivia looked at one of the drawings again. Then, with a hesitancy that charmed Therese, she asked, "I don't suppose . . . I say, have you by any chance made up any of these yet? No, I don't suppose . . ."

"As a matter of fact, I have," Therese said.

"Do you know, it would be jolly to see it *on* someone, *madame*."

It was a stunning idea, one that had never occurred to Therese before. "That can be arranged, at once," she assured the princess. And she knew just who the model would be—one of her junior designers had just the figure for it. "I won't be a moment."

She hurried out and found the surprised designer, telling her to put on the navy walking suit with the tiny harlequin insets of magenta, and to come into the display room. "When you enter," Therese suggested, "walk slowly, gracefully. And turn in a way that will display the skirt and the back, particularly. Stand up straight!"

The excited designer hastened to obey. When she came into the display room and walked slowly around, turning, Olivia exclaimed with pleasure. "Oh, yes," she said. "*Yes*. That is absolutely magnificent."

Therese was flabbergasted when Olivia ordered every one of the ensembles, and the accessories, without suggesting a single change. For all her mild demeanor, the Princess Olivia was known throughout Europe and America for being almost impossible to please.

Intoxicated with the triumph, Therese escorted the young women back toward the entrance door. As they were leaving, Olivia turned back to Therese and said softly, "I think you are a positive genius, Madame Pavan."

Therese bowed her head. "Thank you, your highness."

Dimly, she noticed a young boy waiting to enter through the still-open door. After the women had passed him, he turned his fair head.

It was Charles.

The boy stared after Olivia and her attendant, ignoring Therese. She felt an absurd pang of hurt, of resentment. He was her son, and she hadn't seen him since Christmas.

"Excuse me, sir, are you coming in?" the doorman asked Charles with veiled impatience.

"This is my son, Philip," Therese explained, and the doorman looked chagrined. Charles had never been to the salon before.

"Darling!" Therese called out, taking Charles gently by the arm. "Come in!"

The boy glanced at her coolly, but obeyed. "You said 'your highness,' " he remarked, impressed. "Who *was* that, Mother?"

"An English princess," she said carelessly, trying to stifle her exasperation. "But, darling, what are you doing here? I didn't expect you till Friday. Come, come into my office."

She gave him a light kiss on his hair, and put her arm around him. As they walked toward her office, she asked him in a rush, "Why are you home early? Have you been to the house yet . . . do you like it?"

Charles withdrew from her, unsmiling. There was no warmth in his expression, and she felt a little chill of unease. "I've got to talk to you, Mother."

In her excitement she hadn't noticed, until now, that he held a small grip in his hand. "You haven't been home yet, then," she remarked, irked by his reticence. "You came here from the station. Where's the rest of your baggage?"

He followed her into the office, and she closed the door. "Sit down, Charles," she invited sharply, thinking: I've got to get hold of myself. I'm cross-examining him like an attorney, babbling like an idiot.

Charles remained standing, and she observed him with uncertain eyes: his resemblance to Nicholas, in his seventeenth year, was positively eerie. He still wore his hair as Nicholas had always done and, aside from his finely tailored English clothes, he could have been the Nicholas who caught Therese Pavan in the music room at Petit Anse.

"Mother, I am not coming back to Gramercy Park."

She was so struck by the sound of his voice—its unbelievable similarity to the young Nicholas Adair's—that for a second the words' sense hardly penetrated.

Then she realized what he had said.

"Not coming back?"

"I am seventeen now," he said curtly. "I am almost a man. And I have decided to live at Adair's Island, to go to school in that area. I am letting you know now, in the hopes that you and your new . . . husband will not try to stop me."

She was so taken aback that she could not say a word. All she could do, for the moment, was to listen to his cool, young, arrogant drawl.

"I assume that he does not carry a gun, like my . . . wild uncle."

The boy's sarcasm was so stinging that Therese felt the tears gather at the back of her eyes. She blinked, finding her voice at last. "You can't mean this, Charles." She moved toward him, holding out her arms.

"Save that for your lover," Charles said coldly, stepping back.

Pained, she stopped in her tracks. "Don't talk like that, Charles. Anthony is my husband."

"My *father* should be your husband!" He gave her a look of open dislike that cut her to the heart. "Don't you think I knew what was going on all those years while George was sick and my father was waiting and waiting for you? Why, the boys *joked* about you at school."

Her tears broke free at last, sliding down her face. "Your father lied to you, from the beginning. He deserted us before you were ever born. And Anthony and I never hurt George. You know that. Wasn't I at home every night with both of you . . . did I ever once neglect you?"

"Oh, no. You were always the perfect hypocrite."

With a mighty effort of will, Therese let that pass. "Tell me something, Charles . . . if Nicholas were 'waiting' for me all that time, why did he never come near me, why did I not hear from him?"

"Really, Mother. You know quite well you heard from him. What about all those letters from him, that you just threw away, I suppose."

"*Letters*? Charles, he never wrote me a single one." She was appalled at the extent of Nicholas' lies, the relentlessness of his pursuit of the boy . . . and the way he had succeeded in twisting Charles's mind, in putting her son against her.

"That's another lie, Mother. Like all the ones you told me about my father . . . like the adulterous life you lived with McKay."

It was hopeless, she thought, to pursue this further.
It was like battering away at a stone wall with a spoon.
"I see that I cannot reason with you. Let me plead
with you, then. Please don't run away like this, not
today. Not right now. Come home with me . . . let's
talk. If you . . . wish to visit Petit Anse this summer,
perhaps we can arrange that. But don't do this, darling. Don't."

Her son's face remained as impervious as marble.
"It's no good, Mother. I'm going. I'm going to live
with a man who commands my respect. Do you think I
could keep on living in New York? People here—the
people *I* want to know—know that I'm your son . . .
the son of a whore."

The scorn in his voice was terrible, but she could
hear his words almost as a quote of Nicholas Adair's.
A burning ire, a towering resentful pride drove away
her shock and pain. "That's enough," she said flatly.

Charles turned on his heel and walked out, not
looking back. He slammed the door.

Therese stared at the blank face of the closed door,
her son had closed it on all her love and effort, on
seventeen years of anxiety and struggle. She was too
numb to cry anymore.

And she had no heart for work, not even the super-
vision of Princess Olivia's commission. Her whole body
felt weak and tired, as if she had undergone a brutal
beating.

Slowly she walked to the looking-glass and repaired
the ravages of weeping, smoothed her hair, and put on
her elegant spring hat with its sprightly flowers.

Straightening her shoulders, she went out, telling
her aide that she was going home.

She entered the Gramercy house and went into the
lovely parlor, letting its quiet peace invade her. Then
she walked into the polished dining room, consoled by
its beauty; the house began to soothe her very heart.

She went upstairs and changed into a loose, pretty
housegown, wandering into Elianne's exquisite bower.
At least, she thought sadly, her sister would be happy
in this house, even if it never received her own child.

Saving it for the last, because she knew how it would hurt, she went into Charles's handsome, shining room. Looking around, she saw the evidence of her care—the artful arrangement of his treasures, the fixtures of gleaming brass, the plaids and blues and scarlets, that military touch that had always pleased him. And he had left it all.

In her grieving anger, Therese decided she would pack it all up, this very instant, ready all his possessions for shipment to Petit Anse. It would be unbearable to pass this room, day after day, and see Charles's things.

Obdurately she climbed to the attic and dragged down three huge trunks, one at a time, too sick at heart to call the servants in the kitchen.

Methodically, with a grim face, she packed all the fine summer clothes she had chosen for Charles's approval, then his book collection, and the rest.

When she was done, her body was damp with perspiration, and she felt slightly ill. But she went on, removing the curtains from the windows, stripping the bed, rolling up the rugs.

Tomorrow, she thought, she would have the painters in to repaint the walls. Yes, she would even paint out the stormy blue-gray color that was her son's signature. The walls were the color of those rejecting eyes, the eyes of Nicholas Adair.

She knew she was acting irrationally, but it was the madness of pain rather than anger. Every now and then, she was torn by the memory of what Charles had been as a little baby, smiling and bouncing in her arms.

But she would try not to think of that. She couldn't bear it. Her own unintentional neglect, her own driving ambition, and her burning need to provide her son with a life of ease had created the gulf between them.

Not entirely, though, she consoled herself as she went down to the kitchen. Nicholas Adair had captured Charles with lies, destroyed his love for her with an enduring malice.

Downstairs, Therese asked a surprised manservant

to remove the furnishings from the "blue room" and take them to the attic, to mark the trunks with the address she handed him, scribbled on a piece of paper, and take them to the express office for shipping.

Then she sought the haven of her room.

That evening, when Anthony came home for his new brokerage office downtown, he called out as he ran up the stairs. It was customary for him to find Therese, on the nights when they were dining in, reading on her *chaise longue* in the master bedroom.

This evening, to his surprise, she was standing at the open door of Charles's room. "Darling . . . ?"

Anthony looked in the room. "What happened?"

All the frustration of the day—the day that should have been her triumph—gathered into one great cry, and she began to weep. "He's gone."

"Therese . . ." Anthony took her in his arms. "What do you mean? He was not even expected yet."

She told him, in fitful stops and starts, leaning against him as he tightened his arms around her body.

"Therese. Come, darling," he said gently, and led her into their bedroom. Urging her onto the *chaise longue*, Anthony sat down at its foot, stroking one of her ankles.

"Now," he said softly, "tell me all of it, again. The whole thing."

Calmed by his voice and his loving presence, she managed to do that, omitting some of the more awful things that Charles had said, knowing she could not bear to repeat them.

"But now," she concluded, her tears beginning again, "I feel that I was wrong. I've acted like an impulsive fool . . . sending all his things away before I even had time to reflect. Emptying out his room . . ." she sobbed.

Anthony got up and sat at the head of the *chaise longue*, holding her close. "Listen to me, Therese. The boy's seventeen years old; he is ten years beyond the age of reason. He had no right to say those things to you; it was cruel, heartless. I know he is your son. But he is old enough to have some consideration, to *think* a little—think of all the things you did for him:

working at the salon in New Orleans while you were carrying him in your body . . . sewing during your confinement . . . even marrying George so he would have a father."

She listened intently, thinking of what he was saying. It was true.

"Rushing after him to Petit Anse," Anthony continued. "Living with discretion and dignity here in New York for all those long, long five years . . . as much for Charles's sake as George's. Don't you think I realized that, even if you never said it?" he asked quietly.

She nodded.

"My dear, you were not just acting out of pique." He smiled at her. "You were acting from bitter exhaustion."

"Yes. Oh, yes. I have gotten so tired of the unending battle, Anthony . . . and it just seemed to go on and on. I am ashamed, but one thing I feel very strongly now is . . . relief. That's horrible," she said, stricken.

He hugged her close. "It's not 'horrible' at all. You're a human. A wonderful human"—he kissed her hair, and she could feel his warm breath on the top of her head—"who has struggled and worried and worked, and done a thousand things, above and beyond the call of duty." He said the last lightly, as if trying to relieve her gloom and self-reproach. She felt her body relaxing, a little of the guilt dissipate, as if she had dropped a ponderous burden that was almost impossible to carry.

Thank God for Anthony, she thought, leaning against her husband's strong chest. Thank God he will not have to cope, now, with Charles's enmity. Her spirits brightened.

She leaned back and looked into Anthony's face, finding there the wistful and needy expression she had seen before, when she spoke of her anxiety about Charles. Yes, that was the first day they had come to the house, when they had sat together in the park.

And she said what she had said then: "I have *you*, Anthony. I have you, my love. And you are all in life

I truly need . . . you are the only person in the world I could not live without."

She was exalted to see his face clear, the brightness return to his silvery eyes.

"Why, Anthony, we *deserve* it!" she said with the wonder of discovery. "We deserve to be peaceful and happy in our own house. Don't we?"

He smiled at her marveling statement. "Oh, yes, my darling. We do deserve it. You deserve it, most of all. You've been living most of your life for other people . . . it's time you lived a little for yourself."

She moved into his arms again and kissed him. "You make everything better," she murmured. "You always have . . . and you always will."

"That's all I need to know. Oh, Therese, I love you so much. And I need you so badly."

Their kiss began to heal the soreness in her heart. As Anthony held her, Therese inventoried the blessings that remained: the marvel of her life with Anthony . . . all those she loved who loved her in return—Elianne and Charl', Berthe, Madame Dufay and Nell, Odalie.

The future was still bright for all of them: Anthony's financial genius had made him a force to reckon with on Wall Street. His new post, with the most prestigious brokerage house in New York, already placed him near the top in his field. Elianne was graduating from college, and all the others prospered.

Though much was gone, with Charles, so much abided.

After a short silence, Anthony murmured, "You haven't told me what happened with the princess."

As she did, quoting proudly the princess's comment on her "genius," Therese felt her spirits climb again, her hope renew.

No matter what else happened, she was still Pavan.

# 17

## *1890*

On a sizzling morning in July, Therese found her-self possessed by an utter blankness, a vast *ennui*. She put aside a tentative sketch with annoyance, cool-ing her eyes on the vase of white roses on her desk.

She was unsure about the cause of that strange listlessness; the weather was reason enough—she hated it—or perhaps it was because she would soon be forty-eight years old.

She had reached that "interesting age," as the sar-donic French called it, when a woman threatened to become a monument instead of an object of desire. Therese took a small mirror from one of the drawers and examined herself with cool objectivity. *Pas mal.* Not bad, for someone within a stone's throw of fifty. Her pampered skin glowed, and there was not a thread of gray in her hair. If the tautness of her chin and jaws had relaxed somewhat, it was almost imperceptible. It had been a good idea to put on a few pounds; they were excellent camouflage.

The eyes, of course, would always be the same. A bit wiser, naturally . . . but Anthony said they had the same restless brilliance they had had when he first met her.

She smiled and put the mirror away.

Anthony. He would never change. He had always made her feel beautiful and loved.

She was an incredibly lucky woman. And it was nonsense to let her *ennui* defeat her. *Ennui* was one of the prime forces of change. Sheer boredom, as well as changing mores, had put paid to the absurdities of the crinoline. Now the bustle was about to go the way of the crinoline and the horrible layered intricacies of the eighties. There was some talk of the classical Empire style's revival, but Therese doubted that. The waistline was here to stay. Within the next few years she predicted that corsets would be more constricting than ever. Meanwhile *derrières* were going out, shoulders coming in. And sleeves.

*Mon Dieu*, the sleeves. Therese would never forget the grotesque ones of the eighties; the faddists would no doubt exaggerate them so that women would find themselves in the predicament of fourteenth-century Venetians—unable to dine without sweeping all the crystal off the table.

Therese grinned. Good business for the glassblowers, anyway.

Well, nothing could induce her to plan next spring right now. The very idea of a fabric weighing more than an ounce was appalling.

Ah, that white embroidered gown of Odalie's in the summer of 1858!

Remembrance of that dress brought back New Orleans in all its vividness and Therese felt a pang of fresh grief.

Madame Dufay had died, at the age of seventy-three, only months before, and her last rites had been held in Paris, the city of her birth. Therese would mourn her for a long, long time; they had been through so much together, accomplished so much. Even the old Madison-Pavan in Cincinnati still prospered. Madame Dufay had organized it so superbly that her young successor stepped in without missing a beat.

But Therese could not allow herself to start brooding about that, not today; she was oppressed enough already. The best remedy, as always, would be to create something new and utterly frivolous.

She would sketch an 1890 adaptation of Odalie's 1858 dress—why not?

Busily Therese began to draw.

"Therese." She looked up, sensing that Jenny, her

assistant, had repeated her name several times. "A young woman is asking to see you. A young *lady*," she corrected herself emphatically, "named Germaine Broussard. She wants to show you her dress designs."

Therese sighed. She had hired an assistant designer only the week before. "You told her we have no opening at present, of course."

"Of course. But she was so . . . insistent, I just . . . well, I thought I should mention it to you."

That was baffling; there were few callers Jenny could not dispense with. The very oddity of it piqued Therese's interest in spite of herself.

"I'll deal with it," she said good naturedly. "Please show her in."

Therese could see at once why Jenny had insisted on calling the visitor a young "lady": her good upbringing was apparent in the proud carriage of her small, delicate head in its shadowy hat, and the fine, narrow features of her Gallic face. Yet "girl" was more apt. She was little more than an adolescent. And she looked strangely familiar.

"Sit down, Miss Broussard." Therese smiled; the girl was wearing a new summer Pavan, and her fragile figure carried it to perfection. "Will you have some iced tea? It's a perfectly awful day."

The girl sat down, placing her heavy-looking portfolio, bound in white leather, on the floor by her chair. She had such a *serious* expression.

Perhaps that's why she had looked familiar, Therese thought. There was a resemblance to the Therese Pavan of 1857, who had approached the salon Dufay almost as an acolyte.

A sudden smile relieved Germaine Broussard's solemnity. "No, I thank you." She spoke with the Gallic syntax. "I am accustomed to worse weather."

"In New Orleans?" Therese hazarded. Only someone from that drowsy, humid city would have that accent.

There was a flash of consternation in the girl's dark eyes. "Yes," she said briefly, volunteering nothing more.

Therese had seen that look in the eyes of frightened
animals; the little mystery of it teased her. To put the
girl at her ease, she said casually, "Miss Arnett already told you that we have just employed someone.
However, I'm always interested in looking at designs."

Eagerly Germaine Broussard got up and came around
the desk, opening her elegant portfolio for Therese's
inspection. Looking through the drawings, Therese
registered the technical skill of them, but felt a sharp
disappointment: the first few ensembles were totally
imitative of Pavans. "Oh, dear. I am flattered, but not
impressed, Miss Broussard."

She glanced up at the girl's suspenseful face, and
once again was piqued by the familiarity of the pretty
features. Someone she had glimpsed long ago . . . who
*was* it? Germaine Broussard's nervousness, though,
made Therese dismiss the riddle. A faint dew of moisture had broken out on her upper lip.

"Perhaps if Madame would look at the rest . . ."
she blurted in French—flawless Parisian French.

"Of course." Therese replied in the same tongue,
and leafed on through the portfolio. She thought:
Broussard should have put these in the front—the
designs were highly original, quite startling.

Too startling, Therese judged, to be of much use at
all. And there was a childlike, almost amateurish quality about those designs, an unworkable look . . .

"Do you sew, Miss Broussard?" she asked, reverting to English.

"*Sew?*" Good heavens, no!" The faint arrogance in
the answer nettled Therese.

"Well, if you want to design clothes, you will have
to learn," she said calmly. "How on earth do you
expect to create a dress, when you haven't *handled*
it?"

Germaine Broussard looked so doleful that Therese's pity melted her. "Sit down, Miss Broussard, and
let me tell you a few things."

The girl sat down in her chair again and looked at
Therese with respectful tip-tilted eyes. Her heart-shaped
face, with its large eyes, negligible nose, and small

lips, had the look of a kitten's, which was emphasized by her big hat and puffed black hair.

Gently Therese told her something of her own career, reflecting dryly that it was not easy to be brief about a span of more than forty years. The girl looked overwhelmed when Therese detailed a few of the lessons required before one learned the temper of a fabric, the perfection of a seam. Her face fell.

"Miss Broussard," Therese asked abruptly, "how much do you want to become a fine designer?"

"More than anything." There was no mistaking the certainty of that.

"Very well. If I take you on"—a brightness flared in the tip-tilted eyes, and an incipient smile curved the narrow lips—"you will start in our sewing rooms. Is that understood?"

"Yes. Oh, yes. That will be quite satisfactory," Germaine Broussard said in a rush of elation.

"When will you be able to start?"

"Now." The girl got up at once and stood by her chair.

"Excellent, I like your attitude." Therese rose too, smiling. She called out to her aide and asked her to show Miss Broussard to the sewing rooms, where she would report to the senior *midinette*, after filling out the papers for her employment record.

When they had gone, Therese sat down at her desk again, amazed that she had hired Germaine Broussard when Pavan already had everyone it needed.

But there had been something . . . something in those crude but ingenious designs that captured Therese Pavan's imagination. Something that hinted at the wave of the future, at a strong individual gift in the puzzling young woman.

Therese's memory journeyed back over thirty-three years, to her first terrifying interview with Hortense Dufay in the house on Rampart Street; her reverent approach to that temple of beautiful clothes; her amazement over the triumph of the cape made of mattress ticking.

Her fingers encountered fine pebbled leather. She

glanced down at the desk. Germaine Broussard, in her excitement, had forgotten her portfolio. Curious, Therese examined the inner cover. Engraved there was the name of the most prestigious stationer in New Orleans. It had been in business for fifty years when Therese first came to the city, and she recalled looking into its windows with absolute hunger. Germaine Broussard, she decided, was far from poor.

Who on earth *was* she? Therese did not remember any rich family of that name among the patrons of Madame Dufay. Of course, after all these years, there must be hundreds of new settlers in New Orleans. Still, the girl had a strong family resemblance to someone Therese vividly remembered.

Maybe she resembled Therese herself, the Therese who was still a mysterious figure in New York society, not quite accepted in spite of all she had attained.

When the Princess Olivia had adopted Pavan as her official *couturière* in 1875, the popularity of Madame Demorest began to wane, and Pavan catered more and more to royal patrons from other countries. By the year 1890, Pavan was the city's first house of *couture*.

Just as Olivia's support enhanced Therese's professional standing, her espousal by Marian McKay Sloan ensured her first social acceptance. Marian's marriage to Richard Sloan had united two of the most powerful families in New York; their ancestors had lived in the state for nearly three hundred years.

The bitter irony of her sudden rise to relative social prominence did not escape Therese; the very summer Charles left home, ashamed of the woman his mother was judged to be, Therese Pavan McKay was besieged with invitations, and most of New York society was eager to take her to its bosom.

Marian's set was not the "fast" one joined by certain other young members of local society, and both she and her husband, Dick, had bright minds, simple manners, and accepting temperaments that appealed strongly to Anthony and Therese. During the early years of their marriage, they never entertained on a grand scale at home; it was physically impossible in their smaller house, which, Anthony admitted, had weighed heavily with him in its purchase. Their favorite dinners were small ones, bringing Dick and Marian Sloan together with other friends and members of Therese's family. The guests, Marian said, blended as perfectly as the Empire pieces did with the Acadian artifacts in the Gramercy house.

What surprised Therese a little, and amused Anthony, was her discovery that "society" in general was rather dull, composed of drearily similar people. After a few months of the social whirl, both Anthony and Therese began to decline more and more invitations, thereby earning a reputation for attempted exclusivity. That reputation amused them both more than anything else about the social scene.

In the fifteen years since their marriage, Anthony McKay had become one of the most powerful financial figures in New York, and few women were able to resist the famous *couturière* who outfitted duchesses and queens. And they were rich. To be rich, these days, was to be admired and honored. A Massachusetts bishop of the McKays' own faith proclaimed that "godliness is in league with riches," and the noted rector of Philadelphia's largest Baptist church gave his "Acres of Diamonds" lecture across the country, exhorting, "I say, get rich, get rich!" Only the lazy, he said, shrank from the duty of laying up wealth.

A man named Woolworth was expanding his chain of five-and-ten-cent stores; Aaron Montgomery Ward's mail-order catalogs were becoming an integral part of American rural life. There were almost forty-five hundred millionaires in the nation, and many in New York were flaunting their money, building "cottages" at Newport, Rhode Island, that reminded Therese of the vividly remembered "castle" in Tarrytown.

The McKays built a summer house too, but it was on Long Island; they had no desire to take the trouble of traveling all the way to Newport. Their hearts and interests were too firmly connected to the city.

They continued to live in the comparatively small

Gramercy house, because now there were only the two of them. Elianne Pavan had rarely used her lovely room; on her graduation from Holyoke, she had married a likable Harvard professor named Adam Winston, and they lived in Boston. Adam reminded Therese a little of both Anthony and Dick Sloan; his blood was hopelessly "blue," in his connection with the famous shipbuilding family of New England, and yet he had a humorous, intellectual view toward what was known as society. One of the greatest joys of Therese's life had been the publication of her sister's first novel, during the year she was carrying her first child. The book had already been favorably compared with the novels of the great Jane Austen in what a critic called its "mordant humor" and its "antique grace."

On the death of her husband, Berthe Levitsky had moved to New York, happy to be settled in one of the elegant "flats" that were fast replacing houses everywhere; Madison-Pavan still flourished in Cincinnati, the Pavan division benefiting from Therese's growing international reputation. She hardly visited there anymore, but continued to send them her designs. At Anthony's urging, she opened Pavan salons in Philadelphia and Washington, D.C. Their proximity allowed easy travel; she was averse to traveling longer distances, missing Anthony too much when she was away from him. And certainly they were not in need of money, she told her husband dryly; his coups on Wall Street had amassed a fortune for them.

In 1885 Charl' and Nell moved to New York with their two children and to Therese's delight found a house not far from Gramercy Park.

It seemed, in those years, that there was nothing in their lives that missed perfection, apart from the two matters that continued to haunt Therese—the irrevocable loss of her child and the fact that she was not wholly accepted; she still felt as if she stood outside the proverbial mansion, peering in, as she had once stood on the veranda of Petit Anse.

She shrugged. Self-pity was as futile as speculation. If she had traced a resemblance to herself in Germaine

Broussard she hoped, at least, that they differed in one respect— that Germaine Broussard was not pregnant. Therese had a strong feeling Germaine could amount to something, and she would hate to lose her.

Laughing a little at her own fancies, Therese closed the portfolio and went out to her aide's office. She made a note and attached it, with the direction to return the portfolio to the new employee, Germaine Broussard. Therese hoped the girl would stick.

She was gratified, as the summer wore on, to find that Germaine had not only stuck but also was showing promise.

In her giant, delegated enterprise, Therese rarely visited the sewing rooms anymore, but she received glowing reports from the senior *midinette* of the girl's willingness and ability to learn. Therese was moved to hear that Broussard, in many ways, duplicated her own deportment at Madame Dufay's, working longer hours than necessary, intent on absorbing every small scrap of information.

Glimpsing Broussard now and then, Therese was interested to note that she no longer wore anything so splendid as the Pavan that Therese had identified at the interview; now she wore plain shirtwaists and skirts, apparently of her own devising, because the items had a subtle difference from Pavan ready-mades.

When Therese frequently mentioned Germaine Broussard to Anthony, he teased her gently about her extraordinary interest. "I think you're looking for another doll to dress, now that you've lost Elianne."

But seeing that Therese reacted somberly to his small joke, Anthony took her in his arms. "I'm sorry." He was too sensitive not to know that even now she sometimes felt the lack of Charles and Elianne, adult as they were.

When she was first married, Therese had worried that Anthony, too, might feel the lack of children of his own. He quickly disabused her. "I am one of those biological sports," he said lightly, "who have no strong urge to perpetuate their kind. The McKay name will be carried on very adequately by my cousins." He smiled. He had an inordinate number of nieces and nephews. "And Marian will preserve the genes in our immediate circle. Most of all, Therese, I'll never really need anyone but you."

Therese remembered all that as they discussed Germaine Broussard. She said warmly, "You have nothing at all to be sorry for," kissing him. "I think it's my curiosity, rather than maternal longings, that's killing me."

Anthony laughed. Therese was forever speculating about Germaine's origins. She still had no idea of the girl's real age—her employment record gave her age as twenty, which Therese knew to be impossible—and she could swear that the address of her "nearest relative" in New Orleans was a false one. The whole thing reminded Therese so much of her own early history, when she had posed as "Madame Labiche" and hidden her own true age of fifteen, that she wanted to unravel the mystery.

The conversation with Anthony took place in August; it was September before Therese had a significant encounter with Germaine Broussard.

One evening Therese was in her office especially late, working at designs for the spring wedding of the Duchess of Suffolk. The beautiful, extravagant young duchess was in no way like the Princess Olivia, and her trousseau included a multitude of ensembles and countless accessories. As much as she had enjoyed the challenge of Olivia's trousseau, Therese had to admit she was overjoyed by the splendid richness of this one.

At the same time, she had been working with such a fury that she could feel herself going blank.

To clear her mind and senses, she decided to put the duchess's trousseau aside and turn to another project, a series of sketches she was submitting to the Metropolitan for a possible commission for the opera *Lakmé*. It had been revived the past April at the Metropolitan, with the renowned Patti in the title role. And the costumes had struck Therese as particularly unimaginative. When Lakmé appeared to sing the famous "Bell Song," she was dressed as an ordinary dancing girl.

She should, in Therese's opinion, have been clothed in dreamlike jeweled gauze, with hundreds of tiny gold and silver bells sewn on her gown. The composer, Delibes, had used bells musically, blending with voice and woodwinds, to give the aria its peculiar charm. Therese had been sketching a costume that would express the music—glittering and splendid, a vestment of fantasy.

Therese worked late, with a sense of delicious freedom: Anthony had sent word that he would be in his office late, as well, working out an intricate transaction. But she was surprised to hear her little gilded clock chime seven times, like Lakmé's delicate bells.

The whole building had emptied out at six, and doubtless there was no one else around except the caretaker. Therese decided to work on a little longer; Anthony had said he might be as late as nine o'clock. At a quarter to eight, she decided that she had done more than enough, and prepared to go.

She went to seek out the caretaker so he could lock up, but was surprised not to see him. Then she heard his voice from somewhere above. "I will have to lock up here, miss." Faintly, a woman's voice could be heard in reply.

Therese wondered what could be keeping an employee so late—surely if something had gone wrong, she would have been notified. She hesitated.

The creaking of the elevator caught her ear, and when the car reached her level, she saw the grumpy-looking caretaker and Germaine Broussard through the grille. The girl looked astonished to see her.

"Miss Broussard!" Therese exclaimed. "Why are you working so late?"

Germaine looked caught-out, reddening. She shifted her portfolio from one arm to the other. "I was . . . working out something of my own. I hope that's all right. You see, I have so little room at my boarding-house, and . . ."

"Of course it is." Therese smiled at her. "But you have missed your dinner, I imagine." She recalled the dinners at Mrs. Prickett's in Cincinnati; if a boarder

was late, he just went hungry. Germaine Broussard
nodded.

"Well, so have I," Therese admitted, realizing she
was ravenous. "And I forgot to telephone my house."
She started back to her office. "Would you like to
dine with me at home?" she asked impulsively, turning around.

"How kind of you. Yes, thank you, I would."

"Good. Then come to my office with me. I'm sorry,
Gerald," Therese said to the caretaker. "I'll only be a
moment."

He gave her a respectful mutter, obviously hiding
his impatience.

In her office, Therese went to the telephone attached to the wall. In this year of 1890, there were a
quarter of a million of the instruments throughout the
country. While Therese enjoyed the magical convenience, she thought the things were hideous. And over
the protests of her maintenance employees, she had
actually painted the monstrous object with metallic
bronze paint.

"Why, it's *bronze*!" Germaine Broussard cried out
in a blend of approval and amusement.

"I always wondered: why *black*?" Therese asked
with tart humor. "My cook hates talking on it too, but
this time she'll just have to endure it."

"So does ours," Miss Broussard said in an unthinking tone. Therese, with the receiver in her hand, glanced
at the girl out of the corner of her eye: she was
blushing. Why she should, Therese could not fathom.
Surely there was no disgrace in her family's having a
telephone. But it was another small clue to her mysterious background; her family must have money. The
telephone was not a cheap or common convenience.

Distracted, she gave the operator the number of the
Gramercy house and was soon speaking to the reluctant cook, Bridget.

"There," she said, hanging up. "I think Bridget
looks on the telephone as a satanic device."

Germaine Broussard laughed, and it pleased Therese to see how laughter transformed her. Once again

she was overtaken by strong compassion; how awful it must be for this lovely, delicate girl to live in a cramped, lonely boardinghouse. Therese resolved, during dinner, to find out more about her life in the city.

When the carriage stopped in front of the town house and the girl saw the tall white building with its wrought-iron ornamentation, she exclaimed, "This is so much like New Orleans."

"Yes." Leading the way up the stoop, Therese confided. "That's one reason I love it so. You know, possibly, that I once lived there." All of the magazine articles about Pavan included Therese's bowdlerized history.

They entered the pretty foyer. "Of course. I have read everything written about you, Madame."

Therese could not help being touched by the girl's solemn admiration. No human, she thought dryly, could fail to be.

The maid who had admitted them went downstairs to notify Bridget of their arrival. "About ten minutes, Rosie," Therese called out.

She showed Germaine Broussard upstairs into Elianne's old room to refresh herself, and once again felt a small *frisson* of affectionate pity when the girl said, "This is lovely, Madame. As unique as your clothes," her dark eyes taking in the features of the room.

While disposing of her outdoor things, washing up, and smoothing her hair in her own dressing room, Therese pondered her guest's ambiguous reaction to Gramercy Park. An ordinary *midinette* would have been overwhelmed; Germaine Broussard had taken its splendors very much in her stride, not even mentioning the priceless Corot in Elianne's room, and yet judging Therese's innovations with an artist's eye. The reaction, Therese conjectured, of someone who came from a mansion.

The idea was bolstered by the girl's casually perfect table manners. The first course was eaten in silence, and Therese noticed that her guest's dark gaze was often fixed on her own face, apparently indifferent to the well-cooked food, the delicate wine, the glittering table appointments.

"Forgive me," the girl said. "I was staring, Madame. I am overwhelmed to be dining in the home of Pavan."

She said it so sincerely, without the least artifice, that Therese experienced a new surge of that warmth she had felt before. "I am delighted to have you. I lived in a boardinghouse once," she said, smiling, "and it's an experience I would never want to repeat." After an instant, she remarked, "You must miss your family."

The girl's flushed face and wary eyes told Therese a great deal.

"Miss Broussard . . . Germaine. Have you run away?"

Germaine Broussard turned pale; her fork arrested halfway to her mouth. "You would not . . . send me back. You would not tell them." She put her fork down, looking at Therese with anxious eyes.

"How old are you really, Germaine?" Therese asked gently; the girl's first name came very naturally to her lips.

"Sixteen." Germaine put her elbows on the table and covered her face with her hands.

Therese took both of Germaine's hands in hers and pulled them gently downward. "I thought as much. I ran away, with my brother, when I was a year younger than you. I know all the signs."

"What are you going to do?" Germaine asked her with trembling lips.

"Do? I'm going to ask you why you left home."

The girl's relief was pathetic. Her glass shook in her hand when she sipped a little of the red wine. "I ran off because I knew they would never let me be what I wanted to be. My grandmother Broussard, and Great-Aunt Aimee have already chosen the man I'm supposed to marry."

Great-Aunt Aimee. It just wasn't possible, Therese thought. But she stayed quiet. The floodgate of Germaine's secrecy was open; an interruption might stem the flood.

"My family was horrified that I wanted to 'work,' "

Germaine said bitterly. "They want to mold me into the Broussard and de Sevigny pattern."

So it was true: Aimee de Sevigny was the great-aunt of this child.

Noticing Therese's expression, Germaine asked, "Do you *know* them?" She looked frightened again, child-like and uncertain.

Therese took her hand again. "Not as friends. I once waited on your great-aunt at the salon Dufay in New Orleans."

Germaine stared at her. "Good heavens. Then you . . . *you* are the . . ." She looked embarrassed. Reassured by Therese's steady gaze, Germaine went on, ". . . the 'strange dressmaker' who disappeared. The one who made my great-aunt's striped cloak."

"You know about *that*, after all these years?" Therese was flabbergasted.

"Oh, yes. When the matter of my trousseau came up, Grandmother Broussard and Aunt Aimee began to talk about theirs. And my grandmother teased my great-aunt about the 'bizarre' cloaks that became the rage 'way back in . . ."

"Eighteen-fifty-seven," Therese supplied, feeling a sharp nostalgia. "Yes. Your great-aunt admired my cape, at the salon." She smiled.

"And it was made of *mattress ticking*." Germaine grinned at Therese. "I had no *idea* they were talking about the great Pavan. And yet . . . there was something in the way they described you . . ." Germaine shook her head. "I can't believe it."

"Neither can I." You don't know the half of it, child, she thought. If you knew that my best friend was your great-uncle's mistress . . . and that I lived in the house he paid for. "You actually thought I'd 'turn you in' to your people."

"I didn't know," Germaine admitted. "I *couldn't* know."

"Of course you couldn't. But you see, in some ways, my own beginnings were like yours. My brother and I ran away from the Côte Blanche, in Acadian country . . . for the very same reason you did. Our father would never have allowed us to be what we wanted to be."

And I was pregnant, Therese continued in ironic silence.

"But you," she said to Germaine, "are to be admired, my dear. You left a very sheltered, comfortable life."

Germaine shrugged. "I'm not sure it was an advantage. I don't know a blessed thing about . . . doing for myself. When you asked me, that first day, if I knew how to sew"—she smiled her charming, catlike little smile, enhancing the du Lac resemblance that had nagged Therese—"well, the nearest I was ever allowed to come to that was embroidery. Things have certainly changed now," she concluded with shy pride.

"So I understand. I've received amazing reports of you." Therese studied her. "It seems to me you're resolved to succeed."

"I am." The simple declaration impressed Therese more than any amount of extravagant protests.

"Then I shall do everything in my power to help you." Therese was surprised at the depth of her affection for this girl she barely knew. And yet, from the very start, there had been an odd kinship between them. The irony of her family connection was delicious. "When did you first decide you would like to design?" she asked casually.

"When I was ten years old. Even then I never liked the dresses they put on me." Germaine giggled. "Only last year, I had my maid alter a Worth ball gown, and my mother nearly fainted. I wanted a gown by Madame Cheruit for my first ball, but Mother and Grandmother Broussard wouldn't hear of it. 'Everyone who was anyone' "—Therese could hear the sarcastic quotation marks,—"was dressed by Worth. Cheruit and Pavan are much too advanced for most of New Orleans."

"Cheruit is a woman after my own heart." Therese had visited her salon in 1878, on her second trip to Paris. Madame Cheruit had taken over the Raudnitz house on the Place Vendôme five years before; her

creations were the only ones Therese had ever seen
similar to Pavan's. Cheruit was the first Parisian to
launch simple, almost severe models. "Cheruit has
exquisite taste. To prefer her means that you do too,"
she said, smiling at Germaine. "By the way, may I ask
what you were working on tonight? Do you think I
could see it?"

"Oh, of course, Madame!" Germaine jumped up
and hurried out of the room; Therese heard her running up the stairs, then back down again. She reen-
tered with the heavy white leather portfolio.

Therese cleared a space on the table and opened it.
She drew in a quick, excited breath. Germaine had
drawn a revolutionary series of white gowns whose
sleeves suggested wings; their frail fabric was feather-
printed and their lines had an airy, floating quality,
ethereal to an extraordinary degree.

"Why, it's for Elsa in *Lohengrin*," Therese exclaimed.

"Yes. There was a French production in New Orleans, in the spring, and Gadski's costume looked so
cumbersome I was amazed that she could *stand*, much
less move."

"This is so perfect for the Grail motif," Therese
murmured, staring at the sketches. "And the swan
motif, of course," she added. "Did you know I was
interested in opera costuming . . . or is this one of
those amazing coincidences?" she asked, still intent on
the drawings.

Germaine straightened, flushing. "Oh, I heard some
people talking at the salon. I *did* know. And it inspired me to pursue my *Lohengrin* idea."

Therese looked up to see Germaine observing her
with parted lips and shining eyes. "I think," Therese
said slowly, "we can work together. I'm presenting a
whole series to the board of the Metropolitan Opera."

The girl was speechless. Therese had to smile at her
expression. And all of a sudden, she herself was fifteen again, staring openmouthed at Hortense Dufay
when she learned that she would be allowed to make a
cloak for Aimee du Lac and charge her all of fifty
dollars.

Germaine Broussard had become, in the blink of an eye, a good many things to Therese Pavan—a reincarnation of her own bright youth; someone to teach and guide. And care for.

Therese pictured the girl's room at the boarding-house, and then considered the spacious, beautiful room that had once been Elianne's, with its huge desk, its shelves and cabinets, its generous light.

"I . . . I can't tell you how grateful I am," Germaine said at last.

"You needn't." Therese smiled at her. "I know. I felt the same way a long, long time ago."

When Anthony came home, he found them talking earnestly in the parlor. He was charming, as he always was, with Germaine.

After they had sent her home in their carriage, Anthony asked Therese with a smile, "Have you solved the mystery?"

She was about to tell him, when she hesitated, deterred by concern for his reaction. If he knew the girl was a runaway, and only sixteen, he would surely conclude that "hiding" her might place them in legal difficulties. Therefore, for the first time in their married life together, Therese told him a partial lie. "Yes. Some of it, not all. I think she may be an orphan."

Anthony studied her quizzically. "I have a feeling you're going to take a special interest in Germaine Broussard."

"Yes. I am. You know me too well."

He didn't know yet how much of an interest, she reflected. She was determined that before long Germaine would be living in Elianne's old room, but there was no point in springing that on Anthony tonight. She'd work up to it. And she'd get her way, just as she would get her way with the Metropolitan's board.

After all, Anthony had never denied her anything.

# 18

On a crisp afternoon near the end of November, Edmond C. Stanton, manager of the Metropolitan Opera, observed his elegant drawing room with satisfaction. Everything was in readiness for the meeting of the board.

Stanton was delighted that it was his turn to entertain the board at tea; on his own ground, he would enjoy more than his usual self-confidence. And it would be needed to persuade Mrs. Morris to Stanton's point of view.

It was only ten minutes to four: he still had a few moments of leisure. Stanton went to the console table where the portfolio of Pavan designs rested in its shining brocade cover. Stanton smiled, running his hand over the heavy fabric—the sensitive designer had inquired about the color scheme of his room, so that the portfolio would not disturb its harmony. A woman of delicate perceptions, he reflected. And enormous talent and imagination.

Just as the gilded clock struck four, Stanton heard the doorbell sound in unison. It had to be that magnificent grenadier, Elizabeth Schuyler Morris. She was always the first to appear, on the stroke of the hour.

Edmond Stanton arranged his face into its best smile, going out to meet her. Privately he thought with amusement that Mrs. Morris' entrances were made with such a flourish that the triumphal march from *Aida* . . . or better still, the Ride of the Valkyries . . . should accompany them.

Mrs. Morris united in one person two of the greatest names in the history of New York. But more signifi-

cant were her outstanding financial contributions and
her awesome influence over the other members of the
board.

"Mrs. Morris!" Stanton bowed over her hand. "A
pleasure, as always."

"How are you, Edmond?" she inquired crisply, in
the perfunctory tone of one who did not greatly care
about the answer to her question. In line with Stanton's simile, she looked more like a "warrior maiden"
than ever, in a fur-trimmed cloak of metallic gray. The
sharp lines of its oversleeves, extended at the shoulders, reminded Stanton faintly of the Valkyries' winged
helmets, just as the snug pleated torso hinted at a
breastplate.

As she surrendered her wrap and gloves to the
maid, Stanton remarked a bit fatuously, "You are
prompt to the hour."

"I am always prompt to the hour."

Indeed she was. Stanton was annoyed at himself.
He never babbled, yet he had babbled just now.

He was relieved to hear, just as Mrs. Morris was
seated, the arrival of several others.

Stanton endured the customary social prelude to the
meeting with impatience, then the somewhat cut-and-
dried items on the agenda.

When the board reached its "new-business" stage,
Stanton announced, "I would like to bring up a matter
which I think will be of especial interest to this board.
I have discovered someone I believe to be of unique
talent in costume design."

Elizabeth Schuyler Morris stiffened; she took a deep
breath that caused her imposing bosom to expand like
the prow of a great gray forward-thrusting ship. In
tones reminiscent of Lady Bracknell, she repeated with
indignation, "A designer? I fail to see the sense of
that. Signor Masconi has done splendid work on the
last six productions."

Signor Masconi, Stanton reflected cynically, was also
a handsome and insinuating young man who knew
how to flatter Mrs. Morris.

Stanton met the remark with a bland smile. "I feel

that when you, and the rest of the board, see these designs . . ."

He rose and went to the console table, returning with the portfolio, which he set on the tea table before Mrs. Morris, opening it for her inspection.

The other board members, accustomed to taking second place to the "warrior maiden," accepted the gesture with patient resignation. Mrs. Morris leafed through the portfolio, raising her brows now and then, going through the designs without comment. When she closed the book, she remarked, "There are certain *traditions* . . ."

Stanton then handed the portfolio to the other members of the board. Several of them murmured approvingly, and Mrs. Hester Boerum, a woman of equal social footing with Mrs. Morris, but of a more retiring nature, said softly, "I think these are wonderful. I had no idea Madame Pavan could do these things. I dote on her clothes."

Mrs. Morris sniffed.

"She is married, you know, to a McKay," Mrs. Boerum insisted in her gentle voice.

"Be that as it may," Mrs. Morris retorted, "she has no further recommendation. Worth has always been good enough for me."

"Forgive me, Elizabeth," one of the male board members intervened. "I don't see why Madame Pavan *needs* a 'further recommendation.' It seems to me these designs speak for themselves. Masconi never designed anything like this for *Lakmé*, for instance."

"Hear, hear." The hearty addition came from Roger Stuyvesant, another member.

Stanton was gratified by this unusual evidence of support, but all the same wished that the members would be more tactful; such opposition only stiffened Mrs. Morris' famous resistance. And she was not accustomed to having her judgment questioned.

Stanton's heart sank; Mrs. Morris' face had a look that on a less-distinguished face would be described as mulish. "I see nothing in these designs to arouse such enthusiasm. Some of them are positively . . . startling.

Take this *Lakmé* costume, for example. Can you imagine the racket all those bells would make?"

"I believe," Stuyvesant said courteously, "if you will read the note with the sketch, you'll notice that the bells would not contain their clappers. Which seems to me a very clever notion."

"Indeed it is," Mrs. Boerum commented.

"I don't like all this chopping and changing," Mrs. Morris said. "In the first place, the opera has never employed a woman in this position."

Stanton could not help thinking that Mrs. Morris' position as a woman had never been questioned. He couldn't resist remarking, "That's true. But think of the outstanding contributions that you, Mrs. Boerum, and Mrs. Lewis have made to our board."

"An excellent point," Stuyvesant said. His sharp eyes twinkled. Mrs. Morris had never been a particular favorite of his, and he was the member least influenced by her opinions. More than usual, Stanton felt Stuyvesant should be awarded a medal for valor.

But Stanton's impulsive remark had an unhappy effect on Mrs. Morris. She really dug in her heels. "Am I to understand that the other board members are in agreement with Edmond and Mr. Stuyvesant?"

When it was put to them like that, the members reacted less boldly. One of them murmured, "Not exactly," and Mrs. Boerum looked as if she were ready to back down.

"Perhaps," she suggested in her timid way, "we should . . . table this matter until the next meeting."

"So move," old Stuyvesant declared. The motion was seconded and passed, with Mrs. Morris reluctantly making it unanimous.

That was that, for the moment, Stanton thought, as the meeting disbanded. Perhaps at the next meeting, at the end of December, he would enjoy greater success.

Nick Adair was conscious that he was something of an anachronism in the year of 1890, when the nation was turning its back on the old ways and setting out on

new courses, and it was no longer necessary to be
Anglo-Saxon or Nordic to be an American.

Nick disliked everything about the times—young
women displaying their calves on bicycles, playing games
with unattractive gusto, and writing on the typing machines. It was all part and parcel of an industrialization
that had made a good many men millionaires, but was
almost destroying the mine at Adair's Island. It was
next to impossible these days for the mine to compete
with the strongly capitalized operations. And Nick and
his father feared that when the mine went, the estate
would go too.

That would happen, Nick resolved, over his dead
body. Ever since he had left New York and come
down there to stay, he had been the undisputed prince
of the kingdom his father ruled. As far as Nick was
concerned, there was no other possible way to live. He
would save Adair's Island, and pass it on to his children, and his children's children.

The fact that he was thirty-two and still unmarried
did not disturb Nick at all: he had not yet found a
woman worthy of occupying the "castle." As to recre-
ation, there had always been a plenitude of women,
from the locals who visited his *garçonnière* to the avid
older women, and lately the "naughty" society girls of
the moment. A wife, in any case, was only an instrument; without one, there would be no legal heirs. The
"instrument" would have to be from the highest level
of society. No one less would be suitable for the Island.

And she must be elegant and untouched: no child of
his would ever suffer what he had suffered from his
own unthinking and *declassée* mother. It sickened him,
as it did his father, to learn that the McKays had
prospered. For all her callousness and irresponsibility,
his mother's enterprise was praised in dozens of
newspapers and magazines; the financial publications
attested to Anthony McKay's brilliant coups. And when
Nick had changed trains at Washington and, with time
to spare, had walked around the city, it had nettled
him to see a Pavan salon even there.

All that, his father raged, while Adair's Island was

falling to rack and ruin for lack of money. Nick had been concerned lately to see how much his father was drinking, but all of his pleadings were in vain. The godlike man who had made Charles Madison, that nobody, into an Adair, seemed to be changing almost daily before his son's eyes.

But that would end, Nick assured himself, when he had successfully obtained the necessary loan from their New York cousins. And so he had come north, in December of 1890, to accomplish just that.

He liked New York City no better now than he had when he had left it in 1875, and he was relieved to pass through quickly into the refreshing country of upper New York State. However, his reception there was a devastating disappointment: his elder cousin flatly turned them down, saying that Nick was just as much a fossil as his father, living in a dead past. "It's time," he said, "to let the old place go. Only a millionaire could keep a white elephant like that, these days."

Furious and sore, Nick cut short his visit. He didn't know how he was going to face his father. When the train neared Manhattan, Nick decided he couldn't face him, not yet. As much as he disliked the brash, noisy city, it would postpone the inevitable if he stayed there a few days. And he had several former schoolmates who might be glad to see him. Who knows, Nick reflected with faint hope, there might be another way to obtain the money; perhaps some of his friends could advise him.

Therefore, on a bright December afternoon in 1890, Nick Adair strolled along the border of the skating pond in Central Park with his friend at the precise moment the exquisite girl appeared.

That autumn and early winter had been the happiest of Germaine's life; the move into the Gramercy house in September, her growing closeness to Therese, and her increasing immersion in the business of the salon had filled her days and nights to overflowing.

This evening, Therese would fete Germaine at a birthday reception at Chez Raoul, and she knew the occasion would be marked by even more elaborate presents than the ones generous Therese had already showered her with. As a matter of fact, right before Therese had delivered Germaine into the hands of Mrs. Morris, Therese had remarked significantly that she must take care of some "very important errands."

Germaine wished the party could be at Delmonico's. But the little disappointment had been lost in her anticipation and happiness: she was going to have a wonderful life with Therese and Anthony McKay. Anthony was very kind to her, and Therese was full of plans for Germaine's future.

Foremost among these plans was the prospect of the Metropolitan Opera commission. Although the opera board had not acted at its last meeting, Therese was confident of receiving an affirmative notice after the board met again at the end of December. Therese had even presented Germaine's "angel designs," as they called Elsa's costumes for *Lohengrin*, with the portfolio. And she had assured Germaine that they would work closely in the future. Germaine was sure that in that kind of design, her own imagination could take wing.

Therese had even spoken of the "splendid man" Germaine would meet someday. And he would be just the right kind of man, Therese said. Germaine believed that, because Therese's unique position in New York society—something of an artist-bohemian who was befriended by everyone from the very rich to that group of artists living on the "fringes"—would enable Germaine to make a privileged choice.

But that was far in the future: if, now and then, Germaine suffered small pangs of incipient desire, they were soon lost in the bright variety and fullness of her present days. Besides, she was resolved never to marry until she could love a man as much as Therese clearly loved Anthony McKay.

Germaine, who had learned to skate in Switzerland and Germany when she was a young child, executed a graceful figure eight on the gleaming ice of Central Park, feeling so happy she could fly.

Circling, she caught sight of a superb man, an older

man, standing with another man on the border of the lake and staring at her with admiring blue-gray eyes.

He was so handsome he looked like a magazine illustration: his features were patrician and faultless, and his form was lean. Below his spotless hat, his golden hair gleamed in the winter sun, and to Germaine he was the color of the winter day: pale gold, cerulean.

His attire was correct in every detail. He looked like a prince, a nobleman.

Germaine was so intensely moved by his austere beauty that she almost wavered in her finely executed whirl.

"My *Lord*," Nick muttered to his friend Wharton.

"What?"

"That little beauty there, in the brown." Nick gave an imperceptible nod in the direction of the fragile dark-haired girl, skating in tandem now with another young woman. From her neat velvet toque, with its creamy plume caressing her heart shaped-face, to her nipped-in waist in its elegant jacket, and her twirling skirt and dainty feet, she was perfection.

"Umm . . . pretty. A bit too thin for *my* taste," Wharton declared, grinning. Nick knew that Wharton leaned toward the fair Lillian Russell type; to him the woman looked like a fat, hulking peasant, despite her reputation as a *femme fatale*. "I say, Adair." Wharton's merry brown eyes sparkled as he observed the pair with greater interest. "Her partner's a young lady I know. That's Gertrude Morris."

The fair young woman had noticed them, and raised one elegantly gloved hand to wave at Wharton.

"The political Morrises?" Nick asked, alerted.

"Oh . . . sure. As a matter of fact, they are." Wharton sounded a little bored. "Shall we pay our respects? Kill two birds with one stone . . . introduce you to your little beauty." Wharton grinned good-naturedly.

"Why not?" Nick's light reply masked his sharp interest: if the girl were a friend of a Morris, she must be someone it would be no disgrace to know.

He saw the Morris girl say something to her, and then watched them skate gracefully toward a splendid-looking older woman muffled in dark furs and settle on her bench in a pretty swirl of calf-length skirts above neat booted ankles.

Rapidly Nick and Wharton walked around the rim of the pond and approached the bench. Wharton swept off his hat and Nick followed suit.

"Mrs. Morris! Gertrude. This is an unexpected pleasure!" Wharton greeted them in his pleasant light baritone.

Nick glanced at the lovely dark-eyed girl; she was looking at him with undisguised admiration, which set him up no end, even if on closer examination she seemed awfully young.

"You boys put on your hats," Mrs. Morris scolded. "It's cold. May I present Miss Broussard?"

*Broussard.* The name rang an instant bell with Nick; the Broussards practically owned New Orleans, and had intermarried with the du Lacs and de Sevignys. He wondered if she could be of that family. If so, it was very fortunate indeed.

Wharton in turn presented Nick Adair, adding, "of New Orleans." Another irritating inaccuracy which ordinarily would have upset Nick, but right now he was too interested in the parentage of this Miss Broussard to linger on it.

Something peculiar happened when Wharton announced where Nick was from: the girl's smile disappeared, and a little shadow put out the gleam in her tilted eyes. He was puzzled. Nevertheless, when Mrs. Morris invited them to sit down, he deliberately took a seat next to the dark beauty.

"You are a magnificent skater, Miss Broussard." He noticed some of the brightness return to her gaze, and she flushed with shy gratification. It was a marvel, he thought, to see a young lady exhibit so much modesty. She must be very well-brought-up, he decided.

While Wharton chattered away with Mrs. Morris and Gertrude, Nick took advantage of the girl's tongue-tied silence to add, "You are a Southerner too, I take it." He had detected a faint accent during the introduction, and in her softly murmured reply to his compliment. "Do you happen to be from New Orleans?"

Mystified, he saw that slight withdrawal again. She only nodded. He couldn't understand it: surely she had nothing to be embarrassed about. To be allied with such a family could produce nothing but pride in anyone.

For all her loveliness, he was finding the conversation heavy going. It was not that she didn't like him; he had had too much experience with women to be mistaken about that.

He made a fresh effort. "Are you visiting New York?"

She relaxed somewhat, answering, "Oh, no. I live here now."

" 'Now,' " he repeated, smiling down into her eyes, "must mean that you are a recent settler."

"I . . . I've been here since last summer," she said with that same odd reluctance. Then, after another instant of uneasy silence, she asked, "Have you . . . always lived in New Orleans?"

"Actually I don't live there at all." He laughed a little. Curiously, he was sure that he saw relief in her expression. Why relief? "Wharton's always a little cavalier with details. I live on Adair's Island, on the Côte Blanche. I am not as acquainted with New Orleans as I'd like to be."

"Adair's *Island*!" She seemed inordinately pleased. "Why, everyone knows about that. It must be your . . . grandfather who had the sanctuary. I always imagined he must be such a remarkable man."

A quixotic old fool, Nick thought. But he swelled with pride over her reference to Adair's Island. "Yes. Of course he passed away quite a few years ago."

"I feel that I know you well," she said confidingly, "because I have heard so much about Adair's Island. They say that the house is magnificent, full of art treasures." She blushed slightly again, as if realizing she had been too forthcoming.

"Nothing would give me more pleasure than to show it to you, Miss Broussard," Nick said boldly.

He was annoyed at himself, though. He must have

gone too far, because she turned, looking at the others, apparently in an attempt to change the subject.

"Germaine, my dear," Mrs. Morris called out, "Bill and Gertrude and I have just settled it among ourselves . . . we're going to our house for some hot chocolate. You will join us, won't you, you and Mr. Adair?"

"Oh, I would *love* to," Germaine said with real regret, "but I really must go home and get ready for my party."

To himself, Nick thought: Germaine Broussard. What a beautiful name.

"Of course. What am I thinking of? This is the night of your reception." Mrs. Morris' voice cooled a trifle. She added dryly, "If it's half as clever as Pavan's other *fêtes*, it should be quite dazzling."

*Pavan.* Good God. Nick was stunned. This lovely girl, of such high birth, was connected in some way with his whore of a mother, the mercantile queen. The woman who had made him a bastard. It took every ounce of his control not to let the others see what he was thinking.

To cover his sick confusion, he said the first thing that popped into his head. "Is it a special occasion?"

"My birthday," Germaine said.

"Then let me wish you a happy one," Nick murmured.

"I would be delighted," she said generally to Nick and Wharton, "if both of you would attend. I'm sure Therese would be pleased."

*Therese.* So those were the terms they were on. How in hell had his mother managed to draw this girl into her questionable circle? Nick had to exert control to keep his wits together. "I am honored," he said, "but I'm afraid my presence, at the last moment like this, would . . . cause inconvenience." The girl looked very disappointed. "But your invitation is so kind that it makes me bold enough to ask you something: may I hope that I might see you tomorrow?"

Germaine's dark eyes lit up. She does like me, he thought, triumphant. She likes me very much indeed.

"Yes," she said simply. "Why don't you call at the house?" She gave him the number on Gramercy Park.

He was stymied. Call at the house of Therese Pavan? There was only one way out of it—he would have to gamble on sheer bravado.

"I mean no . . . disrespect," he said earnestly, gazing into her eyes, "but I had the wild, reckless hope that I might see you . . . unchaperoned. At luncheon. That afterward we might have a little ride in a hansom." Perhaps in her obvious inexperience the romance of that would win her over, *bien élevée* or not.

To Nick's delight, it did, because she nodded, agreeing. He arranged to meet her for luncheon thinking she was as naive and tractable as a child, not even to question such improper arrangements.

When the party saw Germaine to a public carriage that would take her to Gramercy Park before they all proceeded to the Morrises', Nick's head rang with plots and questions. There was something very strange about her residence in New York, her association with his mother. She had looked positively frightened when she learned where he was from.

Good Lord, she might have run away from home. It must be; people like the Broussards would never countenance her living in New York unattended—or with his mother, which was the same thing.

Nick would give a lot to know, and to advise the Broussards. They were very rich and powerful people, who would look kindly on a wellborn son-in-law.

The rescuer of Germaine Broussard, Nick reflected, smiling . . . the one who could save her from ruin. He wouldn't be at all surprised if he got the whole story from Mrs. Morris.

He would write to his father tonight, explaining that he needed another week in New York to obtain their money. That would give Nick plenty of time. When he was allied with the Broussards, the future of Adair's Island would be assured.

Bill Wharton reined in his buggy, drawling to Nick Adair, "Rotten bore, having to drive this far. No one

else in New York would be at a country house this
time of year. Good of you to keep me company
tonight."

"I'm delighted." As the two young men surrendered
the buggy to a servant and walked toward the Morris
mansion, Nick observed its stately columned facade.
He was surprised at the comparative smallness of the
mansion: Adair House was much bigger. "After all,
Washington slept here, and all that."

"Oh, yes. And Burr lived here to boot. But I repeat, it's a bore. However, where Gertrude is . . ."
Wharton grinned at Nick.

It won't be a bore for me, Nick thought. He was
proud of the honor—a dinner invitation to the Morris
mansion after only three days' acquaintance. It would
be an excellent opportunity to sound out the old lady
on Germaine Broussard . . . and to blacken the reputation of the notorious Madame Pavan. Nick's smile
broadened.

The butler greeted Wharton with respectful warmth
and bowed to Nick. "The family is in the tearoom,
gentlemen," he said, relieving the men of their fur-
trimmed overcoats.

"Must be a small party tonight," Wharton murmured. "We *are* being honored." He added in a low
voice as they walked along the corridor, "I say, Nick,
keep the lady-mother busy, will you? So I can make
some time with Gertrude?"

"Gladly." Nick was elated: that was exactly what he
wanted. Mrs. Morris seemed susceptible to young men
with the right looks and the proper names, and Nick
felt he was no exception.

He took in the polished entrance hall with a dazzled
glance. Obviously what the hall lacked in size it made
up in elegance, furnished with a breathtaking crystal
chandelier and eighteenth-century pieces of exquisite
simplicity.

Wharton and Nick followed the butler to a door on
the left, and the man announced them.

Stepping into the handsome room, Nick felt he was
surrounded by gold: ebonized chairs were trimmed in

gilt, and the gold window curtains were tied high in the Empire fashion. The dramatic chandelier was of gem-cut crystal and bronze. Few young men were as versed in such matters as Nick. This is what he wanted for Adair's Island, he thought swiftly. A little less splendor, a little more elegance.

But now he was obliged to gather in his wandering wits to greet his hostess. He went to her at once and bent over her hand. Mrs. Morris, stiffly arrayed in a gorgeous brocade gown, also with hints of gold, fluttered slightly when Nick kissed her plump fingers.

Nick greeted Gertrude and then Mr. Morris. He had met the latter once before, and the man struck him as a kind of gray presence hovering outside the aura of his forceful wife.

It was a small party indeed; there were only two strangers. Mrs. Morris acquainted Nick with the Boerums. Mrs. Boerum, he thought, was quite pretty in her way, but she seemed to lack spirit. She was dressed in a rather pale green creation. Gertrude, as usual, was vivid in an apple-red gown; she greeted Nick with careless friendliness, her large dark eyes on Wharton.

After exchanging a few pleasantries with Mr. Morris and the Boerums, Nick set himself to charming Mrs. Morris. He sat down beside her on the long Empire sofa, accepting a glass of sherry from the maid. "I am honored to be your guest," he murmured.

"Nonsense," she simpered. "It is good of a handsome young man to attend one of my dull little dinners."

"Time spent in the presence of beauty is never dull."

Mrs. Morris flushed slightly. The fool thought he was talking about her, not the house, Nick thought. He decided to turn her vanity to his advantage, adding, "In such lovely surroundings, as well." He gazed about, then upward at the chandelier.

Mrs. Morris, following his glance, remarked, "You have an instinct for the finest piece in the room. That is a souvenir of the Jumel residence . . . a gift of Napoleon to General Moreau."

"Magnificent," Nick said, impressed.

"I must say, you are a remarkable young man." Mrs. Morris smiled. "Very few of your generation have such taste and perception, Mr. Adair."

"If I may be so bold," he answered in a low voice, "would you do me the honor of calling me Nick? It would be so nice to hear someone call me that. I'm an orphan in a strange land, you know." He gave her one of his most wistful smiles, the kind of smile that was already working wonders with Germaine Broussard.

It worked splendidly, too, with Mrs. Morris. He seemed to have struck a maternal chord somewhere. Her sharp eyes softened, and she said, "How sad. You lost your mother, then, at an early age?"

"She died when I was born. I never knew her at all."

"My dear boy." Mrs. Morris touched his hand lightly with hers. "Why, of course I will call you Nick."

"You are so kind." Nick cleared his throat in a manly fashion, as if he were deeply affected but too embarrassed to show it. "Perhaps you would be kind enough to advise me about something. It's . . ." He stopped again, feigning shyness.

"I would be happy to," Mrs. Morris declared. Nick repressed a smile: Wharton said that advice, asked for or not, was her great pleasure.

"I've mentioned it to Bill, of course," Nick went on with his mock shyness. "But it isn't the same." He gave her another rueful smile. "Best fellow in the world, of course . . . finest family . . . but there are some things only a mother can really know. And I have no one else here in New York."

"What is it, my boy? Do tell me," Mrs. Morris urged.

But at that very moment, there was an untimely announcement of dinner. Nick very nearly swore. "You will sit by me at dinner," Mrs. Morris directed, "and we shall have a nice long talk."

The party proceeded into another golden room, a Georgian dining room draped in damask, and were seated at a lace-covered table set with glittering appointments and a centerpiece of orange hothouse roses.

Nick pulled out Mrs. Morris' chair at one end of the table, sitting between her and Mrs. Boerum.

"I fear we are an uneven number," Mrs. Morris said. "Another guest failed me at the last moment."

"Then I must try to be as amusing as two," Nick retorted, smiling.

"You should have invited Germaine, Mama. She is most dependable," Gertrude said, with a mischievous glance at Nick. Mr. Morris frowned, and Mrs. Morris chided sharply, "Gertrude! I'm surprised at you."

An unattractive, mottled flush crept up his hostess's neck and face, and Mrs. Boerum seemed deeply embarrassed. "Really," Mrs. Morris said, "I must apologize for my daughter's shocking manners. These modern girls . . ." She confided to Nick in a lower tone, "Germaine is a lovely young lady. And I could tell, that first day, you were charmed with her. But as long as she is under the guardianship of that Pavan woman. . ." Mrs. Morris' flush deepened. She seemed to recall her duties as hostess, and turned the conversation.

Nick endured it patiently until the dessert course arrived. "Perhaps," he began tentatively, "this is not the proper time . . "

"Yes. You wanted my advice. You shall have it." Mrs. Morris announced the adjournment of the women to the drawing room for coffee. "Leave the men to their port and cigars, Nick. You shall come with us. It makes me feel positively daring," Mrs. Morris said gaily.

Nick doubted that; Wharton had also told him that Elizabeth Schuyler Morris was a law unto herself. As a matter of fact, the other men seemed to take the change in protocol calmly.

"In that case, Mama, you should let me stay with the gentlemen," Gertrude said in an impudent tone.

This time it was Mrs. Boerum who responded amiably, "Behave yourself."

Nick followed the women into the drawing room and once more seated himself beside Mrs. Morris. Gertrude and Mrs. Boerum sat a little apart from them, beginning an animated discussion of fashions.

Nick caught the name of Pavan repeatedly. He turned
to Mrs. Morris.

"I was pained to hear you say that Miss Broussard's
. . . connection is doing her social damage," he said
bluntly. "You are absolutely right, of course. You see,
I . . ." Nick assumed his role of embarrassed swain. "I
have every intention of asking her to be my wife."

Mrs. Morris looked astounded. "But . . . good heavens, my boy! You have just met the young lady."

"I know." Nick fervently wished he could blush to
order. "It was extremely sudden." He saw Mrs. Morris' eagle eyes soften. Even she, apparently, was not
immune to a romantic situation. "I not only care for
her deeply, and wish her to bear my family name, but
I am aware that her own family is one of the finest in
the South. But the Broussard name is in peril because
of her connection with this Pavan woman."

Nick almost laughed; he sounded like a romance
novel. He could tell that his words affected Mrs. Morris. She was listening with sympathy and intentness.

"It is also a matter of, well . . ." He laughed a little.
"I'm afraid I sound pompous. But a matter of *rescuing*
her from this ambiguous position." He lowered his
voice, glancing at the other women. "You see, this Pavan
woman's reputation, in the South, is notorious. She came
to the North to escape it. I fear Germaine is so young, so
innocent, that she has fallen victim to the woman."

"I knew it! I knew it!" Mrs. Morris' expression was
indignant, avid. "I knew there was something wrong
about that woman. I'm shocked. Appalled."

"So am I. You can imagine my feelings when I
learned that such a lovely girl, from such a fine family,
had been 'adopted' by a woman of that caliber."

"You poor boy. No wonder you needed advice."
Mrs. Morris shook her elaborately coiffed head. "What
do you plan to do? Am I to assume that Germaine
returns your feelings?"

"Yes. She has done me the honor of telling me so,"
Nick said, greatly enjoying his absurd role as a
lovestruck suitor. "I plan just to . . . steal her away,"
he confided.

"I think that is the most romantic story I've ever heard," Mrs. Morris confessed. "Why, you have swept the girl off her feet, in no time at all. But how on earth have you *managed*? Do you mean to tell me you have already been alone with the girl?"

"That's the most shocking thing of all. This Mrs. Pavan—McKay, or whatever her name is—actually allows Germaine to go out unchaperoned."

"No!" Mrs. Morris' small eyes rounded with shock.

"Oh, yes. If my intentions were not the most honorable . . ." Nick murmured.

Nick noticed that Gertrude and Mrs. Boerum had been glancing at them uneasily from time to time. No doubt they had heard the names of Germaine and Pavan. "What *are* you two gossiping about, Mama?" Gertrude demanded.

"Hush, child. Harriet, come here," Mrs. Morris ordered. Mrs. Boerum obeyed, taking a chair next to the sofa.

"What is it, Elizabeth?"

Gertrude, looking extremely curious, also approached and sat in a neighboring chair. "Yes, Mama, what on earth . . . ? You sound so excited."

"I want both of you to hear this," Mrs. Morris said severly. "Perhaps now, Gertrude, you will not accuse me of 'tyranny' as you did when I forbade you to go to Germaine's party."

Gertrude's dark, graceful brows shot up, and she darted a surprised glance at Nick. Apparently, he thought, such airing of intimate family business was usually unheard-of.

"And you, Harriet"—Mrs. Morris fixed Mrs. Boerum with a steely glance, utterly unperturbed—"will realize why I took the stance I did at the meeting of the board."

The board, Nick repeated silently. This was going even better than he had expected. It sounded as if his mother's business was involved.

"Please tell them what you have told me, Nick."

With relish, pretending to embarrassment and gallant reluctance, Nick repeated what he had said to

Mrs. Morris, with some new embellishments. He hinted with great delicacy that Madame Pavan had had unsavory associations in New Orleans that were "common knowledge" because some of her escapades involved prominent families, leaving the impression that she had practically been run out of town. He added that Michel Pavan, whose family lived near his own estate, was a highly respected man, now brokenhearted by his daughter's disgrace, and that the woman had refused marriage to one of the best young men in the area.

Gertrude and Harriet Boerum stared at him in amazement; to his annoyance, the girl looked skeptical and Mrs. Boerum quite upset.

"You see?" Mrs. Morris triumphed. "*This* is the . . . person who had the unmitigated gall, the sheer effrontery to present her designs to the Metropolitan Opera board."

Ah! So that was it, Nick thought. It appeared that his stone was killing several birds. He was exultant.

"Are you satisfied now, Harriet?"

"I am deeply disturbed," Mrs. Boerum said in her gentle way. "There's never been a breath of scandal in New York about Madame Pavan. She seems such a nice woman. A perfect lady."

Mrs. Morris snorted and Nick remained wisely silent, assuming an air of discomfort.

Gertrude said bluntly, "I can't believe it."

Nick could feel fury rising in him. Was the little bitch calling him a liar?

The other women looked at her in astonishment.

"Gertrude!" Mrs. Morris's tone was scandalized. Exasperated, she asked, "How could you say such a thing? Gracious heavens, child, I think you've taken leave of your senses."

"Really, my dear . . ." Mrs. Boerum said weakly.

Nick could almost hear their thoughts: How could the girl doubt the word of an Adair, whose New York branch was beyond reproach?

But Gertrude was undeterred. "I beg your pardon, Nick. I did not mean I doubted your word. I just feel there's been some . . . misunderstanding. I have always admired Madame Pavan tremendously, and she has been extraordinarily generous to Germaine. It's just that . . . it's hard to reconcile your picture of her with mine." When Gertrude said that, she bit her lip, shooting an uneasy glance at her mother. Obviously she had revealed something she hadn't intended to, Nick decided with amusement. So much the better. It served her right for insulting him, even obliquely.

"I am at a loss to understand your close acquaintance with Madame Pavan," Mrs. Morris said coldly to her daughter. "I was not aware that you knew her so well."

Gertrude reddened. "I . . . don't, of course. I am only going by what Germaine has told me."

"I devoutly hope so." Mrs. Morris gave Gertrude a penetrating look. "In that case, Miss Broussard is the one who has been fooled. And that can hardly be her fault; she is a young girl without proper guidance."

Gertrude maintained a sullen silence.

Harriet Boerum leaned forward with a timid, nervous expression. "All this is quite upsetting, of course, Elizabeth. However, it does not alter the fact that Madame Pavan is a . . . masterful designer." Nick gathered that for her, this was an extremely courageous speech, but it irritated him almost beyond endurance.

Mrs. Morris looked as if Mrs. Boerum had struck her. She took a deep breath, expanding her prowlike bosom, and said in a cold voice, "As far as I'm concerned, Harriet, the subject is closed." She glared at her daughter, including her in the statement.

Agitated, the girl got up and flounced out of the room.

Mrs. Morris shook her head. "Closed, that is, except to say to you, dear boy"—she smiled at Nick— "that I am grateful to you for this . . . vital information. As to the other little matter we discussed," she added coyly, "you may rely on me to aid you in any possible way."

"Thank you. Thank you very much. I will always be grateful to you." Nick took up Mrs. Morris' hand and kissed it, managing to speak with an appropriate *tremolo*. He was amused and gratified to see the old harridan's eyes grow soft again and actually moisten.

The tableau was interrupted by the return of the three other men. Wharton looked dismayed when he surveyed the room for Gertrude and found her absent.

The conversation became general and Mrs. Boerum was prevailed upon to play on the handsome eighteenth-century piano set between two of the windows.

Nick glanced at Wharton. His friend's face was glum. Wharton got up quietly and whispered something in Mrs. Morris' ear. Smiling, she whispered back, and Wharton resumed his seat with a relieved expression. Inquiring about Gertrude, no doubt.

Nick dismissed his friend's consternation and the unexpected opposition of Gertrude Morris.

He himself had triumphed tonight beyond his wildest expectations. The old woman, metaphorically speaking, had dropped into his palm like a ripe fruit. His hostess's *avoirdupois* made that a highly amusing idea, and Nick was hard put not to laugh aloud. He felt wonderful, absolutely wonderful. He had succeeded, he was sure, in ruining the opera commission for his mother. If he knew women, the story would be all over fashionable New York by tomorrow night. Maybe her wretched business would eventually go bankrupt. God, he hoped so, with all his heart. It was little enough to atone for what she had done to him and to his father. And essentially he had told the truth: she had refused one of the best young men in Louisiana. His father, Nicholas Adair. Furthermore, she was no better than a woman of the streets, from any viewpoint.

At the end of the evening, after he had made an elaborate farewell to the ladies and expressed the wish that Miss Gertrude would recover from her indisposition, Nick followed Wharton to the buggy in gratified silence.

Wharton drove off without a word.

After they had driven a few miles, Nick said, "Bad luck that Miss Gertrude was suddenly indisposed."

"She's *never* indisposed," his friend returned. "I

just wonder what's behind it. What were you talking
about, all that time, with the women? Was something
said to upset her?"

"We discussed all sorts of things. I can't imagine
what could have upset her."

"Well, at least you enjoyed your evening," Wharton
said gloomily.

"Oh, yes. More than I could tell you." Nick smiled
in the darkness.


Therese frowned at the sketch. "I don't know what's
gotten into that girl," she muttered. Impressed with
Germaine's design for an evening dress, Therese had
allowed Germaine to submit other ideas for the all-
important Suffolk trousseau, with the assurance that if
they measured up she would be given full credit, as
she had been for the seamless-sleeve idea.

But this—the design was unimaginative, boring.
Worse than that was the execution, which was positively slovenly. And Germaine had been asked to submit three sketches, not one.

Ever since her birthday, Germaine had been a different person. The confidence between them had evaporated overnight; Germaine had been coming home at
odd hours, and once, during the past week, had even
disappeared for hours from the salon without a word
of explanation beforehand. They were going to have
to have a talk, Therese decided. Her head began to
ache. On top of the opera board's continuing silence,
Germaine's defection was the last straw.

"Jenny," she called out, "would you ask Germaine
to come in here a moment?"

Her aide came to the door with a letter in her hand.
"She's . . . not in, Madame Pavan."

"Not *in*! It's eleven o'clock." Germaine had over-
slept that morning, and had assured Therese she would
be in "in no time" when, a bit annoyed, Therese left
the house without her. Something was definitely wrong.
"Is that for me?"

"Oh, yes. It was hand-delivered just now."

Jenny gave her the letter and went out.

It was from Edmond Stanton.

The manager of the Metropolitan Opera.

Therese's hands shook as she tore the envelope open. "I deeply regret . . ." it began. Reading on, Therese had a cold, queasy feeling in her stomach pit.

Mr. Stanton declined the services of Pavan in the most tactful manner, but declined them all the same, stating that the board's ultimate decision had been to continue with its present designers for the various productions.

Therese replaced the letter in its envelope and thrust it in her handbag. She ached with disappointment. And there was still the matter of Germaine.

Exasperated, she ordered the carriage to drive her home. If Germaine had gone back to sleep, Therese was going to give her what-for. Where, Therese raged inwardly, was all the girl's original dedication . . . all her loyalty?

Rosie admitted Therese, respectful as always, but surprised. It was a rare thing for her mistress to come storming into the house on a weekday morning. Without questioning the maid, Therese went upstairs. Germaine's door was ajar.

Calling out her name, Therese went in.

The room was empty, the bed meticulously made. The girl's drawing materials were gone and the top of the dressing table denuded of her dainty accessories.

Sick at heart, Therese went to the big chifforobe and opened its doors. It was empty too. She closed the doors.

Only then did she glimpse the fat envelope on the desk between the two big windows. Weighing it in her hand, Therese judged that there was a long, long letter inside.

With a fateful feeling, she sat down on the bed and tore open the envelope. The date on the letter was that day's.

"My dear Therese," she read, "you will forgive me when you know how happy I am. By the time you read this, I will be Mrs. Nick Adair."

Therese stared at the name, barely comprehending.

Nick Adair.

Charles.

Germaine was marrying her son.

Holding the letter in nerveless fingers, Therese made herself read on.

"I wanted so much for him to know you, and yet I was afraid. I know you would have tried to stop me because I am so young." Eerily, Therese heard an echo of Charles quoting Nicholas, long ago. She had a strong feeling that the reason was Charles's, not Germaine's.

"But he is the man of my dreams, Therese. He is more elegant, more romantic, more beautiful than any prince of the realm. We met that day I went skating with Gertrude Morris, and I fell in love with him right away. He is so courteous and proper that he wouldn't even come to my party, although I invited him and Bill Wharton."

Poor child, poor child, Therese mourned. She had no idea of the real reason.

"He asked me to meet him the next day, unchaperoned, because he longed so for us to be alone. It was a daring thing to do, but I did it, and, Therese, it was like heaven. I knew it would be all right, because he's from such a good family. And it was true: he acted like a perfect gentleman, even when we drove through the park after luncheon. He gave me a lovely leather-bound book of poems for my birthday, perfectly proper, although he confessed that very first day that he wished he could be allowed to give me something more 'significant.'

"And, Therese, he proposed to me the second day we were together! It's the most exciting, most romantic thing that ever happened to me in my life.

"I know now that my career will have to wait; that I am not the genius you are, and never will be. Therese, I know now what I was *born* for . . . and I have found the love like the love you have for Anthony.

"Someday you will meet him, and I know you will love him as much as I do, for you won't be able to help it."

The irony of that last sentence was too much for Therese: the tears streamed down her face. How could he, how could he? He had not even told Germaine that she, Therese Pavan McKay, was his mother. But of course, he would be too ashamed.

Through a blur of tears, Therese returned to her reading of the devastating letter.

"He came to New York, he told me, to try to borrow money to save his father's estate, Adair's Island. He was unsuccessful. This is to be a secret from my family, because Nick is afraid that they might disapprove of our alliance. But I am telling you because I have always told you everything."

Everything, Therese reflected bitterly, except this—this mad act that could destroy you. It was apparent to her that "Nick" had married Germaine only for her connections and the Broussard and du Lac money.

"I'm not worried, though. Even my high-and-mighty relatives could not disapprove of an Adair. It's a splendid joke, isn't it, that I am going back willingly to the kind of life I ran away from?

"But oh, Therese, it is so different now. It is true love that is taking me home again. I know that my family will press us to live in New Orleans rather than at Adair's Island, but I don't care where we live as long as we are together. In any case, Nick has said that he is not at all averse to living in New Orleans, if that will please me and my family."

I can well imagine, Therese retorted to herself. Nick Adair was his father's son; he would go to any lengths to preserve the kingdom of Adair's Island, knowing he could persuade Germaine to live there later.

There was a great deal more to the letter, but Therese didn't have the stomach for it now. She read its fond conclusion, her tears starting all over again.

"Please do not be angry with me, Therese. Write to me to tell me you have forgiven me. I will send you the address as soon as I know it myself. I am so grateful to you, and I will always love you, you know that . . . for all the things you have taught me, all that

you have done for me out of the sweetness and generosity of your heart. I will never forget you."

The letter was signed "All the love of Germaine
that can be spared from Nick."

Therese got up from the bed, smoothed it, and walked
into the master bedroom with the letter still clutched in
her hand. Folding the letter, she slipped it back into
the envelope and put it gently on her dressing table.

Though still in her outdoor clothes, Therese hardly
felt the warmth of her heavy cloak as she paced back
and forth over the luxurious carpet.

Suddenly she recalled a line from Germaine's letter,
something about meeting Charles the day she had
gone skating with Gertrude Morris.

Gertrude Morris' mother was Elizabeth Schuyler
Morris, the most influential member of the opera board.
It was just a little too coincidental. The Morrises probably had met Charles. And Charles could have told
them . . . anything.

Furthermore, in his letter, Stanton had repeatedly used
"I" rather than "we." He had praised her talent and imagination, implying that the board, not he, had rejected Pavan.

It all came together: Charles meeting Mrs. Morris
just before the board turned her down for no apparent
reason. Charles must have had a hand in that.

It will never end, she raged in silence. Charles had
deprived her of that longed-for commission. Worse,
he had done what Nicholas had done before—stolen
from her a beloved child.

Germaine had been her substitute for a daughter,
but more than that, even, a shining hope for the future
of Pavan. She had dreamed that someday Germaine
Broussard might be its head.

Suddenly the heat of her heavy cloak overwhelmed
her. With trembling hands she removed it and took off
her hat. Looking in the glass to smooth her hair,
Therese caught the reflection of her hurt, angry eyes.

Then she remembered that Germaine's letter said
that Adair's Island was in financial trouble.

Transfixed, she stared into the mirror with unseeing eyes.

By God, she'd buy it. She'd buy Adair's Island and make it Petit Anse, that name the island had carried so many years before it was invaded by the Adairs.

Yes, she'd damned well buy the whole thing, estate and mine; and she'd see that the mine operated at a profit. Obviously, under the slack reign of Nicholas Adair, the mine had to be going to seed too.

It would work no hardship on Germaine, with her rich and powerful connections. Her family could buy her any house she liked in New Orleans. In any event, it would save her from having to live in the country; from their earliest acquaintance, Germaine had told Therese how much she loved cities.

And buying Petit Anse would be the perfect payback to the damned Adairs.

She had enough money of her own now to accomplish it, whatever Anthony might think of the enterprise. But he wouldn't object; he never had objected to anything she wanted. He *couldn't* object to what she did with her own money, the money she had worked so hard for, for nearly thirty-five years.

Yes. Therese Pavan was going to buy Petit Anse, and the sooner the better . . . before Charles swindled the Broussards out of the money.

She would turn Nicholas out. She would fill Petit Anse with Pavans. Berthe would love to spend her declining years in the midst of its splendors; many times, in recent years, she had expressed nostalgia for the bayou. So had Charl'. There was every likelihood Charl' might enjoy living there too, with Nell and the children.

Therese laughed, a sudden, hard laugh. And someday she might open a Pavan in New Orleans. How Charles would love *that*, she decided with malice.

She hurried downstairs to the telephone in the hall, and asked the operator to connect her with a particular firm well-known to her and Anthony.

When she was connected with the man she sought, she said coolly, "There is a certain Southern property I have an interest in . . . the owner is eager to sell. . ."

*     *     *

Nicholas Adair stared at the bank statement through alcohol-hazed eyes, triumphant and elated. He had deposited the check, signed the accompanying documents with hardly a glance—legal language bored him increasingly as the years went by—and mailed them back at once to the New Orleans firm acting for the Northern corporation.

Wait until the boy sees the statement, he exulted. This will show him Nicholas Adair is not finished . . . the young puppy, failing so abysmally in New York.

Well, not altogether. He'd had the good sense to marry a Broussard, at least. A fine name, a valuable connection. Not that the Adairs needed anyone now, with this splendid investment arriving as if by magic.

And this nonsense about the newlyweds living in New Orleans—well, that would pass. Nick would knock some sense into the girl. She was besotted with him, and would probably turn out to be a good, obedient wife.

Might be a good idea to go to New Orleans himself he thought. The condition of his jacket reminded him that he ought to refurbish his wardrobe.

He swayed, debating, in the middle of his office.

The sound of voices reached him from the entrance hall: one of the voices was the boy's.

The decision was made for him. He would go to New Orleans another day. He couldn't miss a visit with his son; it was an unexpected bonus, to be able to flaunt the balance.

Nicholas staggered toward the door. Before he could open it, the boy strode in, and his face was like a thundercloud.

Nick closed the door without speaking. Then he demanded, "What in the name of God have you done?"

"That's a fine greeting. What do you mean, what have I done? Don't take that tone with me."

He recoiled from his angry-looking son and grasped the back of a chair; underneath his bluster, he was almost frightened by the boy's expression.

"You drunken fool," his son said coldly, "you've sold Adair's Island . . . to that whore."

Dumbfounded, Nicholas supported himself on the back of the chair, putting his weight on his hands. "You must be crazy," he protested. "We have just had an enormous investment from a corporation in New York."

"Investment!" his son spat out. "Who would invest in this enterprise, with *you* running it? Good God, you didn't even read the papers, did you? Why didn't you consult me . . . how could you *do* this to me?"

Nicholas recoiled from the battery of shouted questions: he was so confused, terribly confused. But he *hadn't* read the papers. He was so eager to get the money, he would have signed anything. "What . . . what do you know of this?" he asked his son.

With a look of utter hatred, Nick threw himself into a chair. "Everyone in New Orleans knows about it now . . . and just when I was about to bring old Broussard around, goddamnit!" He ran his hands distractedly through his hair. "Germaine's pregnant— apparently she already was when we married—and the old man would do anything for her. And she'd do anything for *me*. If you'd only waited. But no, you had to sell my inheritance out from under me to that whore."

"What 'whore'?" Nicholas beat his palms on the back of the chair. "You keep saying 'whore,' and the investors are a corporation!"

"Liquor has rotted your brain. My *mother*—one of your numerous intrigues. *She's* the corporation."

*"What?"* The older man, keeping his hands on the high-backed chair for support, brought his trembling body around it and collapsed onto its seat. "I . . . I don't understand," he said in a broken voice.

"Of course you don't." The answer was heavy with contempt. "The bitch lied from the beginning, to everyone, from the firm in New York, to the agent here in New Orleans. They were dealing with Souzay first, a reputable outfit; when Souzay got wind of what she was plotting, he withdrew, and so did the New York firm, who are also reputable. But that didn't stop her. She went direct to Thibedaux, here—and you know what sharp-dealing varmints they are. Thibedaux, of course, claims now that they were deceived.

"Deceived, by God!" Nick brought his fist down onto the arm of his chair, and his father winced. "She even had you investigated. *Investigated*. Discovered that you're not competent anymore. And she gambled on your incompetence—and won."

Nicholas had never seen his son's face so furious, or so desolate.

"Won the only thing I love, or will ever love," his son muttered. "And now she will turn you out . . . and I will never see this place again."

Nicholas' fuddled mind absorbed only one phrase. "Turn me out? How can that be?"

"She's the owner. Don't you understand that? She can do anything she likes now; she owns the whole place, down to the last stick of furniture."

The enormity of that was so great that Nicholas rejected it as impossible. And his thoughts turned to that other terrible thing his son had said—that Adair's Island was the only thing he had ever loved. He mumbled the phrase aloud, thick-tongued, staring at the boy he had always idolized.

"It can't be true, Nick. You have always loved me. I am your father."

The boy got to his feet and stared down with sheer hatred. "Love *you*, you drunken wreck? It was for Adair's Island I came, never for you. I've been waiting for you to die ever since I can remember. Now there's no reason to come here anymore, and I don't give a damn if I never see you again." He turned on his heel and walked out.

Nicholas slumped in the high-backed chair, his hands on his knees. It was all too much for him, too much.

He could hear the deceitful boy speaking calmly to the butler, and the butler's polite farewell. Then the great front door, closing quietly; the butler's step receding somewhere, over the still-shining floor of the shabby foyer.

The boy had not even had the decency to close the office door behind him. Weak and trembling, Nicholas struggled to his feet and shut it.

Then he lurched to the beautiful sideboard and poured a tumblerful of whiskey from the cut-glass decanter, laboring back to the velvet chair with its thronelike back and half-falling onto its softness.

He raised the tumbler to his lips and drank; some of the liquor spilled over onto his chin. This time the drink did not bring the instant relief he was used to. For a brief moment his brain seemed to clear; his thoughts were too clear, and must be blurred again; he could not bear them. Returning to the sideboard, he replenished the tumbler, and this time he managed to carry the decanter, too, and set it on the table by the velvet chair.

But the last drink brought no more ease than the one before. The pain was still there, sharper than ever.

The boy had said he'd never loved him.

And all those years Nicholas had waited . . . waited for Nick to grow up so he could be released from that whore and those peasants . . . take his rightful place at Adair's Island. The hurtful pictures of those years began to flash before his eyes: Nick's arrival, his splendid young manhood, his years of school. How Nicholas had ached with longing for the holidays, for the boy's return.

Now Nick was married to a Broussard . . . and Nicholas would never see his own grandson, the rightful heir to their green kingdom.

Nicholas Adair the Third.

Nicholas began to cry.

And now that whore was going to turn him out.

There was nothing left at all. It was better to be dead than to give her the satisfaction.

Nicholas got up and lurched toward the gun rack on the wall. Choosing a pistol, he placed it to his temple.

The world exploded in his brain.

# 19

Germaine Adair observed that Nick had been far more upset by the loss of Adair's Island than by the death of his own father. As soon as the estate passed into the hands of that Northern company, she began to see her husband change before her very eyes.

Before, he had been vital and tender; now he was languid and absent, with bitterness dragging down his mouth. Once he said to her in a fit of despair, "I am no one now, without Adair's Island."

Eager to raise his spirits, Germaine protested that she had loved him before she even knew his name, much less that his father owned the Island. But her reassurance fell on deaf ears. It seemed to her he mourned Adair's Island as he should have mourned his father; bizarrely he spoke of the lost land the way a lover speaks of the beloved.

Yet, sympathetic to that mighty blow to his pride, Germaine tried to forgive his preoccupation. She knew that it humiliated him to be without the occupation of managing the salt mine and the estate, to have to have her father obtain a post for him with the powerful Sugar Exchange. Worst of all, perhaps, was the fact that the Broussards had purchased a house for the newlyweds, when Nick had dreamed, he said, of carrying her over the threshold of his family mansion.

He worked hard at the Exchange, going there early in the morning, not returning home until late at night. She endured the discomforts of her confinement with little consolation from her husband.

That stung. So did Therese's continued silence. Germaine had kept her word, writing as soon as she and Nick were settled in the new house, but in all these months there had been no letter. And Nick himself had mailed all her letters for her, saying they'd go more quickly from "downtown."

Tired of his unalloyed gloom, she was annoyed when a letter arrived for him at home one morning, showing the return address of the Thibedaux Company, the agency for what Nick called the "rape of the Adairs." It had to have something to do with the estate. Germaine dreaded letting Nick know of its arrival, but she could hardly keep it from him.

When she handed it to him that evening, his face darkened angrily; he ripped the envelope open savagely. As she watched him read, Germaine saw his golden brows draw together in an infuriated frown and his fine mouth tighten. Cursing, he balled the letter up in his fist and threw it on the floor.

Laboriously Germaine stooped and picked up the crumpled letter, smoothing it out. "The new owners," it stated, "offer their condolences on your father's demise. And they wish to assure you that the furnishings of the houses at Petit Anse have been set aside for you, and are now in storage in New Orleans."

Exasperated, Germaine asked Nick why he was angry. It seemed to her that the new owners were being very decent. Extraordinarily so, as a matter of fact—the furnishings and art objects, she had heard, were priceless. And the new owners had even included condolences. "How can you be angry about *this*?" she repeated.

Attached to the letter, she noticed, was the receipt for the furnishings, marked "Paid."

"Why, they've even borne the expense," she added.

"You're a fool. You don't understand at all," he growled, snatching the letter and the receipt from her hand.

She was furious over the epithet, but he was right—she *didn't* understand his attitude.

She became increasingly depressed during that wretched summer of 1891 when she was carrying the child. She prayed that when it arrived, it would soften

Nick's distress over the loss of his precious Island, whose very name she was growing sick of.

On November 4, 1891, in the famous Touro Infirmary, she had a perfect, healthy child.

The baby was a girl.

She was racked with disappointment. However, when the little thing was placed by her side, Germaine was overcome with love for her beautiful daughter.

The baby could not be another Nick, so Germaine named her Nicole.

Weakened by the difficult birth, Germaine found her recuperation was maddeningly slow. But at last, in January, 1892, she was elated to feel her strength return.

She decided to visit some of the salons and department stores.

She had again written, finally, to Therese. No matter how long they had been out of touch, Germaine knew that Therese could not be indifferent to the news of the baby, and she had been thinking of Therese more and more.

She could drop the letter off at the post office on the way to the stores.


Riffling through the mail on the hall table of the Gramercy house, Therese read the return address on one envelope and dropped the others.

Mrs. Nick Adair.

Germaine . . . after all this time! Therese stared at her writing, incredulous. Holding the letter tightly in her hand, she took it upstairs with her to the boudoir.

It was positively eerie: only that morning, reacting to the horrible current "chest-out" look—it was bound to lead to a sort of one-huge-bosom effect, like the prow of a ship—Therese had begun to sketch out a romantic new "Bayou Line," soft and slender, for spring and summer.

Thanking heaven that many elegant women refused to look like pouter pigeons, Therese had restored the natural lines of the female body. There were gowns the color of the water hyacinths along Côte Blanche, the hue of flying flamingos; slender gowns with spring-green fringe like the swaying meadow grass of Petit Anse.

Some faint, sharp nostalgia had prompted the designs. And now, here in her hand was a letter from Germaine.

Therese impatiently disposed of her hat and, tearing open the envelope with eagerness, unfolded the thick letter.

"My dear Therese." The note of unchanging affection moved her deeply.

"Even though you have never answered my letters, I have never forgotten our friendship, and I hope by this time you might have forgiven me."

*Never answered her letters.* My God, it didn't seem possible for this to be happening again. Nick must have intercepted Germaine's letters; no one else would have had reason to. That had to be it. Why, her son was as big a liar as Nicholas Adair, who had told him that his mother "ignored" his own nonexistent letters.

Therese forced her concentration on the letter.

"I had a beautiful little baby girl last November. Her name is Nicole. I think her eyes will stay blue, like Nick's, but she already has quite a head of dark hair, like the du Lacs and Broussards."

My grandchild, Therese thought with an astonished feeling. *I have a granddaughter name Nicole Adair.*

Her real name is Nicole Pavan. The oblique, swift thought came out of nowhere.

Greedily she devoured the rest of the letter; there was a great deal more about Nicole, and oddly, little mention of Nick. What's more, Therese caught an undernote of nostalgia in Germaine's repeated and carefully unemphatic references to the old days at Pavan.

There was something wrong there, Therese decided. Perhaps Germaine's love for Nick had undergone a drastic change.

"I want to see them, I want to see them," Therese inadvertently said aloud.

"*Do* you? See whom, Madame Therese?"

Therese looked up, surprised. Anthony was standing right by the *chaise longue*; she had been so intent on the letter, and her deep thoughts, she hadn't even heard his silent entrance on the thick carpet.

"Oh, Anthony! Read this." She thrust the letter in his hand. Smiling at her, he sat down beside her and glanced over the letter rapidly.

"Good Lord." Anthony looked at her.

Therese nodded, meeting his gaze. "Nick Adair is up to his father's tricks, it seems."

"Obviously. And now, your granddaughter's arrived. Germaine still doesn't know. And . . ." he said, taking her chin in his hand, "you want to see Germaine and the baby. It's strange, but I had the feeling you were thinking of Petit Anse when I saw this."

Only then did she notice her portfolio, propped against the *chaise longue* beside them.

"You forgot it and left it on the hall table," he said. "So I brought it up to you." In recent years, Therese had begun doing a good deal of sketching at home. "But I couldn't resist looking, first." He grinned at her. "They're beautiful—your dresses from the 'Bayou Line.' "

"Thank you."

"Come here," he commanded softly. She leaned against him, resting her face on his chest. Anthony stroked her hair. "At times like this you're almost like a little girl yourself," he murmured. "And I love the way your eyes light up when I compliment you on your work. Amazing . . . how modest the great Pavan is."

She was silent, relaxed, enjoying his nearness.

He said quietly, "You've been wanting to go to Petit Anse, haven't you?" She nodded, and his arms tightened around her.

How remarkable it was, she thought, to revel in his affection still, after all the time they had been together. How remarkable *he* was; sometimes he knew what she was thinking practically before she thought it. "You are the greatest gift life ever gave me," she said.

He kissed her forehead and squeezed her closer to him. "You're the *only* one it ever gave me." His tone changed then and he asked in a businesslike way, "When shall we leave?"

She leaned back and looked up at him, and began to laugh. "You don't waste any time, do you?"

"Why should I? I would like to waste some advice, though. I'm all for Petit Anse—I could take some quiet time myself. And I know you've been wanting to spend more time there, too."

She had been wanting to visit the bayou in recent months, and told him so. Learning of Nicholas' death right after the final sale, she had avoided going to Petit Anse; she left it in the hands of caretakers, with the servants pensioned off or employed elsewhere. The mine had been left to flounder, under the direction of a foreman; Nick had apparently just walked away from it, and from the house, taking nothing.

She could not stomach the idea of seeing or possessing the Adairs' effects, and specified that the house be totally empty for new occupation, with the contents going to Nick Adair.

Then Charl' and Nell had surprised her by expressing their desire to move south with Berthe. It was the perfect solution; Charl' could take over the mine, with which most Côte Blanche boys were familiar—old man Adair had allowed them to see its operation—and Berthe and Nell would take charge of the house.

Since then, Therese had visited Petit Anse only briefly; then, lately, she had begun to feel an uncharacteristic need to go for a longer stay.

The "Bayou Line" was the expression of that strange homesickness. After thirty-five years, she was suddenly hungry for the bayou she had believed she hated.

Now she and Anthony were silent, thinking their own thoughts.

Finally he said, "It'll be good to go down there again. Even after the war, when it was so shattered, there were always things about that place I loved." He paused. "About my 'advice' "—he smiled—"maybe I should make it a *question*. Are you sure you can . . .

take it all up again with Germaine? It might be very awkward."

His courteous elision made her smile. "To say the least." Awkward indeed, to break it to Germaine that Therese was her mother-in-law, Nicole her own grand-child. Admit to her that she had bought Petit Anse right out from under her own son.

"Look here," she said, "perhaps we should just *go*. By the time we get there, maybe I'll know what to do."

Anthony seemed amused at her audacity, but he followed her suggestion. With the quickness with which he handled everything, he had them in a private com-partment on the southbound train the next afternoon.

Glancing at him as he leaned back, luxuriating in the peace of their compartment, she noticed how tired he was. And she decided to say no more of her di-lemma until they reached New Orleans. She touched his hand. He enclosed her fingers in his with a tender, companionable pressure, and with his eyes still shut, he smiled.

Therese looked out at the passing scenery, but all she could see were the faces of Germaine and Nick, the friend who had become a daughter, the son who hated her.

Anthony had fallen asleep. Therese picked up the new novel she had brought along. But the words made no sense at all; over the clacking of the train her own thoughts intruded. Nothing existed beyond the worri-some problem of Nick and Germaine and the grand-child whom it might be catastrophic to claim.

The solution would not come. All throughout din-ner, and later, when their beds were made up, she had still not decided what to do.

The next morning, she reread Germaine's letter slowly. That undernote of loneliness and frustration struck her again, like a human cry. The decision was made: Germaine needed her: Therese had understood her as no one else could. She would go to Germaine.

As the train was pulling into New Orleans, she told Anthony what she planned. "I think," he said judicially, "you should be sure that Nick isn't at home. And if you wish me to, of course I will go with you."

"I think I should go alone."

He checked their baggage at the depot and accompanied her to a telephone. After speaking into the instrument, Therese turned to Anthony with shining eyes. "She's at home, with the baby. Nick isn't expected for another hour."

That was cutting it fine, but she was resolved to go. She and Anthony made plans to meet at Begue's for dinner. He hailed a public carriage and drove with her to the house.

"Good luck, my darling," he said, kissing her.

Therese walked up the stairs without looking back, suddenly depressed by the sound of the carriage driving away. The prospect of telling Germaine what she had to tell was so daunting that Therese was no longer sure she had the courage.

Of course, when the letters were explained, that would open up the whole Pandora's box—

Her anxious reflections were interrupted by the opening of the door. A neat little quadroon maid asked courteously for her name. "I am expected," Therese explained, smiling.

Then, behind the girl, she saw Germaine coming down the stairs, bright-faced, welcoming. "Therese! Oh, *Therese.*"

The maid withdrew and Germaine embraced Therese. "I couldn't believe it when I heard your voice! I just couldn't believe it. This is such a pleasure, such an amazement . . . you are here. And that means you have forgiven me."

Hugging her close, Therese thought: It has begun already. It's no good at all; I can no longer deceive her. I won't take the blame for what Nick has done.

She stepped back. "Let me look at you." She heard her own voice grow uncertain, because Germaine was sadly different from the girl she had known in New York.

Germaine was not yet eighteen; she looked twenty-five. She had been slender and blithe, now she was thin and tentative. Even her color was not as vivid, nor her hair so glossy. The dark, tilted eyes seemed to have gained wisdom at a high price.

However, she was dressed, as always, in the height of fashion. "How elegant you are," Therese said. She had an idea that the sharp Germaine could see through that; she smiled a little ruefully.

"It's not a Pavan, of course," Germaine said with a forced gaiety that gave Therese a pang. "But come . . . would you like to go up to the boudoir and see the baby? Or would you prefer the parlor for a while?" She laughed, adding, "Mothers are so terribly boring about their offspring, I'm afraid." She took Therese's cloak.

Therese felt as if a knife were twisting in her heart: Germaine had never even known that Therese was a mother too. Germaine did not know, now, that it was Therese's own granddaughter she was joking about.

"By all means," she said, proud of the steadiness of her voice, "let's go up and see the baby right away."

Germaine's face lit up. She led Therese up a graceful, curving stairway to the second floor, and into a spacious bedroom with spring-green walls. A superb rococo postered bed with ivory and coral hangings dominated the room. The springlike colors were repeated throughout the room and the late-winter sun streamed in through three huge windows.

"What a lovely room," Therese said. "It looks like you." Then she saw the gauze-draped cradle by a brocade chair at the other end of the big room. Before Germaine had the chance to invite her, Therese hurried to the cradle and gently drew back the gauze.

The baby was sleeping, with her tiny fists curled at either side of her heart-shaped face, just as Elianne had slept when she was small. Nicole's perfect head was covered with a precocious down of black hair.

Therese addressed the baby silently: You darling. I am your grandmother.

Almost as if she understood, Nicole immediately opened her eyes and smiled up at Therese, waving her minuscule fists in welcome. Her eyes were the shape of Germaine's, but they were the color of the Adairs', that beautiful bluish-gray, faintly greened from the reflection of the walls.

Therese could feel Germaine's steady regard. "She's beautiful, so beautiful. May I pick her up?"

"Of course. She's very good-natured when she wakes up. She hardly ever cries."

Therese was conscious that Germaine watched her every movement as she lifted the baby with extreme care and gentleness, cradling the child against her breast. Therese sat down in the neighboring chair, still looking down at Nicole.

Germaine perched on the end of the upholstered chaise opposite. "She seems to like you," she murmured. "Therese . . . you never told me, but . . . surely you have had children of your own."

Therese looked up at Germaine, knowing that the moment had come. "Germaine, your husband is my son. My son, Charles."

Germaine's half-smile froze foolishly on her lips; she blinked. "My *husband*? 'Charles'?" She pronounced the name with a kind of unbelieving distaste. "What are you saying?"

"I know it sounds strange to hear him called that," Therese said, astonished at her own calm. What an enormous relief there was, she thought, just saying it, having it come out at last. "He adopted the name Nick Adair when he left home at seventeen and went to live with his natural father."

Germaine sat like a statue, very straight, with her hands on her thighs, the fingers spread lax and motionless.

"Therese . . ." Germaine said slowly, as if she were struggling against an opiate or sleep, "I wrote to you. But finally I gave up. Nick mailed my letters."

Therese made no reply.

"*Nick* mailed the letters," Germaine said again, in the tone of one talking to herself. "And kept your letters from me."

Two women sat looking at each other.

"He . . . he must hate you," Germaine said finally. "Why? Why, Therese?"

The baby made a restless sound. Therese put her back in her cradle. "I'll try to tell you."

And slowly, choosing her words with care, she began to tell Germaine the story of Nick's early life.

Germaine shook her head. She looked like someone who was trying to understand a foreign language.

"I know this must be a terrible shock for you," Therese said gently. "But I couldn't let the deception go on. I've always loved you, my dear. I had to claim you . . . as my daughter-in-law. And Nicole as my granddaughter."

She could see the stunning variety of emotions succeed in Germaine's dark, bewildered eyes, disbelief giving way to pain and confusion.

Germaine said abruptly, "It was you who bought Adair's Island! That was why the 'owner' was so generous."

Therese nodded, feeling the quick, hot blood suffuse her throat and then her cheeks.

"When I remarked on it, he called me a fool and said I didn't understand," Germaine murmured. She put her face in her hands and through her fingers said faintly, "Therese, I have been so unhappy. Marrying him was the biggest mistake of my life." At once she dropped her hands, flushing, not looking at Therese.

"Oh, my dear child." Therese got up and went to her, taking Germaine's head between her hands with enormous gentleness, drawing it to rest against her body.

Muffled against the fabric, Germaine spoke again. "I have missed you so much . . . missed New York. He makes me miserable, Therese. And yet I can't quite hate him." Therese fondled her head, feeling the slender body shake with sobs.

Germaine drew away from Therese and looked up at her with a stricken face. "Sometimes . . . many times, I've had the most wretched suspicion that he. . ." She stopped, her voice breaking. "That he married me for the Broussard money. Just to save Adair's Island."

"What are you doing here?"

Startled, the women turned and looked toward the wide door next to the great postered bed.

Nick stood there, his tall body filling the doorway, dwarfing the height of the canopied bed. His hard eyes looked like gray stones, and his mouth was twisted with anger.

"What are you doing here, in my house?" he shouted at Therese. "Why are you poisoning my wife against me?"

"Nick," Germaine said feebly. "You're early."

"Be quiet." He took a few steps into the room, facing Therese. "Is that what you told her—that I married her for the Broussard money?"

Therese stood up. "I never said that at all." She was amazed: he had lost all his power to hurt her. "I am leaving now, so you need not be upset. Germaine did not conspire with me. I came of my own accord." She glanced at the baby once more. "I came to see my grandchild."

Nick was standing by Germaine now, with his hands on her shoulders, almost pushing her down into the softness of the chaise. "She will never be known to the world as your grandchild. I would not wish her to bear that disgrace. And I'll thank you never to intrude in my house again."

"This is my house too," Germaine cried out.

"Good-bye, my dear," Therese said softly to Germaine, and walked out of the room. The hot tears, sternly repressed, broke free, blurring her vision so completely that she had to hold on to the polished banister to find her way down the stairs.

Nick Adair waited to hear the front door close before he knelt down on the Aubusson carpet by the chaise. "My poor darling," he said to Germaine. Lifting her hands in his, he kissed them. "I am so sorry . . . so sorry you had to be exposed to that."

She regarded him in amazement. "Why did you never *tell* me? Why did you . . . confiscate my letters?"

He let go of her hands and grasped her around the

hips, stroking her body. "Because, my beloved, I wanted to spare you. I never wanted to bring my shame on you and our child."

Victorious, he thought he could feel her weakening. He sat down on the floor, caressing her thighs. "She has always lied, Germaine, from the very beginning. My father wanted to marry her, but she ran away to pursue her 'independent life.' And for years she kept me away from my father, my rightful heritage. Do you know that she was the one who stole Adair's Island from us?"

Germaine gave no gesture of assent.

"There. You see?" Nicholas said in triumph. "She is lying still, to you." He was puzzled by the blank look in Germaine's eyes. But wishing to press his advantage, he rushed on. "Now that she has discovered that we have a child"—and the bitch, he thought, had probably "investigated" that too, just as she had detected the incompetence of that old sot—"she will set out to steal her and you from me."

He was sure of it now: there was a disbelieving look in his wife's eyes. He carefully altered his tone.

"How can I allow that?" he asked her tenderly, kissing her legs through the fabric of her dress. Ah! That was more like it: he could feel her respond to his touch. There was no woman in the world he could not win over, not with the skills he had learned at Victorine's and in the *garçonnière*.

He felt his own body respond to the memories of that golden octoroon flesh, in the shuttered, heated afternoons . . .

"I love you, Germaine," he whispered. "You are my life." Nick's stroking hands grew more urgent. Germaine's body softened.

"If I could believe it. If I could believe you love me. . ." Her breath had quickened, and her face was flushed.

"How can you doubt it?" He stood and, taking her hands in his, invited her to rise and come into his arms. Pressing her close, he thought: She still has a splendid body, despite the birth of that little wriggly worm. "Oh, Germaine, it has been so long," he said into her ear, his tongue darting out to touch the soft flesh of her neck.

She trembled in his arms. Smiling, Nick let go of her and strode to the door, shutting it firmly, turning the lock.

He came back to her and held her close again, kissing her repeatedly. It was so easy, he thought with amusement, so terribly easy. He ran his hands up and down her body, hearing her murmur, and unfastened the neckline of her dress, down to the waist.

Her breasts, bare for nursing, were quite round and satisfactory to his hands, a big improvement over what they had been before she gave birth. Nick played with the nipples, watching them bloom.

Then he unfastened the rest of her buttons and gently pulled the dress from her body. She was wearing only a thin petticoat, and the sight of the shadowed darkness beneath excited him. With growing desire, he peeled the petticoat away, leaving her nude except for her shoes and stockings. Lifting one of her small feet, he slipped off one shoe, then the other. When she made a move toward the stockings, Nick said, "No! Leave them on."

Smiling up at her, he stroked the silk of the stockings and then the bare flesh above them. And with expert swiftness he moved to her and performed the kiss that drove the women wild; the caress, his father had told him, that had kept the little bayou trash after him like bitches in heat. Nick didn't especially like it, but it sure got the women hot.

With contempt, he watched Germaine's face break into that gargoyle mask that marred her beauty, and her eyelids flutter; heard her squeal.

He held her firmly. Well, *that* was over, and he could pleasure himself. He picked her up in his arms and carried her to the bed, throwing off his own clothes with savage impatience.

At last: he entered the vibrant, silken, pillowed haven that was worth all the fuss and nonsense, the only thing the foolish females really had to offer . . .

And it was fine, so fine, so fine . . .

Just before the time came, he took the action that would ensure there would not be another brat to swell her up, clutter up the house.

God.

He let out a cry, subsiding.

He gave her the obligatory kisses and pulled her into his arms, idly looking down at her naked body.

He had to give her that—she was beautiful. And she didn't yammer at him afterward, like the lower-class ones had a tendency to do.

In that regard, Germaine was as good as the whores. Good as them in other ways, too, not out of learned skills but inspired by her fortunate but pathetic passion.

He was sure he had done all right, but he wanted to hear it from her. "My darling, have I proved it to you . . . what I said before?"

She nodded against him, stroking his naked flesh.

That was the way he had to keep it; old man Broussard was no fool. He knew that Nick, like him, deserved his little distractions. But let him get a hint that his precious daughter was unhappy, and Nick Adair's name would be mud in Louisiana and for seven states around.

"I'm so glad," he said softly, fondling her breast. "Because I've got to leave you soon. I just came home on impulse"—he gave that its full significance, feeling her incipient laughter against him—"but I still have a lot of work to do."

He had just remembered that tonight the new Hungarian girl would be debuting at Victorine's. He wasn't going to miss that for anything.

Nick raised himself on his arm and looked at her with all the earnestness he could muster. "I don't want you to brood over that . . . incident this afternoon. That woman is not a part of our lives anymore. And, Germaine," he said, fondling her breast, pleased with her quick reaction, "it could only harm our child if the world discovered the truth of my . . . origins. It would break your family's heart."

She gave a murmur of assent, and yet he could not fully read the expression in her eyes.

He hadn't quite won. He would have to keep working at it. He'd have to be damned careful that that woman stayed away from them.

Everything depended on it.

# 20

## 1905

"Thanks, Jenny. This is lovely." Therese examined the curly bronze frame her assistant had bought for her and slipped the new photo behind the glass. "I can always count on your taste."

"Well, I learned it from Pavan." Jenny smiled. "These are the swatches for Kronstad." She put the squares of fabric on Therese's desk and went out.

Therese carried the framed picture to her little gallery in the corner of the office and set it down among her huge collection. There were already a dozen others of Nicole; some represented snatched visits, in New Orleans or at Petit Anse. Others had been sent during the constant correspondence with Germaine over the years.

Therese looked at the latest one with special pleasure. She hadn't seen Nicole for the last two years, and she couldn't wait for this summer's visit. It was hard to gauge the color of her eyes from the sepia picture, but they already seemed lighter. When Therese had last seen Nicole, her eyes had been very blue, a brighter blue than the Adairs'. Germaine said her own mother's eyes were that color. With the jet-black Broussard hair, the girl's eyes were very striking. And she already had that look of mischief that was pure Germaine.

Therese went back to her desk, reflecting on the intervening years—years crowded with new griefs, new losses.

Berthe had lived to a contented seventy-nine before

340

being stricken by a fatal heart disease during the last year. She had been buried at Petit Anse. With her sadness, Therese had felt an odd peace; her mother had had such happy years, first with the gentle Mr. Levitsky, then as a widow among the splendors and comforts of Petit Anse. Therese was gratified that she had been able to do so much for her mother.

In these last years, there had been triumphs and pleasures too, new trips with Anthony.

Somehow the best had been the stolen meetings at Petit Anse. Each encounter presented Nicole in another fascinating stage of growth. Ever since she was four, the child had had ebullient spirits; combined with her beautiful manners and her lapses into dreamy thoughtfulness, they made her a complex person.

To the mutual delight of Therese and Germaine, Nicole had shown a talent for drawing since she was seven. Among the photos in the "gallery" were examples of Nicole's tentative art. In the early years, Germaine had taught Nicole; now she was studying with professionals.

During those years, it seemed to Therese that Germaine grew with her daughter; the more distant she seemed to grow from Charles, the more Germaine regained her old independence. It was a pity, Therese thought, that she went on accepting that farce of a marriage. But apparently she stayed with Charles for the sake of her daughter.

A drastic error, in Therese's opinion. A father like Charles would never encourage Nicole's gifts; he had certainly stifled Germaine's.

On the other hand, a divorce was still possible. Germaine had hinted that last year. And she was still so young, only thirty-one . . .

"Therese." Jenny came in, with a yellow envelope in her hand. "This just came." She started out.

Tearing it open, Therese read it and turned cold.

Charles was dead.

He had been killed in a hunting accident in Virginia. Therese made a strangled sound.

"What is it?" Jenny asked her anxiously. Therese

handed her the telegram. Glancing at it, Jenny laid it
gently on the desk and took Therese in her arms.

Emotions almost half a century old awakened in
Therese. She felt the innocent baby-weight of Charles
in her arms; saw the bright, impertinent little boy with
sunny hair and eyes the color of a stormy sky.

She leaned against Jenny and felt the tears begin, in
a warm, relieving flood.

"Do you want me to call Mr. McKay?" Jenny asked
softly. She handed Therese a handkerchief.

Therese wiped her eyes. "No. Thank you. I'll do
that. Have Marie take care of Kronstad."

"Don't worry about anything here." Jenny pressed
her hand and went out, gently shutting the door.

And Therese made a sudden, irrevocable decision.

Her son must come home to Petit Anse. It was all
he had ever wanted.

The funeral party was invited to refresh itself in the
drawing room at Petit Anse. There were minuscule
glasses of the McKay amontillado for the women,
tumblers of old Scotch and bourbon whiskey for the
men. Therese had found blessed distraction in arrang-
ing all the petty details.

The service was a nightmare: it was grotesque to
remain in the background, posing as a friend of
Germaine's. But any alternative was out of the question. If the truth came out, Nicole and Germaine
would reap the whirlwind. Therese could picture the
reaction of the du Lacs, de Sevignys, and Broussards.

When the endless affair finally drew to a close,
Aimee du Lac de Sevigny moved to Therese, extending her clawlike hand in its glove of black lace. Aimee
was nearly seventy, but Therese could see traces of the
imperious beauty of 1857. The pair of them had traveled a long way from Madame Dufay's salon, where
Therese had knelt at Aimee's feet, putting on her
shoes.

Therese caught that memory reflected in Aimee's
cynical black eyes. "At first we thought it . . . strange
when my grand-niece elected to have the interment

here. But of course, she was the one who knew him best of all. And she said he would have wished it."

Therese could only nod; her throat had closed up.

"It was a most delicate and generous act," Aimee added, "for you to allow it."

I'll scream if she says another word, Therese thought. But she managed an even answer. "Not at all. After all, the Adair burial ground is here, and it seemed appropriate."

At last, after further effusions, the outsiders were gone. Therese slumped, weak with release.

Anthony came in from the hall, where he had been saying good-bye to the last parting guest. "You look done in. Maybe you ought to go up to bed." He put his arm around her. She looked up at him with affection.

He was even better-looking now than when he was young; lean, not gaunt, and his good bones were more prominent with the superfluous flesh melted away. His hair was all white now, but still thick and lively.

"Not yet," she said gently. "I think I'll take a walk outside. I'll be back soon."

She went through one of the open French windows onto the veranda, hearing a ripple of the piano from the music room. It had to be Nell playing; the touch was so delicate. Therese recognized a silvery nocturne of Chopin's.

Therese went slowly down the stairs toward the sequestered *garçonnière*.

When she had first taken possession of Petit Anse, she hadn't had the heart to set foot in the place, that site of her lost innocence, of agony and betrayal. Eventually she had turned the little house into a studio, and the ghosts were exorcised.

But now, in the falling dusk, the phantoms drifted back. And for one uncertain moment she thought she heard the servants' long-ago laughter, the contemptuous voice of the boy who had fathered her child.

Undaunted, she went into the small house and entered her workroom. The sketches she had brought along from New York were spread out on her drawing table—brilliant sketches. There were no ghosts here,

she exulted. This had always been the room of the
future for Therese Pavan, with the old furnishings
forgotten, the walls painted in happy colors, the im-
print of her personality everywhere.

She sat down on her stool, surveying the designs.
They were sketches of opera costumes commissioned
by the famous Madame Kronstad, who would appear
this winter at the Met in a revival of *Tristan*, and had
insisted on her own designer.

Elizabeth Schuyler Morris still queened it over the
Metropolitan board, but there had been sharp changes
since 1890: the board was obliged to accede to the
demands of its star performers. And Kronstad had not
been the first to choose Pavan over the opera's house
designers. Therese had been similarly honored by Farrar and Galli-Curci, among others, and even male
performers. The imperious Caruso had commissioned
Therese to costume him for *Pagliacci*, declaring that
her concept of colors had the resonance of music.

Kronstad had been dazzled by Pavan's interpreta-
tion of costumes for the tragic Queen Isolde. Therese
had painstakingly researched ancient Celtic costume,
blending antique designs with her own freedom of line
and brilliant color. The Valkyrean Kronstad was ecstatic. "They make me look like a willow wand! And
the *movement*, Madame—these are the first costumes
I've ever had I could *move* in."

Squinting at the display, Therese was inspired to
alter something. Unconsciously, she began to draw,
and everything else went out of her head.

The next time she looked up, it was almost dark,
the air outside the window a pale charcoal color, with
tints of blurred lilac.

Amazing. All her life the work had offered sur-
cease, from the first lonely nights in New Orleans until
this moment, when her son lay beneath the rich earth
of Petit Anse.

It was hard to see through the falling dusk, but
Therese made out a pale, narrow figure, a smudge of
black. It was Nicole, in the black velvet dress that
Therese had brought her for the funeral.

Therese went out to meet her.

"I hope I'm not disturbing you," Nicole said with her usual politeness, in her precise, cool voice. "I wanted to see the studio."

"Of course not! Come in." Therese led the way. Nicole looked around with fascination while Therese observed her. The girl's tilted eyes, blue as an October sky, sparkled with excitement, her wealth of black hair glistened. There was an odd maturity in her demeanor, none of the awkwardness of adolescence in the lines of her slender body.

Nicole studied the sketches. "How beautiful. Like clothes from a fairy tale." The girl looked up and smiled; her curious intelligence glinted in the bright blue eyes.

"They are, in a way. Costumes for *Tristan und Isolde*."

"Oh! I didn't know you were doing that. I love opera. But I've never seen *Tristan*. And these *colors*." Nicole gazed at the sketches.

"You like color."

"I adore it. I hate black and white." Nicole turned, flushing. "I didn't mean it like that. This is an exquisite Pavan." She fingered the black velvet with a delicate hand. "I do appreciate your bringing it."

"I know what you mean. It's all right. There was a time when I wore so much black I was starved for color," Therese said warmly.

"Therese. What is *this*?" Nicole bent to look at a crystal figurine set on a chest in front of the window where, by day, it could catch the light.

The figure was a young woman's, not unlike Nicole's. Its draperies were timeless. On the base of the fine Steuben crystal, engraved in narrow capitals, were three words: ELEGANCE AUDACE PAVAN

Nicole read the words. "*Audace*," she repeated.

"I was born audacious," Therese commented. "Elegance has to be achieved."

Nicole read the tiny words on the side of the figure's base: " 'Olivia to Therese, 1875.' Who is Olivia?"

"Princess Olivia of England."

Patricia Strother

Nicole straightened. "Of course. Mother said she was helping design Princess Beatrice's trousseau when she ran away to get married . . . and Princess Olivia had sent Beatrice to Pavan."

"Yes." Therese was overcome with nostalgia. She had had such high hopes for Germaine.

"You know," Nicole said in a confiding way, "I think Mother's always regretted running away from Pavan. She's been talking about it more and more."

"She has?" Therese's heart gave an excited lurch and began to hammer.

"Yes. She's even been doing some designing. She taught me some of the things that you taught her." Nicole smiled, and her face was so charming it warmed Therese's heart. Even with her black hair and tilted eyes, her small straight nose reminded Therese of Charles's. "I'd rather become a designer than anything else in the world."

Therese felt another *frisson* of excitement. She started to speak, when she heard a soft rapping at the front door, and went to answer. Germaine was standing on the miniature veranda. She was pale but her dark eyes shone with a new confidence, an odd peace. "Is Nicole here?"

"Yes." Therese put her arm around Germaine and urged her into the studio.

"I'm glad. I have something to say to both of you."

Therese was mystified by Germaine's look of anticipation.

Nicole was sitting on the drawing stool. "What is it, Mother?"

"Something very wonderful." Germaine's tone was soft and conspiratorial. "I want to present your grandmother, Nicole. Your dear *grand'mère*, the great Pavan."

Therese could not believe what she had heard. She stood there staring at Germaine, then turned to look at Nicole. The girl's lips were parted in astonishment. "My *grand'mère*? Pavan?"

"Yes," Germaine said, smiling at Therese.

"Oh . . . I can't believe it," Nicole whispered. "It's too good to be true." Slowly she came to Therese and put her arms around Therese's body. "My *chèregran*."

The invented word was so moving that Therese's words froze in her throat. Her arms slid around Nicole. When they released each other, Germaine said rather shakily, "Nicole, I'd like to talk to your grandmother alone for just a minute."

"Of course." The girl kissed Therese, then Germaine, and went out. There was still an expression of wonder in her widened eyes.

Therese sank down into an armchair, looking at Germaine for an instant in silence. Finally she asked, "Do you know what you've done, my dear?"

"Repaid you," Germaine answered with perfect calm. "Repaid you for all you've done for me, for us. For what you did today for . . . Charles."

Therese was moved to tears by her use of his given name. "Nick," she corrected. "We'll call him Nick from now on. It's what he always wanted. As for repayment—nothing can compare with what you've done for me."

Germaine sat down on the drawing stool. "But it must have been a nightmare for you today."

Therese retorted, "Nothing like the nightmares we'll have when your family hears this."

"I don't plan for them to hear. We're moving to New York."

"New York!" Delight piled on delight.

"Therese, you know what it's been like for me all these years. I've been in a cage. For a while I thought my talent, my very brain, was gone. But it isn't."

"Nicole told me," Therese interjected.

"I was hoping that, perhaps, there might be a place for me at Pavan."

"It's a dream," Therese murmured. "Of course there's a place for you. There always has been. And someday, I don't doubt, for Nicole."

They looked at each other, dazzled.

Then Therese rose to put the studio to rights, with a song in her heart. "Can you imagine what it will be like . . . the things we can accomplish together?"

# 1911

Somewhere a clock struck two: the black Rolls purred downtown on Fifth, an avenue of dimming golden light.

Therese relaxed against the scarlet leather of the car's back seat and leaned on Anthony's shoulder. "Thank you for this night," she murmured.

He smiled down at her. "Thank you for all the nights."

As always, she was struck by his good looks. "My handsome husband."

"Who would have looked like a threadpaper—like the other McKays—if it weren't for you. You've always kept me a little off balance. Kept me from drying up . . . kept me young." After a minute he said happily, "You and Nicole were really surprised."

"Very. I haven't been that surprised in years."

The "little dinner" to celebrate her birthday and Nicole's, which occurred within days of each other, had turned into a big reception in one of the ballrooms of the Plaza Hotel. Her favorite people, people she hadn't seen for ages, had been gathered there. "So was Nicole."

Her granddaughter had never looked more beautiful. Therese thought of the hyacinth-blue gown Nicole had designed for herself. Its brightness glorified the blue of her tilted eyes, accentuated the black, glistening hair drawn into coils on the top of her shapely head.

"Nicole of Pavan," like Therese and the great French designers Cheruit and and Poiret, campaigned against current detail. Her dress had been starkly simple; with

it she wore only a rope of the Broussard pearls, clasped
high on the left side of her neck with a sapphire clip,
an arrangement as casual as a red bandanna.

"She has something I've never had."

"What could that possibly be?" Anthony asked with
a gallant inflection.

"I like your tone," she teased him. "Natural chic.
Something I always had to work at. She certainly
impressed her kissin' cousins." Therese grinned. "I
can't get over the McKay boys. They look like Arrow
Collar ads."

"Amelie's boys turned out well," Anthony said com-
panionably. "She even *looks* better since the divorce."

Therese made a fervent sound of agreement. She
had survived being Hector's sister-in-law as long as the
Rocailles had lived in Texas. Now that Amelie was
free of him, she could live at Petit Anse, and her boys
were free to develop as they should.

"It was so dear of you to bring them all here," she
said, recalling the joy of seeing Charl' and Nell, the
Sloans, Elianne and her husband, Adam Winston. "To
the very scene of the crime."

Anthony laughed. Four years ago, soon after the
opening of the Plaza Hotel, they had spent a romantic
weekend there. The desk clerk had been shocked when
they gave a local address. "I know that man didn't
believe we were married. And to have a furtive
rendezvous, at our advanced ages . . ."

"I love that place," Therese said. "To me it will
always be new." She had always been fond of its
balconies and balustrades, its piled-up roofs and log-
gias, controlled with classic discipline. "I love this
*night*."

They fell quiet as the Rolls hummed by the just-
completed public library, massively commanding the
avenue with its great *couchant* lions.

"Anthony . . ." Therese spoke low, so her voice
would not reach the chauffeur, John. "Were *you* behind that introduction at the *Follies*?"

One of the highlights of their celebration had been
the abrupt and startling spotlight on their box at the

"new" *Ziegfeld Follies*. Flo Ziegfeld himself had introduced not only Therese but also "Germaine and Nicole of Pavan."

"Well, I happened to mention to Flo that it was your birthday, and almost Nicole's."

"I love you." His arm tightened around her.

As they drove leisurely south toward Gramercy Park, Therese reviewed her years with Florenz Ziegfeld. Pavan had been his costume designer since the first *Follies of 1907*. There had been enormous changes—the main one, Joseph Urban. That master colorist and punctilious craftsman brought to the Follies a subtlety and imagination never seen before. Working with him, Therese had been able to use her talents to an awesome degree. The phantasmic *pointillage* he used in painting his sets was harmonized with her inventions, in dye, on fabrics.

After the fiasco with the "Met" years ago, it was a joy to deal with Flo Ziegfeld, a man of taste and generosity, and Joseph Urban. Both men were severely professional; she was sure that the two of them waved gossip away like so many gnats. All that counted with them was the work; as far as they were concerned, nothing else even existed.

The car turned at Gramercy Park. The town house, as always, welcomed. They got out and John drove off to the stable. Therese smiled. She and Anthony still called it that, despite John's unfailing reference to "the garage."

"Sleepy?" Anthony asked when they were in the foyer.

"Oh, no! I'm still too 'tuned up' for that."

"Good. Just let me get out of this armor." She hung away their coats and he went upstairs.

Therese glanced in the console mirror and ran a comb through her brief silver hair. She approved the effect of her velvet dress with its long sleeves and high collar, that hid a multitude of time's sins. Its color was "bitter chocolate," a distinctive brown-black from one of her own dyes. The color did good things for her pale skin and hair, her still-dark eyes. Her only orna-

ments were the peacock brooch Anthony had given
her in Paris—now her professional signature—and the
harmonizing bracelet he had given her tonight.

Putting away her comb, she glimpsed among the
pile of letters a yellow envelope.

Oh, not bad news, she pleaded, on a night like this.
Perhaps it was a birthday greeting. She tore open the
envelope on her way to the living room, where a fire
was burning cheerfully on the hearth.

Her glance flew to the close: "Jamal Fahmi, Direc-
tor, Cairo Opera." Perplexed, Therese sat down and
read the message: "Am empowered by the Khedive of
Egypt to commission you for the creation of costumes
for an outdoor production of *Aïda*, before the Great
Pyramids, in the month of April 1912, if you would
consider undertaking such commission."

A telephone number and a cable address followed
the signature of Jamal Fahmi.

She sat staring at the telegram, hypnotized.

"Therese?" Anthony returned in his old smoking
jacket, looking at her with great concern. "Is it bad
news?"

"Oh, no." Therese shook her head so hard her
short hair swayed bell-like back and forth, softly brushing her cheeks as her smile broke out; she could feel it
stretch widely across her face. She held the telegram
out to him.

Reading it, he looked up at her, and his piercing
eyes lit up with gratification.

He sat down next to her and put his arm around her.

"What do you think?" she asked with a calm that
amazed her.

"I think, at last, you are getting the recognition you
deserve." He kissed her hair.

"I won't go without you . . ." she began.

"You're damned right you won't," he retorted. "I'm
not going to be away from you that long . . . besides
all the other considerations."

She knew he meant all the unrest in Turkey and
elsewhere in the Middle East, the assassination of the
Egyptian prime minister in the winter of last year.

"As usual," she said dryly, "my knowledge of current events stops short of actual war. But you must be talking about Ghali . . . and the 'little troubles' in the Balkans."

"Yes. Fortunately, the *Orient Express* is 'way out of our way," he teased her. In the last few years riding that great train had been a dangerous business. "I'm sure small border skirmishes would not deter Pavan, with her '*audace*.' " Anthony smiled as he quoted the tribute engraved on her crystal statue.

She glanced at the figure, set on a table near the hearth, where it reflected the orange of the dancing flames.

He sobered. "Therese, this makes up for so much."

Yes, she thought, it atoned for the rejection by the Met, years ago; the puzzling decline of business at Pavan after that rejection; the panic of 1907. But the decline had just as swiftly and mysteriously reversed, and Pavan had not only survived. Now it had triumphed.

The dubious Pavan, who had been "good enough for the scandalous *Follies*," had now been chosen over all the great designers of the world to design *Aïda* for the Khedive of Egypt.

Anthony filled two glasses with old amontillado and handed one to Therese.

They lifted the goblets without a word, and touched rims.

His eyes expressed the moment in a way that no word ever could.

# 21

In the first of his numerous communications, Fahmi informed Therese that the royal performance of *Aïda* would take place during the festival of Shem-el-Nessim, which celebrated the first day of the Egyptian spring. They agreed that Therese would arrive in February, with Anthony and Nicole.

Therese wanted the long weeks to absorb the country's atmosphere and to study technical problems such as the effect of the strong natural light, in which the opera would be performed, on fabrics and on dyes. Fahmi made much of the Egyptian light, writing, "My country is a land of golden brightness. Our *faïence*, our scarabs, are the color of bright water; frequently, when travelers take the scarabs home, to America or England, for example, the color becomes less vivid in the grayer air."

Therese made careful note of that, remembering the different colors of the air in various European capitals: Vienna had been silver-green, Paris pure silver, London at times an almost lilac-gray. The color of New York, which she loved, was a steely blue-gray, as unlike the imagined color of Egypt as a hue could possibly be.

Therefore, in November when she began her careful preparations, Therese relied on her experience with the *Follies*, experimenting with various golden stage lights as she and Nicole examined fabrics of many different colors. Urban, who knew Egypt, praised Therese's "remarkable instincts," advising that stage lights were indeed a splendid approximation of the desert brightness.

Therese and Nicole haunted the Egyptian wing of
the Metropolitan Museum, with its noble tombs and
godlike figures, its objects of *faïence* and gold, of glass
and alabaster. "I'm growing fonder and fonder of the
Egyptians," Nicole confided. So was Therese; their
artifacts displayed a great reverence for beauty, a tender feeling for animals. And it touched her that their
women had been buried with their favorite trinkets, so
that splendor might go with them to the lonely under-
world. "They made their designers immortal," Therese replied, smiling.

It was the happiest winter of her life, working in
such close concert with "Nicole of Pavan." They had
dismissed the idea of university study for Nicole, and
she had been allowed to concentrate exclusively on
her profession. Ever since the disclosure at Petit Anse
after Nick's death, Nicole had immersed herself in
history. That interest, with her specialty in costumes
for the performing arts, made Nicole an able partner
in the latest enterprise.

At twenty, Nicole was already a prodigy of design;
overseen by Therese, she had been designing costumes
for minor theatrical productions for the past two years.
They agreed that Therese would design the major
singers' costumes for *Aïda*, Nicole would handle those
for the less prominent characters and the large number
of supernumeraries.

The family was overjoyed by the news of Therese's
triumph. Germaine, the Sloans, and Elianne and her
husband would come to Cairo for the performance.

In deference to Elianne's Winston connection, as
well as their own preference for the fine Winston
ships, Anthony booked passage on the *Regina II*. She
had been afloat for only two years, and was one of the
queens of the sea. The very names of their ports of
call enchanted Nicole and Therese; the *Regina* would
take them first to Spanish Morocco, and on through
the straits, touching Oran and Algiers, Tunis, Tripoli
and Benghazi before landing at the ancient white city
of Alexandria, named for its founder—Alexander the
Great—more than two thousand years before.

It was an exciting journey, a time of lazy enjoyment, too, for the three of them. One late night on deck, as the great ship left Benghazi, Therese and Anthony were sitting alone.

"This is the first real journey we've taken in years," Anthony murmured. "It makes up for the trip around the world we never had."

"More than makes up," she said, glad to see how rested he looked.

So many obstacles had stood in the way of that often-discussed trip—family matters, Anthony's business. But most of all, Pavan. Therese always felt a strange uneasiness after being away too long, as if Pavan were a beloved and exacting lover whose absence left her empty. Now, with Anthony and Nicole, she had it all.

And as the ship moved toward Alexandria, her heart was high with anticipation.

The port was everything she had dreamed, its white grace appearing before her eyes like a mystic vision, and she was immediately conscious of the innumerable years of its existence.

Even the bustle of landing, the meeting with the gallant Westernized Fahmi and his able retinue, could not dispel Therese's sensation of fantasy. Fahmi and his aides, who all seemed to speak perfect English in addition to flawless Parisian French, whisked them off with miraculous efficiency into the boat that would bear them down the Nile.

Therese saw at once the justice of Fahmi's description: spring was far off, yet the air *was* gold, and the newcomers feasted their eyes on the sights along the banks of the ancient river, the river that had borne the royal barge of Cleopatra and the Ptolemys. The country held her spellbound—people in sandals and long white robes, camels with blasé faces moving like comic dancers.

The party had courteously declined Fahmi's invitation to stay in a wing of his palatial house. Therese explained that a small hotel would enable her and Nicole to come and go at their "inconvenient artists' hours" without disturbance to Fahmi's household. The truth was that she felt constricted as a houseguest anywhere, and was almost embarrassed by the largess of the opera company, under the auspices of the Khedive. Pavan was receiving an astronomical fee, and impressive aids, such as the design studio in Cairo which had all the assets of a Parisian salon. Fahmi, resigned to the odd ways of foreigners, she supposed, had gracefully accepted her decision. But it was understood that the family would be frequently entertained both at Fahmi's house and at the palace of the Khedive, as well as at the palace of the new governor general, Lord Kitchener of Britain.

They were escorted to a hotel which looked out on the Nile. The yellow Mokattam Hills could be seen from Therese's window, and she listened in wonder to a muezzin, from the top of a minaret, calling the people to prayer. It was the most plaintive, most haunting air she had ever heard; there was a prickle of excitement along her nerves. As she fell asleep that night, the scented breeze brought her the exotic odors of the ancient land; the big moon's path, through the window, made the night almost as bright as morning.

Therese's last waking thought was: How wonderful—the moon will be our spotlight for the last act of *Aïda*.

In the weeks that followed, Therese and Nicole, sometimes with Anthony, made repeated visits to the awesome pyramids, testing fabrics and colors in the varying desert light, from sun to sunset, and sunset to the moon's first brilliance.

Both in the looming shadows of the giant monuments and in the museum of Cairo, Nicole and Therese steeped themselves in the Egypt of the pharaohs; they studied the original manuscript of the myth of Rhadames and Aïda, and invaded the bazaars, reveling in the strangeness of savage music.

Driving in small horse-drawn traps called *arabiyas*, they watched the fellaheens work in the fields with buffalo and oxen, labor that had not changed in two thousand years, passing robed men with noble profiles like those they had seen on temple walls, and veiled women revealing nothing but dark, enormous eyes enlarged by the *kohl* around them.

The three were received with great cordiality in the house of Fahmi and in the Khedive's palace. The ladies of the palace were fascinated by the fragile looks of Nicole and by Therese's panache; in turn the Americans were dazzled by the women's sophistication. They knew Paris as well as Cairo, and could not get enough of the talk of fashion.

But it was in her long conversations with Fahmi that Therese took the greatest delight: he spoke of Amneris and Aida, Rhadames and Amonasro as if he had met them last week. And gradually the characters of the opera took on new life for Therese and Nicole.

The weeks advanced toward the festival of Shem-el-Nessim, which Mrs. Fahmi translated as the "smell of the breeze."

For the women from the West, the breeze was compounded of colored aromas—the perfume of royal purple flowers, flowers the hue of flame, whose spirit they would capture in the vestments for *Aida*.

One of the terraces outside the palace of the Khedive faced on the ancient Nile. The night after the performance, during the dancing, Therese slipped out alone to watch the dazzle of moonlight on the storied river.

Her ears still rang with the voices of *Aida*. From the first gemlike aria, the *"Celeste Aida,"* to the "Triumphal March" with its company of warriors on elephants and camels, to the moonlit good-bye of the lovers, the performance flashed again before her eyes in a shining vision.

After all the months of anxious preparation, the magic interval had gone with the quickness of a flight of hummingbirds . . . like life itself.

Images flared in her mind: Amneris like a splendid serpent in her changeable golden gown, a coronet of solid gold on her imperious head; Rhadames armored in actual silver, his tunic like blue fire, playing against the crimson gauze and gems of the passionate Aida

. . . the last lyrical encounter, and the *"Terra addio"* . . . farewell to earth.

The pictures flickered out.

If only life, and magic, could go on and on. The nearer Therese approached her "earth's farewell," the more reluctant she was to give it. The years of her life had passed like hours; in the wink of an eye, she was nearly seventy years old. The young Therese—and Charles and Berthe, Madame Dufay and George, so many others—had passed across the stage into the darkened wings.

Therese heard a light footstep on the terrace. Germaine joined her at the balustrade. "You have always created beauty, but today was your greatest moment."

Studying Germaine's sculptured profile in the moonlight, Therese marveled that nearly a quarter of a century had passed since she first saw Germaine Broussard, whose face had looked like a white flower. She was still a lovely woman, with her deep black eyes and hair and magnolia-pale skin.

"And Nicole's," Therese added. "And yours. You have been at the heart of Pavan for the last seven years."

"I was away from it all too long." Germaine spoke without regret. "I've gotten quite enamored of the practical details."

"You're superb at them. I don't know what we would have done without you." Whereas Nicole and Therese frequently got carried away, Germaine always held it all together. She had developed into an outstanding businesswoman.

"Do you realize what this will mean to your career?" Germaine demanded. "The Met will be clamoring for your services."

"Yes. I suppose it will." Therese said it so indifferently that Germaine peered at her in surprise.

"You're suffering from anticlimax," she said gently.

"I am," Therese admitted. "All I wanted, after the opera, was just to be quiet and alone."

"I know. But that would never do for the Khedive's

guest of honor," Germaine said lightly. "As a matter of fact, here comes Anthony to find you."

Smiling, he crossed the terrace and took Therese's arm. "Fahmi tells me that your presence is requested." He mocked his own solemnity. "The Khedive Abbas Second is about to toast Pavan."

Therese walked back toward the ballroom between Anthony and Germaine. She caught sight of Nicole, elated and glowing in a dress the colors of a bird of paradise.

Or a phoenix about to take wing.

A shining tomorrow lay before Nicole. She would have the stature of a Cheruit, a Doucet, or a Paquin; she could even surpass them.

Therese would place the mantle on those smooth young shoulders . . . and go home, with Anthony, to Petit Anse.

But tonight was hers. Her somber mood was gone, evaporating like the mist from the bayou morning.

The orchestra began the *"Ritorna vincitor."*

For the victory of Pavan.

# Author's Note

To set fashion history straight, New York's Madame Demorest, and not Therese Pavan, originated the first paper dress patterns.

Harper's Bazar (the original spelling) debuted in 1867.

Joseph Urban did not join the Ziegfeld Follies until 1915. Mr. Urban designed not only the Follies' sets but all its costumes.

# About the Author

*Grand Design* is the author's second novel as Patricia Strother. Her first, *The Constant Star*, is also available in Signet. She has published eighteen other novels under various pseudonyms, ranging from astrological fiction (which she invented) to historicals, family sagas, and romances. An Alabama native, Ms. Strother began writing at the age of ten, and initially published as a poet and short-story writer. After college in Tennessee, her occupations included radio and TV announcing and writing, a stint for a New York weekly newspaper, and a twenty-year career with a New York labor union. Ms. Strother lives with her husband, Bob, and their four cats, in New York's Greenwich Village, where she now writes full-time.

**A sweeping saga of a passion that would not be denied, and a marriage that was the ultimate test of love . . .**

*The Constant Star*

*Patricia Strother*

Their love defied their worlds. She was blonde and beautiful, regal and young, the perfect product of New York WASP aristocracy. He was hard, lean, darkly handsome, shaped by the poverty and pride of the Jewish Lower East Side.

Spanning two continents and five dramatic decades of dreams and desires, conflict and change, this emotion-packed saga is a powerful reading experience you will never forget . . .

---